A SPIRIT MYSTERY

a

SPIRIT

of

MURDER

Christmas

TODD VOTER

For Tammy

Chapter 1
December 24th
Christmas Eve Day

Evergreens accented the interior of Saint Wenceslaus, leaving the scent of pine hanging lightly in the cool air of the old church. A large wreath hung over votive candles next to the altar. Matt Jager sat alone in the last pew listening to the small private service. Father Vu and the family gathered around a closed casket. His voice was soft and melodic standing against the harshness of death and loss. The Father wore the white vestments he wore at Dawn's funeral. White to celebrate life rather than black to mourn death. That was fine with Matt then. Dawn's loss belonged to him, it was his pain. He had no intention of sharing it. She was his life, and the overwhelming grief would be his alone. And yet, despite everything he knew about them, the family here on Christmas Eve gathered around the altar shared their grief. They pulled closer together and supported one another. And that's exactly what worried Matt. The Moscow family, united in grief and anger, was not a good thing for Fillmore County.

His mind wandered into the past. An image of his beautiful bride walking down the aisle at their wedding faded into Matt sitting alone in a crowded church during her funeral. Jet lag and the lingering pain of their life interrupted were distracting him from the reason he was here. Father Vu raised his hands and blessed the family with the words, "Go in peace," bringing Matt back fully to the present. He stood as Frank Moscow turned from the altar and walked down the aisle. Like the rest of the men in his family, Frank was dressed in jeans and a flannel shirt. Matt had added a tie to his normal workwear of a dress shirt, jacket, jeans, and expensive running shoes. He extended his hand.

"I'm sorry, Frank." They gripped tight. "I was out of town, or I would have said something earlier."

Moscow, mid-forties weathered older by a lifetime of alcohol, drugs, and hard living, looked better than when Matt had last seen him, but the weight of loss was evident on his face. It sat heavily in

1

his eyes and clenched jaw. He had to wait a moment before he could speak. "You just don't know what it's like to lose your kid." He looked Matt square in the eye for the first time, then nodded. "Well, maybe you do. Appreciate you coming by."

Standing on opposite sides of the law, Matt and Frank had somehow managed to form an understanding, if not an actual friendship. Neither held any illusions about the other, but they could cooperate on a narrow neutral territory. Matt hoped this was one of those situations.

A woman in a long white puffer jacket walked past, questioning Frank with her eyes. He nodded that he'd be with her in a minute, but Matt's attention was drawn to the girls wrapped in her arms. Light blonde hair and thin faces, red rimmed eyes, and an unsure gait made it clear that these were the daughters left behind.

"You and your wife have the girls?" Matt asked when the children were nearly out the door.

"Yeah. Wouldn't let anybody else raise them. Their mom went through some rough times, but she got herself together and was doing right. It's going to be hard for them, but they've got family."

It was the opening that Matt was looking for. The transition from his sincere condolences to the reason Sheriff Catharine Allemande called him this morning, twenty minutes after his flight landed in Cedar Rapids, and told him he needed to talk to Frank. "You should concentrate on those girls."

Frank shook his head, knowing what other shoe was about to drop, and he didn't want to hear it. "Nikki's been clean six months. I put it out that anyone deals to her, they have to deal with me."

"Supplying drugs that lead to an overdose is a felony, Frank. We find who did, and I promise you, we'll go federal and put them away for a very long time."

"I can put them away," Frank blurted.

Matt moved closer. "And what, Frank? You're a felon, and you've been out for three months. You get sent up again, it's not for nine months or a couple of years. They'll put you away forever, and then what about those girls? You want CPS to take them away? Let us handle this. You know I've never lied to you. I want whoever did this. If they can be found, I'll find them."

2

Anger rushed to Frank's face. Matt could feel it coming off the man. "Like you're just going to let someone else find who killed your lady? Like you're going to let them go to the pen and not deal with it yourself? No, counselor, you and I, we're just alike." He emphasized the point by moving inches from Matt. "Except I ain't waiting."

And there it was, what the sheriff feared and what Matt was sure was coming. Frank Moscow, the closest thing the extended family better known locally as the Russians, had to a leader was going to take the law into his own hands and hunt down whoever gave his daughter the fentanyl that killed her. If he had to drag the entire county down to do it, that would be fine by him. Frank stuck out his hand again, gripping Matt's in an extended shake. "I do appreciate the personal thoughts." He was gone in a moment, hands deep into his pockets, shoulders hunched against the cold as he shouldered his way through the doors.

Matt sat down alone in the church and made the sign of the cross. He added Nikki Moscow and her girls to his normal prayer for Dawn, before grabbing his wool jacket off the pew and heading out of Saint Wen's with fading hopes that the death of Nikki Moscow wouldn't lead to more pain and suffering.

Chapter 2

Warm air blowing on his face, combined with the tinkling of frozen drizzle on the Jeep's windshield, threatened to send Matt into a deep sleep. He half regretted rushing back to Iowa after toying with the idea of spending the holidays in Singapore. Prompted by the news of Nikki's death and a text from the sheriff, he settled on coming home and caught a fifteen-hour flight to San Francisco. Add the four-hour layover before flying to Chicago, then another hop into Cedar Rapids, and he didn't even have fumes to be running on. Back in Mannheim, he had enough time to shower and feel how utterly empty his house and life were without Dawn before heading to the funeral. Even his cat was gone, having abandoned him for his niece's apartment. Christmas only deepened his feelings of loss and how much he missed his wife. That they had been together, in a way, twice since she was killed when her car was run off the road couldn't undo that damage. It couldn't replace her presence in his daily life.

The crunch of tires on gravel brought him around again as the universe conspired to keep him awake. Caddie pulled her Sheriff's Office truck up next to him, waved, then disappeared from view as she climbed down on the opposite side. Matt grabbed a Brewers' baseball cap off the passenger seat and met her out in the wet cold.

"Welcome to Iowa." She gave a small smile from underneath her black cowboy hat with its Sheriff's gold star. He grunted in answer. "Back this way." She led him to the side of the Patriot's Inn. Fronted in bright red, white, and blues, the back of the highway-side hotel held all the charm of a semi-abandoned New Jersey warehouse. Its most distinguishing features were thin gravel, two battered dumpsters, and peeling grey paint. Caddie flipped up the collar on her leather jacket against the drizzle, prompting Matt to unconsciously mimic her. "You get any sleep?"

"What I could on the plane. My system is completely screwed up."

She stopped short of a back door and the dim square of yellowish light it threw out onto the gravel. "We could do this tomorrow, if you're not up to it today."

"I just got back and you're trying to get rid of me." They fell easily into their working partnership, something they both enjoyed despite the circumstances. Caddie's responsibilities as sheriff naturally put a distance between her and the other deputies. Matt had his outside work for a firm that specialized in representing defense contractors, which took up most of his time, but with each other they could just be investigators focused on a case.

But seeing her also brought back a nagging sense of guilt. When the sheriff nearly died from an assassin's bullet seven months ago, Dawn returned and helped Matt save Caddie's life. Then in the maelstrom of a storm, Caddie clearly saw Dawn, leaving Matt with a choice. He could tell his friend the truth or hoard Dawn for himself. He chose selfishness and repeatedly lied to her until the fleeting nature of Dawn's existence here helped her hold on Caddie's memory fade. The voice that told Caddie to fight for her life slipped away into a half-remembered fog.

"No, I don't think we have a lot of time." He recounted his talk with Frank and the clear message the grieving father had sent. "I'm sure Nikki's death has been overwhelming the last few days, but now he's a man on a mission." Frank was right; they understood one another. Better than three years on from Dawn's murder and he wasn't giving up on proving who was responsible. Frank couldn't do any less, he just wouldn't be as constrained by the law and the need for evidence as Matt. "I guarantee, he's going to find someone to blame and make them pay."

"Kill them, you mean."

Matt nodded, then motioned to the expanse of rain-slick gravel in front of them. Caddie was the sheriff and spent more of her time leading and administrating than investigating, but Matt never forgot that she had been a darn good detective with Cedar Rapids for years. He'd managed to download the reports before he left Singapore to read on the flight back, but he wanted to hear it from her, including any personal take that didn't make it onto paper.

"Short version, Nikki leaves the front desk at two-fifteen and doesn't appear on video surveillance again. Her relief found her body back here a little after six that morning. Everything is consistent with a fentanyl overdose. Toxicology confirms it. She had a concentration of over 58 nanograms per liter, which is more than fatal. No other signs of struggle, no bruising, torn clothing, no reports from guests about noise, nothing. Her body was slumped against the building. She had a jacket on, unzipped, cigarettes and a lighter in her pocket. There was a cigarette stub still in her fingers. I had that sent to DCI, but my running assumption is that's how she ingested the drug. It's the most common method for ODs, and we didn't find any pills on her and she didn't have any needle tracks."

"Any other drugs in her system?"

"No. She was clean otherwise. Claire reviewed the security footage, and Nikki normally took two or three what look like smoke breaks a night. Usually, fifteen minutes or so, occasionally she's gone for an hour. So everything fits. She was looking at her phone about fifteen minutes before she takes her break, but from the camera angle, you can't tell what she's doing. And before you ask, nothing on the phone so far, no calls or texts that night, but she has two different messaging apps we can't see. DCI has the phone, but I'm not hopeful."

Matt glanced up at the small, dark bubble above the door that concealed a security camera. Caddie shook her head. "It's out, same as the one on the north side. We have coverage of the front desk, two on the front exterior, and one on the south side. The manager said they have repairs planned, but it isn't a priority. Apparently, these places run on thin margins and they were waiting on a yearly maintenance visit to fix the cameras."

"Interior halls?"

"Same, spotty coverage, and Nikki doesn't show up," she said, her flat tone passing judgment. "The way I read it, they don't want to know what's going on."

That was something Mat hadn't considered. "You think someone's moving dope through here? It would provide a drug connection." Maybe Frank's search for who supplied his daughter wouldn't last long.

"There's nothing specific," Caddie answered. "But DEA has put out products suggesting smaller towns are being used as transshipment points for everything from meth to opioids. Traffickers are avoiding the major routes like I-80 as troopers step up enforcement. Instead, they're using alternate routes that attract less attention. Mannheim is a straight shot from Cedar Rapids or Iowa

City to Dubuque, then onto Chicago, so it makes sense. And last month, Jones County busted an escort service that set up shop in their Patriot's Inn. The crew moved in, advertised online, and booked customers within hours. They normally move on after a week or two, but HSI was trailing them and set up a sting. No reason that couldn't have happened here. In any event, the red, white, and blue of Patriot's Inn doesn't want to know."

"But nothing specific about Mannheim?"

"No."

Matt was wondering what he expected to find in a rain-drenched backlot days after a victim was killed because her luck ran out. Putting street drugs into your system was always going to be a deadly game of roulette. That black ball lands on the wrong number, it's too strong, not what you were expecting, or your heart just gives out and you die. If you're lucky, a cop or someone else with Naloxone brings you back, and you get more spins at the wheel. For Nikki, all the numbers came up wrong. The soaked and weathered remains of cigarette butts were the only evidence left here of her passing. "Did you get any info from the family on who Nikki was seeing or potential sources?"

Caddie motioned them back toward her truck and waited to answer until they were inside with the heater running. "I drove out to the Moscow place an hour after the manager found the body. Mom was huddled up with the girls crying, and Frank had already put out the word not to cooperate. We haven't gotten a word out of them since."

"So nothing on current contacts?"

"Claire's working on network analysis charts from what little we're getting, but so far it's either outdated, or if it's recent it only shows her involved with work, her kids, or classes she's taking at Kirkwood."

"She went back to school?" For some reason that hit Matt hard. Frank said she was clean, she was working at a crappy hotel, and now he learns she was going to school to improve her life. He knew addiction didn't care about any of that, but the fact that she was getting her life together and doing her best for two young girls made her death sadder for him.

"A couple of classes at a time. She was studying for a hospitality services degree."

"Crap," Matt said.

"Yeah," Caddie agreed. They let the pinging of sleet against the window fill the void for a time.

"So, how was Singapore?" she asked, her voice making that subtle transition from sheriff to friend.

"Warmer," he laughed. "A lot warmer and uneventful. Our client's customer checks all good. HGS files end user certificates and other export docs with State and Commerce, a company in Singapore gets advanced ground radar imagery systems for mining, and I get to write a lengthy report covering everyone's backside in case the radars end up in China or Iran." But Singapore was already in the past for him. "Frank says she was clean," he said, changing the subject back to Nikki.

"Frank is where I need your focus." Back to her sheriff voice. "Anything we can get on who Nikki associated with, who her old drug connections were, anything that could unlock this."

"Pump Frank for information and keep him from running roughshod over the county at the same time?"

"That's what I pay you for." They laughed at the long-running joke. The D.C. job paid him far too well, and the county barely anything. He wasn't wearing a deputy's badge for the money.

"Man, I'm hungry." He buttoned the top of his coat. "If Jill's is still open, I'm buying."

Caddie's answer was cut off by the voice of dispatch coming out of the radio. "Unit One, we have to 10-50 on the Victory Road exit to State One-Fifty-One. Three vehicles, minor injuries. Roads are getting slick, Sheriff, over."

Caddie sighed and pressed the hand mic clipped to her jacket. "Responding, I'm five minutes away."

Mat grabbed the door handle to leave.

"Rain check?" she asked. Matt nodded. "Plans tonight?" For some reason, she seemed unwilling to let him go. He knew what it was. She had the job tonight, she had Mama Allemande in Cedar Rapids to visit over the holidays, and he had an empty house that could only remind him of what was missing.

"Sleep," he said.

"Don't forget tomorrow night. "

A little Christmas get together at the sheriff's house didn't fit his mood at the moment, but that might be exactly the point. "Be there with bells on," he said, stepping out. She laughed and waved before heading toward her accident. Matt decided eating at Jill's by himself was more depressing than being alone in their house on Christmas Eve. His mind wasn't clear enough to think about Nikki's death anymore; he only hoped there was something in the freezer to eat and that he could fall asleep quickly tonight.

Chapter 3

A wall of cold, dripping trees bracketing the running trail blocked the wind, but rain shifting into freezing drizzle and back again came at Matt whichever direction he turned. He hadn't lasted long enough in the house to do more than change into layers of water-resistant running gear and pick out a pair of heavy-duty trail runners. His earbuds were dead after nearly two days of travel, so he left his phone and music in the Jeep at Waumandee Creek landing and headed north. He quickly lost himself in the rhythm of breathing and his lonely footfalls through empty woods.

––––––––––

It was their first Christmas in Germany. Dawn wouldn't start her job at the Department of Defense school for another six months and money was tight. They had a quiet Christmas Eve with white wine from a local shop, opened the three present limit they had given themselves, and watched a choral concert on German television. They had plans for a long walk in the woods behind their apartment in the morning. Content and ready for sleep, they crawled into bed.

"Do me a favor," he said, "and turn away from me."

She popped one eye open. "Why?"

"Just, turn that way."

Dawn slowly rolled away, her head turning to keep an eye on him. "This isn't going to get weird, is it?"

"A little," he nodded. "Trust me."

"Okay." She finally turned and listened to the scraping of his nightstand drawer opening, then Matt clearing his throat.

"Marley was dead, to begin with. There is no doubt..."

Dawn flipped back, mouth open, eyes wide. "You're reading to me for Christmas?"

"I'm trying to," he said, "but I'll feel weird if you're looking at me."

She kissed him. "You silly, clever soldier. I love you so much."

"I love you. Now, turn the other way."

She pecked him on the cheek again, fluffed her pillow, and turned away. "Start at the beginning again. I want to hear all of my story."

"Marley was dead, to begin with." It would take more nights in bed with Dawn facing away before they would finish Charles Dickens' A Christmas Carol. From that night on, every Christmas season, Matt read to Dawn. Some years, it was a cozy Christmas mystery filled with clever amateur detectives in small snowy English towns. In others, it was Christmas poems filled with faith, love, and wishes of peace. More than once, it was back to Dickens and Scrooge and Marley and the promise of redemption. Every year until she was taken from him. Every year until Dawn's death blew a gaping wound through his life. He would have given anything to read to her again.

————

Matt let the Jeep's heater wash warm air over him as he flexed feeling back into his cheeks. Six miles total out of town and back, past open ponds and dewy woods, produced heavy legs and an overall exhaustion that gave some hope he would sleep tonight. Part of him didn't want to come in from the cold, though. Part of him wanted to keep running, letting the memory of Dawn and their life propel him in his own frozen fantasy land. But he had to go home now. He had to face tonight alone.

Chapter 4

The freezing rain had turned to fog and hung heavily outside the windows of the house that had been in Dawn's family for nearly a hundred and forty years. Large windows intended to let in morning light instead filled the kitchen with a melancholy gloom matching the night outside. A haunted London Christmas had nothing on the mood permeating Matt's evening. He sat at the kitchen island staring out vacantly into the dark, the light over the sink behind him the only illumination. He picked at microwaved chili still in the Tupperware he found in the back of the freezer, unable to remember when he made it. The first bottle of Vogel's Premium was empty in front of him with the second well on the way to joining it. He shivered and swore the cold clung to the old house refusing to retreat in the face of the best efforts of the furnace. Twenty-first-century heating losing the war with nineteenth-century homebuilding.

At least in Singapore he didn't see Dawn's face everywhere he looked. But in this home, in this town, she was everywhere. That had mostly been a comfort since she left, her miraculous returns populating his mind with new images of their lives, and afterlives, together. Christmas this year, though, he was finding it a gut punch. He pushed his chili away and finished the beer, clinking it loudly on the counter, and then stood ready to blow right past his two-beer limit.

Opening the refrigerator door let out a flood of light for an instant, before it died along with the light above the sink. The hum of the furnace fan quit. Glancing out the window confirmed it was just his house. "Crap." You could never upgrade the electric in the house enough to make up for it being built in the 1880s. The first flashlight in the drawer was dead. "Crap, crap." Grabbing a long pink candle, he lit it and headed toward the basement door before a thought, a barest of hopes, entered his mind. "Dawn?" He could hardly get the word out. There was no reason for her to return. Whatever allowed her to cross over, he knew, was based on her overwhelming ability and need to care for and love others. But everyone she cared for and loved was safe. He wasn't in any danger. But he called again, "Dawn?"

Ignoring the basement and the fuse box that promised to restore power, he wandered through the front rooms, then up the stairs of the home she had lovingly restored to its original glory. To a sinking heart, he realized that there was no one in the bathroom, no love of his life standing in the hall. All was as it should be.

Disappointed, he headed downstairs for the long descent to the basement. As his foot landed softly on the bottom step before the front door with its descending squares of colored glass, the sharp electric tingle of the doorbell sounded. Matt expected and wanted no one here tonight and considered quietly retreating up the stairs. But Dawn wouldn't do that. Not on Christmas Eve of all nights. He held the candle up as he quickly brushed away melting wax dripping onto his hand.

"Hello." The porch was empty. A wind blew a sheet of drizzle, clearing the fog for a moment. Darkness extended out into the yard until it was rudely interrupted by colored light from his neighbor's inflatable twelve-foot Santa. He laughed at himself. Old house with an old electrical system, and he was searching for ghosts on Christmas. "Bah humbug," he muttered.

A voice called from the dark in the sitting room next to him. His heart stopped. "If you compare me to an undigested bit of beef, you're in trouble, dear."

"Dawn." He turned. Unable to step forward, he lifted the candle, allowing its warm yellow light to reach across the gap of darkness. His love, his bride, his Dawn stepped from the shadows with a shy, warm smile radiating love, and all the darkness and cold left his world.

"Hello, soldier." She tilted her head, part cute come on, part soft caring, reminding Matt that wherever she might be, he remained loved. Tears streaked down his cheeks.

"Baby." Dawn stepped to him, all her plans for cute banter washed away with his release of longing. "What's the matter?" Reaching for his cheek, tiny sparks of electric discharge jumped the gap between them before dying painlessly.

"I really needed to see you." He could finally move and stepped into her as if they could feel one another. "It's supposed to get easier, but it doesn't."

"That's because you love me, silly. It will get easier, I promise, when we're together again. But I'm here now. I'm here for you."

Those words tripped Matt's mind from the emotion of seeing the love of his life to the question that lay behind it. "But I don't need you."

Her smile slumped into slack-jawed disbelief. "Pardon me?"

———————

Dawn knew she wasn't thinking straight. Crossing over took more energy, more life force, or whatever it was, than she could describe. It also required a great deal of love, the energy that held the universe together. *Gravity, as if.* Which told her she wasn't thinking straight, because she hadn't used the phrase 'as if' since she was a teenager. "You want to try that again, my dear sweet soldier?"

The pain in Matt's eyes was his first answer. "That's not what I mean." He looked so cute being pitiful, she almost didn't want to let him off the hook. She must have shown forgiveness as his shoulders relaxed, and that sly boy smile touched his cheeks. "I just meant, I'm not in any danger or trouble, and no one's trying to shoot me."

"Are you sure?" She leaned against the door frame, knowing it would accentuate what curves she had. She wished she were wearing a skirt to show off her legs. Back from the beyond, married for more than twenty years, and they couldn't help flirting with one another. "Some people have found you very shootable lately."

"I've been working on that. But no, I'm okay, your family is fine."

"And our friends?"

He hesitated a second. "They're fine, everyone is as they should be."

"Stop quoting *A Christmas Carol*, dear. You know, I remember every line of it." Time didn't exist where she was, at least not in the way you could think of on this side. Over there, everything was eternal in a sense that the word couldn't describe. She and Matt were together there. From the moment they met, they had always been

14

together, but there was a tenuousness to it. What Matt did in this life would change his eternity. Her mind settled back into the here and now. Leaning back, she looked out the front window to the sight of a far too big, far too bright Santa swaying in a pelting wind. Up the street, more lights outlined roofs and filled in bushes. A nativity cutout was silhouetted in a white spotlight. She looked back at Matt. "What day is this, exactly?"

"Christmas Eve." He said it like he was confessing to a gross misdemeanor. He wasn't going to jail, but he knew he was wrong.

She made a show of looking around the room for any sign that it was Christmas. No tree, no lights, no Nativity set on the mantle. There was no Christmas in their house. "You are so wrong, dear. You really do need me."

Chapter 5

Convinced that for once murderous high school principals or insane deputies weren't gunning for Matt, Dawn focused on fixing the one thing she knew was wrong with her husband; he was spending Christmas Eve alone in a dark house drinking beer. There were people who cared for him that he should be turning to. She thought he had figured that out last time she was here. Seems her work on this man was never completely done. Luckily, she loved him beyond measure, and he was still cute. Dawn climbed into the Jeep wearing tall white boots and a short white wool jacket trimmed in white faux fur over a short skirt that left her trim legs exposed. A white knit cap jauntily angled on her head completed the look. Not something she would ever normally wear. She felt like a pinup girl straight out of a 1940s auto parts calendar. "Are you thinking naughty thoughts?"

"You would if you could see from where I'm sitting."

"You are a naughty soldier," she grinned. "Now tell me about this case you have. It's not murder, but maybe that's why I'm here."

Matt took his time driving through the neighborhood. She knew it was to let her see the lights. Part of their first Christmas was spent doing the same thing, only with hot chocolate in a Thermos and Christmas music on the radio. Before he answered, he tapped the radio on, pressed two preset stations before finding Vince Guaraldi's *Linus and Lucy* from the Charlie Brown Christmas Special. It was practically their song. Cute and sweet.

"You know Nikki Moscow, Frank's daughter?"

Dawn had to think. The fuzzy brain from crossing over had faded, but she was tired. That's the way it went on this side. She would need to rest if she was going to help with Christmas and whatever else Matt needed from her. "I don't think so, other than the last name, of course."

Matt turned down another street, delaying their arrival at the Sheriff's Office so they could keep talking easily, explaining what he knew about Nikki's life and death. "I need to dive in deeper. I was gone when she died, and I haven't seen the notes on associates who might be dumb enough to defy Frank's order to not provide her drugs."

"Off working for HGS? Somewhere nice doing something exciting, I hope."

"Singapore, which is nice. Working on confirming end user certificates for sensitive exports, which isn't exciting. My plan was to start working this more tomorrow after a decent night's sleep."

"On Christmas?" Dawn admired and pitied Matt for wanting to work on an overdose on a day they should be together, enjoying being together.

He shrugged. "It's only going to get harder to find her source. Either Frank runs them off, and we never get them, or worse, Frank finds them, gets convicted of murder, and those two little girls deal with another loss. CPS might take them, and who knows after that."

"Little girls?" The name Nikki was coming back to her. "Little blonde things, skinny as can be?"

"One's not so little, but that sounds like them. I feel terrible for them." It sounded like a confession. "And there's a woman dead because of bad dope that could be out there waiting to kill someone else, and Frank is threatening to burn down the county to find out who's responsible."

He finally turned toward Government Road and the Law Enforcement Center. "Maybe that's why you're here, my little Christmas miracle. You can help me give those girls some peace of mind and keep their criminal grandfather from blowing up their world even more."

"That's right, let's make the world safe for Frank Moscow to raise more kids." She would try to help with the case, but her job, then and now, is to protect Matt. He had the same job for her, but it was his turn to be protected.

Chapter 6

Blinking in time to unheard music, purple and green lights were strung along the walls and workstations of the Sheriff's Office dispatch center. A paper Santa in his sleigh pulled by reindeer arced across the back wall, while a collection of small plastic snowmen grinned from the tops of filing cabinets. Matt and Dawn stood in the doorway as Claire Henderson handled a call about an accident, this one a very slow-speed affair in the Walmart parking lot. Caddie's voice came over the radio, acknowledging the call and saying she was two blocks away.

"She shouldn't be working on Christmas Eve like some cooler female version of Bob Cratchit," Dawn said, her warmth for the young woman coming through.

"That's just who she is," Matt whispered. "She volunteered for dispatch tonight so no one else has to work on Christmas."

The sound of Matt's voice tilted Claire's head before a quick turn. The headphones were off in a blur, and she rolled her wheelchair to the door faster than he could react. He'd grown closer and more protective of Claire in the months they'd known each other. There was a lot of personal baggage they each carried, from the accident that took the use of her legs and her parents' lives, to the emotional toll Dawn's death took on him, which drew them together. It also helped that they genuinely liked and respected each other. Their hug was tight and longer than Matt planned. An eye up to Dawn saw her waving understanding. "She's practically your daughter," she said. "Papa should be home for Christmas, and I hope you got her something better than a T-shirt from Singapore."

Matt held Claire at arm's length, inspecting her for a moment. "What happened to your hair? It's brown." He was so used to her changing shades of green, purple, and blonde that he'd come to think of them as her natural state.

"I know, weird, right? But I saw too many grandmas with their hair dyed wild colors, and I had to go another direction." She pulled up the sleeve on her "Santa Rocks" T-shirt with its cartoon image of Santa, two elves, and a reindeer crossing a street like the Beatles on the Abbey Road cover. Her right bicep was covered by a vibrant tattoo of Rosie the Riveter flexing her muscles. Claire flexed hers to go along with it. "What do you think?"

Dawn had once suggested getting a small ankle tattoo and Matt freaked out, if only a little. He just wasn't from a tattoo generation. His wife saved him again. "The only right answer is how awesome it looks. And, dear, it is pretty awesome."

He nodded, thanking Dawn for the check on his gut reaction and agreeing she was right. "That is awesome. When did you get it?"

Claire rolled toward the breakroom next to Dispatch. The building was full of breakrooms and well-appointed conference rooms thanks to a former sheriff who purposely ran up the cost. "Before Thanksgiving. You've been gone for a while, Matt, but at least you're home for Christmas."

"Yes, dear," Dawn said. "You've been gone too long."

Settled with mugs of tea with honey from Claire's personal stash, they spent a few minutes catching up before diving into work. Dawn sat on the workspace behind Claire, her feet dangling in the air, kicking easily back and forth. Claire was still dating Bob, a contractor she met in June, who was a good guy, but on the shy side. He was also seemingly entirely devoted to Claire. "Honestly," Claire said, "part of volunteering for dispatch tonight was to take the pressure off spending the entire holidays with his family. I mean, they're great, but a girl needs a little space."

"Let it go, babe," Dawn said. "She's not looking for advice, just venting a little. And, we should have bought her present. You did get her a present? Right?"

"I've got your present at home. How about work tonight, present at Caddie's party tomorrow?" Matt asked.

"Caddie's party?" Dawn did not sound thrilled.

"Sounds good," Claire said. She quickly caught him up on her Nikki Moscow work before sending him to the office where she spent most of her time as the Sheriff's Office intelligence analyst. Matt wanted to see her charts, it was the reason they came here, but he also wanted to ease the frown on Dawn's face.

"The party is for anyone in the SO who wants to attend," he said as they headed down the hall. "It's not some, whatever."

19

She let out a deep, long sigh. "That sounds fun, and I shouldn't fuss that you have plans for Christmas with your friends since I was just fussing about you not having plans for Christmas with your friends." She paused. "Caddie, friends, right?" The last was accompanied by a raised eyebrow, tentative in its reach.

"Yes, dear," he said as they passed through an empty deputies' bullpen. "Friends."

"Thank goodness." She let out a long breath that led to a broad smile. He remained all hers. A second thought stopped Dawn in her tracks. "I'm sorry, I completely forgot. Caddie's okay now, right? And what does she remember about me? What did you tell her all about the mystery woman?"

"I was going to tell her everything. But with the storm damage and everything, I didn't see her in private for a couple of days, and by then it all seemed nuts. What would she even do with the truth? A lie felt easier. I told her there was no woman, that between the pain drugs she was on, she'd imagined it."

Dawn stood open-mouthed waiting for more. When it didn't come, she closed her eyes and slowly shook her head. "The lady cop, with as much experience as an investigator as my dear husband, bought that?"

"I think so. She argued a little at first, but it seemed like the memory was fading already. Between it being impossible that she saw my wife and the nature of whatever you are, dear…"

"Besides, cute."

"Besides, cute. Finally I think her memories of you kind of slipped away."

"You think so," she said. "But we have no idea if she'll still see me."

"Claire doesn't," Matt said.

"She wasn't on death's doorstep while I whispered words of encouragement in her ear."

"No." Matt motioned to continue to Claire's office. "Let's focus on Nikki and talk about Caddie later."

"I'll add it to the list of things to talk about," she said.

Matt set down the oversize printout of the network analysis chart on the table in the back of the Dispatch Center. It painted a clear

20

picture. In the middle was a DMV photo of Nikki Moscow with a slight smile. She looked as good as you could in a driver's license picture. To the left of her picture, lines led to a tangle of driver's license photos and booking shots with short bursts of words below. Jesse Moscow, assault, burglary; Sarah Highland, check fraud, meth poss, OWI. Cousins, high school friends, and the perpetually troubled and addicted you could find in any small Midwest town. Mannheim had more than its share, and Nikki had hung out with every one of them. Above that tangle sat Frank Moscow, represented by an old booking photo, looking far worse for wear than he did today. The list of abbreviations below his name was long and still incomplete: intent distro meth, assault, burglary, fishing w/out lic, added just for fun. Lines from Frank's photo reached down through the web below him. If someone in Fillmore County was in on the drug trade, dealer, buyer, or both, they were connected to Frank.

The picture of Nikki had its own list for shoplifting, driving under the influence 2nd offense, and assault for punching a bartender at the Hawk's Nest. Below her were two squares with blue outline images instead of photos. Megan and Bella Moscow. "I want to see pictures of the girls," Dawn said. "It shouldn't matter, but I want to be sure if one of them was the little girl I called CPS about. It shouldn't matter, but it does."

Matt pointed to the blue outlines. "No pictures for the girls?"

"I didn't want to put their pictures on a chart along with people their mom might have been doing drugs with. If that ever found its way into court or was released, I'd feel horrible."

"That's very sweet," Dawn said, giving her husband a wink. "You've done a good job raising her, Papa." Ever since they'd found that Matt, along with Caddie, were listed as Claire's emergency contacts, Dawn had decided that Matt was responsible for Claire. She was going to make sure he lived up to that. "She's right about the pictures on the chart, but I still want to see them. But let's finish looking at these spaghetti charts you two love so much."

"You're right about their pictures on the chart," Matt told her. "I wouldn't have thought of that. But I'd still like to see their pictures."

Claire jotted a quick note on a sticky and stuck it to her dispatch work station. "I'll email them as soon as I get a chance."

Matt pointed at the less populated right side of Nikki's chart. The manager of the Patriot's Inn, two younger-looking women labeled as students, and three brothers and a sister. The Moscow kids had their little rap sheets below their pics, the least being the sister's public exposure; the manager and students were clean. A thick black line ran down the center of the chart, dividing the two sides with the word rehab along its length. "Are you saying that she has no association with all of these other people in what, the last seven months?"

"No. I'm saying statements we've gathered since her death do not put Nikki with any of her old friends once she left rehab."

Matt's eyes were drawn again to the picture of Nikki looking out at him with the slight smile allowed for a driver's license picture. "Frank insisted she was clean."

"I don't know if she was clean." Claire tapped the chart. "But it looks like she was trying, anyway. From everything we've found so far, she kept her distance from people she used to associate with. None of the Russians are talking to us, but everyone else says she went to work, went to school, or was home with her girls."

"What about from her phone?" Matt asked.

"Those connections are shown here." Claire pointed to the small cell phone icons in the middle of arrows connecting Nikki to a few of the entities on the chart. "Her call history went back about a month, in that time, she's been in contact with her mother, Frank, the oldest daughter, Megan, the manager at the Patriot's Inn, and two students she knew from Kirkwood." She pointed at the two images of women whose DMV photos had that glow of getting your first driver's license. "Neither has any record, no one in their family has a record. Both were shocked at Nikki's death. They swear they never heard her talking about drugs. To them, she was the cool mom in class who they shared notes with. Sometimes they got coffee after class."

Caddie's voice came over the speaker, clearing the fender bender in the Walmart parking lot. She was taking ten in McDonald's before they closed.

"I'm not sure what's sadder," Dawn said. "Eating Mickey D's on Christmas Eve or working there." She gave Matt her soft smile. "Sorry I fussed about your little party tomorrow."

22

He gave a small shrug that Claire caught as she turned around. At least she hadn't overheard him talking to himself, but with Dawn back, that was probably coming, too. "What?" she asked.

"Sorry, just thinking. Maybe she was clean, but it doesn't always stick, and it only takes one bad dose. Was there anything else on the phone? Search history, texts, apps?"

"Search history was wiped a month ago. It could have been a major system update, or she just didn't want people seeing what she was up to. In any case, what is there is all about country music, Caitlin Clark, and her daughters' schools. Texts are the same people as her calls, again going back thirty days. Nothing there. Normal shopping, music, and game apps. From what I could see in those, there was nothing. One slightly odd app was Yadda, an anonymous text service."

"Yadda? And who's Caitlin Clark?" Dawn asked.

"I hadn't heard of that one," Matt said. "What's its trick?"

"Texts disappear as soon as you read them," Claire said. "There's also a photo option that bypasses the phone's built-in photo software, so the image only appears in the app. You can send nudes and not worry that someone will post them later. There's a basic service that's free and allows a limited number of texts a month. You can pay for an upgrade that includes video, voice, and group chat."

"Dear, you know I think you're cute, but please don't send nudes. No one needs to see that," Dawn said.

Matt ignored her. "Payment could be traceable," he said.

"Unless you buy a gift card or use an anonymous payment system," Claire said.

"Oh," Dawn brightened, not able to hold back from interrupting. "I get it. Yadda, yadda, and I'm exhausted this morning." Matt's eyes scrunched in puzzlement. "Seinfeld, you know. Yadda, yadda. Anyway, I guess that was obvious. Go ahead, dear, I'll try to be quiet."

Claire went on, her words mixing with Dawn's. "The boss said to write up a subpoena for Yadda, but they're based in Romania, and their system wipes the data when it disappears for the users. Even if they respond, it probably won't do us any good."

A call into 911 pulled Claire back to the desk, giving Dawn a chance to talk. "If you were texting to get drugs, you might use

Yadda or something like that. Besides that, I could see getting an anonymous text app so the government, people like you, dear, don't peek at what I'm texting."

He wanted to laugh. The idea that Dawn would be doing something that needed spying on struck him as funny. But she wasn't making an 'I'm cute and being amusing' face. She was entirely serious. "Really?" he mouthed.

"Yes. We've given up a lot of privacy for convenience. Maybe a girlfriend wants to talk to me about an affair she's having, don't you get any ideas, or some medical issues, or whatever. It's nobody's business and shouldn't be sitting in a server until some corporation or government comes along and snaps it up."

His wife the rebel, but he knew a lot of people would agree. It was easy for him, sitting on this side of the law, to be glad law enforcement could reach back and read your texts or see who you've called for the last year. It made the job easier, but there was a cost to people's sense of freedom from nameless snoopers. "So maybe it's not that odd," he whispered exactly at the same time Claire finished her 911.

"What?" she asked, turning her chair in place. He explained Dawn's thinking. "I get that," she said. "I thought about getting Yadda. Bob said he's caught his mom checking out his phone. Which is really weird. Who wants to know what's on their twenty-five-year-old son's phone?"

"I shudder," Dawn said.

Matt glanced at the charts but decided they'd done enough for the night. Better to start fresh in the morning. *Christmas morning*, he thought, *at work with Dawn*. Despite the circumstances, it brought him joy. Not exactly in the Christmas spirit. "Sounds a little clingy," he said.

"Maybe that's why I'm here on Christmas Eve." She spread her hands out in front of the dispatch station and its monitors and comms equipment.

"That's not why," Matt said. "You're a nice person, and you wanted everyone else to have a happy Christmas."

"That too," she said.

Matt's eyes went to Dawn, who had tilted her head and narrowed her eyes a little. She wasn't done, even if the two paid Sheriff's

Office employees were. "How'd Claire get into the phone if the Moscows aren't talking? I hope they didn't use Nikki's finger to unlock it."

"Huh, I hadn't thought of that," Matt said.

"It's okay, dear, you're tired from all your world traveling exploits."

"Hadn't thought of what?" Claire asked.

Matt shook his head. He was out of practice having secret conversations with his wife in public without looking like a bit of a loon. "Sorry, internal conversation. If the Russians aren't talking, how did you get on the phone?"

"I have a confidential source." She tried not to smile but didn't succeed.

"You what?"

"I have a source." Claire sat up straighter, ready to defend herself from what she knew was coming next.

"You don't have sources, Claire," Matt said, sharply. "You're an analyst, not a trained officer. Any confidential source with the code to get into Nikki's phone is not to be trusted and is inherently dangerous."

Dawn hopped down from the table and zipped up her jacket. For someone who was reluctant to leave a minute ago, she seemed ready to walk out now. "Settle down, Papa Bear," she said. "I have a feeling Claire knows precisely what she's doing."

Matt barreled through Dawn's warning. He did that at times, and almost always regretted it. "And the sheriff is good with this? You out there recruiting sources in a family of drug dealers and thieves?"

A wince of pain flitted across Claire's face before it reset in determination. The look came together with Dawn's warning letting him know he'd messed up, he just wasn't sure how yet. "Yes, Matt, she approves, and I'm not some idiot off the street. I have a vague idea of what I'm doing. And, in case you have forgotten, I can take care of myself."

"Listen to your wife," Dawn said in a stage whisper before she got louder, "and you won't hurt the feelings of a young woman who, for some inexplicable reason, looks up to you. She's not a dummy, dear."

Matt let out a very long, audible breath and rubbed his forehead. "Sorry, let me try again. Claire, can you tell me who your source is?"

"I think I can do that," she said, holding on to her irritation a moment longer. "Megan Moscow. We've kept in touch since her grandfather used her to pass a message to you." Any hurt or anger at Matt faded with the triumph of being right. "I sent her a text the day after her mom passed, telling her if she needed anything, she only had to ask. I wasn't thinking of information, just a girl who lost her mom." She shared the pain of losing her own parents, a pain shared by Matt and his grief after Dawn's accident. "She's a good kid who already had it rough. I just wanted her to know that I cared. She called me that night and said Grandpa Frank put down the law, and no one was going to talk to us. The Russians will handle their own business. She knows what I do, we've talked about what it means to be a criminal analyst, just to give her ideas beyond the family business. Anyway, she asked if I had her mother's phone. I didn't see any reason to lie and said yes. She gave me the code, which we would never have gotten because it's not a birthday or anything like that. Megan's been keeping tabs on her mom since she got out of rehab and checked the phone regularly. So, I got in, copied the phone's drive, and sent it off to DCI for a tech to examine when and if they ever get to it."

"Jesus," Matt said, knowing the moment it crossed his lips what was coming next.

"Dear, let's not take the Lord's name in vain," Dawn said. "Not on Christmas." She'd broken his habit of saying GD first. He could barely think it now. Then she went after the variations of Jesus, especially the one with an obscene middle name. F bombs and scatological vulgarities she left alone.

"That poor kid," Matt said. "That's good work, Claire."

Caddie came back on the radio. She was heading downtown and available for calls. Claire rolled up to her station and answered. Christmas Eve was only going to get busier, and Matt decided that he and his bride needed some rest. With a fresh start in the morning, they could figure out their next steps.

"I'm going to leave you to it," he said, headed for the door. "If you have a chance, call me tomorrow. I'd like to talk about Megan and how she might be able to help. Sorry to work you on Christmas."

"It's the job," Claire said as another 911 call came in. At least half of them tonight wouldn't be true emergencies; someone playing Christmas music too loud to accompany their yard decorations, or a little one worried the sheriff might mistake Santa for a burglar and shoot him. Between that, accidents, and the always present possibility of a domestic, Claire was about to hit a very busy few hours. She answered the call and waved to Matt at the same time.

"Merry Christmas," he said.

"Merry Christmas," she mouthed back.

Dawn followed Matt out the door, a little purple Santa hat on her head, the white ball dangling perfectly to the side. "I think it's time for more Christmas, dear."

Chapter 7

Matt continued on to Main, avoiding the direct route home. He'd contracted with Mannheim's Iowa's Best Flowers months ago, before the Singapore assignment, and his own dread of Christmas had set in. He hadn't even seen it yet himself, but he knew from their niece, Sam, that it had gone up the week before Thanksgiving. They drove past Jill's Diner with its windows painted with a Nativity scene. The same artist decorated Isabella's with a Christmas tree and presents in one window, and children battering a reindeer piñata in the other. Overhead, street poles were hung with candy canes, stockings, and silver bell lights; a garland of green suspended across the road held a large red bow. Even the Hawk's Nest bar got into the act with Merry Christmas painted on one window and Happy New Year on the other.

Dawn kept up her happy chatter, putting the death of Nikki and the fate of Megan and Bella to the side for a moment to enjoy her hometown in full Christmas adornment. "Oh, that's just wrong," she laughed at the yoga studio window with Mrs. Claus, elves, and a decidedly skinny old Saint Nick stretching on a sunny beach. Matt crossed the street and pulled the Jeep over, facing the wrong way. Dawn was about to ask what he was up to when the sight of his office caught her eye. The one-hundred-and-twenty-year-old brick building she had bought, tying them to a second mortgage they really didn't need, was decked out in a massive Christmas wreath suspended along the front of the second story. It was large enough that the tall former warehouse window in its center could act as a light, filling the wreath with an otherworldly glow. The red bow at its bottom hung just above a door with a frosted glass window with gold letters reading Matthew Jager, Attorney at Law.

Nothing from their plans when they opened his office seemed to have worked out. He practiced very little law, she didn't have a chance to finish rehabbing the upper floors into apartments, and he regretted paying for the Christmas display when Sam texted him the picture last month. But the beaming smile and mitten-dulled clapping of his wife made at least that expense worthwhile.

"Ah," she laughed. "And you said bah humbug. It's beautiful."

"Yeah. I thought about canceling, but I got busy working and forgot."

"No." She made a little pouting face. "You can't cancel Christmas. You're a sweet boy, and you should just admit it."

"Well, it's a little easier to get into the mood now that you're here." He put the Jeep into drive, ready to pull away.

Dawn stuck her arm out. "Wait. Turn it off."

He did it without a second thought, the dumbest idea coming to his mind. He was tired after all. "If you want to park and make out, we need to find a better spot."

Her eyes reached the ceiling. "No, dear, we're not necking on Christmas Eve in downtown Mannheim. It's probably already started, but I want you to take me somewhere."

Matt looked around at the empty sidewalks and closed businesses. The time had gotten away from him again, and with it being Christmas Eve, everything in town was shuttered up for the night. Everything but the Hawk's Nest, and there was zero chance she wanted to go there. Then he saw it on the next block.

Light spilled out of open double doors, down a flight of steps, and across the street as the last stragglers hurried into Saint Wen's Catholic Church. Dawn loved Christmas Eve mass, a tradition she insisted on from their first Christmas together at Fort Lewis. They'd even taken in a midnight mass in Germany at a church older than America, the pews removed for the night, Germans crowded in, the service in a language neither could keep up with. She loved it.

"Are you sure?" he asked. "We can drive around and look at more Christmas lights." Dawn's funeral, last summer's service for a fallen deputy, and then Nikki Moscow's small, family funeral. That was the extent of Matt's Saint Wen's experience in the last three years. Being surrounded by worshippers celebrating the birth of Christ should have been a comfort, but it wasn't. Not when Dawn wasn't here.

"It will be good for you, you'll see." Her smile was sweet and managed to say he had no choice at the same time. There was even a touch of pity in it for his inability to resist her.

By the time Matt was outside the Jeep, opening her door, Dawn had changed into a knee-length wool jacket open at the chest, revealing a dark green satiny dress and white flower brooch. Her hair hung perfectly down her chest, curling in enticing waves. Her skunk stripe was back in full force, adding a streak of white down one side. "Now, I really do want to make out," he said.

"Silly." She took his offered arm, neither feeling the comforting weight of touch, but happy in what this night had given them.

The outside air, wafting in wet and cold, barely made a dent in the warmth generated by hundreds singing O Come All Ye Faithful as Father Vu, in green vestments, walked the center aisle, gently swinging a metal lamp emitting incense smoke. Of all the things to remember from Catechism class, the word thurible came to Matt. Dawn stood next to him along the back of the side wall, the service standing room only by now. Saint Wen's did good business on a normal Sunday; Christmas Eve and Easter, it did Black Friday level business. Matt kept his head down, hands clasped in front of him, listening to Dawn sing. The joy in her voice was the most beautiful sound he'd ever heard.

The flapping of paper drew him out of his own mind. Jaylee Rainer, the oldest daughter of the deputy they'd buried in June, a man he and Dawn had tried to help, was holding out a Missal. She smiled and mouthed Merry Christmas as he thanked her and whispered Merry Christmas back. Ensuring she and her sisters received the full line-of-duty death benefits for her father had tied Matt further to his Beltway law firm working for defense contractors. Her Christmas greeting and a quick smile from her mother were good reminders that he'd made his own fate. He had no regrets.

The mass took on a rhythm that had become innate to Matt over his life, a hypnotic ritual that lulled him into the ability to pretend his life was normal for a few minutes. That Dawn had never left, that their lives continued on together, that she would grow old with him in this little town, nothing changing. Nothing that was important. They loved one another, they were together, they would always be together. Her prayers and answers to Father Vu's calls reinforced the deception. He let himself believe, knowing that coming here tonight was the wrong answer for him. Not because he didn't believe, but because it made it too easy to believe. Believe his life was still whole.

Time had gotten away from him again when pews began to empty as the line for communion formed. Bev, the owner of Jill's Diner, was the first to greet him with a tight hug around the neck. "Welcome home, Matthew," she whispered. "Merry Christmas." She squeezed again, her heartfelt happiness showing with a smile that pushed her light brown cheeks high on her face. "I expect you to stop by," she said.

No one else was as forceful or as happy as Bev, but a stream of people nodded or said Merry Christmas. A few he knew well, including Luke, home from the art institute in Chicago to see his dad; a school district employee he practically accused of murder once; and Miriam, their neighbor from across the street, who looked surprised and worried when she saw him. Neither of which was an unusual look for her. The sight of Jaylee Rainer sliding back into her pew after receiving communion prompted Matt to ask Dawn if she was ready to go with just an expression. She knew the look and waved him toward the door. The bracing cold outside air broke Matt's spell.

"Did you enjoy that?" he asked.

"Yes, dear, thank you. Are you okay?" They made their way down the steps and across the street toward their Jeep.

"Yeah, I was thinking, though. I want to talk to Megan Moscow."

Dawn stopped, her hands to her very cute hips. "You spent Christmas Eve Mass in that beautiful church with those lovely people thinking about the case? That's not why we went."

"I thought you looked beautiful singing, if that helps."

She nodded and started walking. "It does, a little anyway. You don't think Megan would have told Claire if she had any ideas about who might have given drugs to her mom?"

"Maybe. Or maybe it's someone in the family, or she's seen something not knowing how important it could be. But what really got me thinking was the fact that she told Claire how to get into Mom's phone despite what I'm sure were very explicit instructions from Grandpa not to cooperate with the cops."

"So, why did she do it?" Dawn asked mainly for Matt's benefit.

"One, she's worried Grandpa is going to find them first and kill the dealer. Then someone else in her family is dead, or they've pissed off another family by knocking off their favorite drug-dealing

31

relative. Or," Matt stopped outside the Jeep, "she called because she's been snooping on Mom's phone and knows something is in there. She's hoping Claire can find it, and she doesn't have to snitch on anyone."

"Snitch, dear? She's a child."

Matt opened the car door for her, waiting as Dawn arranged the long coat around her as she sat. "She's a Moscow, dear." He had to wait until he was around the Jeep and seated himself to hear the reply.

"That's unkind."

"Maybe. But the sooner we talk to her, the better. I need to get Caddie to have Claire set up a meeting."

"You are not bothering that child on Christmas Eve, Matthew. Even with her mother gone, maybe she and Bella can have something close to a normal Christmas. She'll still be there in a day or two."

Matt cranked over the engine. He was tired and finally believed he could actually sleep. The fact that Dawn would be next to him made it easier. "And if there's bad dope out there, someone else could be dead in a day or two."

"But you can't pressure her into talking to you; there's no shark mode for a child who's lost her mother."

"Don't worry, I'll have an education professional by my side to keep me straight."

"Darn right." They both smiled at that. They would be together.

Chapter 8

Matt cranked over the Jeep, ready to head home and sleep and snuggle as best they could. The whoop of a police siren made him jump.

"That's just mean." Dawn turned in her seat to look out the rear window at a massive black truck inches behind them. Caddie waved and stepped out.

"I wanted to talk to her anyway," Matt said, opening his door.

"Me, too." Dawn slid through the passenger door without waiting for Matt.

Caddie was waiting on the sidewalk. "You know, parking facing the wrong direction is a twenty-five-dollar fine?"

Dawn waved from the other side of the Jeep. "Hello." She spoke loudly enough to get a tiny jump from Matt. Caddie didn't react. "Caddie," Dawn called. Matt tried keeping an eye on his wife and the sheriff at the same time. The expression on Caddie's face remained a half grin. Then Dawn was next to him on the sidewalk, the three of them making a small circle.

"Caddie, Caddie, Caddie!" Dawn added a hand wave inches from the sheriff's face.

Slowly, Caddie's head tilted and turned toward Dawn, her eyes blinking in an attempt to focus. "I…" She let out a long breath and shuffled her feet.

"Caddie," Dawn whispered. "I'm right here."

"I…" she looked Dawn directly in the eyes, on the precipice of a thought. Then her head snapped to Matt. "I forgot what I was going to say." She gave an uncomfortable laugh. "Did you just come out of church or the Hawk's Nest?"

"What!?" Dawn stepped between Caddie and Matt. "Caddie!" she yelled, breaking the word down into three syllables.

Caddie looked away, her eyes closing and hand rising to her temple. "Cold must be getting to me, I'm getting a headache."

"Ugh," Dawn said, her voice falling in disappointment before she spun on Matt. "Look what you did, you broke Caddie's brain."

Caught between Dawn's anger and disappointment and Caddie's headache-induced squinting, Matt could only think to answer the sheriff's question and hope to move on. "I went to mass. It was nice."

"It was nice," Dawn said, stepping aside. "That's what you've got, dear? You fritz Caddie's brain, and all you can say is that church was nice?"

Matt decided to keep the conversation moving forward and talk to Dawn when they were alone. He did feel guilty. He could have told Caddie the truth, despite it being completely unbelievable. He could have shared a bit of Dawn's love and light instead of holding it close for himself. It may have meant something to Caddie to know that the voice she heard as she lay close to death was real, not flesh and blood, but real. And that even in impossible circumstances, Dawn cared for Caddie and wanted her well. He also hadn't considered what it would mean to Dawn. All that love and caring to give, and she had a chance to connect to another person in this place and he blocked it. Not nice.

"I want to talk to Megan Moscow," he said.

"Wow," Dawn said, tossing her hands in the air. "Not even a smooth segue out of talking about your breaking Caddie's brain. This conversation, dear, is not over."

Matt had heard that warning before. The conversation was definitely not over, but one problem at a time, and then he could try to distract Dawn with some cute Christmas something or other.

"I don't love that idea," Caddie said. Her face cleared, and her voice grew steady. Whatever effect Dawn had on her seemed to have ebbed. "We really want to talk to a kid who could get blowback at home if her grandfather finds out?"

"The kid was worried enough about her mom to spy on her phone," Matt said. "We can run down every doper in town," he put up his hand to cut Caddie off, "and we should, but let's not put our best potential witness to the side because she's a kid."

"But she is a kid, dear." Dawn's words were softer. She was Matt's literal conscious sitting figuratively on his shoulder, Jiminy Cricket style. "I kind of agree with you, even though you're in trouble, but convince the boss lady, who I swear is giving me the stink eye, that you understand that, too. And I wonder if she'll see me if I bop her on the nose."

"Can we even do that?" Caddie asked. "Pull in a minor without a guardian and question them about the overdose death of their mother?"

Matt reverted to his now rarely tapped legal education. "Yes, we can. She's not in any way a suspect. We're not trying to jam her up or get her in trouble. We treat her as a confidential source. Even then, we work to backtrack whatever information we get out of her and come up with it another way. She may not even have anything for us, but we need to try."

"I don't love it," Caddie said.

"Me either," Dawn echoed.

"I promise," Matt told them, "I feel for the kid. I'll take it gently, and if she doesn't have anything, end of the story. If she does, we do everything we can to keep her clear of it."

"You have a lot of experience interviewing children in CID?" Caddie asked.

"No, not really," he admitted. "But, I'm guessing you wouldn't let me do this alone anyway."

Caddie was emphatic with her head shake. "No. We do this, it's a team effort. Megan trusts Claire. She needs to be there, too."

"All right, all three of us then," Matt said. "I want in. For better or worse, I've become the office expert on Frank Moscow." Besides, he knew Dawn would want to be in on any questioning of the child, and she had more experience dealing with kids than any of them.

"I'll talk to Claire and get it set up," Caddie said.

"Sooner the better," Matt said.

Caddie nodded, waved a silent goodbye, and headed back toward her truck.

"Hey, lady!" Dawn yelled one last time. "If you can hear me, give us a sign. You'd be saving Matt a butt chewing."

Caddie shook her head in seeming to answer before speaking. "I'll let you know when it's on. But, you're right, the sooner the better."

"Well, dear, my list of things to fix keeps growing," Dawn said. They waved as Caddie climbed back up into her truck.

"Am I on the top of the list?" Matt asked.

"Always," she said. "I love you the most, and you are the most in need of fixing."

She's not wrong, he thought.

Chapter 9

Parked behind the carriage house garage, their house loomed up in the darkness before them. Dawn told Matt they would talk about Caddie and Megan, and the death of Nikki, tomorrow. "Part of me wants to open a bottle of wine and snuggle with you in front of the fireplace," Matt said.

"That's the sweet part," she said. "But the fuzzy-brained, tired part needs to go to sleep."

"Do you notice you spend a lot of time on your visits trying to get me into bed?"

She laughed and pretended to pat his leg. "You're still way ahead in that department, buddy."

"You can't blame me. You're adorable and sexy."

"While I could listen to that all night, we do need to get you some rest. Me, too."

Matt grabbed the door handle when a brief flash of light shone through their kitchen windows. His flirty voice gave way to Army cop. "Someone is in the house." His hand went automatically to his belt. "Shit, I'm not carrying."

Dawn leaned forward, squinting through the windshield. "You didn't need to be carrying in Saint Wen's, Matt. And what do you plan on doing, going in guns a blazing on Christmas Eve? What if it's Santa?"

"Okay, you're the one who needs sleep now. Last time someone wandered around the house in the dark, Caddie got shot."

"Yes, dear. Caddie was the one wandering around," Dawn said, watching the house intently for movement. "Go ahead. Dig into your little mobile Batcave back there, but let's not start the gunfight at the OK Corral unless absolutely necessary."

"Only if I really need to," he said, turning off the overhead light and popping out.

Back from pulling a 9mm Beretta from the mounted gun case in the Jeep's rear, Matt found Dawn with what could only be described as a festive expression on her face. "Put that silly thing in your holster, dear. You won't need it."

He didn't like it, but why break decades of precedence and not do what she told him now? "Ghost powers?"

She scrunched her face at him. She had done and felt things on her visits that weren't exactly in the normal realm, but jokes about ghost powers still rankled her. She had them, but without a clear understanding of how any of this worked. They just seemed to work when Matt needed them. Besides, sometimes it wasn't about powers; it was about seeing things differently than her Army CID-minded husband. "Yes, dear, it's the ghost of Christmas past to show how to keep the Christmas spirit."

"So I get to see us together again on a snowy German Christmas?" He slid the weapon into his overcoat. "I'll take it."

Dawn followed him down the walk toward the back door. "How can I fuss if you insist on being so sweet?"

"You'll find a way." He unlocked the kitchen door quietly, his hand automatically resting on the handgun his wife insisted he didn't need.

"Hello, hello," Dawn called. It was so happy and loud in Matt's ear that he turned and shushed her, only to be met with an even broader smile. Of course, he was the only one who could hear her. "Who knows," she said, "if it's a Christmas ghost, they may answer back."

The house was bathed in deep shadow, the momentary light he had spotted through the window nowhere to be seen. "Maybe it was just a car passing on the street."

"Maybe," she smiled from a perch on the kitchen island, her dress boots replaced by puffy slippers with kitty faces on the front. She looked down, a little surprised herself. "Makes sense, this house is always so cold in the winter."

A bang in the basement brought the pistol out and pointed at the open door to the stairs.

"Finally noticed the open basement door, detective?" Dawn leaned sideways, lying lengthwise along the island, propping her head up with one hand. "Put the gun away, dear, before you hurt yourself." In the next instant, the darkness of the home was shattered as half the lights on the first floor snapped on.

"Dawn?" Matt gave her a side glance as he kept his focus on the stairs.

38

"That was not me." Her sly but entirely visible happiness forced his weapon back into his pocket. Laughing and clomping came up the stairs. "Noisy ghosts, it seems."

Sam Janda, Dawn's niece and Matt's business partner, hit the top stair and gave a startled yelp of surprise and happiness. Matt quickly found himself pushing a purple Santa cap and a face full of dishwater blonde hair away from his face as Sam enveloped him in a full-body hug. "Uncle Matt, we were trying to surprise you." Allison Dutch, a corporal with the Fillmore County Sheriff's Office, was a step behind Sam but definitely not going in for a hug.

"Matt," she said. While Sam was fully into the Christmas spirit with a sweater emblazoned with Chevy Chase being electrocuted in *National Lampoon's Christmas Vacation*, complete with functioning tiny lights, Allison was in jeans and a black flannel shirt.

"Ouch." Dawn sat up. "You clearly have not been putting in the effort to charm Allison. Not that I want you to, or that I think it would work. But it's the effort that counts." She nodded emphatically.

"You shouldn't be sneaking around in the dark," Matt said to Sam. "I could have shot you."

"Not very nice considering why we're here." She led him by the hand to the front of the house. Dawn happily bounced along, full of questions about Sam's outdoor adventure business, her relationship with Allison, and whether young people still watched *Christmas Vacation*, all rattled off at a speed that expected no immediate answers. Allison followed, hands stuffed in pockets, a partial smile on her face more for Sam and her enthusiasm than their mission tonight. "You didn't even let me know you were back in town. I might not have seen you until tomorrow at the party. You are coming to Caddie's party, aren't you?"

"She is rather exuberant, isn't she?" Dawn said.

"You are rather exuberant," Matt said.

"It's Christmas." She turned serious, stopping them in the living room. "I know how much Auntie Dawn loved Christmas, and I was worried about you stuck in Singapore during the holidays, then when I hear through Alison that you were home." She poked him in the chest. "And not from you. I was not about to let you hold up in this big old house by yourself drinking beer in the dark."

"I like beer," he said.

"I know." Dawn and Sam echoed one another; Dawn in slight dismay, Sam in complete agreement.

"But it's no way to spend Christmas Eve," Sam said. "Anyway, you weren't here, and Allison and I got to work and finished when the lights all blew."

"It wasn't me," Dawn protested. "This time, anyway."

Sam rushed to the front of the room, flicked off the light, and waved Matt forward. There in the sitting room across the entry way sat a full Scotch pine, decorated with the ornaments he and Dawn had gathered through the years, lit in glowing bands of white lights. It was the room where Dawn sat and read, where she enjoyed her morning coffee watching the town wake up around them. Where when she returned to Matt the first time, they had danced by candlelight, though neither could feel the other.

"It's beautiful." Dawn clapped, hopping up and down in the most dignified possible way for a woman in her forties filled with an innocent joy. "Hug her, Matt, hug her for me right this instant."

Matt had no choice but to obey, pulling Sam to him as they faced the tree. He wished their niece could see Dawn practically dancing around the fir. "Thank you," he said. "I can't even explain how much I appreciate this." He turned to Allison, who'd hung back. "Really, it was very thoughtful."

"It was Sam's idea."

"I know, still," he said.

Matt watched Sam performing the hot chocolate making ceremony, her aunt unseen and unheard at her shoulder offering suggestions and general merriment, while he and Allison sat at the kitchen island, helpfully out of the way. Sam was shorter and broader in the shoulders than Dawn, blonde rather than brunette, and you wouldn't easily pick them out as related, but he saw it now. It was in the way that they cared, in the way they threw themselves into a moment without an ounce of self-consciousness. Sam smiled at them, a look echoed by Dawn, as milk warmed on the stove.

"You know who you remind me of?" His voice cracked when he said it. Even with her standing right there, talking about Dawn brought out more emotion than he could easily contain.

"That's sweet," Sam said. Dawn touched her heart and blew her husband a kiss.

"I'm sorry," Allison said softly. Matt wasn't sure if Sam heard now that she'd turned her attention to pouring the milk.

"What?" He could see that her concentration was on Sam before she looked him in the eyes.

"I think I'm starting to understand."

He patted her forearm, their version of a deep hug. "I'm glad. For both of you."

"Marshmallows?" Sam called out.

"Yes, yes," Dawn said.

Matt's eyes flicked between his wife and a grinning Allison. "I don't think I have marshmallows."

Not waiting for an answer, Sam was plopping miniature marshmallows in their cups. "She brought them," Allison said.

Matt blew across his cup as they listened to Sam call up from the basement, sure that the vintage Christmas wreath with the bubbler candle in the middle had to be down there somewhere. He'd assured her and Dawn that he hadn't gotten rid of it; he just didn't know where it was. Allison had unexpectedly stayed in the kitchen with him. Dawn, who still couldn't help but radiate Christmas joy, wouldn't like it, but Matt suspected he knew why the deputy took the moment to be alone with him. He and Allison were never about to be best buddies, and they didn't have the connection he and Caddie had during an investigation, but they both tended to put the job first, even if they disagreed on how to do it.

"You have any thoughts on who might have supplied Nikki?" he asked, earning a full frown and a finger wag from Dawn.

"It's Christmas Eve, dear," she said quickly, but fell into silence to hear Allison's answer.

"I've talked to a few people who float around that crowd, people Nikki used to party with before she went to rehab. They all agree on two things: she hasn't been around that crew since she got out, and Frank threatened anyone who dealt to her."

"You think that's going to stop an addict who's dealing on the side to support their habit?"

"I don't know," she admitted. "But at the very least, they'll be quiet about it, and they definitely won't talk about it after it killed her."

Dawn leaned forward on the counter. "Ask her if she knew Nikki." So much for Christmas Eve for his wife, too.

"Did you know her?"

She shook her head. "By reputation. I think she was a senior when I was in seventh grade. That whole crowd was wild partiers. Dope, speed, ecstasy, anything they could get their hands on. I'm not surprised she developed a problem. When I started with the office, I had a couple of run-ins with that bunch. Same story for all of them. Employed for a while before they're fired for showing up high or not showing up at all. Petty theft, ripping off construction sites, credit card fraud. Anything to earn a buck to get high, including dealing. If she fell back with them, there's a dozen people who would have sold to her, whatever Frank's warnings."

"Uncle Matt," Sam called from the bottom of the stairs.

"Yeah."

"You know you have a lot of power tools gathering dust down here."

"Those were your aunt's."

"I do love a good power tool," Dawn agreed.

The echoes of Sam climbing the stairs hurried Matt and Allison's conversation. "If you have time tomorrow, let's talk again."

Allison nodded. "I'm on shift in an hour, but if nothing else, we can find time at the party."

"Look at your two, conspiring to ruin a perfectly good Christmas party with your police talk," Dawn said. "Remember, dear, the chains you forge in life."

Sam emerged from the doorway, a plastic wreath with a bubbler candle triumphantly in hand. "Straight from 1969," she said, insisting that any more retro Christmas decorations Matt found were hers. "And you know, if you gave me those tools, I could do some of the apartment rehab myself and keep costs down."

"Still on about fixing up the rest of the building and renting out apartments?" Matt said as an answer to Sam and to fill Dawn in about their niece's latest business idea. "I don't love the idea of being in the landlord business, and I don't know if the math works."

"It can," Sam said. "And I take care of everything."

"We'll talk about it," Matt said.

"Yes, we will," Dawn agreed.

Allison made a show of checking her watch, a bulky plastic affair only a cop could love. "I need to change for shift."

"I've got to go, too," Sam said, gathering their coats and hats.

"Aww." Dawn didn't sound too upset, though she loved seeing her niece.

"Allison isn't the only one working. I have to be at Saint Wen's at 5:00 A.M. to help with Christmas lunch. We had so many applications, they added a third shift. Nearly two hundred people in a small town like this need help just to get a decent meal on Christmas. And with Bev running the kitchen, I can't afford to be late."

"See, dear, the Christmas spirit is alive and well." She thought for a second, money didn't solve everything, but it sure as heck helped. "Maybe you could offer some of your ill-gotten booty. If it is ill-gotten, and don't make me say booty, again."

Matt nodded agreement. "That sounds expensive."

"It is." Sam was ready to go, bundled up against the wet, chilly night. "Sam's Adventures made a donation, so you've already helped."

"It is desirable that we should make some provision for the poor and destitute who suffer greatly at the present time," he said.

A puzzled Sam kissed his cheek and called Merry Christmas as she stepped out onto the porch. Allison gave Matt a head nod and a slight salute. Dawn reached for his hand reflexively as they watched the young couple walk away. A weak spark of electricity jumped the gap between their fingers, neither minding nor surprised. "I was sure you were going to ask if the Union workhouses were still in operation."

"And the Treadmill and the Poor Law still in full vigor," he said, finishing Scrooge's answer to being asked for a donation to the poor. "Hard to do that with you and Sam beaming Christmas spirit at me like a flood light."

"Are we going to keep quoting Dickens?"

He shut the door and looked deep into his wife's ever-familiar pale green eyes. "Yeah, I think so."

Chapter 10

The sun shone weakly through clouds, feeding a morning haze that grew into a heavy fog. With no stockings stuffed with small gifts, and a big pancake breakfast a waste for Dawn, they went straight to their traditional Christmas morning walk. The cold never stopped that. Matt stepped carefully across the ice-sheeted parking lot while Dawn strode confident that she wouldn't slip, a small benefit of her being here, but not entirely. The crunch of tires across ice broke the final strands of the winter spell they had been under as a black Fillmore County Sheriff's Office SUV rolled slowly in their direction, stopping a few feet away. Allison lowered her window. "Good morning."

"Merry Christmas," Dawn corrected her.

"Morning," Matt said. "Rough shift?"

"Not too bad." Allison gave a head shake that said it was nothing but deputy stuff. "A couple of OWIs early."

"Merry Christmas," Matt said.

"Merry Christmas," Allison answered in the exact same unmerry tone.

"That's not how you say that, dear." Dawn jumped her butt onto the cruiser's hood and leaned against the windshield, propped on one elbow. She was every ounce an adorable, mischievous Christmas spirit. "You can't say Merry Christmas full of skepticism at your fellow man, even if they are blotto behind the wheel."

"Luckily, by the time temps really started dropping and roads turned seriously bad, everyone was nestled all snug in their beds," Allison said.

Dawn popped up straight, puffy mittened hand pointed at Matt. "Do not answer her with another line from *The Night Before Christmas*. I'll not have you two cooperating to drip your cop sarcasms all over Christmas."

Matt, a half-formed, not very good crack about a fat man on the roof dying on his tongue, answered with the ever-ready nod of acknowledgment. "Hopefully, we get some sun to burn this off before everyone gets out on the roads."

"Somebody else's problem in," Allison checked her watch, "forty-three minutes. But look, the reason I pulled over when I saw your Jeep was I got a call to the ER at 3:00 A.M."

"Oh," Dawn leaned forward for a better look at the deputy. "My spider-sense is tingling, dear. We may hear a clue." She winked at him, getting the grin she wanted, which could only confuse Allison and reconfirm her opinion that her girlfriend's uncle might possibly be insane. The pause before the deputy spoke said Dawn's prompt worked perfectly.

"Um, anyway, the call was about a possible assault victim. I show up to interview him, and he wants nothing to do with talking to a cop. He said he slipped on the ice, but somebody worked him over good enough to send him to the ER for stitches to the back of his head. They also took X-rays of his hand, which had been stomped, but it wasn't broken."

Dawn sat up. "Well, that's not a cute, cozy clue."

"And?" Matt asked.

"NCIC check on the victim comes back with a dozen arrests, including an intent to distribute in Rock Island that got dropped, and he's on Claire's chart of old friends of Nikki Moscow."

Matt tapped on her windowsill, close to being a pat on the back. "Frank sent his elves out on Christmas Eve to work over dope dealers looking for who supplied Nikki."

Dawn let out an exaggerated sigh. "You two are going to Grinch the magic right out of Christmas."

"He wouldn't talk to me, but I bet he talked to the Russians," Allison said.

"They left him healthy enough to get to the ER," Matt said.

"Which means he convinced them he didn't supply Nikki," Allison said. "I thought you talked to your buddy."

"Frank said he'd find who gave drugs to Nikki. He never promised to be nice about it. You think it would help if I try to talk to your guy?"

Allison looked Matt up and down before she answered. "No, everyone thinks you and Frank have some deal going on..."

"We don't," Matt objected. Allison waved it away.

"He's very much a local. If you want, I'll make another run at him."

"Your call," Matt said.

Allison shifted in her seat, signaling that she was ready to move on. "There's not much, but I wrote it up, and you can find the victim's history on that. But it's not about him. It's about your friend Frank being ready to do whatever he thinks it will take to find who's responsible for Nikki's death. If we're not lucky, they're going to kill somebody."

"I'm not sure what else I can do about that short of finding who supplied her drugs," Matt said. What he kept back from Dawn and Allison was that he understood Frank's anger. He didn't exactly condone his methods, but he didn't blame Frank for wanting justice or revenge or whatever you decided to call it. But he'd come to know that Dawn was right, it had to be justice, it had to be done right or the cost would prove too high. Which is how he found himself in a position of trying to save the county's crime boss from himself.

Chapter 11

The lively chattering girl they heard approaching from the back of the building disappeared the moment she stepped into Matt's office and saw him and the sheriff waiting. Megan was blonde to the point of being nearly washed out. Pale hair curling off in every direction, skin translucent except for the wind-burned red fading on her cheeks, eyes a shallow ice blue. Claire was right behind her, assuring the teen that it would be all right and that Matt and Caddie only wanted to help. Megan was willing to meet, but not at the Sheriff's Office, whether from fear her grandfather would find out, and he probably would, or just a general family aversion to law enforcement. They set the meeting for Matt's private office and used the building's back entrance to Sam's Outdoor Adventures' office.

"That's one of them," Dawn said from her perch on the desk behind Matt. "Now that I see her in person, there's no mistaking it. I called Children's Protective Services for her sister, Bella. Poor little thing was being completely neglected. There's no mistaking those two being related."

Matt gave a quick look over his shoulder as Megan settled on the couch. His wife understood the question in his eyes.

"I think so," she said. "Somehow, I must have a connection to Bella. Not really the vice principal's job, but I cleaned her up and combed out her hair and made sure she had food in her backpack when she headed home." The children they didn't have, the future denied them by Dawn's death, filled those simple actions of caring with greater weight. "Offer her a drink, dear. Poor thing looks like a puppy who fell into a lion's den."

"Before we start," Matt said, and leaned forward, trying to present himself as non-threatening to the girl who looked like she could have blown here on the wind. "Can I get you something to drink, hot chocolate or a pop?"

Dawn groaned at the word. Despite being a Midwesterner herself, besides taking the Lord's name in vain, she found pop the most objectionable word in the American lexicon.

"I've got diet, but Sam has everything in her office."

Megan hesitated until Claire added, "Matt's got a little kitchen back there with a pod system and every kind of hot drink you can think of. He doesn't even know half of what's back there." It set Megan at ease and told Matt the way this interview would go. Claire would be on Megan's side. She would be the ally in the room with the two cops. That was fine, seeing her now in person, he knew Dawn was right. Someone needed to put the girl's interests first and Claire would do that.

Megan started with Matt but quickly looked over to Claire. "I could use a coffee, maybe a mocha."

The two turned into the friends they had become over the last six months, laughing in the kitchen as the pod system gurgled away, cranking out two mochas. Caddie gave Matt a smile as they listened. Claire was proving herself again as an asset they should never underestimate. Dawn, who had been staring at the sheriff during the entire interlude, shifted uncomfortably before jumping down and wandering toward the door to the kitchenette, putting both rooms in view. "Dear, we have a lot to figure out. Let's keep a focus on these girls and finding who hurt their mother, but at some point, we're going to talk about your friend there." She walked back past Matt and stood next to the sheriff, bending close to her ear. "Caddie!" she yelled. "Catharine Allemande!"

The sheriff swung her cowboy hat back and forth on a finger, an inpatient smile on her face. Then slowly, her left hand came up, rubbed her ear slightly before returning to her hat. None of it seemingly at a conscious level.

"Now, you're just messing with me," Dawn said.

Megan and Claire's laughter trailed off as they came back into the office, but Megan had lost the tense, hunched look she'd carried earlier. Sitting on the leather couch, she curled her feet up under her, a move that struck Matt as oddly Dawn-like. It helped remind him that while Megan and Dawn grew up on opposite sides of whatever invisible tracks separated this town, they were both products of Fillmore County. He wanted to believe, and the evidence was right in front of him, that his Dawn was flawless in every way. But he couldn't look at the hand that Megan was dealt, a convicted felon for a grandfather and a mother strung out and now dead, and not wonder how even his sweet wife would have come through that.

Matt gave Caddie a little raise of his eyebrows, and she tilted her head back. She was letting him go first. "Megan, I'm Matt Jager, and I work as an investigator for the Sheriff's Office. This is Caddie Allemande, the sheriff. We asked Claire to see if you could talk to us about what happened with your mom. You're not in any kind of trouble or anything, we just want to do the right thing." Matt avoided words like investigating or punishing the people responsible for her mother's death to hopefully keep the girl from feeling frightened.

That sweet, seemingly intimidated face shot back, "Grandpa says you're a bullshit artist lawyer." She glanced at Claire, winced, and turned back to Matt. "Sorry, bullcrap."

"What an angel," Dawn said. "I like her."

Okay, Matt thought, *I like this kid, too.* "You know your grandfather and I know one another." He wasn't sure what Frank would share with his family about their cooperation. Not much, he assumed, and likely all couched as Frank playing Matt for inside information and favors, which he had to admit wasn't that far from the truth.

Megan nodded agreement. "Grandpa had me pass that message about your wife's car." The quick, feisty Moscow kid disappeared for a moment. "I'm sorry about her. I only had her as vice principal for the one year, but she was nice." She looked down into her cup of cooling mocha before taking an unsteady sip. Behind him, Dawn took in a deep breath, forcing Matt not to look at her. She cared so much about the kids under her care, he hadn't considered how this would affect her, which made him feel selfish. He returned his focus to Megan, he would let Dawn know he had failed her later.

"She called CPS because of my little sister. Mom was really bad then, on meth and oxy and stuff, and drunk and staying out all night or passed out all day. I tried, but I was pretty young, too." She looked up more defiantly. "I made sure Bella was fed, though. Even if I had to steal from Mom. Most the time, I just walked us up to Grandma and Grandpa's house for dinner, but Mom didn't like that 'cuz then Grandpa Frank would get on her case about not taking care of us." However reluctant Megan had been to come here, she had plenty to unload. "Lucky, somehow, Grandpa heard about CPS before they visited…"

"That fricken Sheriff Dubcek," Dawn said, every bit of an F bomb in her fricken. "I wanna know what we're doing about him," she spat out quickly, not wanting to miss what Megan was saying.

"…so Grandma cleaned up our trailer really good and made sure there was cereal and stuff in the cupboards. Mom was such a wreck, they still almost took us anyway. I didn't like that at all." She pointed at Matt, letting him know that she might feel bad about his wife, but in the best of her family tradition, she held a grudge. "Grandpa Frank was pissed off. He yelled at the school, and the CPS lady, and Grandma because she didn't watch us close enough. But mostly he was mad at my mom."

Matt nodded understanding. Claire smiled encouragement. Caddie largely kept a straight face, at this point an observer of the conversation rather than a participant. "You're doing good, baby," Dawn whispered, though he hadn't done much, which he guessed was her point. They said in Fillmore County not to get in the Russians' way. He certainly didn't want to get in Megan's.

"Those two, Grandpa and Mom, were screaming at each other, slamming doors and stuff. He says she's a junkie, she says she learned from the best." Megan grinned at that. Whatever complex mix of emotions she had about her mother at the moment, she admired her fight. "We finally got another visit from the CPS lady who had a big report with all this stuff Mom was supposed to do, like make sure we have food and clean clothes and stuff. I remember the lady left, and Mom broke down crying. That was the start of her trying to get clean." Megan had managed to distill the turmoil of her childhood into a single emotion she would carry with her the rest of her life.

Caddie spoke for the first time. "Your mom loved you. You and your sister meant everything to her. I didn't know her, but I know that. I was looking at the dates, it was still a couple of years before she checked into rehab, wasn't it?" The question was soft but carried authority. Matt could do one or the other, but not both, not in a way the sheriff could.

Megan nodded. "She tried on her own at first, but it never lasted."

"She was sick," Caddie said.

50

Dawn's sigh told Matt her mood had changed again. "Darn it, I like Caddie again."

"She was sick," Megan agreed. "After a long time, she told Grandpa she needed help. He said he'd get her in the best rehab place in the state. Then she said he had to quit—" she looked over to Matt. Somehow, despite the sheriff's uniform, Caddie had come to represent the law less than Matt. "You know, drinking and stuff."

"Did he?" Matt asked. "Quit drinking and stuff?"

Megan made a face that could only be perfected by a teenager saying, 'What do you think?' "He's better. He says he's slowing down in old age." What Megan said fit with what he and Dawn had seen since they first met Frank last year. He wasn't ready for the cover of Men's Health, but he looked a little less like a poster warning of the dangers of meth.

Caddie gave a flick of the finger that was holding her hat. She wanted to stay in control of the interview. Matt caught the movement and leaned back, distancing himself from Megan. "It's okay, baby," Dawn said. "Let the girls talk for a bit." He nodded to her. It wasn't hard for him to remember that Caddie, and for that matter, his wife, were as good at this as he was, maybe better when it came to questioning Megan.

"How did your mom do in rehab?" Caddie asked. "It's not easy and a lot of people have slips, and it's not their fault." She held up a coffee mug. "I can't even give this up."

"That's the thing." Megan was fully turned to Caddie, mimicking the sheriff by sipping from her mug. "Mom killed it. We didn't get to see her for like three months, and that was super hard, especially for Bella, but the first time we went there, it was like Mom was a whole new person, you know."

Caddie's face was soft and welcoming. "She was doing good."

"She was." Megan laughed. "Her hair looked so much better. I'd forgotten how pretty her hair used to be. It's blonde like mine," she said, slipping into the present tense, maybe something only Matt would notice, "but not all crazy frizzy. Her hair was," she said, slipping back to the reality that her mom was no longer with her, "thick and laid perfectly. Lots of times, she was too busy and would just comb it out and put it in a pony, but it was still perfect. She had model hair."

"I'm jealous." Caddie's auburn hair was cut into a bob that touched below the bottom of her collar. Being a cop and having long, luxurious hair weren't the most complimentary things in the world.

"Me, too." Megan's excitement at the memories came back down. Matt understood. Moments of joy at the memory of a lost loved one faded quickly when confronted with the reality that they were gone. He couldn't help himself, and for a moment didn't care how it would make him look. He turned and took in the image of his wife. The long hair cascading down one shoulder, creating a soft curve over her breasts. The stripe of white highlighting the contours and waves. The eyes, pale green and alive with concern for this girl in front of them, then down to him and shining with her love. A soft smile that told him he was loved and would always remain so, and that she understood, that she cared and was his, and that when this moment faded into the next and this day was gone and she disappeared again, he would remain loved. He wanted to kiss her and cry. He wanted to push the world and death and this child's pain away so he could hide himself away with Dawn and treasure every moment. He wanted to be selfish. Not that she would ever let him make that mistake.

"Pay attention, sweetie," she said. "You'll have time to make googly eyes at me later."

He winked and turned back to the conversation. If anyone had noticed his mental absence, they didn't show it. Megan was in the middle of explaining how her mother had spent her time in rehab, not only getting clean but in learning how to live the way she wanted to.

"Every time I saw her, she had a new book. Sometimes two or three. Lots of books about living clean from people who'd been there. Then all these old classic books like Pride and Prejudice and stuff. She was so excited about reading. Said she used to read all the time when she was a kid. She said it was a way to escape and that escape could be good, but only if you dealt with the real world and your problems at the same time."

"Your mom was smart," Caddie said. "She got herself clean, she took care of her girls, she went back to school, got a good job. You should be proud."

For the first time that day, the weight of grief and loss showed fully on Megan's face. It slacked as if the muscles had lost all their strength to hold together. Her eyes went lost, then filled with tears until they ran down her cheeks. "I am."

There was anger in her voice that Matt had taken far too long to recognize in himself. It wasn't directed at anyone, at least not at first, so it ate away at him. Then he found a target for it, the former sheriff, Jimmy Dubcek. He and Megan's grandfather were far too much alike. The only thing that kept him from putting a bullet in Jimmy's head was a combination of knowing it would hurt Dawn and twenty years carrying a badge with the idea that he was upholding the law. Frank didn't have either of those constraints holding him back. In the end, Matt wasn't sure they would hold him back either.

"She did get clean and she stayed clean," Megan concentrated on Caddie. She needed the sheriff to believe her. At the same time, she reached out to Claire, who grasped her hand and held tight.

"You think your mom stayed off drugs?" Caddie managed to ask the question without challenging Megan's memory of her mother.

"I know she did." She looked over to Claire. "I had to make sure after what we went through, after they threatened to take us away--," there was a glance at Matt.

"I don't think she'll forgive you for me calling," Dawn said.

"I watched Mom when she got out of rehab. I got her phone combo and checked her texts and search history." She laughed and finally wiped away the tears that had stopped running for now. "I was the nosy mom watching the kid. I don't know what I would have done, guess I would have told Grandpa Frank, who would have beaten up anyone giving Mom drugs. But I didn't see anything. I know people talk in code and stuff, but if you're on drugs, you're not that smart. I would have known."

Caddie nodded; she was on Megan's side, and they believed each other. A fleeting glance at Matt told him it was his turn, and he knew exactly what she wanted him to do. Good cop, bad cop with a grieving kid, and he drew the bad cop straw.

"Are you sure about that?" He tried to keep his voice firm without being harsh. He may have missed.

Dawn nearly hissed. "If you go shark mode on this child, you are going to be in real trouble, mister."

Great, no winning this one, he thought. "If she slipped, it doesn't mean she wasn't strong or there was something wrong with her. It happens. And she did overdose, Megan," he left the rest unsaid. Nikki Moscow died from a fentanyl overdose; of course, she was doing drugs. "Maybe she didn't know she was doing hard drugs and thought it was just marijuana."

"No." Megan was sharp and empathic. "Mom said she couldn't do any drugs or drink. That was a mistake she made before. She said she had to be all the way in. No halfway. She smoked like crazy, but she said she'd quit that too eventually. None of the stuff I saw on her phone was about her getting high or needing drugs or talking about partying or anything. She was texting her school friends about assignments or her boss about work."

"Nobody else? No one she used to hang out with when she was using? No one you didn't recognize?"

"No."

"No cousins or someone else who might have given her drugs?" Matt knew this was dangerous territory. He was asking a Russian kid to tell on a relative, a relative who could become a target of her grandfather. The conflicting loyalties might be too much to cross.

"No, nobody like that. Mom even kept her distance from some of the family," Megan insisted. "She was doing everything to stay straight. And she did it."

Matt hoped this interview would point them in the direction of who Nikki was communicating with, who could have supplied her drugs, or if she had been partying. Instead, it had devolved into a child refusing to believe her mother fell off the wagon and managed to hide it from her.

"If you need to ask about the Yadda account, do it gently," Dawn reminded him.

"Megan, you know about apps that let you communicate privately, that are designed to keep people like law enforcement from seeing what you're talking about? Your mom had one of those, an app called Yadda."

Megan nodded agreement, but the look of defiance didn't leave her face.

"Did you ever get into that app?"

She brightened, but only for a second. "I did. She used the same password on too many accounts, and it was in a little notebook."

Caddie shook her head. They didn't have a notebook. Even if they got a search warrant for Nikki's trailer, Frank probably cleaned the place top to bottom by now. There would be no notebook.

"Did you see any messages?" Matt asked.

"No. They disappear after you read them. But her phone isn't the only reason I know she was clean. She was smart and funny and took care of us. Even if she worked all night, she would make sure we had breakfast and lunch for school, then she would sleep a few hours before driving into Cedar Rapids if she had class. And I searched the house, too. It's not that big, and I know all the good hiding spots. I swear, Mom was not on drugs. She drank coffee by the gallon and sucked down cigarettes like a maniac, but she was off drugs."

"Then why the Yadda account?" Matt knew the question came too fast. He could see the look from Claire, and he could feel Dawn's eyes drilling into the back of his head, but an anonymous texting system didn't jive with a rehabbed mom staying on the straight and narrow.

"I think, maybe, she had a boyfriend." The answer was reluctant. That's what Megan had been concealing.

"Why did you think that?"

Megan looked to Claire for support. Her friend squeezed her hand and nodded for her to go on.

"I didn't say because, I don't know. You know this shitty town." She didn't apologize for her language this time. She let Claire's hand go and focused on Matt. "You were at Mom's funeral."

"I was."

"Who else was there?" That Moscow temper showed, though Matt completely understood the source. "A cop dies and Mannheim is flooded with people, and they have a giant funeral. I bet they packed Saint Wen's when your wife died."

"This poor baby," Dawn said. "You need to let her know it's okay to be mad. She's right, for her this is a shitty town."

"They did," Matt said. "But it didn't help me. I was still alone. All those people telling me how great she was, how they remembered her as a flag girl for the marching band, how beautiful she was, how she helped somebody. I didn't care. I didn't want them there. That was mine. She was mine, and she was gone, and no church full of people could change that." Yeah, he had far more in common with the Russians than anyone would think.

"But they came," Megan said, suddenly not seeming fourteen anymore. Years of caring for her little sister in the chaos of an addicted parent, worrying the state would take them away and split them up, watching after a mom who was always trying, worried there would be a slip, then that slip kills her. You can't stay fourteen going through all of that. "All those people who you didn't want to share your wife with came. All those teachers and busybody bitches couldn't take an hour because my mom was just another druggie Russian. Town was probably better off without her."

"I—," Claire's face was stricken, Megan's words stabbing at her.

Megan was up, hugging Claire tight, speaking into her ear. "I know, you had to work, and you called. I wasn't talking about you."

"Still," Claire hugged Megan tighter.

Matt started to speak when Dawn cut him off. "Give them a minute, dear. Megan will get back to you." He waited until the embrace was over and Megan sat, her composure returned when she looked back at Matt. "It's stupid, but I didn't want it to get out that Mom was seeing some guy. Then she's a druggie and a slut. It's stupid, but anyway."

"But if she was seeing someone, he could have been the source of the drugs," Matt said.

"She was clean."

"Okay. What makes you think she was seeing someone?"

"The Yadda app. And I know what you think, that she was using it to get drugs. But I saw her on that phone. She's smiling away, tapping in a little text." Megan smiled, mirroring the memory of her mom. "It was only for a minute here and there, but it was like she was a girl. She was the teenager and I was the mom, and she was keeping her boyfriend a secret. And sometimes, she would say she was going to Walmart, and she would come back with Pokémon cards or something for us, but it doesn't take two hours to go to Walmart. She wouldn't exactly dress up, but she made sure her makeup was perfect, and she did this thing where she," her hands went up around her unruly curls, "like shaped her hair perfect. She was so proud that her hair was back. When she got back home, I was pretty sure she had got some."

The words were nearly as startling to Matt as Dawn's loud laugh in his ear. "I believe her on that."

"Why hide a boyfriend from you?" Caddie's question was back to the soft tone she'd established earlier. Matt was thrilled the sheriff was saving him from following up with the teen girl about her mom getting some.

Megan considered her answer before speaking. "Bella and me. We got the same dad, but they never married, and not long after Bella was born, dude just ghosts us. I don't really remember him, but it's weird I remember when he left. Like that really hurt my mom. She never had a serious guy after dad. I kind of think she didn't want him around us unless it got super serious. I told you, she was all about taking care of us. I think this was taking care of us."

"Any phone calls from this guy?" Caddie asked.

"You can talk on Yadda, I know that. But I never heard her talking to the guy."

The questions went on for a while more, Caddie exploring Nikki's home life, Matt interrupting occasionally to get back to a potential drug connection, but the forward momentum was gone. Dawn finally slipped off the desk and walked to stand between Claire and Megan. Matt's breath caught in his throat. In the light bouncing off the office walls from a sun peeking through the windows, he swore she glowed; his Christmas angel come to life. "It's time to let her go, Matt. This girl needs your help, but she's told you everything she can." He agreed with a blink of his eyes. "I love you, dear," she added, because she knew he needed it.

Megan begged off a ride home despite the weather; someone from the Sheriff's Office dropping her off wasn't a great idea. She got here on her bike and would get home the same way. Claire followed her out of the office as Megan agreed to call or text her if she needed anything at all.

Caddie stood, played with her hat for a moment, and seemed ready to say something, but changed her mind. "Do you believe her?" she finally asked. "About her mother being clean."

"I think that's what she believes. I don't think she's covering for someone, if that's what you're asking."

"I believe her," Dawn joined in. "I don't know what that means, but I believe her."

Matt held back from arguing the point, partly because he wanted to believe it too. The mom who got herself together, fought her personal demons, and took care of her girls. But that's not what the evidence said. Matt believed in his Dawn because she was here; he believed in the evidence because that's what twenty years of being an investigator taught him. "She may have held the line a long time," he said. "But one slip and it could have pulled her back in. It only takes once."

"Yeah," Caddie agreed, putting her hat on and heading for the door. She turned at the last moment. "See you tonight?"

Matt smiled. "See you tonight." And she was gone with the sound of the outer door closing.

Dawn stood in the office doorway, her head cocked to the side and a questioning look on her face. "Do you feel as sad about this as I do?"

"Yeah, baby. I do."

Chapter 12

The common room of River View Estates turned out to be a pleasant surprise, a homey Christmas scene that could fool you into thinking you weren't in an assisted living community. The tree was large and real and full of homemade decorations. Lights hung on every surface as Santas fought for space with snowmen, reindeer, and a dozen wreaths of every color hanging on the walls. A large white creche sat in one corner, a Buddy the Elf cardboard cutout from a theater in another. The music was a little on the loud side, but then Dawn imagined it was no louder than the television in here on an average night.

Caddie, in full sheriff's uniform, waded through the crowd of family, wheelchairs, and walkers to greet them at the door. She handed Matt pink punch in a clear plastic cup.

"You don't even like punch," Dawn said.

"Heck of a party," Matt said. "I feel like I should have a beer."

"No," the women flanking him said.

"Thanks for coming," Caddie said softly. "Sorry about the last-second invite, but last election, they bused all the residents to the polls. You're looking at a ninety-plus percent turnout room. I could use your help."

"Politics," Dawn said in automatic disdain. She didn't care for it when she was here before, and her opinion hadn't changed. But Caddie deserved the job, and her being sheriff meant Matt could continue as a part-time investigator. Her hubby needed that; she'd kiss babies herself if there were any here, and she could actually kiss them.

"You want me to charm the old ladies?" Matt asked with an eyebrow wag.

"Yes, actually," Caddie laughed. "And there are a couple of older men with military pins on their jackets, go talk Army with them."

Matt took a sip of the punch and shook his head. "That's atrocious."

A woman, centered in a clutch of fellow residents dressed in identical red sweaters with puffy green Christmas trees sewn onto the chest, caught Caddie's attention with a wildly waving arm. "Go talk to the voters," Caddie said low, then added, "and thanks, Matt, I do appreciate this."

Dawn hung onto his arm the way she had at more parties in more places than she could count. "Come on, soldier, let's go get our friend some votes." She couldn't feel the weight of her Matt, the solidness of his arm, the warmth of his body, and she missed that, but none of that compared with knowing how much he loved her. This existence was not everything she could want, but his love was.

Matt did well, focusing more on saying Merry Christmas and telling the ladies how nice they looked and how wonderful the party was, than pushing for them to vote for his boss. From the snippets Dawn could pick up from the sheriff, she was doing the same. Caddie was thinking about the election; she had no choice, but Dawn knew the woman would have been here anyway, and probably would have drug Matt along for his own sake. For her part, Dawn was enjoying the scene, and she liked the idea of her husband giving back to their community. She followed along closely, suggesting nice things to say, which he sometimes did. But her soldier was running out of steam with lots more retirement community party fun still in front of him.

"I think I saw a tea kettle in the little kitchenette across the hall," she told him. "Tea and cookies, baby?"

He covered his mouth with his hand. "You love me, don't you?"

"More than ever."

With a steaming paper cup and a small plate stacked with cookies, Matt found a corner, his favorite party spot anyway, with an open chair.

"You can fuel up and get back to your wild campaigning," Dawn told him.

Matt sipped his tea and grabbed a cookie before looking at the elderly couple next to him.

"Introduce yourself, dear," Dawn said. "I think they could use a little Christmas conversation."

Matt set his plate on his lap and extended his hand. "Matt Jager, I'm a deputy with the Sheriff's Office."

"John Everson, I haven't had a job in twenty years." He grumbled a bit about the party; the music was too loud, and the punch wasn't spiked, but his wife was enchanted and clapped along as the staff led a round of *Jingle Bells*. Caddie was awkwardly joining in, and Dawn would have sung at the top of her lungs if she could. Not that she was great at carrying a tune, but she knew the residents would appreciate the enthusiasm. Matt looked comfortable and at his best grumbling along with the older man.

"Tell you the truth," Matt confided to Everson, "the only reason I'm here is as a favor to the sheriff. She's good at the job and needs all the help she can get next November."

"I know your name," Everson said. "You're the one who shot the other deputy, and you were married to Dawn Mann, if I'm right."

"Still is," Dawn cut in. "Though it's weird that the two things you're known for are catching me and shooting people."

"Yeah. I was pretty darn lucky on both counts."

"I was lucky in marriage, too." Everson gently patted his wife's leg. She smiled at him before returning her attention to the sing-along. "I met Barb in high school. Then, like an idiot, I volunteered for Vietnam. Lucky for me, she was still willing to marry me, and we did it the minute I got back."

"Two tours in Afghanistan." Matt extended his hand again, and the veterans gave a hard shake that made Dawn want to hug them.

"Can I ask you something?" Matt asked.

"Shoot," Everson said.

"You look in pretty good shape, and you're clearly sharp enough not to want to be at this party. Why do you live here?"

Dawn was ready to fuss at her husband. That wasn't the kind of question you asked, but Matt and Mr. Everson understood one another. He answered without hesitation.

"I'm here because Barb needs to be here." His wife continued clapping at the same rate and volume, even as the song changed to *O' Christmas Tree*. "She started forgetting simple things a few years ago. Nothing you'd notice, car keys or an appointment. She put her purse in the refrigerator once. But she was still my Barb. Then one day, she couldn't remember our daughter-in-law's name for ten minutes, and we knew she had a problem. She was diagnosed with Alzheimer's. Not long after that, she was diagnosed with cancer."

"I'm sorry, John," Matt said.

"Thank you. It's not curable, but it's manageable. But between her memory and the cancer, I couldn't care for her myself anymore." He put his hand on Barb's leg and left it there. "But, I'll be damned if I'll let that separate us. If she needs to live here, I'm living here."

"That had to take a lot of the burden off you," Matt said.

"It did. Now I concentrate on being here for her and not getting frustrated. Mind, they don't get everything right. She went through issues with her pain meds this fall. It's fine, then it's not strong enough and she's in pain, then it's too much and she's zonked out, but seems like they figured it out now. Anyway." He changed the subject before it became too emotional for him. "Your wife, I'm sorry, too. Barb knew her grandmother. We went to the funeral. That was tough."

"It was, it can be," Matt said. "But you know, I remind myself that I married way out of my league, and she loved me, and I still love her."

"Couple of lucky G.I.s," Everson agreed.

Dawn wasn't sure she'd ever been more proud of her husband. Army and cop stuff came naturally to him, he'd sacrificed and worked hard, and she was to very proud of that, but finding an emotional connection to another veteran, both of them opening up like this, that didn't come easy for him. She bent so she could whisper to him, not that she needed to do it for him to hear, but she wanted him to feel how much it meant to her. "You are a good husband, Matt Jager, and I will always love you." That made her husband look up to the ceiling in an effort to keep his emotions under control. He'd learned to open up, but not too much.

Any chance to dig deeper was interrupted by a tall blonde in form-fitting jeans and a pink scrubs top decorated with Christmas pins, including a large Rudolph whose nose lit up when you pulled its string. In the middle of her chest hung a delicate heart pendant formed from small diamonds. She gave Matt a friendly, apologetic smile before crouching in front of Barb. "How are we doing?"

Barb, frail and tentative, was torn between the sing-along and the staffer. Dawn wasn't entirely sure Barb understood the question. "Leave her alone, she's having fun," she said, her heart softening for the woman who reminded her of Nana near the end. So much had been stripped away, but not the sweetness and joy.

"It's Christmas," Barb said. Her husband spoke, gathering her attention.

"Do you want to stay or are you tired?" John asked over the sound of the singing.

"Oh." Barb looked again at the singers. "Can we stay longer?"

"Of course we can." He lifted her hand and kissed it, her attention already back to the show in front of her.

"I'll wait here and get her to the room as soon as this is finished," the woman in the pink scrub top said. "We're really stretching her limits, but she's definitely enjoying herself. That's nice to see."

"Then why are you bugging her?" Dawn asked.

John joined in with his wife watching the sing-along, Barb glancing at him occasionally as if needing confirmation that he was still there. Ignored for a moment, the staffer turned to Matt, extending a slim hand with well-manicured nails polished in Christmas colors. "Denise Kohler. I'm Barb's RN. We approach resident care with a team concept. I'm Barb's team leader. It is wonderful to see her having a good time, though I'm afraid it will catch up to her later. Did I hear right? You're the deputy who was married to Dawn Mann?"

"He still is, so back off." Dawn wasn't enjoying the Christmas show anymore.

"Still am," Matt said. The remark confused Denise for a moment, then she nodded. "That's nice. We see that attachment with some of our couples here. It's reassuring in its way."

Dang if she knew what her boy had going on, but she swore every time she came back, some woman was eyeing him up. From dark-haired, tattooed strip club owners to over-bleached blonde nurses. She'd hate to think what would happen if Matt ever went wild. It wouldn't be good for him.

The song ended, and a teen volunteer brought up a large edition of *The Night Before Christmas* and began to read, showing the room the first page.

"I'm sorry, John," Denise said. "It's time for Barb's pain meds, and I really think she needs to get some rest. As nice as this is, we don't want to make things worse for her for the next few days." She gripped the handles on the back of Barb's wheelchair and smiled goodbye to Matt. "It was nice to meet you." Then pushed Barb away with John a few steps behind.

"I hope Denise got coal in her stocking," Dawn said.

Chapter 13

The Casey's on the highway connecting Cedar Rapids and Dubuque was busy with holiday travelers gassing up, or, like Caddie, locals hitting the store's liquor and food stocks. Two parties on the same day was a lot, but she didn't regret it. River View was good for her and Matt, for different reasons, and it felt good to give a little back to the community that had taken both of them in. And after what they'd been through the last year, they really needed tonight's party. Unfortunately, a quick inspection of her kitchen revealed a potentially dangerous deficit of booze. Worst of all, her only beer was from Saint Louis, and she was not in the mood for Matt's lecture on the superiority of Wisconsin beer.

A low rumble grew quickly louder, turning Caddie's head before she reached the convenience store door. A phalanx of motorcycles, all Harleys, swung into the parking lot's far edge along the frozen grass. *Not exactly bike weather*, Caddie thought before the cop in her kicked in and she sized them up. The bikers had Iowa rockers on the backs of their leather jackets. This was an MC, motorcycle club, one-percenters. The only bikers who could wear a state rocker without it being beaten off them were the outlaw clubs who claimed Iowa as their territory. The upper patch read Road Demons with a cartoon devil on a bike below it. Caddie was very aware of the fact that she was still in her sheriff's uniform, including the cowboy hat with its shining gold star.

It being Iowa, and bikers having the God-given right to not wear helmets and splatter their brains all over the highway if they crashed, she got a good look at the crew, concentrating on the riders at the front. The ones who, by custom, would be club leaders. They were everything she expected. Long hair, beards, bigger guys, though lots of that was gut. They strode across the lot, not exactly menacing, but certainly with a sense of owning wherever they walked. The one thing that surprised her was their age. Most of the one-percenters she'd dealt with before were getting up there in age, many in their fifties or sixties. The thrill of joining a biker gang had lost its appeal for the young long ago. But not this group. There were a few graybeards, but most looked to be in their thirties or forties, a few even younger. The biker at the head of the group wore a president's patch on one side of the vest front and his nickname, Strangler, on the other. She'd be surprised if he were much over thirty-five. He was a big guy, and his stomach strained against the leather of his jacket, but he was more than solid enough, with broad shoulders and thick arms. Not someone she would like to get in a street fight with. He looked her up and down as he approached.

"Howdy, Sheriff," he said over his shoulder. "I thought it was Christmas, not Halloween." The club members laughed as if they had a choice, though they probably found it clever anyway. Strangler stopped a foot in front of Caddie, holding the door open as his club filed into the store. She ignored the jibe.

"Doesn't seem like good weather for a club ride." If they were just passing through, that was fine with Allemande, but she did not want an outlaw MC setting up shop in Fillmore County.

"We make a Christmas run if the weather's good. Might be the last time we can get on the bikes until spring." He grinned at her as if the very idea of a short redheaded woman sheriff was cute. "Don't worry, we're dropping off presents at homes of brothers doing time. Just stopping in for some coffee."

She glanced behind her into the store where the bikers were gathered around the booze section, grabbing bottles. "I don't want anyone spiking their coffee before you move on."

"Wouldn't think of it." He kept the grin. "That's for later. Now, if you don't mind, I need to take a piss. That Harley engine does a number on your bladder."

She motioned him inside, and he gave her a tip of an imaginary hat. She'd wait for them to leave before she hit the liquor shelves herself. Standing elbow to elbow with bikers picking over tequila options didn't feel right. As she filled a large coffee, she couldn't help thinking about how outlaw motorcycle clubs made their money. Robberies and bike thefts, extortion, prostitution, money laundering, but on top of this list by a long shot was drugs. Meth fueled them for decades, both literally and figuratively. It was what took down much of the previous generation. All those old bikers she'd helped investigate more than a decade ago. She wasn't up on MCs like she should have been, but there was no doubt in her mind that they jumped on the opioid epidemic full throttle. That meant pills from Mexico, diverted legal drugs, and fentanyl, where the real money was. She took a sip of coffee as their bikes roared to life. Strangler saw her in the Casey's window, raised his hand in salute, and led his men out of the lot. Caddie stood there for a minute thinking. If Frank Moscow ever got the idea that the Road Demons dealt to his daughter, war wouldn't be a figurative description.

Chapter 14

Despite only being separated from the dining room by a low counter, the kitchen felt quiet compared to the rest of the house. Matt and Caddie leaned back against the counter next to the refrigerator, watching the scene in front of them play out. Dawn, in a knee-length green dress bordered in white fur, sat on the counter, her feet crossed at the ankles above a pair of short green boots. She looked the epitome of Christmas present. She knew the pose accentuated her calves, something only her hubby could see, but it still pleased her immensely. Caddie silently toasted Matt with a beer, who answered with a tip of a steaming mug. She silently questioned him with a look.

"Believe me, I was looking forward to a Leinenkugel's. They don't sell the good Wisconsin beers in Singapore. But my rhythm is all messed up, and I thought I'd start with caffeine before alcohol."

"My idea," Dawn said, looking around her husband to talk directly to Caddie, still hoping for a breakthrough in reaching the sheriff. Caddie blinked twice in response. "Is that code, Caddie? You're safe among friends."

Any reply, conscience or not, was interrupted by Lieutenant Dubcek calling goodbye from the dining room. He had one arm around his wife, a diminutive dark-haired woman, while holding up a rather expensive bottle of whiskey that had been a present from Caddie. Matt didn't even know the man drank before tonight.

"You're not a whiskey boy, dear," Dawn reminded him, cutting off any future sipping sessions with the LT. He knew she was right and wished she was always around to take care of him, and wished this Christmas would last as long as the impression of Dickens' London Christmas.

Claire rolled into the kitchen, and Matt asked where Bob was to no answer other than a soft admonition from Dawn. Sam and Allison stood on the other side of the counter, arms around each other's waists. The rest of the guests had quickly followed the LT, and the house had quieted. Dawn smiled, knowing everyone her husband cared about was here. She couldn't have orchestrated it better herself.

"I guess it's time," he said, reaching across Dawn, grabbing a small gift-wrapped package. He got the sounds of kisses blown in his ear for his troubles. The others had already opened theirs. A jeweled flower broach from Singapore for Claire and the latest in heavy-duty GPS hiking watches for Sam. Even Allison, who'd objected, got a present from Matt. She laughed and took her objection back when she found the box was filled with gift cards from Downtown Coffee. "Merry Christmas," he said, handing Caddie her gift.

"I would say you shouldn't have…" Everyone laughed as Caddie tore into the square with a joy she rarely showed. She let the paper drop and held up the clear cube with a baseball darkened by age mounted in the center. It took a moment of squinting at the scrawled ink before she made out the first name. "Joe Tinker." She gaped at Matt in genuine surprise, turning the cube as she read on. "Johnny Evers, Frank Chance."

"Tinker to Evers to Chance," Matt said, quoting the famous baseball poem about the Cubs' smooth operating early twentieth-century infield.

"Aww," Dawn said. "You did good, baby. I'm not going to ask what you paid for an old used baseball, but you did good."

Caddie hugged him around the neck, which elicited a "Back off, Sheriff," from Dawn before she disappeared into her office and came back with a small gift-wrapped cube topped with a bow. In seconds, Matt was holding up a clear plastic cube containing a baseball autographed by Rollie Fingers, Milwaukee Brewers' great and namesake for his cat.

"Look at you two baseball nuts. God Bless us, everyone," Dawn said. "You could probably even have one of those beers you've been eyeing, dear. It is Christmas after all."

Matt was still digging in the refrigerator for the exact right beer when the phone in Caddie's back pocket announced itself. He and Dawn exchanged looks.

"It's probably Mama Allemande," she said, but didn't believe.

Caddie answered with a "Yes," as her body language transformed from party host to sheriff. She nodded with a series of "okays" before hanging up, reaching out, and gently pushing the refrigerator door closed. "You haven't had anything to drink tonight, have you?"

"No."

"You're in charge then."

Chapter 15

A tall, peaked ceiling reached beyond a second-floor balcony. A glass wall separated the room from a dark Iowa winter sky. A Christmas tree blinked slowly in white lights, the reflection in the massive window creating the illusion that the room spread beyond its confines deep into the night. The reflections of red ribboned wreaths hanging along the balcony were fainter, fading away against the light. It could have been the setting for a Hallmark Christmas movie about the rich girl who falls in love with the local veterinarian. It all would have fit except for the body of a blonde middle-aged woman lying sprawled on the floor, dwarfed and alone in death.

Matt and Dawn arrived as the EMTs ended their attempts to revive the victim. It played out like actors on a stage, everyone fulfilling their role to the pre-determined outcome. The husband, stricken in shock, stood to the side. Deputy Taggert was slightly behind him. The female EMT, sweat dripping off her forehead, compressed the victim's chest violently while her male partner called out, "Final dose, that's twelve milligrams." The woman pumped as her partner checked the victim's pupils with a penlight. He motioned for her to stop the compressions, placed his ear low to listen for breaths, then felt for a pulse. His partner did the same. They shook their heads and said they were sorry. It had been too long.

Caddie had only nursed two beers tonight, but Matt was stone cold sober, which put him in command. He would sign off on reports, make any statements to the court, and, if necessary, testify to tonight's events, though he had nagging doubts that they'd ever get this in court. The EMTs gathered their equipment and stepped back to the edge of the room.

"Unless we get a call out, we'll wait here until you're done to transport her," the woman EMT said. Then she made excuses about packing their gear away, and they left for their truck.

The husband remained well away from the body. Matt already had their names: Tracy and Kyle Everson. One look at the man, and Matt didn't need to ask if he was related to the John Everson he had met that afternoon. They were clearly father and son. But there didn't seem to be a point to bringing it up. The son's shock rooted him in place, while despair and pain patiently waited their inevitable turn. "Sir, is there another room where you'd like to wait?"

When Dawn died, Matt fought to get to her side and collapsed on the floor holding her hand. He didn't want to deny Everson any final moments, but he also didn't want him to see his wife being treated like evidence of a crime, which she most assuredly was.

His head snapped up, taking in first Matt, then the prone body on the floor. He looked like he was going to be ill. "I'll wait in the basement," he stuttered and turned away. Matt motioned for Taggert to follow.

"I'm not sure what I was expecting." Dawn crouched down near Tracy Everson. "You hear OD and you think of a dirty abandoned building with needles and trash everywhere." She looked back up at Matt. "She looks peaceful, despite everything. I hope she is at peace."

Despite the violence of the EMTs' futile attempts to revive her, and what Matt was sure would be confirmed as fentanyl that had coursed through her system, you could find a sense of peace in Tracy's face if you looked hard enough. But it wasn't there at first glance. She lay heavy and lifeless on the light tan rug next to a light tan sofa, her long blonde hair splayed out in a fan. An irregular red wine stain crept out across the rug, creating its own blood splatter pattern. She'd been holding the glass when the opioid crashed her out and she fell hard. The EMTs had flattened her back to apply CPR, but one leg was still bent at the knee to the side. In life, she had been trim and healthy-looking. She wore light makeup on her face and expensive jewelry on her neck, wrists, and fingers. A small gold crucifix hung from her neck. A red sweater and black jeans were the only interruptions to the color palette. Matt slipped on rubber gloves and knelt next to Dawn. He ran his fingers along the outside of Tracy's jeans. "Not feeling anything in the pockets."

"You don't think she's a needle user, do you?" Dawn asked. "She doesn't look like an addict, as wrong as I know that is."

"I don't know about needles, but you're right, she doesn't look like an addict, if that even means anything anymore."

72

He moved the hair that had become partly wrapped around her neck. "I don't see any bruising on the neck or face."

"I guess you need to check everything."

Matt nodded and moved to examining her hands, pushed her sleeves up, then lifted the sweater to expose her stomach. "No track marks, no bruising. Doctor Serrano will have to confirm, but I don't see any obvious signs she'd been assaulted. I think this is what it looks like, an overdose."

Matt had gotten the basics from dispatch on the drive over. Tracy was forty-five, married, had been in a residential drug treatment at some point, and was supposed to be clean. If it weren't for the differences between a gravel lot behind a cheap hotel and a home that easily ran seven figures even by Iowa prices, the deaths of Tracy Everson and Nikki Moscow were mirror images. A woman fought addiction, relapsed, and paid the ultimate price. Dawn's voice in Matt's ear startled him. He had to stop getting lost in his own thoughts.

"I know my ideas of addicts are all wrong, but this house and the way she looks, Christmas and a beautiful view and a glass of wine, that's not what I expect for an overdose death scene."

Matt stood, still looking down at Tracy, inert and heavy against the carpet. "She was playing Russian Roulette with the fentanyl out there."

"We need to find who loaded the gun before they fire another round," Dawn said. "That was a rather movie detective line, wasn't it?" She shrugged. "It's true, though."

Matt gathered Caddie and Allison, both newly arrived and in uniform, in the kitchen away from Tracy's body. They'd want to examine the scene, but he wanted to keep a tight control on tonight's investigation.

"What have you got so far?" Caddie asked.

Matt looked at Allison first. "Have you had anything to drink tonight?"

She shook her head. "No, I was supposed to be on shift at midnight anyway."

"And you're okay?" he asked Caddie.

"So in charge, baby." Dawn leaned forward across the granite kitchen island, beaming up at him.

"Two beers all night, and it's your scene, Matt. We're not taking any chances. But that doesn't mean I'm not going to ask questions."

"So kind of in charge, baby," Dawn said. "I still think it's sexy, though."

"Fair enough." He suppressed a grin as Dawn winked her best sexy, silly wink at him. "Taggert is sitting with the husband in the basement. From his initial statement, he was out visiting his parents for a few hours, returned home shortly after nine, and his wife was lying on the floor unresponsive, not breathing, no pulse. He attempted CPR, then called 911. Paramedics arrived about nine-forty-five. Someone needs to talk to them more in-depth, but the victim was gone. Despite that, they attempted CPR while administering the maximum dose of Naloxone to no effect. The female EMT said the victim had been dead for at least an hour when they got here. Then she decided maybe she shouldn't be giving me her opinion." He glanced at Dawn for support and to ask if he'd missed anything.

She gave him the smallest possible pucker of the lips, the littlest of air kisses. "Sorry, I don't have anything adorable to say."

"You question the husband?" Caddie asked.

"Not yet," Matt answered. "Interestingly enough, I met the parents at the River View party today. Mom has cognitive issues, but the dad is a good guy. I haven't mentioned it to the husband, yet."

"Small towns," Caddie said. "Any signs the wife wasn't alone when she died?"

Matt shook his head. "Not yet, but it's on my list, Caddie."

Dawn stood straight. "You sounded a little snippy there, babe. Better watch that."

The sheriff put her hands up. "Got it, your scene."

"Got away with it that time," Dawn said, slipping onto the counter so she was a head taller than Matt. Her smile was still there, but slight and sad.

"How long before you figure Frank Moscow knows about this?" Allison asked.

"Trying not to think about that." Matt had been keeping the broader implications of tonight from his mind, trying to concentrate

74

on this woman's death. "Knowing Frank, he'll know by morning." He clapped his hands together, startling everyone, including himself. "Okay, let's get to work. Allison, get video and good stills of the scene. Collect her wine glass, the bottle, samples of stained carpet, anything you think could be helpful. Once you're done with that, you can release the body—"

"Tracy," Dawn corrected him, keeping the focus on the victim. He nodded, she was right.

"Tracy," he said. "You can release Tracy to the EMTs. And get all their contact info. I want someone to interview them tonight."

Allison was already shifting away from their meeting, ready to begin working the case in earnest. "I know this crew. Let me see how long they'll be on duty. Either way, I'm on tonight, so I'll make sure to catch up with them."

"Good," Matt said. "I know they were concentrating on their jobs, but anything they can tell us about the victim, what they saw, particularly any indications someone else might have been here. We want good, solid statements. If we get someone into court, an EMT's testimony could be powerful."

Allison nodded. "Anything else?"

"Come find me," he said, sending the deputy on her way satisfied to have a mission.

"Whatcha going to do with the other one, boss man?" Dawn asked, absolute mischief in her eyes. "Now remember, you may only have one shot at telling her what to do, but she will be back in charge tomorrow, so you don't want to push it too far. Dilemma."

Matt motioned his wife and boss to follow him. "Let's go talk to the husband."

"Chicken," Dawn said.

Kyle Everson sat on the edge of his chair, head down, foot tapping but not hitting the floor. In the harsh lights of overhead fluorescents, his attempts at looking younger, hair dyed blonde, face too tan for an Iowan in December, teeth too white for anyone, made him look older than his late forties. His eyes were clear, but he had the slack-jawed expression of someone about to be sick. Matt sent Taggert off with instructions to help Allison. He wanted to make the interview as private as possible. He was about to ask this husband, who had just lost his wife, some very uncomfortable questions. The fact that he'd met the man's parents less than twelve hours ago didn't help. He liked the senior Everson and appreciated the couple's love. He wanted to feel the same about the son and his wife.

"I should have seen this coming," Everson said. "I should have been here. She could have gotten help in time."

Matt sat on the couch next to him. Caddie took the other end. He couldn't see her, but Matt could feel Dawn behind him. She wasn't perched on the couch or standing still, but wandering in a short loop. He wished she would just come out and say it, whatever it was.

"Mr. Everson, I am very sorry for your loss," he said. "I'm Deputy Matt Jager, I'm an investigator with the Fillmore County Sheriff's Office." He motioned to Caddie, who gave Everson a sympathetic smile. "This is Sheriff Caddie Allemande. She's asked me to take point on this investigation, but she'll be involved every step of the way."

"You have my condolences, Mr. Everson," she said.

Matt waited a beat to hear from his wife, but she remained resolutely quiet.

"I need to ask you some questions so we can understand what happened to your wife."

Emotion flared up in Everson. "I know what happened." He looked down and blew out a long breath. "She got back on dope, and it killed her."

"I know how tough this is, Mr. Everson," Matt said. He wanted to tell the man that he understood because he had felt the same pain of losing his wife suddenly. He understood the shock and desperation, the feeling of being unmoored from your life. But part of being a good investigator is understanding when to distance yourself from a subject. There were times and people when a more personal approach was more effective. Making a personal connection and letting yourself become more vulnerable would get you closer to the truth. This didn't feel like one of those times. Everson wasn't looking for a safe harbor; he was blaming himself, and there was an undercurrent of anger in his words; anger at himself and probably his wife. He didn't want to hear about Matt's pain, and with the love of his life wandering in circles behind him, Matt wasn't inclined to share it. "Anything you could tell us could be important to finding out who supplied drugs to your wife. If that is what happened."

The remark got a dismissive wave from Everson.

"I know," Matt said. "This could be the second overdose death in the county in less than a week. And if we can learn anything that might prevent another, we have to try."

The anger from a moment ago was replaced again by pain in Everson's eyes, his emotions whiplashing across his face. "Someone else has died?"

Matt nodded. "Yes, so you can understand why we need to talk to you tonight despite everything you're going through."

"Who died?"

"Nikki Moscow."

Everson acted surprised. "Nikki Moscow? When was this?"

"Last week," Caddie said.

Everson shook his head as he ran his hands through his hair. "I didn't know. We've been so busy with work and the holidays. Tracy knew her."

"How?" Matt asked taking back the interview.

"They were in rehab together. Tracy never said anything to me about Nikki dying. I don't know if she knew, but..."

Maybe we can get this into court, Matt thought. It was tragic, but the death of Tracy Everson made it easier to solve the death of Nikki Moscow. "Where were they in rehab together?"

"Decorah Hills Recovery Village. Spring this year. I've got all the info here somewhere."

"Did they remain in contact?" *They must have,* Matt thought. You go away and meet someone local in a rehab center, and come back to a small town like Mannheim, you have to keep in touch to some extent. It was hard to imagine that Tracy hadn't heard of Nikki's death.

Everson shrugged, said he didn't know, groaned, said maybe, then said he didn't know again.

Dawn stopped pacing. "You would know."

Not everyone had our marriage, Matt wanted to say. The connection between Tracy and Nikki instantly became the focus of the broader investigation, but it didn't seem worth pressing at this point. For now, they would concentrate on tonight and what was right in front of them. "Okay. Do you have any idea where your wife may have hidden drugs in the house? Having a sample to test may tell us something about them and where they potentially came from. This isn't a judgment on you, we just really want to stop more families from having to go through this."

Dawn closed behind him, her arms crossed, and leaned forward to better see Everson.

"No, I don't. If I had, I'd have flushed them and gotten her back into rehab. Not that it worked the first time."

Dawn cleared her throat. She'd never felt the need to warn Matt she was about to talk before, but she was clearly feeling the delicate nature of this conversation. "I'll have questions, dear, but I don't want to interrupt you."

Matt gave a quick nod. He'd always make room for Dawn to ask whatever she needed to.

"Do you mind if the sheriff looks around? You never know what will help." Matt kept the request purposely vague and open-ended.

"Sure," he said to Caddie. "She's got her own bathroom on the second floor right off the master. But it's a big house," Everson said, perhaps not realizing he had just given the sheriff permission to search the entire house for anything she could find.

Caddie stood and tugged down her leather sheriff's jacket. Matt decided not to interpret that as a sign of Caddie being peeved.

"If you find anything, leave it in place and get Allison to photograph it."

She straightened her jacket again.

"Oh." Dawn leaned over the couch, her head swinging from Matt to Caddie and back. "She looks peeved." She caught her husband's reaction. "You just thought the word peeved, too! Baby, you and me." She pointed at her head, then his. "Like we're operating on the same wavelength."

"Anything else?" Caddie asked.

"Yep," Dawn said, "you've peeved her."

"No." He hoped she'd understand he was just doing the job. They had grown used to working with her in charge, but a little look in her eyes told him they'd be fine.

"I'll grab Taggert and get him looking too," she said, which was her way of letting Everson know they planned on searching far more than his wife's bathroom. If he wanted to withdraw consent, now was the time. She gave him a moment before heading upstairs.

"Now, back to the serious work, babe," Dawn said, disappearing behind him once again.

For the first time since sitting down, Matt considered the space around them. While the first floor was sleek with a touch of McMansion, the basement felt very Iowa, in a good way. A bar ran along the back wall with collector beer signs and bottles from brands that hadn't been brewed in fifty years. The obligatory Hawkeyes posters, all neatly framed, and an oversized print of Caitlan Clark nailing a logo shot in an Iowa uniform. The furniture was leather, the television massive, and the pool table half covered in boxes. It was like the house was caught between a family that had done well and one that was rich.

"He looks like he could use a drink, dear," Dawn said from behind him, leaving Matt wondering what kind of drink she meant.

"Before we go on, do you need a drink, or can I get you anything? I know this is difficult, but I appreciate what you're doing."

Everson stood, walked behind the bar, and came back with a tall can of Budweiser, popping it open and drinking half before he sat. Not the reaction Matt was expecting. Dawn said, "Mmhmm."

Everson answered as if he'd heard Dawn's rebuke. "Sorry. My wife dies from an overdose, and the first thing I do is pick up a beer. But you asked if I could use a drink, and I thought hell yes, I could use a drink."

"It's okay," Matt could barely trust himself with two beers all these months later. He understood the draw of drowning your emotions, but he'd been afraid that if he went under, he'd never surface again. "Believe me, no one is judging you."

"I am," Dawn said.

"This isn't about blame, Mr. Everson. It's about stopping it from happening again."

Everson took it in, had another drink, and set the can squarely on the coaster on the chair's side table. "I want to help. I don't want anyone else to go through this, and whoever's out there selling this poison needs to be in jail." His voice was steady, more assured than it had been all night. The beer doing its trick, Matt thought. "Let me start at the beginning. I've known Tracy since we were kids. I grew up here in Mannheim. Her family was from up by Dubuque, but our parents had gone to high school together, and when we were little, we saw each other during summer on the river or on the Fourth. We started dating in high school, then through college, and got married young. It was like we were always meant to be."

Matt expected to hear from Dawn on that, but she was back to being resolutely quiet.

"Like anyone our age at the time, we partied and drank and smoked dope. I'm not proud of it, but I admit I tried coke. But it was experimenting," he said, brushing it off. "Honestly, I'd rather have a beer." As if to emphasize the point, he took another long drink of his Bud, then went back to his story. "After school, we started the business, and I got more serious about growing up."

"When was this, just so I understand the timeline, and what business are you in?"

"It started as Iowa Aviation," Everson said. "We do business now as Flightline Avionics." He shrugged. "Thinking big. We rehab aviation equipment, everything from small engines to communications, hydraulics, instrument panels, and now advanced navigation systems. We mainly work with smaller regional airlines, in the U.S. and overseas. We started in '95 with a grass airstrip and two large metal sheds overhauling engines." He anticipated the question Matt wanted to ask. "Tracy's family has money. My mom worked at a yarn store, and my dad installed HVAC systems. I got my mechanical aptitude from him, we got the money for the business from her parents."

"Tracy was more of the partier. I'd like to say her addiction came from getting hooked on prescription meds, but that would be a lie. She was willing to give anything a try once." He took a deeper breath as a sick look entered his face again. "I was right there the day she tried oxy for the first time. I didn't take any, but I didn't exactly try to stop her either."

Matt opened his mouth to speak when the sharp zap of an electrical discharge shivered his shoulders.

"Oh, sorry," Dawn said quickly. "I went to tap you, not that you'd feel it. Guess I'm still full of energy. Anyway, babe, I know you want to focus on today, but we need to hear this. Trust me."

Matt rubbed the back of his neck, but kept quiet. If Dawn said it was important, it was important, and he didn't want to get zapped again.

————

Caddie ran her hands quickly through the pockets of another jacket before moving on. The walk-in closet was larger than her office and filled with expensive clothes. She couldn't guess how much all of this cost, but that was the third leather jacket, none of which looked off-the-rack. If Tracy had been using again, she undoubtedly knew she needed to hide it from her husband, and a house this size presented thousands of potential spots to stash pills that could easily fit in the palm of your hand. Once she'd cleared Tracy's bathroom, a natural hiding spot, Caddie knew the odds were stacked against finding anything. But it was worth the effort, identifying the actual pills that killed her could be key to the investigation and a potential prosecution.

She grinned to herself as she went through the motions. Showing a little irritation had ruffled Matt's feathers a bit. He'd probably led as many investigations as she had, but they had a routine; she was in charge, and he tried to do his own thing until she reined him in. It worked for them, and she was beginning to realize that was part of why they were friends as well as boss and deputy. Their egos and personalities bumped up against each other's, but in a way that helped move things along rather than impeding them. She bent down and started running her fingers inside a pair of blue low-heeled pumps. Two shelves of shoes running the length of the bottom of the closet awaited her, but she stopped for a moment.

There had been a fleeting moment, no two moments tonight, when she almost saw something or heard it, but that wasn't right. Felt it was a better description. Felt something on the edge of her mind, which again didn't make sense, then she got that buzzing little headache. Matt had been there both times. When they were alone in the kitchen before they unwrapped presents, then again in Everson's kitchen. She would definitely talk to Serrano, even though she didn't want to. Her worries went back to the injuries she sustained in June; she'd lost a lot of blood, which couldn't be good for your brain. Then again, maybe she just needed glasses. Whatever it was, it would have to wait.

Chapter 16
December 26th

Everson took a long final pull from his beer before tapping down the empty can. "I didn't think much about it for years. We went on with life. The business was growing, and we were both working eighty hours a week. It wasn't like drugs were interfering with our lives."

Risking a zap, Matt interrupted him. "When was this? When she first started using opioids?" He wanted to jump ahead and get to something that could be helpful now. A long dive into the Eversons' arrested party years wouldn't get them closer to finding who had supplied Tracy a lethal overdose today. But, besides not wanting to be zapped, he assumed Dawn had a point in wanting to listen to this. She always did.

"I don't know. 2010, maybe the first time."

Which put them into their thirties, Matt thought. He wasn't supposed to be judgmental of a victim. Dawn was probably sympathizing with Everson and how his past had come to haunt him in the worst way. But Matt couldn't help himself. Kyle had been too busy slamming Buds and working to keep his wife safe. He knew the arguments he would hear from Dawn and Caddie if he said it out loud. Tracy was a grown woman. Men are not here to protect women from themselves. He didn't care if it marked him as hopelessly outdated. His thoughts were on the lovely ghost lady pacing the floor behind him. He hadn't protected her from an unseen threat that took her life. She loved him; it was his job to protect her. The threat to Tracy's life wasn't as hard to see. You didn't play around with opioids and excuse it as partying gone wrong.

Dawn cleared her throat as Everson was momentarily lost in thought. Matt raised a finger, telling his wife he knew to be quiet. He would try at least.

"It wasn't until about 2018 when I realized she was using regularly." He paused, looking over to the empty beer can, then opening the wooden box on the table and pulling a cigar from the humidor. He rolled it in his fingers before setting it back. "I lied to myself and said she wasn't an addict. Not Tracy. She put in the hours at work running the office. You saw her even now." He motioned to the floor above them. "She was a good-looking woman with a great personality. If we were working on a new client, I would handle the hardware and she handled the software. Not computers and stuff, people. I could give all the specs, the options, the prices. She charmed them. And it didn't matter if they were a Mormon from Utah or an Eastern European businessman looking for a night on the town, she knew exactly how to handle them and brought the deal home." A look of pride flashed quickly across his face.

"I know what that sounds like, but I didn't care. I was proud of her." Everson picked up the beer can, remembered it was empty, and set it down further away. "I'm sorry, none of this is helping you."

"It's okay," Matt said. "Take your time."

"I have thoughts," Dawn said. They didn't sound like good thoughts to Matt. Not what he was expecting from his normally empathetic, caring former school teacher.

"Anyway," Everson said, wiping away the years, "she hid the problem for a long time. No impact on her work, she kept her looks. Then COVID locked everything down. We opened back up as fast as we could; we didn't have a choice, but the business was hit hard. No one was traveling, and airlines were mothballing their fleets. Swear if that had gone on much longer, we would have lost it all. We nearly did. I was working insane hours back on the floor rehabbing equipment, and Tracy was mainly at home with nothing to do, which was hard for a social person like her. Then she started complaining about back pain doctors couldn't explain, and next thing I know, my wife is an addict."

"She was doctor shopping?" Matt asked.

"Yeah, and she was good at it. She used those looks and people skills on doctors from Dubuque to Cedar Rapids pretty effectively at first. There's some system that's supposed to catch that, but it either doesn't work or she charmed her way around it. At least that's all I hope she did."

"Yuck," Dawn said. The word was low and guttural. *She certainly must have thoughts*, Matt thought. *Maybe she's blaming Everson as much as I'm trying not to.*

Everson went on. "After the docs cut her off, she hooked up with someone she knew in high school in Dubuque who scored for her. I mean, I get it. Whatever she did to keep supplied, that wasn't her, that was the sickness. But I only learned that later when she was in rehab."

"That's the second time he's done that," Dawn said.

Matt wasn't entirely sure what Everson had done and didn't have any way of asking. "Who's the connection in Dubuque?"

The name came quickly to Everson, but he just as quickly brushed it aside. "I saw in the news where he got convicted of drug dealing last summer, federal, I think. He got sentenced to twelve years. In any case, he's in prison and didn't supply Tracy with whatever killed her."

"I need a list of the doctors who prescribed to her," Matt said.

"I don't have that." Everson shook his head. "It should be in her medical records. But I don't know everything she did to get drugs or who she got them from. Once she finished rehab, I just thought it better to forget everything about her addiction, put it all behind us, and pretend it didn't happen."

"Sounds more like ignoring," Dawn said. "Maybe that was the problem."

"We'll want access to medical records, including from the rehab clinic." Even as Matt said this, the strictures of doctor-client confidentiality were running through his mind. The doctor's responsibility to safeguard the patient's privacy didn't end with their death. But there were public safety exceptions; he just didn't know if a substance abuse counselor would be willing to waive that to name potential drug sources. He jotted a note to research the question before he went to sleep tonight.

"Sure, whatever you need," Everson said. "Doctor Kashvi Prijat is the director and she was Tracy's counselor. I can call up there if you want."

"No," Matt said. "We'll draft something up for you to sign. You have more than enough to deal with." He didn't need the deceased's spouse in the middle of the investigation. Everson seemed calm tonight. That may not last, and his going off on Tracy's doctors wouldn't help. The image of the EMT pumping on Tracy's chest and her partner calling out another Naxalone dose hit Matt, and he changed directions on the questions. "After rehab, did you consider having Naxalone in the house, just in case?" The drug wasn't magic, but sometimes it seemed like it.

"We never talked about," Everson said.

"Okay," Matt said. "You don't know about Nikki Moscow, do you know if Tracy remained friends with any other patients, or is there anyone else who she's particularly close to who might be able to help us?"

"I don't think so," Everson said quickly. "Most of those patients are out of the Cities or Chicago. It's a pretty exclusive place. I've got the bills to prove it. The only reason it's in Iowa is to get those people away from the environment that got them hooked in the first place."

"Okay," Matt said, though he would follow up with fellow patients. "When did Tracy get out of rehab?"

"June."

"What about the friends you used to party with?" Matt asked, taking a slight turn of direction.

"No." Everson was emphatic. "We lost touch with most of that crowd, except for a few who'd outgrown hard partying. Besides, Tracy's focus had changed completely. She joined the yoga studio in town and went all the time. She ran and had a strict, healthy diet. She was into some crazy daily meditation routine. Other than the occasional glass of wine, she was as straight as could be."

Dawn stepped forward so Matt wouldn't have to turn his head. "If she was having the occasional," she gave the word an upward tilt, "glass of wine, she wasn't straight."

Matt nodded. From what he knew, you couldn't be half in on sobriety, which may have been Tracy's problem.

"Did your wife go back to work?" Matt asked, thinking of another potential pool of drug sources.

"Yes, in September. I didn't think the pressure would be good for her, but she insisted. It was her business, too."

"Any chance someone at your business supplied your wife?"

"No," Everson said. "None. We deal with sensitive aviation equipment; I can't afford to have drug users working for me. Everyone passes a background investigation, that includes office, cleaning staff, everyone. Wherever she got her junk, it wasn't from anyone at the company."

"How many people do you have working for you?" Matt asked, not giving up on the idea.

"Twenty-four right now. All good wages, profit sharing, everyone with an incentive to make the company grow. I'm telling you, nobody there would risk their job selling dope, especially to my wife."

"Okay," Matt nodded. "Let's focus on the last few days. We'll work our way backwards. You got home around nine and found Tracy. Where were you?"

"My parents. I left here around six-thirty. You can check the outdoor cam if you want an exact time. They were watching *It's a Wonderful Life* for the millionth time."

"Why didn't Tracy go?" Dawn asked, leaning forward on the couch. "No chance I'd visit family on the holidays without dragging my sweetie along with me." She smiled at Matt. "Even if he'd rather be reading one of his new books."

"Is there any reason Tracy didn't go?" Matt asked. Dawn was right, he would have rather stayed home with a cup of tea, digging into whatever new read his wife bought him for Christmas. She was also right that she'd drag him along, and he wouldn't complain because that's what you did when you loved someone.

"My mother has memory issues. She doesn't know who I am half the time, and that can make her difficult to deal with. It was just easier for me to visit by myself. Tracy understood."

"Hmm," Dawn said and pulled back.

"When you returned, did you notice any signs that someone else had been here?" Matt asked.

Everson pulled his phone out of his back pocket, manipulating the screen as he spoke. "No, I didn't really think to check. But here." He handed Matt the phone. The screen showed a live feed from a camera taking in the wide expanse of the front drive, showing their Jeep and two Sheriff's Office SUVs. The EMTs and the ambulance were gone, which meant Allison had released Tracy's body. Matt scrolled back, looking for alerts that motion had been detected. It showed the response to the discovery of Tracy's OD in reverse order, from the Sheriff's Office to the EMTs to Everson, all the times roughly matching what they already knew. Before that, there was Everson pulling out in a long-cab pickup, with personalized Flightline plates, shortly after six. The only other notification during the day was for three deer wandering across the drive around noon, until Matt hit Everson jogging up the drive just after nine that morning. He handed the phone back.

"I would like access to that," he said. "We'd go back at least a week to see if anyone visited that you can't account for."

"Whatever you need."

"What about yesterday? Did either of you go out?"

"I went in to work in the morning. It's Christmas, but I needed to check on where one of our big orders stood. We've got tight deadlines we're trying to meet. I was out from about nine till one. As far as I know, Tracy went in for yoga and then hit Fareway for fresh lunch meat. Maybe she stopped at Downtown Coffee, she does that a lot. Other than Fareway, I'm not sure of any of that, but she was home when I got back. We had a quiet afternoon. Everything seemed fine. She didn't seem high or anything," he said, shaking his head. "At night, we had a little wine."

"Great idea for an addict," Dawn said.

"Then we exchanged presents." He lifted his wrist to display a watch the size of a brick. "I got this. I bought her earrings and matching necklaces. We're boring now, in bed by ten-thirty."

Matt flipped the page over on his notepad, ready to walk Everson back a week if he needed to, when Kyle leaned as far forward as he could, putting his head nearly between his knees. "I know you need to do this, and I want to help, but honestly, I just can't. Not tonight. I think I'm in shock, and I feel sick to my stomach. My chest hurts."

"Do we need to call you a doctor?" Everson did look like he was going to be sick. Under the artificial tan, his skin was losing color. Matt had been inconsolable. Everson might be showing it differently, but those same forces were working their path of destruction through him.

"No. I don't need a doctor. I need to take a sleeping pill and lie down. Let me forget for a few hours."

Matt didn't think more pills were the answer, but it wasn't his place to judge this man's reaction. They had more to run down than they could possibly accomplish in the next twenty-four hours; letting

88

Everson go now wasn't the worst idea. Tracy and Nikki's relationship was at the top of his list. Patients at the same clinic at the same time die of ODs days apart; that's not a coincidence. Whatever its path, there was a common link in the drug chain that killed them both, he was sure of that. Then there was Everson's company, background checks or not, twenty-four employees were a lot of possibilities, he'd be surprised if there wasn't a Russian cousin somewhere in the mix.

Matt stood and pulled out a business card, checking to make sure it was one with his personal cell number. He held it out. "If you think of anything, call me anytime. If you just need someone to talk to." He didn't say the rest, still unsure if Everson was looking for a personal connection. Matt was more than willing to talk about what losing Dawn meant to him: the pain, the anger, the sense of being lost in your own life. But he was also leery of putting his own feelings on this man.

"Thanks." Everson read the card, his eyes flicking up to Matt after a moment's consideration. "I've heard of you, you know."

Matt nodded, not knowing what else to say.

"You killed that deputy that shot the sheriff."

That wasn't the reference Matt had expected, but it shouldn't have surprised him. A deputy killing another deputy who'd kidnapped the sheriff, all in the middle of hurricane-force winds and driving rain, had managed to pop to the top of national news for a few hours. It dominated local coverage for a month. Matt wondered if he'd morphed from the man who'd lost his wife tragically to the killer of a crooked, insane cop.

"We're going to work this hard," he said, a non-answer being his best answer. "For your wife and Nikki Moscow, and to keep it from happening again."

Everson stuck out his hand and they shook. A look passed between them, and Matt was left with the feeling that Everson knew the rest of his story, too.

"We'll clear out of the house in a few minutes," Matt said before leading a strangely quiet Dawn up the stairs.

Chapter 17

Matt waved, and Dawn stood with her arms crossed, as Caddie and Allison pulled out of the drive. They agreed to meet in the morning to review notes and plan out their next steps. Matt already passed on the information that Tracy and Nikki had been in rehab together, making that connection their obvious, but not only, starting point. Dawn had that fleeting thought again, the same one that hit last June. Maybe she should push her Matt to move on and find love in this world again. Watching Matt and Caddie working together put the last of that away. They were good partners, but they would never be together. That was not their path. At least now, Dawn could say to herself that it wasn't selfish of her to hang on to Matt. Dawn waved and Caddie looked quickly away. Then Matt was beside her, holding a flashlight that was far too large for anything less than spotting bombers over war-torn London.

"What are you up to, silly boy?"

"The surveillance camera Everson set up only covers the front drive. If you know that and you're secretly supplying dope to Tracy..."

"You avoid the cameras and come in the back?"

"It's an idea."

"It wouldn't be the first time we've found a killer using a path in the woods."

"Killer?"

"You sell someone fentanyl and it kills them," she said, and Matt nodded agreement.

"Look at it this way," he flicked on the light and held out his hand for her to hold and not hold, "it's Christmas and you're dressed as cute as can be and the weather is a degree or two above bitter cold."

She could see a smile reflected in his eyes. Despite everything, he still found a way to make her presence in the middle of a death investigation an opportunity to show how much they loved one another. How much they missed the simple pleasures that built and confirmed that love. A Christmas-time walk was something they'd always enjoyed. He'd probably try to do the same if they were in a driving blizzard. And she'd probably let him.

"Okay, baby. Let's go for a walk."

He swept the light across snow-covered grass shining green through a sheen of thin ice left by the freezing rain. If anyone walked back here in the last few days, they would have left a trace.

"I was thinking," Dawn said.

"I knew that," Matt nearly laughed. He'd been waiting for this.

"Okay, smarty." The boy always thought he knew what she was thinking. Just because he was right most of the time didn't mean she liked being so easily pegged. "What was I thinking?"

Matt stopped, the beam of the flashlight following tracks leading away from a garbage can and recycle bin. The frozen crust clearly showed tiny, almost human handprints. "Trash bandits."

"A clue," she said. "And what was I thinking?"

"You don't like Everson. I'm just not sure why."

"I was trying not to dislike him," she said, correcting Matt without telling him he was wrong. "When I took the vice principal job, we were trying to enlist local business leaders to fund an upgrade to our gym and auditorium. They needed it, but more important, getting someone else to pay for that could have freed money to hire positions focused on helping bring up reading and math proficiency for fourth through sixth grade."

Matt stopped, his light shining on Dawn. Despite its brightness, the light didn't bother her eyes, which she didn't exactly like. It reminded her that she wasn't entirely here with her love. She put up a mittened hand, miming pushing the flashlight away.

"Sorry," he said. "It's just that even now you continue to amaze me."

Oh, he was going to get sweet. She loved it, and any idea of telling him to move on fell even further from her mind. "Tell me how, baby."

"You're just perfect. That's all. Figuring out how to get people to do what you want by getting them to do what they think they want. It's an impressive skill."

Yeah, not letting this boy go. "It's how I got you. Unfortunately, we didn't raise enough money, then they decided to try for a bond to build a new elementary school after the new high school got built."

He nodded, motioning for her to move beyond the evidence of a raccoon attack on the garbage cans. "So, what about your ultimately unsuccessful fundraising made you not like Everson?"

"He hit on me."

"Wait? What?" Matt stopped, shone the light on Dawn, then quickly moved it away. "When?"

"Remember that little cake and coffee gathering in the gym where I stood in front of everyone for ten minutes, pitching how wonderful it would look and how proud people could be seeing their names on the supporters' wall?"

Matt shook his head; he honestly did not recall.

"Sometimes, dear. I'm not surprised. Remember, you swept the floor with one of those giant fuzzy brooms after complaining about crumbs everywhere?"

Recognition dawned on his face. "Oh, yeah." He raised a gloved finger in his defense. "You were wearing a green sweater and a pair of jeans that made your butt look very nice."

"Thank you, dear. You don't remember my speech, but you remember my butt. I'll take that as a win. Anyway, while you were lost in whatever bad boy thoughts my bum inspired, I was walking prospective donors around the gym, talking about what needed repair and what the new gym could look like. Kyle Everson was one of those people. I didn't recognize the name or the face until he mentioned that their business refurbishes aviation equipment. That I remember."

"You were seeing dollar signs," Matt grinned.

"For the school," Dawn emphasized. "And darn right, I was. Well, we were off in a corner where I was pointing out cracks in the wall that had been patched over, and telling him that a total replacement would eventually be required. Everson suggested he would be interested in discussing it further. Somewhere else. Another night. Alone."

The flashlight swung toward the house, making Dawn wonder if she should have mentioned the incident that hadn't made a lasting impression until it was dislodged by Tracy's death. "That SOB." The light swung back. "And I was there?"

"Yes, dear."

"You didn't tell me. I would have remembered that."

It was Dawn's turn to start them walking. "Matt, if I said something every time some idiot guy made a weak pass at me, we would have spent half of our paychecks bailing you out of jail. We weren't rich like you are now."

"I wouldn't have--"

"Yes, you would."

"Yes, I would." Matt shone the light out across a narrow stretch of backyard. Heavy woods and what looked like a steep drop off, not twenty yards away. It turned out the home was situated at the end of a narrow ridge, allowing for the rare nearly three-sixty-degree Iowa hilltop view. "And Tracy? Was she there?"

"I don't think so, but with someone like Everson, it wouldn't have made a difference."

"So, you don't like the guy because he cheats?"

"It doesn't help," she said. She knew her Matt was devoted to her and would never, but the betrayal of a cheating husband still stung. It was all tied to the same instinct that made her mad when she thought Matt had been visiting strip clubs, even after she was gone. She could almost admit to herself that this touch of jealousy was rooted deeply in her love for Matt. The same instinct that made her want to hang onto him even now, when it wasn't entirely fair.

"That can't have been all that was bothering you," Matt said.

Dawn could see the red rising in his cheeks, thinking at first that her husband was becoming angry. Not at her, but the idea that some man who meant nothing to her made a clunky pass five years ago. Then she caught sight of his breath hanging frozen in front of him before it slowly fell, drifting apart. She was reminded that they inhabited different worlds with only their love maintaining this connection. He was cold, and she needed to get him back into the Jeep. She couldn't have Matt freezing to death. "It's not, but let's talk about it with a heater running."

The drive from Everson's home took them through frost and snow-shrouded evergreens. A wall of green and white bracketing the road. Dawn pointed at the radio. "Christmas music."

Matt had an AM station out of Cedar Rapids on and Bing Crosby playing in seconds. "Okay, babe. I'm warming up, Christmas tunes are on, and we're driving through a winter wonderland. What else is bothering you about the man who just lost his wife to a fentanyl overdose?"

"Well, when you put it like that." It may not have been what he was getting at, but Dawn was well aware their being happily together now meant someone had died. Not exactly a heavenly tradeoff. "At first, I was trying to listen and be quiet so you could do your job."

"That had to be hard."

"Be nice." She could feel her own smile, silly boy giving her a gentle hard time. "First, I couldn't help noticing that despite the fact that his wife was an addict, the house was full of alcohol, and he didn't seem to have a problem using sleeping pills. I think if your wife spends time in rehab, you could do without mind-altering stuff in your house." Everson didn't take care of his wife, and that bothered her even more as she said it.

Matt nodded agreement. "I know, I had the same thought. But judging him doesn't do any good in moving the investigation forward. We can't focus on that. Besides, that will catch up to him sooner or later. At some point, he's going to ask himself what he did wrong, what he could have done differently. Right or wrong, he'll pay a price for that eventually."

"That's just it, dear. He didn't seem to be paying much of a price for finding his wife dead in their home. I don't understand his reaction." She mimed patting Matt's hand resting on the gear shift. When she was fully here, she would rub the skin on his hand between two of her fingers until it drove him crazy. She wasn't sure why; she just liked it. "You told me how my leaving," she said, using Matt's favorite euphemism for her death, "made you feel. You said, you sobbed and fought off deputies to get to me, even though I was already gone." Heater or no, being here entirely or not, the thought of her own violent death sent a heavy, cold weight through Dawn's soul.

"That's true," Matt said, finishing her thought so she wouldn't have to. "I couldn't even stand. I knelt there holding your hand, racked with sobs. Eventually, Doctor Serrano led me away."

"I didn't know she did that," Dawn said.

Matt shook his head as he slowed the Jeep to a stop as the long drive intersected with a county highway. "I'm not sure I even realized it myself until now. It was a blur. She took me to another room, got me water, and a washcloth for my face."

"You must have been a real mess, baby." She couldn't help it, but warmth entered her voice. She loved hearing about how much this man loved her, as much as she was pained at the torment her death put him through.

"Yep, that was me. A complete mess. But the thing is, baby, everyone reacts differently. The first month, it was like I was in shock. I was numb, but I could function. I could watch TV or read a little. I mean, I was torn up, but I could go through the motions of life. Then, about a month in, I was checking out at Fareway, loading stuff on the belt, and this cashier, this girl, asked me if I found everything I needed. I looked at her, my head screaming, No! I didn't find everything I needed, you stupid twit. Dawn's not here, she's gone."

"You didn't?"

"No. I didn't scream at an innocent cashier. I held it in and checked out, made it home, even put the groceries away, and the entire time, my head was exploding. And I went up to the bathroom, lay down on the floor, curled into a ball, and cried. That's when I fell off a cliff. I didn't know I could hurt that much. I went from crying to breaking down four or five times a day." He looked at her with his eyes matter-of-fact despite his words. "And it didn't make me feel better either. It emptied me out only to fill again. Running is the only thing that helped, a little anyway. Then, very slowly, I started getting better. After a few more months, I started reading everything I could about grief, particularly about losing your spouse. Joan Didion—"

"Oh, I love her writing."

"I know, dear. She wrote *The Year of Magical Thinking* about her husband's sudden death. She kept his shoes for a year because part of her mind couldn't accept the idea that he wasn't coming home and wouldn't need them again."

"That's sad. And you with a garage full of my clothes in boxes," Dawn said.

"But I wasn't playing that mental game," he said. "I couldn't. That way leads to madness. Anyway, there was another book written by a psychologist and a minister who both lost their spouses in their forties. They ended up married eventually and wrote a book about grief."

"Not sure I like where this is going," she said.

"No, it's not about them getting together," Matt said. "It's what he did. They were writing about their wedding rings. He wore his for six months after his wife passed, then took it off, thinking it was time to live again."

"Huh." Dawn had no idea what to think of that, so she didn't think about it.

"Yeah. Well, that really pissed me off."

"Really?" She could hear the slightest touch of anger in his voice. He wasn't kidding about the story's effect on him. "Why?"

"Because he was wrong. He was grieving wrong. He didn't love his wife enough if he could take his ring off after six months." He looked away from the road to connect with Dawn. "I hated the guy."

She glanced at Matt's left hand, but it was hidden beneath a glove as it gripped the steering wheel. Resisting the urge to ask, she let him go on in his half briefing her on a case and half baring his heart way.

"It took a while, but I eventually realized that he was mourning his wife the way he needed to. I felt a little bad for judging him. Joan kept shoes for a year. The minister had to make a decision to move on. I cried like a baby and ran as many miles as my knees would let me. Everson has a long road in front of him. He may wake up a month from now and be a total wreck, and I might be the one hitting on hot elementary school vice principals."

"Not many of those around," Dawn said. But she couldn't take her eyes off Matt's gloved hand and no longer felt like holding it in. "Take off your gloves."

"My hands are still cold." Matt suppressed a smile. Her man knew exactly what she was thinking. The only thing she was unsure of was what she'd see. She told herself to be happy with him either way. He'd more than paid the price he insisted Everson would eventually pay. If he had to take the ring off at some point, that's okay, she told herself.

"Dear," she insisted with the single word.

He slipped off the right glove first, teasing her with how slowly he managed to do it.

"Other one, silly."

He took it off quickly, showed her the gold band on his ring finger, and began tapping the steering wheel, far too happy with himself. "I told myself, I'd take it off when the time felt right. It never felt right, and I don't think it ever will."

"How did I not notice before?" She asked herself as much as Matt.

"Because, dear, it's what you expected to see. We don't notice what we know is supposed to be there. We see what's missing or what we don't think belongs. I'm your husband and have always worn the ring. It's what you knew belonged."

She leaned over and kissed his cheek. The electric discharge made an audible pop. Matt rubbed his cheek, laughing as Dawn sat back.

"And yet, nurses, strip club owners, and small-town waitresses still hit on you."

"Men get sexier with age," he said.

"Who would have thought," she laughed along with him, loving him for all his faults, "that the sweet young soldier I saved from getting airsick would turn out to be so vain?"

Chapter 18

The Hawk's Nest, stinking of sweat and beer, was packed, the pressed bodies creating a hot humid zone despite the frigid temperatures outside. Allison made her way deeper into the crowd. So far, the Nest had been quiet without a single call to dispatch over noise or a fight on the street. She was hoping the sight of a sheriff's deputy would help keep it that way when the place closed down in twenty minutes. The parked cruiser across the street might also convince some to walk home or call for a ride instead of getting behind the wheel.

"Last call," one of the bartenders yelled over the din. He was a big beefy man with a pit-stained Hawk's Nest T-shirt and a lit cigar in his mouth in defiance of Iowa's prohibition against indoor smoking. He caught Allison's eye as he poured another pitcher. She shook her head, and he just grinned back. His smoking wasn't going to be a priority tonight.

A cold burst fought its way through the heat drawing Allison's eyes to the side door. Three men were moving out through it, one of them looking like he was being half-dragged against his will. Helping a drunk friend out, she thought, until she recognized the tall blonde with long hair as Jesse Moscow, one of Frank's many nephews and by extension a cousin of Nikki's. He had a firm grip on the man he was most definitely not helping. Jesse's arm partly blocked her view of the jacket, but not enough that she didn't recognize the Road Demons patch.

"Coming through, coming through." She pushed her way through the crush, the uniform and her words not helping at all. Finally clear of the crowd trying to get to the bar, she was out the door in three quick steps. A blast of cold hit her in the face. Glancing left, she was just in time to see the Road Demon held up against the wall as Jesse and his companion screamed at him. In a flash, Jesse punched the Demon in the stomach, doubling him over in pain. The MC member vomited, emptying his stomach on Jesse's shoes. Jesse tried skipping back before cursing the Demon and hitting him again.

"Hey!" Allison yelled as she unsnapped her holster before breaking into a trot. "Sheriff's Office, don't move."

Jesse's partner didn't waste a second spinning and taking off running. He was beyond the corner of the alley before Allison's weapon cleared the holster. She leveled the pistol at Jesse as the Demon sank to a knee in his own puddle of puke. "Hands on your head, Jesse!" she commanded.

Jesse grinned. Then he winked and ran.

"Dammit." Allison holstered her weapon and took off at a sprint. The Road Demon retched again as she ran past. "Don't go anywhere."

Reaching the end of the alley, Allison caught a glimpse of Jesse rounding the far corner of the building, doubling back towards Main. "Shit." She turned back into the alley. Jesse and his partner were probably parked on the street in front of the Nest, and they had a head start. "Stupid, stupid," she muttered out loud as she passed the Demon staggering back toward the Nest's side door. "I said don't go anywhere," she called, picking up speed.

The rumble of an engine coming to life echoed down the alley, and Allison knew she was too late. Reaching the street, she saw a truck thirty feet down Main picking up speed away from her before she could get a good look at the plate. Jesse leaned out the passenger side window, blonde hair blowing in the wind, waved, and then flipped her off.

Allison stood watching, trying to catch her breath. Unless she wanted to initiate a high-speed chase in town over two punches thrown, Jesse would get away with it for now. "Jesse, you just made my list," she said out loud as she headed back into the alley.

The Road Demon wasn't a big man, but with his MC vest, ponytail, and scraggly beard, he wasn't hard to spot in the back of the Nest. He'd shaken off the thumping Jesse had given him, and the ensuing puking, and was talking junk about chasing off a couple of Russians. Allison decided not to bust his fantasy talk, instead guiding him to a semi-private corner to catcalls from his friends. He gave up his ID easily enough. William Sexton, address out of Waterloo, thirty-eight years old. Allison wrote it down and noted the nickname on his vest, Squirts. *Nice,* she thought. As for the assault, he feigned his memory of five minutes ago was already lost in a fog of ignorance and beer.

"So you have no idea why Jesse Moscow and another guy would haul you out of here and work you over?"

He shrugged. "Guess I just pissed them off. What can I say? I do that to people. Look, cop lady--"

"Deputy," she said.

"Deputy lady." Squirts gave a sneer and a laughing nod to his friends, who were still watching. "It's just some dudes who bumped into each other in a bar and got into a scrap. Nothing for you to get all hot and bothered about." The sneer expanded. "Unless that's what you're into. I don't judge."

She wasn't sure if it was harder not to laugh in his face or pop him one. "Do you want to press charges?"

"Nah, it's Christmas," he said. "I'm full of cheer."

She motioned to the one-percenter patch on the front of his vest. "Visiting friends?"

"Always. My brothers got my back."

"I don't see any here tonight," she snapped back.

He shrugged, and Allison decided the interview was over. She held out her card. "You remember anything that could be helpful, give me a call."

Squirts looked at the card, sniffed, and walked past her, the card hanging in the air. She added Squirts to the same list Jesse Moscow was on. With the crowd thinning, Allison headed outside to act as a living reminder to not drive drunk. She figured she'd let the sheriff sleep and wait until morning to let her know that the first shots had been fired in the war between the Russians and the Road Demons. *Merry Christmas*, she thought to herself.

Chapter 19

Matt held his phone up so Dawn could listen in. Without his normal morning run to get him going, he was relying on a cup of tea, which had barely begun to do its job. Caddie passed on Allison's encounter with the Road Demon and Jesse Moscow at the Nest, and he couldn't help thinking she was blaming him. He put that aside, realizing the sheriff was probably as tired as he was. Dawn may be able to push on with angelic energy, but Matt and Caddie would have to rely on caffeine and adrenaline.

"I'm reaching out to Rafer this morning," Caddie said, referring to the FBI supervisor based in Cedar Rapids. Although the SO often dealt directly with DEA and other federal agencies, they found Rafer was the shortcut to hitting all the feds at the same time.

"Did they ever date?" Dawn mouthed. Last time she was here, she insisted Caddie and Rafer would make a good couple and that Matt should make it happen. He didn't, and he didn't know if they had. His blank expression got him a disapproving eye roll.

Caddie went on. "For an MC without a history in Fillmore County, that's two appearances in twelve hours. We have to at least consider the possibility they're the original source of the fentanyl that killed Nikki and Tracy."

"You would think you would have heard about them pushing in," Matt said. Caddie may not be a Mannheim native, but she'd managed to get a pretty good feel for the community since becoming sheriff. A motorcycle club moving in and slinging dope should have hit her radar.

"Maybe this is me hearing about it," she said. "Either way, we need room to work this angle, and I need you to convince Frank to give us that room."

"Caddie," he said in a tone that no other deputy would try with the boss, "I don't control Frank. And if I push him to let us look at the Demons, that's only going to make him think we're onto something and he'll escalate."

The sheriff got irritable right back. This was also a tone she never employed with other SO members. Being friends with the boss meant she didn't feel obligated to treat him as kindly as she did her other subordinates. "I didn't say to give him our entire playbook. Look, you figure it out. Say something about checking on leads from Tracy's death, and that we don't want to scare a suspect into taking a runner. Or threaten him, I don't care. At least slow him down for a day or two, and maybe we can put this to bed before he goes wild."

Dawn made a face. She'd never heard anyone sort of yell at her husband, and then for him to just take it calmly. Another proof of their friendship. They could vent on one another with no harm done.

"Gotcha. I'll do the impossible and calm Frank Moscow down."

"Good," she sounded calmer. "When are you going to see him?"

"Pretty soon." He grinned at Dawn. She gave him a mischievous wink back.

Caddie said she was heading to see Doctor Serrano for early autopsy results on Tracy. Matt promised he'd check in later before he slipped his phone into a jacket pocket and pulled the Jeep back onto the road. The turnoff to Frank's wooded rural spread was a quarter mile ahead.

"You are so bad," Dawn laughed.

A double-wide trailer sat ten feet off the gravel drive against towering pines. The faded blue home was flanked by a picnic bench on one side and a swing set on the other. A wooden plaque mounted alongside the door read Nikki, Megan, and Bella with a rainbow arching through the names.

"It's clear," Dawn said as Matt pulled a silver tool from his pocket, inserted a long, thin probe into the keyhole, and unlocked the door. "Breaking and entering, dear. You are back to being the bad boy of the Fillmore County Sheriff's Office, congratulations." She slipped in behind him, the scene inside chilling their excitement over the minor break-in. The common living room and kitchen area was neat, well, if inexpensively, furnished, and decorated for Christmas. A tree brushed the ceiling next to the television on the far end with a halo of dead needles dotting the red tree skirt below. The ornaments were a mix of hand-crafted, pictures of the girls in small frames, and Disney Princesses. A few presents remained under the branches. Matt made his way over as Dawn remained in place.

"The tags say Mom," he said.

"That's sad," Dawn answered. "It doesn't look like the house of a drug addict."

"You keep saying things like that," Matt said, "even though we know they're not true."

He started searching the room. Unwilling to disturb the peace that had descended on the trailer, he moved quietly, closing drawers and setting couch cushions back when he was done.

"She wouldn't hide drugs out here, baby," Dawn said. "Whatever else Nikki was or had become, Megan says she was a good mom. Looking at this place, I believe her. She wasn't so far gone this time that she would leave something lying around that would hurt her girls."

Matt stood straight and considered his wife. "You like her."

"I do," Dawn nodded. "She loved those girls. I don't know how she got pulled back into taking drugs, but I bet she fought it with everything she had."

"Easy fight to lose, baby."

"And you keep saying things like that, even though you don't know if they're true." Dawn pursed her lips, her exact expression when she wanted to argue with Matt but was holding back. That didn't last. "She decorated that tree for her girls. This place is neater than our house. Nikki did that while working night shifts at a crappy hotel and going to classes forty minutes away."

Matt made his way closer to her. She wasn't right about a neat home meaning Nikki hadn't slipped, but she was right about not finding anything where the girls would easily find it. If she was hiding her drug use from Megan, Nikki wouldn't leave anything incriminating in the living room. "I know you want to believe she was clean, baby. But the OD tells us otherwise, doesn't it?"

She nodded, her lips still pursed in protest to the idea. He blew her a kiss and moved on to the kitchen, quickly opening and searching through cabinets and the refrigerator. They were exactly as Megan had described, filled with food. Nikki tended toward store brands. Great Value cereal and breakfast bars from Walmart, frozen treats from Fareway, boxes of rice and noodle dishes from Aldi. She was on a budget and got the most for her food dollars. He slowed and took his time under the sink, figuring that even a nosy teen like Megan was unlikely to spend much time among the detergent, cleaners, and old sponges. He wasn't exactly second-guessing his idea of searching the house, but he was increasingly doubting they would find anything useful. He wasn't even sure what he was hoping to find. The one thing they learned was that Nikki's relapse hadn't progressed to the point where it was showing in the rest of her life. Nothing under the sink. He stood, ready to hit the back of the trailer and Nikki's room, where he was hoping for better results.

"Notice something different between here and the Eversons'?" Dawn stood next to him at the end of the hall. Her arms were crossed, and her lips had gone from pursed to I told you so. He wanted to say something about wealth and money, but he knew that's not what she was talking about.

"What?"

"Not a drop of alcohol."

He nodded to the cabinet over the sink. "Two cartons of cigarettes and a big thing of Folger's." It was an agreement with her point.

"Like a woman on the straight and narrow," Dawn said. "Do you know if she was attending NA or AA?"

He had to think. Not being in on the first days of the investigation was catching up to him. He should know this. He should know Nikki without having to search through mental notes. He already knew Tracy Everson better than Nikki Moscow. He would have to fix that. "I don't know."

"You need to check," Dawn said. "I see this house and I hear Megan, and I see a strong woman fighting for her girls. If she needed to go to meetings, she would go. She was focused on taking care of her girls and improving her own life. That's what she was using to keep herself straight."

He wanted to agree with her. He wanted Nikki to be straight and for her girls to know that their mother had fought for them to the end. But two ODs in five days said something different. "Then what are you suggesting, dear? Murder?"

Dawn raised her eyebrows and motioned to head down the hall. "You said it first, Matt, not me."

"But I don't believe it," Matt retorted, wishing he'd softened his tone. He did not want to argue with Dawn. He loved her deeply and had never won an argument with her in his life, whether he was right or wrong.

104

The first door on the right opened onto a small bedroom decorated in pink, camo, and pink camo. "Megan," Matt said.

"You are a detective, dear," Dawn whispered in his ear.

He waggled his eyebrows at her as he turned and entered the bathroom a little further down the hall on the opposite side. He searched quickly but thoroughly.

"Any better luck, babe?" Dawn asked.

"Not really expecting any," he said. "If there's anything in the house, it'll be in Nikki's bedroom, but you just never know what you might find."

"A scrap of paper with a drug dealer's name and number on it?"

"If it was 1985, maybe." He ran his hand deep into the shelves in a narrow closet crammed with towels and sheets. He shook his head and followed Dawn down the hall.

"Babe." She held out her arm as if she could have stopped him. The gesture was enough, though. In a room even more pink than Megan's, a small bundle was curled up in the bed, a short shock of blonde hair sticking up from under a cover decorated with teen versions of DC Comics superhero girls: Wonder Woman, Harley Quinn, Batgirl, and more, all with big eyes and bright smiles. "It's Bella," she whispered.

"Poor kid," Matt said softly. The trailer's furnace clicked on and a gentle breeze of warm air from a vent overhead ruffled her hair. He looked to the end of the hall and the master bedroom that stretched across the width of the trailer. "A quick search?"

"No, dear." Dawn was emphatic. "We're not going to have this child waking up to the sounds of someone in her mother's bedroom. It'll either terrify her or convince her she's been living in a terrible dream. Either way, we are not doing that. Your choice, you can wake her very gently and take her up to her grandparents' house, or we can sneak back out of here and let them find her later."

He looked toward Nikki's room again. It had been his idea to come out here, you didn't investigate a woman's death without trying to know everything about her. Searching her house was part of that puzzle. They hadn't found anything, but they'd learned a lot. Megan was right to an extent; her mother was trying to live a straight life. But it didn't mean she was successful. She'd fallen, probably recently. That could cut down on the number of suspects who could be supplying her and Tracy Everson at the same time. Tracy's death was a tragedy, but it made it more likely that they could solve Nikki's. Maybe even before her father set the county on fire.

"No." Dawn was stern, even if her voice was soft.

Matt gave up on further searching. "It's too cold out, we can't take any chances."

Dawn gave him a 'good job' smile. She knew where she was leading him the entire time, the smile was for him figuring it out. "I'm sure she knows the way just fine, but no, we can't let her go by herself." She stepped back to let Matt in. "Now be very careful. Let's not traumatize the little one."

Matt knelt, putting himself on the same level as the bed. Bella was facing away, curled in a tight ball. The cover rose and fell slowly with her breath. Pulling the badge off his belt, he held it up so she could see it when she woke. "Bella." He kept his voice gentle. "Bella, wake up."

The girl turned her head slowly, her eyes wide awake. She'd been playing possum. Searching the room behind Matt and seeing nothing, her focus fell back on the gold badge. "I just wanted to come home," she said. The words broke Matt's heart. "I couldn't sleep in Mom's bed, but I wanted to be home. Am I in trouble?"

He put the badge away. "No, Bella, you're not in trouble. That's not why I'm here. You want to know the truth? I didn't even know you were here."

She sat up, gathering the covers around her waist. "You're the man who was at Mom's funeral. The one Grandpa Frank said was a sneaky cop."

"I was there," he said. "I didn't know your mom, but I know your grandpa, and I wanted him, and you and your sister, to know how sorry I am about what happened to your mom. I also wanted him to know that I would do everything I could to find anyone responsible," he slowed, realizing that Bella may not know or understand everything about her mother's death.

"Just be truthful," the conscience in the form of his wife said over his shoulder. "You don't have to say everything, but whatever you say has to be the truth."

"I want to find whoever gave your mom drugs that took her away so I can stop them from giving them to anyone else."

106

"She wasn't taken away," Bella corrected him, angry that he'd tried to soften it. "Mom died."

"You're right," he said. "And I know how much that hurts."

Dawn was closer and no longer speaking softly. "Do not start questioning this little one, dear. I will not have it."

He wanted to protest that he wasn't going to, but he wouldn't have found that believable himself. "I think I should drive you up to your grandpa and grandma's house. They'll be worried about you, and it's really cold outside."

"Grandpa said a bunch of curse words about you, but he said he could trust you."

Matt stood. "Sounds about right. You need to get dressed?"

Bella nodded and waved him out of her room, a gesture well beyond her age. It was hard not to like the kid.

"You would have made a good dad," Dawn said.

Matt searched her face for any sign of sadness or remorse. He would have made a good dad, but she would have made a great mother, a hall of fame mom. They had put the Army and his career first, always putting off children until later, then it never happened. They could have fixed that with more time, but never had the chance. That was his fault, and if it pained her even after death, he would have to carry that burden, too. But he didn't see that, he saw pride and happiness in her look. That helped.

"I guess we'll just have to settle for you being Claire's pappa for now."

Bella came into the living room, sat on the floor near the door, and slipped on her pink, flowered snow boots.

"Missed that clue someone was here, detective," Dawn said with a smile, pointing at the boots.

Bella was up and in a puffy pink jacket in seconds.

"Do you need a hat?" Matt asked. He figured most children needed hats most of the time.

Bella pulled her hood up and picked up an equally pink backpack she'd crammed with more of her stuff. "Wait," she said, running back down the hall.

"She takes as long to get ready as you do," Matt said. Dawn stuck out her tongue through a smile. When Bella came clopping back, she was rolling up the pink camo blanket that had been on Megan's bed.

"She really likes this blanket," she said.

"You're a good kid," Matt said, opening the door to a blast of cold that cut into the trailer and forced his and Bella's heads down. Dawn adjusted her white knit cap and walked out first.

"Oh dear. Company, Matt."

Matt stepped out onto the steps to the sight of Frank Moscow blocking their Jeep in with a massive truck, pulling just far enough forward that he could open his own door. He didn't look happy climbing out. The passenger door creaked open as Megan joined him, her mane of frizzy blonde hair corralled under an orange wool cap. She stared stone-faced at Matt, saying nothing.

Dawn reaffirmed what he was thinking. "Megan doesn't know you, dear. She's never met you, and you don't know her name."

Matt nodded at Frank and in agreement to his wife. "Good morning, Frank."

"You're trespassing, counselor." He stayed close to the open door of the vehicle, something Matt definitely didn't like, particularly with the look in Frank's eyes. For the first time since they'd met, Moscow was showing Matt exactly why the man was feared in this county. There was no attempt to establish a connection or play the good old boy role. This was Frank Moscow, a man you did not want to cross.

"You mind stepping away from the truck, Frank?" He tried keeping the request casual, but he wasn't sure if he'd managed.

"You mind telling me what you're doing on private property?" He didn't move, but stuck his hands in his jeans' pockets. Matt took that as a compromise.

"Trying to solve a crime, Frank. I told you I would."

"You got a warrant?"

"You got a gun in that truck?" Matt took a blind shot, but one he felt pretty solid taking.

"Warrantless search," Frank replied.

"Felon in possession," Matt said. "That's ten years federal."

Dawn and the two girls watched the men trade volleys like spectators at a tennis match until Megan broke the exchange. "Bella, come on, crazy girl. Grandma's making French toast."

Bella looked up at Matt with a stern expression on her face. "If you don't find the people who gave my mom drugs, Grandpa said he's going to and he'll shoot them in the nuts."

"He would, too," Dawn laughed.

Bella was off, running down the steps, holding Megan's blanket up to show her sister.

Frank waited until the girls were comfortably back in the truck with its heater running. "Second night in a row she's snuck down here."

Matt nodded. "She misses her mom."

"See," Dawn said, "you and Frank are friends again. Not that that's a good idea, but better than your little frozen standoff."

"Heard about the Everson woman," Frank said. "What can you tell me?"

Matt shook his head. He had used Frank for information in the past, but this wasn't a two-way street. "The Sheriff's Office is committed to finding and bringing to justice whoever is supplying lethal illegal drugs in Fillmore County."

Dawn made a slight gagging sound as Frank spat a stream of brown tobacco juice out onto the clear snow. "Sounds like a lawyer answer," Frank said. "I like you better as a cop. Less bullshit involved."

"We are committed, Frank," Matt said, trying to reassure him. "I promised you that. For those girls, too. Let us do our jobs so you don't end up back in the can." He left the Child Protective Services threat out this time. The girls were deep in conversation, Megan having spread her pink camo blanket over their laps. But her eyes kept flicking between her grandfather and Matt. She knew the threat already, but he didn't want her to hear it coming from him. "Did your daughter know Tracy Everson?"

Frank thought for a moment. Matt figured it wasn't about whether Nikki knew the woman but whether he'd answer the question. "Yeah," he looked back up the road toward his house, hidden on a rise in the woods. Smoke curled up through the trees. The girl's grandmother must have started up the fireplace. "They knew each other from that treatment place. She met the girls. I figured she was a snotty rich bit—," he looked over to the girls, "bit of trash, but seemed almost like her and Nikki were high school kids. Never hurts to have friends on the inside, long as you don't trust them."

"Ah, life lessons from Frank Moscow," Dawn said.

Moscow went on, "As far as I know, they didn't see one another when they got out. She didn't talk about her, but you know it's a small town."

"You got him talking anyway, dear," Dawn said. "Maybe warn him again, real nice this time, about not beating people up and running amok across the county."

"If you find out they've had any contact since rehab, let me know. It could really help find who supplied them." Matt reached out an ungloved hand toward Dawn, she placed her immaterial mittened hand in his. "Give us a chance, Frank. You take care of those girls and let us find who's responsible. Your nephew out beating up bikers is not going to help."

Frank's hands came out of his pockets as he turned to climb back into his truck, a slight chuckle coming out. "You need to hurry up, then. And get the hell off my property."

"Oh, quick, baby," Dawn said. "Ask him about the motorcycle guys."

"What do you know about the Road Demons?"

Moscow paused for a moment, the malicious grin bringing Matt back to the realization that whatever semi-friendly relationship they had established, he had been playing with a cobra. In an instant, that smile was replaced by a grandfather's as he called into the truck cab, "Who wants French toast?"

Frank was headed back up the long, snow-covered drive before Matt and Dawn moved towards their Jeep. "That's not good, baby," she said.

"No. No, it's not," he answered.

Chapter 20

Doctor Serrano's office was sparsely and sharply decorated, reflecting a woman most comfortable in a world of refinement and minimal unnecessary distractions. While others found the doctor cold, Caddie had grown to understand that Antonia cared deeply for her patients and her friends; her professional demeanor wasn't a cover, it was an expression of that caring. The strong, almost sweet smell of freshly brewed Colombian coffee filled the room and began warming Caddie even before the doctor handed her a cup. Caddie took a sip and let the hot liquid hit her system, jolting her awake with the promise of more. *Dang, the doctor knew coffee.*

"I trust you had a pleasant Christmas, at least before the unfortunate call last night," Serrano said.

"It was nice actually," Caddie said, the memory of being surrounded in her home by the people she cared for momentarily joining the comfort of the coffee. It didn't last, though. "Until," she finished.

Antonia let out a breath, the closest she would come to showing her frustration at another needless drug death in her county. She opened the file that had been sitting square on her uncluttered desk.

"I have a very busy day, so I came in early to complete Mrs. Everson's examination."

"Okay, Doctor, what do you have for us?"

"The toxicology screen is not back yet, but everything is consistent with an opioid overdose. I expect we will find fentanyl or a similar potent synthetic drug present in her system. She had consumed wine over a several-hour period. She had cheese, several meats, and crackers in her stomach. Not a great deal, though."

"How much wine?" An addict drinking was one of a number of things that bothered Caddie about last night. Not exactly a good strategy for staying sober, but that might have been the slippery slope that led her back to harder drugs.

"Toxicology will give us a more precise answer, but I expect about half a liter."

Caddie nodded for Serrano to go on. The smell of the coffee in her hands reminded her to drink, and she sipped and listened.

"No external signs of heavy drug use. No needle marks, skin is in good condition, and personal hygiene is high. To eliminate the unlikely, I examined her for defensive wounds; there were none. Similarly with her fingernails. The only bruising is on her left hip, consistent with falling when she lost consciousness and landed on her side. She was otherwise in excellent health. No signs of heart disease or other conditions that could have contributed to her death." She closed the folder, though Caddie doubted the doctor had actually needed to refer to it. "In short, Catharine, there is every appearance that Tracy Everson was a healthy woman who succumbed to her addiction and consumed a dose of an opioid that slowed her respiration and heart rate until she slipped into death. Unfortunately, no one was able to provide her with an anti-opioid in time."

"Will the test tell us how long she's been using?" Caddie knew some drugs, particularly with chronic use, were detectable in the body longer than others, but she'd never worked an overdose, fatal or not. Probation officers who were charged with keeping their probates clean probably knew this stuff hands down; she didn't.

"It is detectable in blood for up to twelve hours, that's where we will receive the first results from our hospital's lab. I should have those in before this afternoon. If it weren't for the holidays, you would know already. To determine if there has been chronic use, I've taken hair samples. Those we're sending to the DCI lab in Ames. They're the experts on this, but opioid use shows up in hair for ninety days. I will let them know that you have questions, and I expect they will be able to provide you with some answers. How detailed, I'm not sure. In any event, I've ordered a complete tox screen on both blood and hair, so you should have as detailed a picture of her drug use as is possible. I will say that the similarities between Nikki and Tracy are striking. Both supposed former addicts, otherwise healthy women with no noticeable external signs of long-term drug use." Serrano's expression and tone changed from presenter to questioner. "If I may, Catherine, what are you hoping to find? If I had a better understanding of your needs, perhaps I could suggest something."

Caddie stared into her coffee, watching as it settled back after a sip. "I'm not sure, Antonia. Maybe if we knew how long Tracy and Nikki had been using again, and assuming they have the same source, we could narrow down a suspect list. If we had a suspect list."

Doctor Serrano shifted uncomfortably in her chair, a movement Caddie easily picked up on. The doctor had gone from presenter to questioner to something else. For the first time since she'd known her, Antonia almost sounded tentative.

"You will find out eventually, I assume, but I feel I must tell you that Tracy Everson was a patient of mine."

Serrano had her undivided attention now, even the coffee half-forgotten in her hand. "What can you tell me?" If the doctor had something on her mind, better to ask an open-ended question.

"Doctor-client confidentiality extends past the patient's death, Catharine."

And still, there was hesitation in her voice. Maybe she'd been wrong, maybe asking the right question, in the right way, would convince the doctor to tell her more. But going at it like a hammer, one of Matt's favorite moves, was not the right answer.

"I appreciate that, Antonia, I do, but there is a public safety exception. Anything you can tell me that could point at who supplied Tracy could prevent more overdoses, more deaths."

Serrano thought about it some more, though Caddie was sure she had wrestled with the question for hours.

"I can treat your information as confidential," Caddie assured her. "If it's that sensitive, I'll do everything I can to keep it out of any reports or at least not release it publicly. This is important."

Serrano nodded once, more to herself than Caddie, and resumed her authoritative voice. "I saw Tracy in mid-November for an unrelated issue. I can tell you that at that point, I do not believe she was using opioids. I, naturally, knew of her addiction. I'm the person who recommended Decorah Hills for her treatment, and I've been watching for any signs of relapse since her return. There were none. As I said before, you can only detect opioids for twelve hours after use, but her blood at that visit was clean. Eyes, skin, mannerisms, everything then told me she was not using."

"What did she see you about?" Caddie noticed the doctor had conveniently left that out.

Serrano gave a wan smile. "I'm sorry, I don't believe that is relevant to the question of her drug use."

"Okay," Caddie said. No reason to beat on the doctor about that. She wouldn't give in if her mind was made up anyway. "Thank you." The movement of her hands reminded her of the coffee, and she quickly finished it, unwilling to let any go to waste. Serrano assured her that she would be available by phone if Caddie had any questions. Caddie thanked her for the coffee. She was halfway to the door, ready to put her cowboy hat back on, when Serrano cleared her throat. Caddie looked back, but the doctor was seemingly deeply absorbed in typing something into her laptop.

"Blood results will likely say Tracy Everson was clear of any sexually transmitted diseases." Serrano kept typing without losing a beat.

Caddie almost said 'What?' but caught herself. Antonio Serrano was telling her the test results that hadn't come in, that Caddie hadn't asked about. On top of that, it was rank speculation, something the precise doctor simply did not do. Despite doctor-patient confidentiality, Serrano had just told her what Tracy was seeing her for in November. Caddie stood there a bit longer, silently willing the doctor to say more. Antonia didn't look away from the screen.

"Merry Christmas, Catharine," she said.

Caddie put on her hat. "Merry Christmas, Antonia." It wasn't a cheery wish, but it was genuine.

Chapter 21

A basket of homemade baked goods sat in the middle of the conference room table. Individual mini loaves of pumpkin and zucchini breads swaddled in plastic wrap, imperfect cookies bulging with nuts, biscotti poking high into the air. The treats were a present from a family whose beloved dog had run away after last summer's derecho and was assumed lost forever until Lieutenant Dubcek spotted a golden tail moving through the woods off an isolated county road fifteen miles from town. It took him three nights, beef treats, and a lot of soft talk before he convinced the terrified animal to trust him enough to get close. Then the golden retriever spent the ride back to Mannheim firmly planted in the LT's lap. Matt told the story to Dawn as quickly as he could before they were no longer alone.

"You could do worse than learn a few things from Chris," she said while deciding whether her husband should have the zucchini bread or biscotti. She went on without having to look at the expression on his face. She knew it would be there. "Persistent with an unfailing moral compass, dear." His chance to argue back passed as Claire rolled in with a stack of files on her lap.

"Oh, treats." She grabbed the last zucchini bread. Dawn shrugged a half-apology and pointed to the rock-hard, twice-baked biscotti.

"Try not to make a mess dunking them in your tea. It can get kind of icky, baby."

Matt made a show of slowly, deliberately dunking the cookie into his black Army mug as the room filled and people grabbed treats from the basket. Dawn was laughing and calling her husband a silly soldier as Caddie came in last, grabbed a cookie, and took the chair at the end of the table.

"She took the boss chair, baby," Dawn said. "So much for your command of the investigation."

"Okay, everyone, I'm going to try and keep this short. We've all got a lot on our plates. I haven't canceled any leaves yet, and I don't want to. Chris, are we still good with patrol if Allison spends part of her time working the OD investigations?"

The lieutenant, dressed in jeans and a pressed flannel shirt, studied the laptop in front of him before answering. "I think so. I assume she's going to be available for part of her shifts; I don't have her as the only deputy on patrol at any time. Barring something else coming up, we're good through New Year's Day and back at full strength on the fifth."

"Good," Caddie said. "Let me know if you need me on the road."

The LT shook his head. "No. You focus on the ODs, I've got the patrol." The sheriff was about to go on when Dubcek raised a hand. "One thing though, there's a chance of a major winter storm later in the week, extreme cold, winds, snow. But this is Iowa, so it could slide north of us, but if it looks like we're going to get hit. I may make some patrol schedule adjustments. At least have an extra deputy or two on call."

"Good. Keep me updated, but like you say, it's Iowa, who knows what's going to happen. And thanks for coming in, I know you're off."

"My wife says I'm underfoot," he chuckled. "She could use an hour's break."

Dawn plopped herself on the conference table next to Matt. "Chris and his wife are almost as cute as you and me." She beamed. Dawn had always loved love. "It's nice."

"I'm sure that's not true, but thank you anyway." Caddie touched her temple and blinked slowly twice, a small glitch, until she turned to Claire. "I know you haven't had a lot of time, and you were supposed to be on leave, but what do you have for us?"

"Not a problem, Boss." Claire set three folders to the side and concentrated on the yellow legal pad in her lap. "I'm still looking at what I can find for background on Nikki and Tracy. As everyone already knows, they attended Decorah Hills at the same time. Between statements from Mr. Everson and what Matt got from Frank this morning, they knew each other."

"Frank said they were close in rehab, but doesn't know about anything since," Matt added. "Everson only said they knew each other."

Claire nodded and went on. "I took a quick look at the clinic online, and it looks like a resort. It has a full pool, a sauna, gym, health food kitchen, private rooms. Pretty exclusive sounding."

116

"That had to cost a lot," Matt said, thinking out loud. Why the cost struck him, he wasn't sure.

Dawn spoke, keeping her voice down to not set off another round of blinking and head touching from Caddie. "Frank would spend whatever he had to for his girl. You can see that in the way he treats Megan and Bella." She almost sounded like she admired him.

"You saw the Everson house," Caddie said. "He could afford it. I'm sure Frank can come up with the cash if he needs to. We work their relationship from both ends. I'll call the director up there and see what they can or are willing to tell us about any relationship between Nikki and Tracy, and who else they knew. Let's identify who in town they were both in recent contact with. If we're lucky, between the two, we can find the fentanyl source."

"I'd rather show up in Decorah, pull out a badge, and start asking questions," Matt said. "A phone call feels like it will be followed up with lawyers and talk of confidentiality and worries about liability."

"Challenging the boss's authority," Dawn said gleefully. "A strong but not necessarily bright move." But that's not the kind of relationship Caddie and Matt had. He could disagree with her, she'd consider it, even argue over it, but in the end, she made the decisions, and he at least pretended to go along with it.

"Lawyers are the worst," Caddie said.

"Hey," Dawn protested. "You two better not be still joking about that law degree I paid for. The one you hardly seem to be using." Caddie blinked the words away. "Sorry," Dawn whispered.

Matt grinned, directing it to Dawn above him. "But chicks dig a law degree." Dawn stuck out her tongue as the room gave Matt a weak laugh

"I don't want to show up at the clinic out of nowhere, badges or not," Caddie said. "I'll call and set something up and try not to give them a chance to stiff-arm us."

"We don't need no stinking badges." Dawn was back to gleeful, knowing her husband couldn't resist a laugh. He didn't, earning a stiff glare from Caddie.

"Sorry," he said. "Just thought of something, anyway, Dr Kashvi Prijat is the clinic director, and Everson said one of his wife's counselors. She's who we need to talk to."

Caddie made a note. "All right. What else have you got for us, Claire?"

"I would like to get bank and credit card records, maybe something would show up. We know Tracy was a regular at the yoga studio, maybe there. I also thought of AA or NA, but I think there's the anonymous part of that, and I have no idea how they would react to an approach from law enforcement."

Allison raised her hand. "I know a guy who leads meetings in Mannheim. I could talk quietly with him. I don't know what he'll be willing to say, but if this is a threat to people in NA who relapse, he may be willing to help."

There was something about the way that Allison looked away that caught Matt's interest. "How do you know him?"

"We dated a few years ago," she answered dismissively. She wanted this part of the conversation over. The sheriff obliged.

"Thanks, do that. Even if he can't point you at a drug source, see if he can confirm if Tracy and Nikki attended, if they acted like they were still friends. Whatever you can get."

"Will do, Boss," Allison said, happy to have it over.

Claire scribbled a note, then made a check mark before moving on. "Home security video. I've sped back through Christmas Eve Day. It seems to match Everson's statement. On Christmas, you can see him leave the house early in running gear, head down the drive, and come back about an hour later. He leaves again at six-thirteen in his truck. The camera gets a pretty clear shot, and it's him. He returns at nine-fifteen, and after that, it's medical and LE response. No other visitors. Going back, Christmas Eve Day, he goes for a run at six-thirty in the morning—"

"Pretty cold and wet for a run," Chris said.

"Wouldn't stop you, baby," Dawn whispered.

"Nothing like running outside," Matt said. "I've run out that way before. There's a whole network of blacktop paths and forest trails in the area that connect up to the old railway right-of-way trail that runs from Dubuque to Cedar Rapids. You can get to half of the county from out there."

"He was definitely dressed for cold-weather running," Claire said. "He left again at eight-twenty and doesn't return until a little after three. Tracy left at nine and was back before noon. One FedEx truck in the afternoon, but we can see the package left on the porch, and the driver had no interaction with Tracy. Going back further is one of my priorities until we get phones and financials in." She looked at the sheriff. "I assume we're getting those."

"Matt, you mind?" Caddie said, but it wasn't actually a question.

"Sure, give me all the fun stuff."

"You can make use of that law degree drafting the subpoenas," she said.

"Seriously, dear." Dawn wasn't smiling anymore. "Do you know how much Marquette Law School costs?"

"Shouldn't take long," he said. "But with the holidays, we're not going to get anything back fast enough to head Frank off."

Caddie let out a long breath. Frank Moscow was not a complication any of them wanted, but he couldn't be ignored. "Gather the evidence, we do it the right way as always. But you're right about Frank. Get the subpoenas signed and out as quickly as you can, but we're not waiting for results. See if the husband is willing to provide access to their financials. It could help point to connections between Nikki and Tracy and track Tracy's movements."

Matt groaned. "If they're joint accounts, we're good. I don't know about his ability to turn over her private financial records. At least not until he gets to the bank and takes control of her accounts. And that's assuming there's not something unusual in her will about who inherits what."

"Do what you can," Caddie said. "We'll get it eventually, but eventually doesn't help us with Frank."

The exchange between Caddie and Matt finished, Claire made another note, and ticked off another line. "Finally, in case everyone hasn't seen it yet. Doctor Serrano emailed the toxicology report for Tracy Everson. Fentanyl, as we suspected. The numbers look similar to Nikki's, if that helps anything. That's it. That's all I've got. I'm going to put in a request to Iowa Workforce for an employee listing at Flightline. In the meantime, I plan on pulling everything I can on the business. That could give us a halfway decent employee list. I'll start looking for any drug convictions, connections to the Russians, anything I can find."

"Good work," Caddie said before pointing to Allison. "Run down last night at the Hawk's Nest for everyone."

Allison started with seeing Jesse Moscow pulling the Road Demon out of the bar and finished with her questioning the MC member. "I don't have anything more on him, no drug convictions, nothing in our records or with the DEA. I spoke to the Cedar Rapids RAC this morning, specifically about the Road Demons, and asked what they have, whether it's in Fillmore County or not. Are they moving drugs? What kind? How much? Any family connections to Mannheim? Anything. He claims that they don't have anything beyond general intelligence that the Demons are involved in low-level meth distribution in the Waterloo and Dubuque areas."

"Claims?" Matt said, picking up on Allison's choice of words.

"Claims," she said, then looked over to Caddie. "The answer was pretty quick. He didn't think about it for even a second. I could be completely wrong, and maybe they already looked into them, but that's not what he said. They could know more. But why hide it?"

Matt didn't let Caddie answer. "Because they've either got a big op planned or they've got a source they don't want to burn."

Dawn purred. "So untrusting, dear."

Caddie pointed a pen at Matt. "If there was an op, they'd wrap us in. Adding potential OD deaths would elevate any charges. But if they have a solid source and they don't think the Demons are involved in opioids in the county?"

"They would do what they have to protect the source," Matt agreed.

The purr was gone from Dawn's voice. "Neither one of you trusts anyone. I guess that's what makes you buddies."

"You want me to push them for more?" Allison asked.

"No, that's on me," Caddie said. "I think maybe an end around with the FBI."

"Oh, you never answered me if she and Agent Rafer got together?" Dawn asked. "I need you to catch me up on gossip since I've been gone, baby."

Whatever look Matt gave her evidently was the wrong one.

"Oh, like you would even pay attention," Dawn said in a sulk.

That over, Allison went on. "I did speak to the EMTs who responded last night. There's nothing additional they have to offer at

120

this point. When they arrived, Everson was administering CPR, but there were zero signs of life. They still went through their protocols with Naloxone to no effect. She had been gone too long for anything to help. I'll write it up this morning. Other than that, I've got nothing. I'll talk to the NA leader and run down anything else you have for me."

"Again, good work," Caddie turned to Matt last.

"One thing to add from my talk with Frank. He was already aware of Tracy Everson's death, which I guess isn't a surprise. He was also clearly aware of Jesse roughing up a Road Demon. They are definitely on his list. I warned him off again, told him we were working this hard and he needed to stay out of the way and out of trouble."

Caddie chuckled softly. "And it stuck this time?"

Dawn echoed the soft laugh. "What do you think?"

"He told me we needed to hurry up, so maybe he'll slow a little, but he's mad. He also knows we're right about this putting Megan and Bella in danger of being taken away, even though that family is the best thing for them right now—"

"As sad as that is," Dawn cut in.

"As sad as that is," Matt said.

"I see you left out breaking into Nikki's house," Dawn teased. "Probably a good idea."

"Let's keep pushing, and maybe Frank gets to raise those kids," Caddie said, shaking her head that this was the best option for them. "I'll call Rafer and see what the FBI has and get him to reach out to DEA and ATF. If anyone has a source inside the Demons, I want them pushed for information. Everyone always wants to protect sources, but what good is protecting them if you don't get information when you need it?"

Caddie ran down what she'd heard from Doctor Serrano, without mentioning her remark about Tracy being clean of sexually transmitted diseases. She'd let Matt know and wait to highlight that for the rest when the tests actually come back. Then she turned to the next steps in the investigation. With Allison already having marching orders, the sheriff turned to Claire. "I know you've got a lot on your plate, but I'd like to make it out to Flightline today, if possible. How long before we can get a rough employee list?"

Claire blew away a lock of brown hair that had fallen across her face, the act as much a sigh as anything else. "Just names? An hour. Something useful, like names and real quick backgrounds? At least two."

"Two hours," Caddie said before turning to Matt. "Can you have the subpoenas done by then?"

"Someone else will have to get them signed."

"I'll talk to my NA guy and come back and do that," Allison offered.

"Okay," Caddie readied herself to stand. "Alibis?" A table of shaking heads, and the meeting was over. Dawn stretched, one arm reaching toward the ceiling, one leg pointed down in a pose that accented a trim form. It caught Matt's eye, which he was sure was his wife's intention.

"That," she said slowly to match the stretch, "was the most boring meeting ever. You didn't cuss or storm out or anything."

"Not every meeting is exciting," Matt said out loud. Chris Dubcek snorted agreement.

Chapter 22

The roar of two large fan heaters competed with the intermittent buzz of power tools and classic rock from an ancient boombox in the corner. Despite the extra effort to heat the dealership's maintenance area, Allison's breath was visible as she walked to the far bay. Still, it felt a good forty degrees warmer in here than outside. A couple of mechanics glanced her way, but the uniform and her purposeful stride convinced them to pay more attention to the autos they were working on than her. She cleared her voice loud enough to be heard over the din as she approached the last vehicle, a small Japanese model with a mechanic bent deep over the engine. He looked up, a touch surprised, then stood and wiped his hands on a rag.

"Hi, Dave," Allison said. "I see you're getting your hands dirty."

"Hey." He was tall and good-looking in an easy kind of way. His hair was gathered loose in a short ponytail, and his smile came naturally. It wasn't hard for Allison to remember why she was attracted to him. "My dad's idea, not that I mind. He says you can't run a dealership unless you know every job inside and out. I'd rather work on an engine than convince someone to add a rust-proofing package to their new car anyway. But I'm guessing you didn't come here to ask about how I'm doing."

Allison detected something in Dave's remark. She wasn't sure if it was a touch of bitterness or humor, but she hadn't exactly ended things well with him. "Is there somewhere we can talk in private?"

Dave led Allison to an office in the back of the maintenance area. The rest of the floor could still see them through windows that ran along the top half of the walls, but between a shut door and the heater fans, it was as private as they could get. He poured coffee and sat on the edge of the desk. "You here about the ODs?"

Allison added sugar into her paper cup, something Dave knew she took with her coffee. "I'm sorry, I know twelve-step programs are anonymous, and I wouldn't be talking to you if it wasn't important, but the more we know about the victims, the better chance we have of preventing more deaths. Are you still leading the groups?"

"There's more than one leader, but I'm still involved in NA and AA. It's how I stay clean."

She felt there was a dig in there somewhere, but focused on the job. "What can you tell me about Tracy Everson and Nikki Moscow? Anything could help, but we're really interested in any connection between them."

Dave sniffed deep and looked away across the repair bay. "I shouldn't be saying anything. People need to know they can come to group and we're not going to run around telling stories on them."

"They're both dead from their addiction, Dave. We're not trying to get anyone who's innocent in trouble, but if we can find who supplied them fentanyl, we could save other people, including maybe some of those people in group." For an easy-going guy, Dave's look hardened, and Allison wondered if coming here had been the right idea. She thought their relationship, to the extent they had one, ended long ago and wouldn't be an issue. But the way she ended it may have left some lingering resentment. "If you'd rather talk to someone else with the Sheriff's, I get it. I can have Matt Jager get in touch with you, but I think you could be useful."

"I'm not talking to anybody else, Allison." His look softened; he'd made a decision. "I'd rather talk to you. First, I'm not giving anybody up in group unless I'm convinced they're doing something that directly hurts someone else, okay?"

Allison relaxed. Maybe she was the one sending off bad vibes. Whatever passed between them, she knew Dave was a decent guy and he would help if his conscious would let him. "That's fair. What can you tell me about them?"

Dave finished off his coffee and set the cup aside. "I know both of them, knew them. They were friends. They always sat by one another." He thought for a moment. "Tracy was first, I remember that. June, I think. Nikki came about a month later, but didn't stick around for long. I ran into her in town later and pulled her aside and talked about how important it was that she attend. She's got—shit, man—had two little girls. I don't think she'd mind me saying, but she talked about them a lot and how important it was to her to be clean for them. But she said she was good. She had a job, which can be tough to get when you've got a record, and she was going to school, and swore she'd come in if she needed to talk. Anyway, you can't force someone to attend, and she seemed good. Not that I ever trust that to last."

He turned away and poured himself another cup and drank before he went on. "Sorry. First Nikki, then I heard about Tracy this morning. Fucking opioids, man. That shit will pull at you. I wish I was surprised when someone stumbles, but it's part of the gig."

"I'm sorry," Allison said. "I hadn't thought about how this would make you feel. I appreciate you talking to me."

He waved it away and dug a pack of cigarettes out of his pocket. "Don't tell my dad. Smoking in here is a big no-no with the insurance company." He lit up and blew out a long puff of smoke. "Tracy, she stuck around longer, a couple of months of nearly every day. Then it was maybe once a week, which works for some people." He had to think some more. "That's right, it seemed like she wasn't attending, but she'd stop by occasionally, listen, and take off before the meeting was over. It was like she needed to hear what others were going through but wasn't up to sharing herself."

That seemed to run against what her husband had said, but that didn't surprise Allison. They seemed like a couple that might not be as honest with one another as they should be. "What about recently, the last two months?"

"Same, I think." He hesitated. "You know, maybe not. I think she came in a little more, a couple of times a week. Not a lot, I mean, but enough that I was going to talk to her about sharing. Then nothing since Thanksgiving."

"Could she have been there to see someone in the group?"

He shook his head quickly. "No. She was always in late, out early. After group, people stand around the parking lot smoking and shooting the crap, but I never saw her out there."

Tracy and Nikki's patterns for attending were interesting, but didn't point to any possible supplier. "Is there anything else you can think of that might help?"

"No." Dave stood straighter and took a half step to the office door. "I hope you catch whoever supplied them, but I don't have anything more for you."

Allison moved so she could leave the office before him. She did not want Dave holding the door open for her like a gentleman. "I appreciate you talking to me." She was at the door, hand on the knob.

"And, I'm sorry how I ended things." She hadn't planned on saying anything; emotional communication wasn't exactly her strong suit, and this probably wasn't the right place or time, but it felt like something she needed to say. "I was new with the Sheriff's Office, and when you told me your whole history—"

"You mean I was an addict with an arrest record?" he said with a smile. That easy look that was so attractive to women.

"Yeah, that." Even Allison couldn't help smiling. "Anyway, I should have ended things better."

His grin broke wide. "Yes, you should have, but I get it. I hear you and Sam Janda got a good thing going."

She turned the knob. She was not about to talk about her relationship with Sam with an old boyfriend. "We do," was all she was willing to say.

"Try not to mess it up, Deputy."

"Thanks, Dave." Allison walked back across the shop floor, relieved that she'd managed some closure, though she hated the word, with Dave, and wondering what might have driven Tracy back to more meetings at the end and why her husband hadn't noticed.

———

Matt typed away, cursed, deleted, and started again.

"Maybe if you slowed down a little there, cowboy, you wouldn't make so many mistakes." Dawn lay on the leather couch in Matt's law office, one leg high in the air, stretching before she let it down, and arched her back. It got him to stop working on the subpoena for a moment.

"What are you doing there, kitty cat?"

She turned on her side, head propped on her hand. Her smile was somewhere between sultry and silly. "Cowboy and kitty cat, those are new." She stood and stretched her arms over her head, arching her back in a side view. "Speaking of cats, where's Rollie?"

Her stretching done, he went back to typing. "Upstairs at Sam's place or wandering around her office. She's always happy—"

"That cat is never happy."

"Rollie's as happy as Rollie is capable of being with Sam. She'll spend hours sniffing fishing gear in the garage. I don't think either would mind if I left her here."

126

Dawn slid onto the front of the desk, her behind inches from Matt's eyes and flying fingers. His eyes flicked up. "You really don't want me to finish this, do you?"

"Is my bum too much of a distraction for you, dear?"

"Yes," he said. "But please don't move it. I like it there."

"Naughty, boy." There was nothing sultry or teasing in the words. She appreciated how much he loved her. He worked, and they talked about Sam's idea to rehab more apartments upstairs. Dawn wanted it done, but Matt argued for looking at the numbers. Before he could say it would be a good idea if they could do it cheaply enough, he'd already lost the argument and agreed to finance whatever Sam wanted. "Matt, spend that D.C. money on helping our niece build nice places she can rent at reasonable prices. It's a good business venture for you guys."

"There." He tapped the return key hard, emailing the subpoenas to Caddie and Allison. Leaning back in his chair, he clasped his fingers across his chest and tried his version of a naughty boy smile. "Do you want to try your kitty cat stretching for me again now that you have my undivided attention?"

Dawn leaned back, reaching her lips out to Matt. He sat forward. They kissed to the sharp spark of static. "Sorry, soldier, the stage show is over."

Chapter 23

The cluster of buildings that made up Flightline Avionics sat on an open field a mile outside Mannheim city limits. The office was a squat adobe-colored building with the logo, Flightline, in sharp forward-leaning blue script, above the doorway. Adjoining this was a long two-story metal building of tan and blues with large windows set high in the wall. Two smaller outbuildings flanked a private airstrip that stretched out across a frozen grass field.

Caddie and Matt huddled outside the sheriff's truck. Caddie quickly flipped up the collar of her jacket while Matt sank deeper into his, hunching his shoulders and digging his hands deeper into his pockets. Dawn bounded happily to a Christmas tune heard only in her head. She promised Matt she'd try staying quiet after another attempt to get the sheriff to hear her. Caddie's grimace ended that effort.

"How about we get inside?" Matt looked to Dawn for support, she offered a silent air kiss instead.

"Okay, Mr. Wisconsin," Caddie said. "A little winter weather bothering you?"

"Oh, baby, she got you there," Dawn said, sending him another kiss before they moved on.

Everson's office, overlooking the floor of the adjoining building, was strictly utilitarian: a workstation, modest visitor chairs, and a nearly empty bookcase that looked like it cost less than fifty bucks at Walmart. A television mounted in the corner silently played a business news channel with its talking heads and a stock price scroll across the bottom. After seeing the Everson house, this was not the office Dawn had expected. Even with her somewhat negative reaction to Kyle, she was still taken aback by his business-like manner this morning. He shook Caddie and Matt's hands, thanked them for coming in, and offered coffee. You would think they were potential clients in for a visit. Caddie and Matt offered condolences again, asked after how Everson was doing, and assured him they didn't suspect anyone in his company of doing anything wrong. She was seeing again how her husband and the sheriff played off each other so well. *Don't be bothered by the things bothering you,* she told herself, and threw a loud air kiss Matt's way.

Everson gestured out to the floor below. "Larger components, mainly small aircraft engines and hydraulic equipment, are worked here on the main floor. Staff in this area fluctuates. When purchases of used equipment and sales line up right, there could be two dozen people working. That was our original business and, in some ways, is still the bedrock of the company. It's not a spectacular earner, but it gives a steady return. It's the work bays beyond that far wall that have fueled our expansion over the last couple of years. Electronic avionics equipment; navigation, communications, even dipping our toes into packaging some AI systems that track and diagnose repair and maintenance needs in aircraft." He turned to the sheriff. "If you need to question anyone from there, I'd prefer if we brought them into one of the conference rooms."

"Is that area classified?" Matt asked. Her husband had made the question casual, but he'd never fooled Dawn. He was worried Everson was trying to keep Caddie out of those spaces for some reason, though Dawn doubted people working with sophisticated electronic equipment generally moonlighted as fentanyl dealers.

"No," Everson said. "If you need to, you can go in, but you'll have to put on protective gear to keep stray dust and dirt away from the electronics."

Dawn nodded along. That seems reasonable, she told herself. Matt seemed good with it, too, letting the point go.

"Did your wife have a lot of interaction with that part of the business?" Caddie asked, picking up where Matt left off. Dawn wasn't thrilled that the sheriff and her hubby were on the same wavelength and promised herself twice over not to let it show or say anything. Her boy needed this connection to Caddie, and if it ever blossomed into something else, she would do the right thing and tell him to go for it. She laughed out loud, drawing a quick look from Matt, which set off a small frown from Caddie, a chain reaction of her thoughts about her husband moving on. *No,* she admitted, *I am not about to tell him to go for it.*

Everson took a beat and steeled his face, holding his emotions in. "No, not after rehab. Like I said last night, she wasn't back full-time, not really, and she mostly dealt with office issues. She used to be the life of this place." He slowed his words. "She was the one who made this more of a family than a business. She knew everyone's birthdays and anniversaries. She made sure there was a nice envelope for graduations and births." He smiled. "She read a book once about leadership by walking around. That's what she did until she got sick. I thought she was headed back to that, but if I'm honest with myself now, it was too much to expect." His words were evenly spaced, considered. "I think letting her come back to work was a mistake. But I thought about how good she was with people. She thrived on it. I thought it would be good for her." He sat at his desk, his face down and away from Caddie and Matt. Dawn stood unseen behind him, looking out to the work floor, listening intently. "I'm afraid I'm responsible for her death." At last, he finally choked, let his head drop lower, and began to cry.

When Dawn turned to the scene, she was more intent on watching her husband's reaction than the man weeping for the wife he lost less than a day ago. Matt was impassive, professional. That worried her. "I am sorry, Kyle," he said after a minute. "I know this is very difficult, and we appreciate your help." That was it, no attempt to connect, no empathizing for someone who's lost his wife, too. It took Dawn a few moments to understand that Matt was giving the man space to grieve and an opportunity to say more. Maybe that was right for Everson and the investigation, but she still didn't like it.

"I shouldn't have come in today," he said, his head nearly between his knees now. "I was numb this morning and thought I should get out of the house and drive in like I do every day, and now," he shook his head.

"Mr. Everson, would you like one of us to drive you home?" Caddie asked.

"Oh, Jesus." Everson sat back in his chair, looking up at the ceiling. "I haven't even told my parents yet."

Matt's eyes met Dawn's. "I don't know, babe." She said softly, hoping not to disturb Caddie. "I think it's all hitting him now. It's hard to watch."

Caddie's movement drew their attention. She was looking straight at Dawn. Unnervingly straight at her. "Would you like one of us to go with you to do that?"

"No." Everson stood quickly, wiped his palms down his face, and sniffed back more tears. "With my mother's memory issues, more people will just confuse her. Coming to work and running on automatic, I was just pretending none of this happened. I can't do that anymore."

"We understand." Caddie's voice carried more sympathy than Matt's. "We'll talk more in the next few days. In the meantime, if you think of anything or if you have any questions or need something from my office, please don't hesitate to call."

"Thank you, Sheriff. Matt." He grabbed his jacket off a rack near the door and was nearly out of the room when Matt stopped him.

"Kyle, I'm sorry, but did you find Tracy's phone?"

"I did. It was on her nightstand on vibrate. I left it on the kitchen counter at home. You can send a deputy later and I'll be there, or send someone now and break in. I really don't fucking care, man. Do whatever you need to do." He was out and moving quickly before anyone could ask him anything else.

"Grab the phone later," Caddie said. "I'm going to pass on breaking into his house. He's not exactly thinking straight."

"Yeah, I got that. I wish I'd caught up to him this morning before it all hit him. He's going to have a tough couple of days now. I'm not sure how much more help he'll be."

It wasn't until they split and Caddie went down to the maintenance floor that Dawn spoke again.

"I'm not sure which of you three is acting stranger."

"What?" Matt half-whispered.

"Nothing, dear. I just find human nature difficult to understand."

His expression went from questioning to confused.

"I love you," she said, knowing that would suffice for now. But they would talk when she had more time to think.

———————

The front office ladies echoed Everson. Tracy made Flightline a family as much as a business and pulled more than her weight with customer relations. Both cried, one hugged Matt, and neither could believe it. They never said they were related, and they had different last names, but they could have easily been mother and daughter.

Mousy-brown hair, chubby cheeks, and a tendency to look at each other to confirm if their answers were right.

"I thought she got better," the older one sniffled.

"We so wanted her to be better," the younger said, handing the tissue box to her office mate.

"What about the last couple of months specifically?" Matt asked. He was having an increasingly difficult time keeping his emotions in check. For whatever reason, the composure he felt around Everson was crumbling in the onslaught of these women's tears. The sympathy in Dawn's eyes helped him act like the professional he told himself he was.

"Pay attention, baby," she said. She knew he was losing his focus. She knew everything about him.

"Thanks," he mouthed to Dawn.

"You're welcome, baby."

She had done her trick again. He was back, not exactly in shark mode, but shark didn't seem the right approach anyway. He sat, pulled his chair closer, and spoke softly. "No one is in trouble, but if you noticed anything about how Tracy was acting or who she might be close to, it could help us prevent someone else from getting drugs that will kill them." He didn't ask a question, letting the plea for help stand as an open request.

"Well," the older woman said, "a few months ago."

"Before Halloween," the younger said.

"Yes, before Halloween, Tracy seemed nervous or preoccupied, her head not really in the game."

"No, not at all," the younger agreed.

Matt very much wanted to ask what they meant, but the very slight 'Shh' from Dawn stopped him. He wanted to press, she wanted to give space. She won.

"I had to remind her of a video meeting with new clients from Hungary."

"She was normally very good with things like that," the younger added.

"Yes. And then her hours were weird."

"Weird," said the younger, "in early, out late, then gone for days. She was normally very reliable." They nodded to one another, agreed that Tracy was normally reliable. That seemed to have finished their description, so Matt pressed on.

"Did you think she was using again?"

The women looked at one another, shook their heads, and then the older woman answered, "No."

"It wasn't like the last time," the younger finished. "Then she was flaky, and you could tell. Something was bothering her, I think. Maybe the stress. It could be that's why she fell off the wagon."

"Stress?" Dawn asked.

"Stress?" Matt repeated.

"Work," the younger said, breaking their pattern. "New business, hanging on to old business. COVID about did us in, but we've been going really good this year. There was a lot of pressure to keep that up. In this business, you always need to be getting new customers. Kyle and Tracy are very good at it, but there's a lot of pressure."

Matt looked up to his wife without trying to look like he was looking up to his wife.

"No, dear, that's all I have for now, thank you."

Matt thanked them, considered asking if they were mother and daughter, and quickly decided that was a trap he didn't need to step into. He stood to leave before asking his last question entirely off-hand, or at least that's how he hoped it sounded. "Outside of the office staff, is there anyone at the company that Tracy worked closely with or seemed to be a close friend?"

"Ryan was closest," the potential daughter said.

"Ryan Gentry was closest," the possible mom agreed.

Matt thanked the duo a final time, wished them Merry Christmas, which he almost regretted when their faces lit up and they said "Merry Christmas" in near unison. He held the door open long enough for Dawn to slip through.

"I have not threatened to bop anyone in the nose in a very long time, but if those two finished one another's sentence one more time, I would have been tempted."

"But they're cute, baby."

"No, dear. I'm cute. Your butt is cute. They're just irritating."

———

Caddie felt the tingling come in at the edge of her senses before she saw Matt through the window in the conference room door. She was almost beginning to believe he was the cause. She told herself again that she would see Doctor Serrano when they got past the crunch of this investigation. She didn't have the time for poking and tests right now. Besides getting shot, then beaten nearly half to death in June, got her enough poking and prodding to last a lifetime. The fleeting thought of Serrano and the hospital triggered another memory just beyond her grasp, but the man across the table talking pushed it away into the ether.

"Sorry." Matt stood in the open doorway until Caddie motioned him in. She was nearly finished anyway.

"Ryan, this is Deputy Matt Jager. He's the lead investigator on Tracy Everson's death."

Matt's eyes flicked to the left before he focused on Gentry and offered his hand. He was about Matt's height but broader in the shoulders and with the hands and forearms of a mechanic. Caddie had burned through the short list Claire had given her far too quickly. No one knew anything or had much contact with Tracy since she got out of rehab. But three of them fingered Gentry as someone to talk to. They'd offered him up pretty quick.

"Ryan," Matt said, "I don't want to retrace what you and the sheriff have already gone over, but I am sorry about Mrs. Everson. I understand she was well thought of here, and I'm sure her death comes as a shock to everyone."

"I heard this morning, and it just makes me sick. She made this place a family."

Not only had Gentry repeated Everson's words about Tracy making Flightline a family, but he'd used the exact same phrase with her about hearing of Tracy's death. "Ryan is the lead mechanic for refurbishing the engines," Caddie said. "And he's also closely involved in the shipping process. That's where he had the most interaction with Tracy. Unfortunately, he doesn't have any ideas so far about where she might have been getting her drugs."

"Not, here," Gentry said. "With liability issues from working on aviation equipment, the insurance company mandates drug testing. Anyone working directly on equipment is tested randomly twice a year."

134

"Would that include Tracy?" Matt asked. Caddie had covered this already and was ready to cut it off, but Gentry kept his answer short.

"I wouldn't know, but I don't think so."

The tingling in Caddie's mind had faded, and she was ready to go. They would hit the employees again later when they knew more. She wasn't about to close off any avenue of approach, but a connection through the company didn't feel right at this point. Between the drug testing, background checks, and the fact that Tracy seemed to have less contact with employees since rehab, it was more likely that she was relying on someone from her past as a connection, or Nikki passed on the drugs that killed both of them. "Thank you again, Ryan, for your cooperation. If you think of anything, you have my number. Call anytime."

Gentry was gone as quickly as he could move. Matt was lost in thought for a minute before turning to Caddie. "Get anything?"

"No." That she hadn't expected much today didn't take away the disappointment. "Tracy made Flightline a family. They thought she was beyond the drugs. She was around less in the last few months. Same story from everyone. You?"

"Same," he nodded. "The front office duo did name Gentry as the person here closest to Tracy."

That gave Caddie pause. "They used that word, closest?"

"Yep. Not worked closely with, closest."

"Huh? He told me they worked together on shipping, but didn't make it sound personal. He also said they hadn't talked much lately."

"Want me to question him?" Matt asked and then he paused and Caddie's head buzzed again. When he went on, it was in half-apology. "Not that I could get anything you didn't. Just thinking out loud, forget it." Then he nodded his head.

Maybe he needs to see Doctor Serrano, Caddie thought. "Let that slide for now. I'll have Claire take a deeper dive on him. You get the phone from Everson while I shake the fed tree and see if I can get anything to fall out."

Matt laughed and said, "You're going to have to shake hard," while the tingle flittered on the edge of Caddie's senses.

Chapter 24

The light over Everson's garage flicked on automatically as their Jeep pulled into the drive. The Christmas tree lights shone white against the dark of the interior and the grey gloom of a falling frozen mist.

"I don't think he's here, babe," Dawn said as Matt put the vehicle in park.

"Could be asleep or in the basement." He called Everson. The phone went to voicemail.

"He's not answering, anyway." Dawn sat back. With nothing else pressing at the moment and Tracy Everson's phone feet away but out of reach, Matt held his hand out and joined his wife in watching the lights of the tree fade in and out in a slow, steady rhythm. "That has to be on a timer, right?" She didn't sound entirely convinced. "He wouldn't turn it on, not after last night."

Matt looked to his right. Dawn's hand rested in his. He felt nothing, but it felt right. "What are you thinking, dear? If I didn't know better than to accuse you of it, I would say you're acting squirrely."

She gave a single giggle. "Squirrely? I've never been squirrely in my life."

In my life, the phrase hit sharply. "Ouch." He should have let her cute reaction stand on its own, be another memory for him to cherish. He was sorry he didn't have better control of his emotions. He hadn't thought so, but the deaths of Nikki and Tracy were weighing on him. The loss that Kyle Everson should be feeling could be working at Matt himself.

"Sorry, dear." She said it sweet, not sad. That was his wife, keeping the Christmas spirit in the face of death, including her own. "He's probably at his parents."

"We could track him down there," Matt said, to a head shake from Dawn. "Or, if you don't like that, we could break in and take it. He did invite me to."

"Let's have one investigation where you don't violate the law."

"Too late. We could sit here for a while longer and let that really big Christmas tree hypnotize us."

"Let's do that." She leaned his way, snuggling his shoulder, all but resting her head on it. The faint reflection in the windshield warmed his heart. He hated breaking the spell and let it set for a time before he spoke.

"You want to tell me what's bothering you?"

"What?" She sat up straight, looking at him. "Nothing. We're together, it's Christmas, peace on earth and goodwill to men, and none of our friends are in danger. It's terrible what happened to Tracy and Nikki, but we'll bring them some justice and stop it from happening again. Nothing is bothering me."

"I meant about Everson, dear." Though he was very glad Dawn was taking what happiness she could from their circumstances. She wasn't the only one who was glad they were together for Christmas. If it weren't for her, he would have tried to put the holiday as far in the rearview mirror as he could.

She relaxed back into leaning on him. In some way, he couldn't understand and wouldn't try, he was holding her up but not feeling her physical presence. "You're the professional," she said. "I'm just the amateur former teacher and vice principal, what do I know?"

"In the cozy mysteries, the amateur solves the case when the inept police can't."

"This isn't a cozy, and you and Caddie are far from inept."

He turned and kissed the top of her head, an automatic reaction to snuggling in a car together. She zapped him for good measure. The kiss did its second job and prompted her to go on.

"It's terrible of me, because I don't like Everson. That shouldn't matter. His wife's death is no less tragic because he hit on me once—"

"Jerk," Matt said.

"Thank you. Or that his reaction to her death wasn't the emotional devastation my husband endured." She looked up to him, though they could see one another in the windshield. "I don't think I ever thanked you for that. Not that I wanted you to be hurt, but," she had to pause. "I knew you loved me. I know I loved you, love you, with everything I have, but it's still nice in this really, really messed up way that your love was so big, that losing me would…" She shrugged, unsure of the words.

"Turn me inside out and dump me upside down," he finished her thought.

"Yeah." She smiled. "That. Thank you. I'm sorry, but thank you."

He kissed her lips, all the static electricity in the world be damned. The shock was sharp and lit the windshield in a small spark, and he didn't care. They took deep breaths and kissed again. In the faintest reaches of his imagination, he was sure he could feel her lips against his. Whether it was memory or real didn't matter at the moment. "Back to Everson," he said, reluctantly.

"Back to Everson." She rested her head on his shoulder, and they watched the lights grow bright, then fade to black and begin again. "He feels wrong, which is unfair and maybe has nothing to do with Tracy's death. I can't help feeling that at least he was complicit in a way."

"He let her fall back into addiction?"

"Yes and no. You can't keep someone else from falling off the wagon, but keeping booze and sleeping pills in the house is practically pushing them. You don't have to drive her back to work, so you can keep the business growing. You can take more of an interest in her daily life. I have the feeling that beyond knowing she went to yoga, he has no idea what she did all day."

"Do you really think he drove her back to work?" Matt hadn't considered it from that angle.

"I think," she said, now sure of her footing, "that he needed her at work. COVID hit them hard, it must have been like starting over again afterward, and she was the people person. She closed deals. You heard the front office ladies, their business needs a constant flow of new customers. People loved Tracy. I think maybe Kyle loved that more about his wife than he loved his wife."

Matt had to think about Dawn's observations. First, as normal, she was right, or at least it felt right. That would also explain Everson's muted response. "Addiction could do a number on a marriage."

"I bet it did a number on the business, too," Dawn said. "He pushed her to get back to work. That's what I think. I didn't say anything because it doesn't get us any closer to finding who gave

Tracy fentanyl. It just means her husband is probably going to move on quickly."

"He's doing it all wrong," Matt said.

"He is," Dawn agreed before sitting up. "Enough watching tree lights, dear. Let's see if there's anything else to do tonight. If not, let's get you something to eat, then go home and watch Charlie Brown and snuggle in the candlelight."

There was nothing Matt could think of that he wanted more. "You're a Christmas bear," he said.

"You're a Christmas bear," she grinned back.

Chapter 25

Jill's Diner was comfortably warm and filled with the hearty smells coming off the plate of turkey slices over a mound of stuffing with chestnuts, sides of mac and cheese and greens, and an extra helping of corn bread. Sitting at the counter made it harder for Matt to talk to Dawn, but eating a Christmas feast wasn't their only reason for coming here tonight. Bev set down a second pot of tea and his dessert. "That, Matthew," she pointed at the orangish-brown pie slice in front of him, "is sweet potato, not some tasteless pumpkin pie."

He took a bite and moaned, "You are something else, Bev."

"And you're killing me," Dawn pouted. "I may forbid you from eating here if you aren't nicer."

Matt did feel bad for his love, but not enough to put the pie aside.

"I imagine you wanted to talk about these terrible deaths," Bev said, her voice lower to keep from disturbing the other customers.

"What do you know about Tracy and Nikki?"

"They were in rehab together," Bev said. "I know that."

"How do you know that?" Matt asked, surprised.

"Bev knows everything," Dawn answered.

"Nikki Moscow hadn't been back in town a week, and her and Tracy met up here for lunch. They was laughing at inside jokes and really seemed to like one another."

"They meet here regularly?" Matt asked. Everson admitted not knowing what his wife was doing when she wasn't at work. He had said Nikki and Tracy didn't maintain a relationship, but then again, how would he know for sure?

Bev thought for a moment. "Some. I wouldn't say regularly. I know they came from yoga. They were dressed for it anyway. Not lately, though, best I can remember. Which isn't really surprising. Tracy had a husband and a business, Nikki had that family to deal with, and her little girls, then a job, and all. She had a lot stacked against her, but I would have put my money on her. She brought the girls in here sometimes. That little one could put away some ice cream."

Matt pushed his plate away, the thought of the girls pulling him fully back into the dark of the investigation. "What about Tracy? You see her around much?"

"Not so much. Check with Downtown Coffee, she seems like an expensive coffee after yoga type." She said she didn't know anything about people selling drugs, mad that they would even do it in her town.

The bell suspended above the door rang. Matt and Dawn reflexively turned in its direction to be greeted by the sight of former sheriff Jimmy Dubcek striding in. He was wearing his normal near-sheriff uniform of jeans and a dark brown leather jacket. He even had a Fillmore County Sheriff's Office baseball hat on. He'd tried to run Caddie out of the job when she lay wounded in the hospital in June, and it had been a near run thing. With an election less than a year away, it looked like he wasn't done trying to recapture the job. The small group with him included his cousin the local bank president, one county commissioner, and the owner of a convenience store chain that covered four counties. Matt stared at him, but Jimmy kept his eyes straight ahead. The group was louder than it needed to be, and Matt was sure that was for his benefit.

"I guess it's time we talk about it, dear," Dawn said.

"Yeah," Matt mumbled. He slid enough cash to more than cover his bill on the counter and told Bev he'd wait for his to-go order outside. He needed fresh air.

"I went up to Orange City a couple of weeks after the last time you left." The only other people on the street were two smokers standing out front of the Hawk's Nest half a block down. Matt kept his back to the window front of Jill's, so no one would wonder who he was talking to. "Frank's source was right. It was your Mustang. They hauled it across the state to keep me from seeing it." He watched her face intently. He'd considered telling her a couple of times already, but didn't want to bring her pain from remembering the moments before her death. That was foolish. She deserved to know, even if hearing the truth hurt. If he didn't know her as well as he did, he would have thought she was taking it in calmly, but he could see the tension around her eyes, the purposeful setting of her face to not betray her emotions. She was probably trying to protect him from the thought of hurting her.

"It's been sitting there in the junkyard for three years, and none of this would stand up in court," he warned her. "But, you were right, you were run off the road."

She took a deep breath in and her eyes grew harder.

"I don't see how that rear-end damage could have been caused by anything else."

She nodded. The memories hadn't come back right away; a truck's headlights appearing behind her on a rain-slicked country road, the crashing of glass and crunching of metal, the fight to keep control of the wheel. When they came back, they came back hard. Matt reached out, but she waved him off. "Go on." She knew there was more.

"I don't think it was Eckhart."

Surprise broke her stoic expression. "What? He had an old truck, he tried running you off the road, he was up to his eyeballs with Jimmy, and he killed two people, and you're saying it wasn't him?" Once they believed her death wasn't an accident, they both assumed that Jason Eckhart was responsible for killing Dawn. The same man who tried running Matt off the road, killed two other people, and was only stopped from killing Matt by a bullet from Caddie. They never had a solid reason why, but assumed it was connected to a plot to somehow profit off construction of the new high school. But they never had a chance to prove it. Dawn's fear and pain were replaced by this new mystery. "Explain."

"There's deep blue paint along the driver's side of your car, from the rear bumper halfway up the side. I think whoever hurt you," he didn't want to say kill for both their sakes, "hit you once, square on. Then, as you went into a skid, he hit you again on the rear driver's side. Then," he stopped, choked back the image of his Dawn being killed. Of her fear and pain. "That's when the truck scraped along the side of your Mustang sending you into the tree line."

They stood quietly on the cold, wet street. She was waiting for him to go on. He was waiting for the ability to go on. His chest hurt and his eyes watered. It took time to recover. "Eckhart's truck, the one he used to ram us, was red. I even found the guy who bought it and checked. It hadn't been painted. I think he got the idea of how to kill me because it worked for someone else with you. Someone else connected to Jimmy."

Dawn slowly turned her head so she could see Dubcek sitting in his booth inside Jill's. His group was confident and laughing. "Jimmy fucking Dubcek," she said.

The fact that his wife had dropped a proper F-bomb surprised Matt. He normally did all the cursing in their family. "But Jimmy doesn't get his hands dirty."

"No, he doesn't. Other people do the killing, he reaps the rewards." Whatever she was going to say next about finding who killed her, or telling Matt not to let it consume him, was washed out by the rumble of motorcycle engines. Four Harleys, two abreast, cruised down the road, Road Demon patches on the riders' jackets.

"Well, look at that," Dawn said. "It's practically like they want you to know they're in town."

"The sooner we find who provided the poison that killed Tracy and Nikki, the better," he said. They were back on the deaths of Nikki and Tracy, on bringing justice for two little girls, on stopping more people from dying, but Matt was not about to forget Jimmy freaking Dubcek and proving to himself that the man was responsible one way or another for ending Dawn's life. Maybe not today, but Jimmy was going to pay.

Chapter 26

Caddie sat at her desk, office door closed, and hit dial on her phone again. She'd steadfastly refused to leave a message on Agent Rafer's voicemail, the string of unanswered calls their own message. The relationship between her office and Rafer, and by extension the FBI, started off promisingly enough in June when the agency responded with all hands on deck to the attacks on the department. Since then, it's been a combination of dead air and vague promises that the preliminary investigation into Jimmy Dubcek and corruption in the county had the FBI's highest priority. Not progress, not specific steps taken, but their highest priority. When she pressed last month, Rafer promised something by the end of the year. She was afraid he was avoiding her because highest priority meant 'we'll get to it eventually, if we get to it at all.'

She was about to hang up before she got the automated recording when a deep voice, partly out of breath, came on. "Hey," Rafer said. "Is this an emergency?"

"No, but—"

"Okay, I'll call back soon. Promise, okay?" And the Senior Supervisory Agent for the FBI's Cedar Rapids office was gone.

"Son of bitch." Caddie slammed the phone down and reached for her temple as the tingling came back. The voice of Arnold Schwarzenegger told her it's not a tumor, and she promised herself to see Antonia. Oddly enough, this time the tingling came with the smell of sautéed onions.

———

Matt and Dawn made their way through the deputies' bullpen toward Claire's office. Caddie's door was shut, light slipping out through the cracks in the drawn blinds the only indication that she was there. Dawn decided to delay tonight's snuggles for a visit before they left.

Her Matt was a tactile person, or at least he was with her. He couldn't pass her in the kitchen without his hand brushing across her rear. Then he would draw her near from behind and nuzzle his nose into her neck. The thought of it drove a shiver down her spine. He loved her beyond the touch of their bodies, he'd proven that. But he also loved the touch. She'd never tried to hide that she did, too. Snuggles that don't touch and old Christmas cartoons weren't a replacement, but they would have to be. Slightly naughty thoughts were interrupted by the strains of classical Christmas music floating softly out of the open door to Claire's office.

"Aww," Dawn said. "That's nice."

"Hey." Matt held up a cardboard food container. "Double smash burger with Swiss and onions."

"Fries?" Claire spun her chair, reaching out for the box.

"Fries," he said.

"You're better than Door Dash."

"Well, it's not Mrs. Cratchit's Christmas pudding, but Happy Christmas anyway," Dawn said. She wished she could know Claire, that Claire could know her, then she cut the thought off. Her time here was short, as one of the ghosts of Christmas most surely said. She wouldn't spend that time regretting things she had no control over. She could be here for her Matt, she would help others by helping him. Claire Henderson would have to be Matt's job.

Claire set her food down, grabbed her water bottle, and started digging in with little more than grunts and appreciative groans.

"What happened to our healthy snack, no sugar added, fair trade chocolate, Claire?" Dawn asked.

"It's a really good burger," Matt answered. Claire nodded emphatically. She washed down a bite with a large swig of water.

"Sorry, I haven't had anything but peanut butter crackers from the machine all day. I'm not built for fasting. Sorry to eat in front of you," she said before diving in again.

"Not too sorry," Dawn laughed.

"It's okay, I already ate," Matt assured her. "What are you working on?"

Claire took a long drink and wiped her mouth with a napkin before answering. "I've tied down the dates for when Tracy and Nikki were at Decorah together. Tracy was there a week before Nikki and left three weeks earlier, but they overlapped for nearly five months." She ate a couple of fries before continuing. "Other than that, I've got a preliminary list of Flightline employees from Iowa Workforce. Over the last couple of years, the numbers add up."

"What about the Decorah clinic director?" Matt asked.

Claire nodded, her cheeks half-full of burger. "I worked up a quick bio. Dr. Kashvi Prijat. University of Wisconsin undergrad, Johns Hopkins medical school, jobs with major medical centers in the San Francisco area, then she opened the clinic in Decorah."

"Another Badger, honey," Dawn said.

"Expensive clinic to open," Matt said, his eyes following Dawn as she wandered toward Claire's computer monitors.

"You want me to dig into who's behind the clinic?" Claire asked before taking a big bite out of her burger. The girl had developed a 'skeptical but I'll do it tone' for Matt. Where Allision challenged her soldier directly, Claire was more subtle and probably more effective. Her Matt was many good things, stubborn among them, but that of course cut two ways.

"No," he said. "Not yet. More thinking out loud."

Claire made a show of wiping her mouth and fingers, but didn't push the burger container away. "I do have something else you're going to like." She rolled to her computer, forcing Dawn to step out of the way, and retrieved a folder, handing it to Matt. She waited, anticipating his reaction.

The folder was thin, holding no more than a few printed pages, but Claire's presentation promised a worthwhile revelation, and Dawn found herself drawn into the small drama. Matt made sure to hold the folder so she could see. Even in the middle of his talk with Claire, he made sure not to forget his sweetie. "Thank you, dear," she said.

The pages looked like copies of a printed newspaper. 'Storm Lake Man Arrested in Drug Bust' the first said across the top. Matt began reading out loud. "Ryan Gentry of Storm Lake was arrested Saturday for possession of marijuana and cocaine in what local law enforcement is describing as a major disruption of illegal drug sales on the campus of Buena Vista University. Gentry, nineteen, originally from Cedar Rapids, Iowa, was apprehended as part of an undercover operation initiated after the drowning death of Lacy Goodwell in July. Goodwell's death and the discovery of alcohol and barbiturates in her system..." Matt trailed off, still holding the folder

146

so Dawn could read, though there was little more of note in the first article.

"You already had his name when we went there today. This didn't show up on his criminal history?"

Claire was grinning. She had caught Matt's excitement at finding new information. Dawn got it, though, even under trying investigations like this, coming across something new and promising was a rush.

"Expunged," she said. "The rest of the story is in there, but in the summer of 2004, Lacy Goodwell drowned at night in Storm Lake. When drugs were found in her system, some people blamed students at the University. That fall, there was a crackdown, and Gentry was popped in an undercover buy." She held up a finger to stop any questions while she ate another French fry. "I pulled the articles from a newspaper archive service. These don't show up on Google."

"Local high school girl drowns, and they bust a college kid for selling weed and coke three months later, and then they parade him through the local news like the two are connected."

Claire pointed a fry at him. "Exactly. The final article talks about the judge ordering a closed-door hearing, the county attorney walking back talk of major drug busts, and the university president talking about how much they cooperate with law enforcement."

"They screwed something up, didn't they?" Matt said.

"I'm not following your little conversation here, dear," Dawn said, frustrated with herself for not picking up what they were hinting at.

"Between law enforcement and the county attorney, they're presenting a small-time college dealer as a major drug bust, but they did something wrong with the buy, or the arrest, or searching his room, or something else embarrassing. But after the big stink of practically saying Gentry killed a local girl, they can't just drop charges publicly," Matt explained.

"Right," Claire said, "and rather than explain everything in open court, the CA agrees to pretend none of it ever happened; defense is happy, college is happy, local judge is happy, and poof, no bust, no record, nothing on Iowa Courts Online. Like it never happened."

"Except," Matt pointed the folder at Claire, "it did, and Gentry forgot to tell us."

Dawn hated to burst the little fun bubble these two were playing with, but she decided popping bubbles must be her job. "But that was twenty years ago, and like you said, he was some small-time college dealer, not a fentanyl source in Fillmore County today."

"We know one thing." Matt looked directly at Dawn as Claire returned her attention to her burger. "Gentry is a liar."

"And we don't like liars, do we, babe?" She couldn't help but get caught up in their excitement. Yes, the tie was tenuous, but Gentry had a history of selling drugs, he had close contact with Tracy, and it was a small enough town that knowing Nikki Moscow wasn't too much of a stretch.

"We do not like liars," Matt agreed.

"Nope," Claire mumbled around chewing, waving as Matt left her office, taking the folder with him.

————

Matt knocked on Caddie's door. He normally would have gone straight in after a quick tap, but with Dawn standing there, he waited for a response. Caddie opened up.

"We're knocking now? That's an improvement."

Matt didn't have to look to know Dawn was giving him squinty eyes. But her attention quickly went to the sheriff.

"Ask her if she's okay. She's not looking so good."

"Hey." Dawn was right, something looked off about Caddie. "Are you coming down with something?"

Caddie dropped into her seat, waving vaguely at the ceiling. "Between the FBI and a nagging headache, I've been better. But I'm fine." She waited until Matt was sitting on the couch. "Thanks, though. You know, when you're gone, I can't complain to anyone. The boss always has to be fine."

"I'm glad I'm good for something," Matt laughed. "What's up with the FBI? Is it going to make me mad?"

"Probably," Dawn said.

"Probably," Caddie said. "I finally got through to Rafer, and he blew me off. He was supposed to call back, but after their foot-dragging on Dubcek, I have trust issues."

"That's Matt's job," Dawn said. Matt repeated it for another laugh.

148

"I'm also playing tag with the rehab clinic. So far, I've made my way up from a receptionist to a counselor to the deputy director." She picked her phone off the desk, looked to see if a text had secretly snuck in, and set it back again.

"Give her some good news," Dawn said. "Tell her about what your top-secret source told you." Matt passed Bev's info on, and the tension around Caddie's eyes eased the slightest.

"Too bad she's dating someone," Caddie said. "Bev is sweet on you. She never tells me stuff."

"Hey," Dawn said. "Teasing Matt about other women is my job. Does no one stay in their lane anymore?"

"You going to try and get up to Decorah tomorrow?" Matt asked. His hand automatically went to the couch between him and Dawn. She patted it. He couldn't feel it, but like everything in her tangible but intangible existence, he knew it was there.

"Me, you, both of us," Caddie answered. "We know Nikki and Tracy were tight in rehab, and we don't have a better place to start."

"I'm not sure she's spoken to Claire about Ryan Gentry's past," Dawn said. It felt like she was talking directly to Caddie at times, as if the two women had a connection that went beyond Matt.

"There's another possibility," Matt said. "Weak, but it's not nothing." He handed her the folder and told her about Gentry's expunged drug bust.

"I don't like being lied to." Caddie leaned back in her chair, reading and talking at the same time. "Twenty-year-old college dealing is one thing, lying to me by not mentioning it pisses me off and makes me wonder why."

"Yep," Matt said.

"See, dear," Dawn said. "Never lie to a woman. We don't like it."

"Good thing I never lied to you," Matt said to both of them.

"Good thing," they echoed each other.

"Sounds like you want Gentry," Matt said.

"Oh, she does, babe," Dawn said. "That man is in trouble."

"I do," she agreed. "I guess the clinic is yours then, approach it however you want. I'll let you know if I hear back from the director."

They chatted a little more, no one in a rush to break up the conversation after it veered away from the investigation. Eventually, the talking trailed off, and Dawn was ready to go, but reluctant to leave Caddie alone in a nearly empty building with winter closing ever tighter around them the day after Christmas. The day after Caddie's party was cut short. Dawn and Matt had snuggles and cartoons to look forward to. She was imagining Caddie heading home to an empty house and fought with herself not to invite her over to their place. Then she thought about the hand that she was patting and not feeling. She was sorry, but tonight she would be selfish. She needed her time with Matt. He would have to take care of their friend when she was gone. "Let's go home, baby," she said.

Matt stood and said his goodbyes. "You need anything, just call."

"Not me," Caddie said. "I'm going home to take a bath and crawl into bed. I'm done for the day," Caddie said in the utter confidence that she had no control over how she would spend her night.

Chapter 27

Lieutenant Dubcek knew Phil Moscow's beat-up Ford truck on sight. He was sure a plate check on another half dozen trucks and muscle cars in the McDonald's lot would come back to one Moscow family member or another. Only the stubborn Czech in him, and an excited gaggle of grandkids and wife looking forward to McFlurries, kept him from turning around. *It's Christmas, and everyone can enjoy McDonald's without any problems,* he told himself. As they reached the door, the roar of engines, followed by a tremor working its way across the blacktop, stopped him. "Get the kids inside and don't come out," he said softly to Ann with a gentle hand on the small of her back. She hesitated as they watched a phalanx of Road Demons rolling into the lot. A quick glance at her husband, and she put on a cheerful voice and herded the children through the door. Chris was a sheriff's deputy; he never went anywhere unarmed, but the Glock 43 nine-millimeter in his ankle holster didn't exactly feel comforting.

Matt pulled the Jeep into the alley behind their carriage-house garage, but his phone gave a triple beep before he could cut the engine. "That's Caddie," he said.

"Oh, done with cute ringtones for the girls?" Dawn teased. "Probably a good idea. You better answer it." She put her finger in front of her lips. She knew not to talk. Caddie might not be able to hear her, but electronics had the uncanny ability to pick up her voice.

"Yeah," Matt said.

"Get to McDonald's, right now." Caddie's breath was coming in fast. She was running. "Chris is in the middle of a showdown between Russians and Demons. It'll be just the three of us for now."

He threw the Jeep into reverse. "Got it. Be careful."

Caddie hung up without further explanation. Russians and Road Demons were enough to send every available unit, but the problem with covering a large county with a small department was covering a large county with a small department.

"I'm going to be very angry if these idiots ruin my snuggle time," Dawn said.

"We should warn them." Matt shifted into drive and sped down the alley.

"Like they would listen."

Chris loved a good Western. He'd seen *Tombstone* and *High Noon* more times than he could count. Right now, he felt more like the nervous Gary Cooper watching the clock tick down to a gun fight than the righteous Kurt Russell bringing hell down on the Cowboys. Heck, he didn't even have a badge on him to flash. The Demons milled around their bikes, watching the door into the McDonald's. Their showing up here wasn't an accident. Movement behind him caught his attention, and he tried looking without taking his eyes off the bikers. Phil Moscow spat on the sidewalk and brushed past him. The Demons who'd been leaning against their bikes stood straighter.

"Get back inside, Phil," Chris grumbled, hoping the sheriff got here before he was forced to pull out his weapon and announce himself to the bikers. At least Gary and Kurt weren't caught in the middle of two gangs.

"It's a public parking lot, Deputy," Moscow said.

For once in his career, Chris wished he were dealing with Frank Moscow. Unlike his brother, age had barely tamed Phil. He may not be the meaner of the two, but he was definitely the more impulsive and dumber. Not good traits right now. "Inside."

"I got my rights."

Four more Russians crowded out the door behind Phil. They all wore untucked flannel shirts or open jackets. Chris spotted at least two bulges from carrying a weapon. "You take one step on that blacktop, I swear to God, Phil, I will run you in and worry about charges later."

"Why are you threatening me? My family's been wronged, and you got outsiders trying to run this town. I'd think you'd want to stand aside and let me do what needs doing," Phil argued, but didn't move forward.

"I got the wife and grandkids in there, Phil. I'm not letting you turn McDonald's into a warzone."

"Wouldn't be my doing."

Chris could feel the eyes of everyone in the restaurant on him. He only hoped Ann was keeping the kids far from the windows. The Demons gathered closer and took a few tentative steps in their direction.

The short beep of a police siren turned thirty heads to the entrance off the highway. Caddie Allemande's Ford F-150 black Sheriff's Office truck pulled slowly into the lot, but a row of parked cars prevented her from putting herself between the two groups. She hopped down, slowly put her black cowboy hat on, and walked to the center of the lot. Chris couldn't help but grin. *Maybe I'm not the one who's Wyatt Earp,* he thought. He'd be happy with the older brother, Morgan Earp's, role. "Don't move," he ordered Phil before walking to join the sheriff.

The Demons stopped but didn't retreat as Phil ignored the LT's orders and took a step off the sidewalk, eight more Russians joining him.

"Sheriff," Chris stuck out his hand to let everyone know they were together.

"Chris." They shook. "What are the chances everyone just walks away?"

He looked between the Demons and Russians, both inching forward. "Doesn't look like anyone wants to be the one to back down."

"Well, it's our job to see that they don't turn this into a shootout in the parking lot of Mickey D's."

Chris looked behind him. Phil was a good four feet off the sidewalk. The lieutenant shook his head. Moscow pretended not to see it. "We got our work cut out for us," he told the sheriff.

"Looks that way," Caddie said, before raising her voice. "I'm Fillmore County Sheriff Allemande." She'd managed to stop both groups from moving forward, for the moment. "I want this lot cleared. There are too many civilians. Someone is going to get hurt."

Dubcek wasn't sure if appealing to the better nature of outlaw bikers and local criminals was going to be effective, but then he didn't have a better idea. If the Demons and Russians were determined to have it out, there wasn't much the two of them could do about it.

153

"Nice seeing you again, Sheriff." Strangler took a step forward, leaving the other Demons behind. "We got rights. We ain't violating no laws, just stopped to get something to eat."

Caddie rested her hand on her sidearm, still firmly strapped into its holster. "Find somewhere else."

A group of teens, noisy enough to draw attention even in the middle of the tension, flooded out of the restaurant, raising their phones to record the most exciting thing they'd ever seen in Mannheim. Chris hated the internet more every day.

Strangler forced his smile wider and took another step forward. He was testing Caddie. "Maybe you and I should talk. I'd like to report a crime. Seems a friend of mine was assaulted in your little town last night. Those folks over there did it, too. I need to see justice done. If that's me or you doing it, I don't care."

"I need you to clear your club out of this lot." Caddie unsnapped her holster.

His heart racing, Chris deliberately bent over and pulled his weapon out of its ankle holster. Standing straight again, he held it at his side. He was really hoping Ann wasn't letting the kids watch this.

The Jeep flew through the intersection, bouncing as it hit the dip running under the freeway, and back up again.

"Good gracious, Matt," Dawn said. He thought she was complaining about his driving until he saw the scene at McDonald's. Caddie and the lieutenant were isolated in the middle of a parking lot holding off bikers and Russians who, even from this distance, looked itching to fight. "Things like this definitely did not happen in Mannheim when I was a kid."

He slowed to turn.

"Don't, baby, you go screaming in there, you could set off a spark."

"Cute and smart," he said, and drove past the turn off, instead driving another twenty yards ahead and pulling into the lot of the farm and fleet store next door. He stopped far enough away not to draw attention.

"Vest first," she said as they climbed out.

"Yes, ma'am." Matt opened the back of the Jeep, unlocked a cabinet mounted into the floor, and pulled out a vest with Fillmore

County Sheriff printed in white across the chest. Next came his Mossberg Pro 940 shotgun. Using the rear door as cover, he quietly loaded the weapon, opting for buckshot, a nice combination of stopping power and spread.

Dawn stood at his shoulder. "Don't you dare quote Doc Holliday out there. I've decided you are not a cowboy."

He winked at her. "Okay, kitty cat," which he knew was not exactly reassuring. Armed, vest on, and with a badge fully on display, he strode across the lot, not caring if anyone saw him. But the Russians and Demons were focused on the sheriff and LT. Twenty feet behind the bikers, Matt whispered to Dawn, "Watch this baby."

"Not a cowboy," she said.

Matt lifted the shotgun to port arms, gripped the stock, and pumped a slug into the chamber. The scrape of metal and the chunk of the shell seating itself cut across the lot, making every head turn his way. "Hi," he said loud enough for everyone to hear. "Whatcha all doing? I'm Deputy Matt Jager with the Fillmore County Sheriff's Office."

Chris grunted a smile. Caddie nearly laughed with relief, but didn't waste a second of everyone's focus and inaction. "Chris, get Phil and his crew inside now. Nobody leaves until we say so."

"Gladly." He turned and marched in Phil's direction, his arms up in a sweeping motion, pushing them back as Caddie turned her attention to Strangler. Part of her wanted to see her sergeant taking command of the Russians, but she wasn't out of the woods yet with the Demons. She moved within three feet of the club president, too close for comfort but close enough to talk him down without embarrassing him in front of his club, who were a good ten feet behind him.

"In five minutes, this lot will be crawling with deputies and state troopers."

"Bullshit," Strangler said, but quietly enough that it was between him and Caddie.

She didn't argue. Let him wonder. "You're not having it out here. Not in my county, not tonight. Even if it's just me and the deputy behind you with the shotgun, you don't walk away clean from shooting cops. And it will all be on the internet in seconds from all those cell phones pointed our way." They looked back at the McDonald's. Chris had his hand on Phil Moscow's shoulder, guiding him to the door. The rest of the sidewalk was clear, but the glass wall was full of teenagers with their cell phones up, catching everything. "Get on your bikes and move on. Do that and nothing has happened here."

"Something has happened here, Sheriff. I'll remember this," he said, but took a step back at the same time.

"Me, too."

Strangler spun and waved his MC towards their bikes. "Whole town can't take a joke. Little sheriff says we got to get on our bikes and ride." Squirts laughed loudest and first, and the rest of the Demons made their way to their bikes. Strangler held his middle finger up for Caddie and then Matt as they roared out of the lot. Caddie's heart was beating faster than the spinning of their tires.

Caddie and Matt sat across from each other in the McDonald's booth. Dawn sat next to Matt as they watched the last of the Moscow clan pull out of the lot. Caddie waited until Phil cranked up his truck, studiously ignoring them despite being six feet away on the other side of the glass, before she flipped open her Big Mac box.

"You're a big idiot," Caddie said, special sauce squeezing out over her fingers. "Acting like a cowboy out there."

"Hey," Dawn said. "Don't listen to her. You're sweet and cute, only a little bit of an idiot, and not a cowboy."

"That was the most fun I've had in a long time," he said.

"Yep, idiot," Caddie said around a mouthful of double patties.

"How long do you think that's going to hold?" Matt took a sip of the hot chocolate Dawn had him order.

"Not long," Caddie said. "We need to find this dealer and fast."

"Maybe I should head north first thing in the morning and hunt the clinic director down."

"Hunting her down doesn't sound good, dear," Dawn said.

Caddie thought about it for a minute before nodding and digging her fries into the heart of the Mac and pulling them out covered in sauce. "You do that. I've got Rafer and Gentry if I have to hunt both of them down."

"Let's take your cocoa to go, dear." Dawn was shooing him out of the booth. "I've had enough with women in your life shoving burgers into their faces for one day."

Chapter 28

A soft white haze from the Christmas tree lights added to the flickering of low flames in the fireplace. It was the first fire Matt had built since Dawn left the first time. The comfort and warmth of the flames would have only reminded him of another time, a time when he'd been whole and happy. She couldn't feel the heat against her skin, but the reddish light still danced across a contented smile. They skipped Charlie Brown, for now anyway, and concentrated on each other. She was talking about a Christmas walk through the forest behind their apartment in Germany when Matt popped up, said "Don't go anywhere," and disappeared upstairs.

"Where would I go?" she called after him. "Silly soldier," she said to the flames.

Matt was back a minute later with a tight stack of square papers in his hand, a red ribbon holding them together. He held them out. "Merry Christmas."

The reflection of flames from the fire in her eyes glistened. "You got me Christmas?" Her fingers flustered over the top of the ribbon until she shook them in happy frustration. "Open it, Matthew."

Matt pulled at the end of the ribbon, the bow coming apart and the ends falling down over his hands. He set the stack down on the couch between them, spreading the envelopes out like a deck of cards. "I told you how I couldn't read for months after you left. These helped me read again."

Dawn bent lower before looking up at Matt. "These are from me."

"Some," he said. "Some are cards I gave you. Lots of Snoopy for anniversaries and birthdays. But most are from you to me when I was deployed to Afghanistan."

"Where were they?" She held her hands over her heart.

"I found them at the bottom of your underwear drawer when I was making room for running shorts. It was like finding a treasure. I spaced them out, reading one card or letter a day. I could hear your voice." His throat constricted, forcing him to slow his words. "When I was in Afghanistan, you told me you loved me, and you talked about being alone and afraid. All you wanted was me home so you could hold me. You thought about God a lot and you prayed."

Dawn watched, absorbed in Matt's telling of his grief and reaching back to a time when she was dealing with a different kind of loss but experiencing the same emotions. Then Matt's sadness at the pain turned to gratitude.

"You were talking to me more than a decade later. You were comforting me, telling me that I could get through it. You were saving me again, baby."

"Oh, sweetie." She reached out, placing her palm on his cheeks, setting off a tingle of static. "I was scared, and I so wanted you back in my arms, but I got through it. You will, too."

He smiled, leaned his head closer. "You came back for me." They kissed and ignored the shock.

"My love never left you."

"Never," he said. Then he slipped the first card out of its envelope. Snoopy danced across a bed of rose petals, Woodstock a step behind. "To my wife on our anniversary," he read, holding the card so Dawn could see. She wiped away a tear with the back of her finger. He opened the card. They read them all. The cards from him, the letters from her. They laughed at Dawn's stories of her little students. Matt was more honest about his experiences in Afghanistan than he'd ever been in life. They spent the hours connecting their pasts to today, an unbroken chain of love represented in aging sheets of paper.

Chapter 29
December 27th

Caddie got up early, sacrificing an hour of sleep for exercise, promising herself she wouldn't check her email until she'd worked up a good sweat. Head down, legs pumping and sweat running down her temples, a text dinged on her phone and popped up inches from her face. JT. Never should have rested the phone on the exercise bike's display monitor. She tapped to see the entire text.

'Sorry didn't get back to you. Catching flight out of DC back in CR by afternoon. See you at Fed LE party tonite?'

She let her head drop as sweat gathered and rolled off her nose. She was not going to answer right away. Let him wait this time. But the urge to respond was too much. Grabbing the phone, she sat up straight, slowed her pace, and thumbed in a reply.

'Too busy for party. Can't talk over phone?'

He pinged back immediately. *'In person I can come there tomorrow.'*

'Tonight then.'

'Okay bring Matt if you can'

She set the phone down and ignored his thanks and see you later, her legs picking up speed again. Rafer wasn't the kind to pull pretend rank as a fed, he must have commitments to the job at the party tonight for him to push meeting there. His request that she bring Matt brought another possibility beyond information on the Road Demons. JT had something for them on Jimmy Dubcek. She spun harder, sure the news wouldn't be good. She wanted, needed, Matt's focus on the ODs, and now Rafer was threatening to drop a bombshell that could only distract him if not set him off completely. She couldn't do anything about it now but sweat more. Her thighs were burning, and the back of her shirt was damp and growing heavy when her phone pinged again. It was Matt.

'Heading north to rehab clinic. Call to talk strategy when you're up'

She peddled faster. She'd told him the clinic was his and she'd take Gentry and the factory, but she'd wished he'd called before taking off. Keeping Matt on track and on target could eat up too much of her time, and she didn't need it today. It wasn't the first time she wondered if she gave the man too much leeway because they were friends or because he was a damn fine investigator. But over time, she'd found that giving Matt a long leash brought results. This time, she waited until the bike's timer crossed forty-five minutes and she entered the cooldown phase before responding. Too late to tug on his chain today anyway.

'OK will talk. Also you're going to LE party in CR tonite'

Taggert sat in one of the deputy cubicles, typing away at a report. "Hey, boss," he called without looking away from the screen. "Got an OWI this morning that turned into a prohibited person in possession." He hit a final key triumphantly and turned around. "I stopped at Walmart before work, the wife wanted me to grab Christmas wrap and stuff on clearance, and I saw this idiot nearly hit someone in the parking lot. I pulled him over and he smelled like a brewery. Blows a point-one-one."

Caddie was enjoying the story, real, everyday cop work was a nice change. "At eight-thirty in the morning?"

"Said he just had one, hair of the dog. Anyway, when I run him, he comes back with a felony domestic."

"And you asked to search the vehicle?"

"Didn't need to, I could see a shotgun in a rack on the back window of his truck." They enjoyed a good laugh together. Days like this, it was fun being the sheriff. "He's in interview one. You want to talk to him and lock in his claiming the gun?"

"He invoke, yet?" she asked, wondering if he'd asked for an attorney.

"No. I read him his rights for the OWI. I'm guessing he thinks there's no use in fighting that."

"Okay," Caddie said. "Your catch, you take it all the way. Do the interview. You're asking about the shotgun to make sure it's his. Then ask him about the domestic. See if you can get him to admit he knows that he has a felony conviction. It's not necessary, but it helps with the felon in possession charge. When you're done, let's talk and figure out if we want to take it state or go federal."

He smiled wider. Every cop likes to see a case to the end. "Schott is out on patrol now. If things stay quiet, I could have this wrapped up this morning."

Caddie turned toward her office when a thought hit her. She didn't need one of her deputies in trouble with his wife. "Did you get the clearance Christmas wrap?"

"Dang." He tapped his forehead. "Never got in the store."

Caddie slipped into her command voice. "You need to get there today, Deputy."

"Yes, ma'am. Soon as I talk to this mope."

Caddie's computer hadn't finished the login process when Claire knocked and rolled in at the same time. Her analyst didn't look as cheery as Caddie felt. She handed over a folder.

"Everything I could find on Gentry. He grew up on a farm, went to Buena Vista for a year before he was arrested. He dropped out and never went back after the charges were expunged."

Caddie let the folder sit. She would read it, but would rather focus on what Claire was saying at the moment.

"It looks like he was an original hire at Flightline or close to it anyway. He owns four acres and a three-bedroom outside of town, but there's nothing there to suggest anything off about his financials one way or the other. Never married, his only law enforcement contacts since Storm Lake are two speeding tickets, one here, one in Dubuque County. That's it."

"Thank you, that's helpful."

Claire was rolling herself backward. "Iowa Workforce said they would have a complete company roster for me today, and I'm still waiting for Tracy Everson's phone. Then I have to get ready for dinner with Bob's family tonight. I was kind of wondering if you'll need me to work."

Caddie never had kids, but even she could read Claire's need to talk. It didn't sound like she'd be upset if she had to work. Being sheriff could wait a few minutes. "Talk to me."

"You've got enough to worry about," Claire said, but stopped rolling away.

162

"Claire." Caddie stopped for a moment, thinking about how to put it into words. "There's no one more important to me than you. You know that, right?"

Claire nodded, her lips going tighter. She had to look away before speaking. "I know." She let out a big gasping breath. The more emotional part over, she went straight to the problem. "I'm not supposed to be with Bob. I mean, he's great, he's kind and nice, and treats me like a princess."

"Sounds rough."

Claire began to smile. "I know. And he's so attentive that he's too attentive. If you care for someone, if you love them, it shouldn't feel too attentive."

Caddie laughed. "You know I've been married three times? Maybe you should have this talk with Matt."

"No, I am not talking boyfriends with Matt." Claire was laughing now. "He wouldn't know anyway. He had the perfect wife and the perfect marriage."

"Nobody's marriage is perfect," Caddie said. "Is this about how Bob treats you or how you feel about him? You can talk to him about how he treats you, how you feel is something else."

"So I'm supposed to tell him it's me, not you?"

"I thought about letting my first husband's car on fire, with him and his girlfriend in it. Instead, I told him to get out; it was over. But Bob's a good guy. You need to tell him how you feel."

"During the holidays?"

"It's not going to be easier on January 1st."

Claire agreed, saying she would talk to Bob, and the conversation drifted from there, covering two out of three of Caddie's divorces. She promised the last story for another time. Alone in her office after Claire demanded a hug and left, Caddie wondered about Matt's marriage. Was he holding on to a memory that was too perfect? For some reason, she couldn't explain to herself, she didn't think so.

Chapter 30

The valley that held Decorah Hills Recovery Village was softened by a carpet of white from an overnight snowfall. A cross between a high-tech company campus and an Alpine resort, the clinic was made up of low, scattered buildings capped at the far end by an unobtrusive two-story office building. Doctor Kashvi Prijat pointed out residents' housing, counseling centers, exercise rooms, and what she claimed was the best health food kitchen between Minneapolis and Chicago. The doctor was of medium build, dark hair, deep brown skin, and a distinct Wisconsin accent.

"It isn't only patient confidentiality that makes me reluctant to talk to you," Kashvi said as she waved to an older man quickly making his way between buildings. It was impossible to tell if he was a patient or staff member. "I chose Decorah for the clinic because it would help isolate our patients from the world around them in a setting that promotes healing."

"Sounds like the back of a brochure," Dawn said.

"But it wasn't easy convincing everyone we would be good for the community. Some locals fought us, saying we wanted to bring drug addicts into the town. When we explained the reality of our clientele—"

"Wealthy people," Matt interrupted.

"That's part of the reality," Kashvi agreed. Despite ambushing her by parking in her designated spot, a trick he learned from Caddie, the doctor acted friendly enough, but her insistence that they walk the campus instead of going to her office hinted that the interview would have its challenges. "We also reserve beds for middle and lower-income patients and run outpatient counseling for local residents, but the fact is, this facility is expensive to run. Which is why we were attacked by people on the other side who claimed we were nothing but a resort for rich people, so they could avoid jail time. But we worked through it. Building this place provided construction jobs, and now more than fifty good-paying positions. Our relationship with the local community is good, but on rare occasions, one of the patients runs into trouble from alcohol or drug consumption, and some of the old prejudices reappear. We are in the midst of an epidemic of opioid abuse, Deputy. Synthetic opioids become stronger and more available every day, sweeping up everyone from every background. It destroys lives and families. Then there's meth and cocaine, and alcohol which still outpaces other drugs for the destruction it does. Treatment is our only way out of this, and I want to avoid anything that makes it harder for us to treat people. Stories about the clinic being connected to two deaths will not help our mission."

"She's worried about bad PR, dear," Dawn said. "Not very cool."

"Investigator Jager," Kashvi started, softening her posture the slightest.

"It's Matt, Doctor," he said.

"Matt, please call me Kashvi."

"Ugh," Dawn grunted, "return of the flirt monster. You two would have such beautiful babies, I can't stand it."

"Kashvi." Matt wanted to sound friendly. He needed the doctor on their side. Dawn could be right. Prijat was more worried about keeping the pipeline of rich patients flowing than she was about the lives of two former patients. Or she simply saw the bigger picture, drug rehab was difficult and more than a few would fall to their illness, but you had to keep treating those who remained. He decided he wasn't here to judge. He also expected Dawn would accuse him of being taken in because Kashvi was undeniably attractive. "I'm for attacking this from every angle. Precursors coming out of China need to be stopped. Cartels in Mexico need to be attacked. The border needs to be tighter. We have to put drug traffickers in prison. And yes, we need to treat addicts. None of those works without the other. The last thing I want to do is harm your clinic or your patients. But you gave Nikki Moscow and Tracy Everson a chance to live normal lives. Someone took that away from them. We owe it to your patients to find out who that is."

"I wonder, dear," Dawn said as the doctor considered Matt's words, "would you have been so impassioned for a chubby, balding, middle-aged man?"

That didn't take long, Matt thought, but the self-satisfied smile on Dawn's face told him she was simply stating fact, not scolding her husband. That might come later.

Kashvi led Matt onto a path wandering toward the tree line. Dawn walked alongside Matt, leaving no trace in the snow. One of those moments that drove home the oddness of her existence.

"Tracy and Nikki were close," Kashvi said. "That's not unusual here. Patients are isolated from their old lives while they go through intense counseling. For those physically able, there's also a rigorous exercise regime."

"A good run can solve just about anything," Matt said.

"No, it can't," Dawn said.

"I wish it could," Kashvi followed. "But it can be part of the process. We often find that patients will gravitate towards one another and form very deep, meaningful friendships."

"Foxhole buddies," Matt said.

Kashvi nodded. "It's very similar. The shared experience of going through a difficult situation together. Nikki and Tracy reinforced and supported one another. They did yoga and aerobics together. They went for long walks, and it wasn't surprising to find them staying up late talking. Near the end of Tracy's stay, I did something I don't often do, I encouraged them to keep in contact with one another."

"I think she just admitted to personally counseling both of them, Matt," Dawn said. "It would be good to know if she normally did that."

Matt hadn't picked up on that. "Being director must keep you busy. Do you personally treat a lot of patients?"

"Some. I'll never give up clinical work. It's the reason I spent years raising the money and working the politics to build the clinic."

"Lots of money and time," Dawn motioned to the buildings around them. "But that's something for another time. Keep your focus, dear. Nikki and Tracy."

"Did you have any contact with either after they left?" Matt asked. "Do you know if they stayed in touch?"

Kashvi stopped on a concrete circle at the edge of the woods. A picnic bench covered in six inches of snow sat in the center. They were about as far from the clinic's buildings as they could get and still be on campus grounds. "You said they did. I have no direct knowledge of that. And before you ask, even if I thought it fell outside of doctor-patient confidentiality, I wouldn't know who to name as someone who could have been supplying them with opioids.

166

The overwhelming percentage of our patients are from out of state, lots from the Twin Cities and Chicago, but St Louis too, and as far away as California and the East Coast. These are not people you're likely to find in small-town Iowa.

"What about some of those low and middle-income patients you take in?" Matt asked, knowing he was letting the rich off the hook in favor of looking at people from working families, but the doctor was right. The clientele that kept this place afloat weren't generally hanging out in Fillmore County. But maybe people with real lives.

Doctor Prijat shook her head. "I don't think so. Certainly, no one comes to mind."

Dawn circled the doctor, a little like a very cute wolf sizing up her prey. "She's got something, babe. She's wrestling with telling you, but isn't sure." She stopped, hands on hips, a sigh of resignation escaping her lips. "In case of emergency, break glass. Deploy your charm, dear. I'll try not to look."

"Can I ask you where you're from, Kashvi? I saw you went to UW-Madison." Matt didn't know if this qualified as charm, but the doctor was beginning to open up. What he wanted more than her being charmed was her trusting him.

"Eau Claire, Wisconsin," she said, starting to explain where in the state it was.

"I know Eau Clare," he interrupted. "I grew up in Fountain City, it's across the river from Winona, Minnesota. I got my bachelor's from Maryland, but went to Marquette Law when I retired from the Army."

"And you work as a sheriff's deputy?" She seemed intrigued; maybe he was charming, or at least interesting.

"Mannheim is my wife's hometown. After following my Army career around, we followed hers for a vice principal position. Then she left."

Dawn moved closer, putting herself between Matt and the Doctor. "I love you, soldier," she said.

"Left?" Kashvi asked.

"Car accident," though he didn't believe it was. "Losing her broke me." He felt his eyes watering, and he couldn't blame the cold.

Kashvi studied him with a look of clinical interest. "You cover it well. How long?"

"A little over three years." He looked directly at his wife. "There are times it seems she's right next to me. Whispering in my ear."

"You silly," Dawn said.

"Other times, I'm empty and crushed." He decided to get to his point. "I have a two-beer limit rule, and most of the time I won't have the second."

"Because you don't trust yourself," Kashvi said.

"Too easy to crawl into a bottle and not come out." He looked back at the clinic campus, low lights filtering out of windows fell across pristine snow as heavier cloud cover rolled in. "It's not exactly the same as the pressure your patients feel, but I get it. Every day they get up, move through life, and fight the urge to dull the pain or chase the high."

"Or just not feel sick," the doctor added.

"Yeah," Matt said. "I don't want to add to that pressure. What I want to do is bring justice for Tracy and Nikki's deaths because being an addict doesn't mean your life is disposable. And maybe I can help prevent someone else from dying."

"I appreciate that, Matt, I do, but I still won't violate their privilege."

Dawn clicked her tongue. "You were so close, dear. And so I don't forget, very sweet and charming in a broken soldier kind of way." Snow began falling heavily. Whatever impulse had prompted the doctor to bring them to this spot seemed to fade. She shuffled her feet, looking down, ready to suggest the interview was over. "But I think you're losing her, dear. Ask her about Kyle Everson while you still have time."

Matt wasn't sure if a question that could go straight to Tracy's counseling sessions was the way to go, but Dawn was right, Doctor Prijat was ready to call it any second. "I get that you have to be careful about what you can say, but what can you tell me about Tracy's husband? I can't help thinking there was a disconnect between them the last few months. He hardly seems to know what she's been doing with her life unless it dealt with their business."

Prijat considered the question as she turned her back to the wind. "This falls outside anything she may have told me," she said. "It varies from patient to patient depending on their needs, but we don't allow visitors for at least the first thirty days of treatment. Kyle

168

Everson didn't visit until several weeks after Tracy was allowed to have visitors. I was told that he was in Europe on business and was very busy. He was apologetic to me, not so much to her, from what I observed."

"He was more worried about what the cute woman doctor thought of him than how it made his wife feel," Dawn said, back to her skepticism of Everson. Matt repeated the thought, leaving out the part about Kashvi being cute.

"That's the way it appeared to me," she agreed. "It was another month before he returned, but after that, he was here every week."

"What changed?" Dawn asked.

Feeling a bit like a sign language interpreter, Matt began repeating Dawn as the words came out.

"On his third visit, Tracy and Nikki already had plans to walk into town for lunch. Nikki begged off, but Tracy insisted that the three of them have lunch together."

"Don't repeat," Dawn said, cutting off Matt's translation, "but I'm pretty sure she just violated that confidentiality. Keep pushing, this is what she wanted to tell us when she took the attractive boy deputy into the snowy woods."

"And after meeting Nikki, Kyle Everson became a regular visitor?" Matt asked, pushing Dawn's point.

"Yes."

"And did they include Nikki in these visits?"

"Tracy liked Nikki a great deal. She admired Nikki's strength, and she adored Nikki's children. The Moscow family is not like most of our patients' families. Her father was in prison when she was here. But her mother or one of her siblings brought her girls nearly every week. Tracy longed for that connection, that tight family support. Having Nikki with her gave her the strength to begin demanding that level of support from her husband, even if she didn't put it in those words."

"Definitely therapy session info," Dawn said. "Ask her what Nikki thought of Kyle."

Prijat didn't need prompting. "I found it transparent, but I think Kyle Everson has a certain charm that appeals to some women."

"Stupid charm," Dawn said.

Matt repeated it, and Dawn sighed, "That was just for you, dear."

But Kashvi laughed. "Yes, but he's successful and decent-looking in a way."

"Not your way, babe," Dawn said. "And in case you're confused, that was just for you, too."

"For someone from Nikki's background, that level of seeming stability and, well, lack of criminality, could be very appealing," Kashvi said. "From the outside, Kyle Everson could appear successful, loving, supportive. From the outside, anyway."

"You think there was something between Nikki and Kyle Everson?" Matt asked before Dawn could get the question out.

"I don't know that, and as far as I know, Tracy didn't believe so," she said, giving away that she'd been passing on Tracy's thoughts.

"But?" Dawn said, quickly getting there before Matt

"But?" he said more softly.

Kashvi brushed snow off her shoulders as it came down even heavier. She turned into the wind, ready to walk away from the interview. "I don't know anything for certain. Nikki didn't say anything, but on a Saturday, after Tracy left and Nikki was here alone, I saw Mr. Everson's truck downtown in the lot downhill from The Hotel Winneshiek."

"Lot of trucks in Iowa," Matt said.

"Not with Flightline plates." Doctor Prijat picked up her pace. She had violated her patient's confidentiality and pointed Matt and Dawn at the connection between Nikki and Tracy that had always been there, and she was finished talking.

"And Nikki?" he asked, falling in step, Dawn walking beside him.

"Signed out until ten that evening," she said before turning uphill to head to the office building.

"But Tracy and Nikki were so close to one another," Matt said. "Do you think Nikki would betray her that way?"

Kashvi gave a knowing smile. She had given enough away. "None of us is perfect, Matt. We make mistakes, we betray people close to us. Being addicted doesn't fix that." She began walking away from Matt, her head down. "You should talk to someone about your wife."

"I talk to her," he said without thinking.

She stopped and looked back at him. "Call me if that stops working."

170

"Oh, doctor," Dawn answered for him, "you have no idea how close you are to a bop in the nose."

Chapter 31

Caddie didn't bother checking in with the admin ladies at Flightline. She knew her way around and didn't want Gentry to have a heads-up she was here. A twenty-year-old tossed bust for dealing in college was hardly the stuff to crank up an investigation over, but the lying gnawed at her. Then there was Doctor Serrano tipping her off about Tracy getting tested for a sexually transmitted disease, and the office ladies pointing to Gentry as the person in the company closest to Tracy. Add that all up and Gentry put himself squarely in the interesting zone. The mechanical work floor was busy today. A line of heavy open crates sat along the far wall. A three-person team in the center of the cavernous room was carefully swinging an engine over a box resting on a forklift. Gentry appeared from behind the lift, his head down, concentrating on a tablet. When he looked up, he was staring directly at the sheriff. She saw it then, the disappointment that she was back for him. Squarely interesting.

"I was a kid, and they were trying to pin some poor girl's death on me. It was all garbage, and the judge wiped it off my record," Gentry pleaded. "And honestly, I didn't think it mattered." He leaned across the conference room table toward the sheriff with a look of supplication.

"There's nothing honest about any of that," Caddie said. Gentry just failed his second test. She'd started soft with a question about why he didn't tell her about his arrest in Storm Lake. No accusation of lying, no connecting him to Tracy's death. He could have confessed that he was scared and had made a mistake in not telling her. Instead, he went with that it didn't matter and had the gall to attach the word honestly to it. "People around here tell us that you worked closely with Tracy. They say you're friends. And this woman you work with, who you're friends with, dies of a drug overdose, and you don't think the fact that you once sold and were busted for drugs would matter to me?"

"I didn't mean that, sorry." He ran his hand through his hair and looked up at the fluorescent lights above. After a deep breath, he

172

tried again. "Of course, I knew you'd be interested, but I hoped you wouldn't find out. I checked when I got this job, there's no record of the arrest, nothing in the court system. It's like the judge told me, it's like it didn't happen."

"And you didn't think we would find out," Caddie stated.

"No, I didn't. But I had nothing to do with Tracy's death. I sold some weed and a little speed in college for the money. I didn't come from wealthy parents, we could barely afford school. Dealing gave me carrying cash. I never even met the girl who drowned, but they were looking to blame someone, and I was a good target." He looked to Caddie for understanding, but she gave none back. It wasn't her job to soothe his conscience; besides, as long as he was talking, she wasn't going to get in his way.

"I didn't want to be a target again," he said, filling the silence. "I haven't had anything to do with illegal drugs since then. You can check the company's drug tests if you want."

"I might," Caddie said before slipping her leather jacket off and hanging it on the back of the chair. That was her warning to Gentry that they would be here for a while. "Let's start over. How well did you know Tracy Everson?"

Caddie spent the next thirty minutes bouncing between Gentry's work at Flightline, what he knew of Tracy's drug use, his bust for selling in Storm Lake, and why he hadn't been straight with her yesterday. Nothing significant changed. He insisted the dealing was a college thing and his brush with the law had kept him far away from any drug use, much less dealing. No, he hadn't put the bust down when he applied for this job. The judge had said it never happened. He liked Tracy, and they got along well. She oversaw the administration side of the company, which included scheduling and tracking shipping, and that's where they worked together.

Tracy hid her drug use well the first time until she completely fell off the edge. When she got out of rehab, she seemed physically healthier but less sure of herself as time went on. "I was worried about her. She was always full of life, like a bubbly personality. Until she got really sick before rehab. When she got out, the real her was back kind of, but it slipped away." A look of pain crossed Gentry's face.

"Did you think she was using again?" Caddie asked.

"I don't know. It didn't seem the same. She seemed down, I guess. Like maybe she thought the world was going to be great when she got out, and it was just the world again with work and life. I don't know," he said again.

Caddie heard a plaintive sadness in Gentry. She didn't think he'd supplied Tracy with the drugs that killed her, but she also wasn't sure he was simply a work friend. "I've been told that Tracy wasn't around much the last couple of months."

"Less," he agreed. "She was only really back the one month, then in October or so, she started coming in less. She used to like working here, getting together with everyone, dealing with clients, and growing the business, but it wasn't doing it for her anymore."

"Did you see her outside of work?" Part of her wanted to ask straight out if he'd been sleeping with Tracy, if he was the reason she was concerned about an STD, but easing into the idea felt the more sure path. He didn't answer right away, getting caught in the last lie of omission had its impact.

"A little," he finally admitted. "Not before she went to rehab, but when she got back, and Kyle wanted her working again. She was in charge of shipping, and some stuff still needs real signatures. I took the forms out to her at the house. We might have a cup of coffee or something and talk for a while. That's it. But she was still engaged with the work. She wouldn't sign the papers right away, she wanted me to leave them so she could read them over and I'd come back and pick them up a few days later."

"Why not have Kyle bring them in ?" Caddie asked. It seemed a better answer than having Gentry run back out to the house. Unless, of course, it was about seeing Gentry again and not the papers themselves. She had thought she knew the answer to the next question, but now she wasn't entirely sure. "Did you and Tracy have a physical relationship?"

Gentry's head went back as if he were reacting to a soft slap. He hadn't expected the question. "What? No, never. Why would you ask that?"

"What did you talk about?" Caddie asked, trying to redirect the interview. Whether or not he had an affair with Tracy Everson, she thought the question should have been an obvious one; for Gentry, it came from nowhere.

"Nothing," he said. "The company, the weather. Nothing that mattered. Look, I admit, I liked Tracy and found her attractive, but she was not putting out any kind of vibes to me. I was concerned because she seemed down and alone. That's it. I was trying to be her friend."

"Do you think she could have purposely overdosed?" Suicide by fentanyl hadn't been on the top of Caddie's list, but it was a possibility they had to consider, even if it didn't fit into Nikki's death.

"No," he said, quickly. "I think she was down about something, but the real Tracy was still in there. I don't think she'd given up. Whatever she was going through, I thought she would come out the other end and be herself again."

Caddie's questioning took a subtle turn in her mind as Gentry went from the longest-of-shots suspect to more of a witness. "Adjusting to sobriety can be tough. Did she give you any idea at all about what might have happened that was weighing on her?"

Gentry rubbed his hands together. They were the tough, calloused hands of a mechanic. He may have had a crush on Tracy, but Caddie bet he thought the woman wouldn't have been interested in someone like him. She had no idea if he was right. "She didn't say anything, not directly. I didn't ask."

She let him sit alone with the answer in his mind. It came in time.

"I don't think Kyle was paying much attention to her," he said. "He wasn't around the house, and I know he wasn't here. She seemed lonely."

"This is just between us right now," Caddie lied. "Is there any talk about Kyle with other women?"

Gentry sat back. "I went on a trip to Vegas with Kyle once, this was before Tracy went to rehab. I don't know what he's been up to in town, and I haven't heard anything. But I'll tell you, his first words when the plane touched down were 'What happens in Vegas, stays in Vegas.' He wasn't joking."

"What did happen in Vegas?" Caddie asked, blowing through the cliché.

"It was an avionics convention with everyone from Boeing and Airbus to little outfits like us. We had a small booth and spent most of our days talking to potential clients. He wanted me there to

175

discuss details on mechanical systems. Don't get me wrong, Kyle knows his stuff, but having the lead mechanic there can help."

"Sounds like an event where Tracy would have been useful," Caddie said, thinking of Everson's description of his wife's role in attracting new business.

"She would have been, but her being there would have interfered with his nights. He went at it pretty hard. I couldn't keep up."

"Including women?" It was looking like her husband's philandering was the reason Tracy asked to be tested for an STD. It could also point to an intentional OD, but again, that didn't explain Nikki.

Gentry nodded. "He was playing the odds, hit on enough women, and he figured he'd win eventually."

"And?" Caddie pressed. She wanted a definitive answer. She needed to understand exactly who they were dealing with. Already, his version of their lives together, Tracy as the party girl and he as the grown-up, was ringing hollow.

"First night, we drank for a while with potential clients. But the bar was packed, so we headed to some clubs and from there to strip clubs. I finally bailed to get some sleep. When I was getting ice in the morning, I saw a woman leaving his room. She was a looker. Either he was really lucky or he paid for it. After that, I cut my nights short and he did whatever he did."

"And now?"

"I wouldn't know. We don't exactly hang outside of work."

The steam was out of the interview, asking more questions would just be retreading old ground. Caddie wasn't sure she was done with Gentry; he had clearly been attracted to Tracy, and something between workmates and friends. He wasn't a suspect anymore, but she also didn't think he was being entirely honest with her either. She thanked him, asked him to keep their conversation between the two of them, and walked back out onto the plant floor. Glancing up, she saw Kyle Everson standing in his office window, hands behind his back, looking down at her. She nodded. *Not done with you yet,* she thought.

Chapter 32

Dark woodwork set against white walls and cream-colored marble floors gave the Winneshiek Hotel a nicely dated look. A blazing fire added a Christmas feel. Matt flashed his badge and asked the desk clerk how long she'd been working there. The blonde, very Norwegian-looking young woman, said three years.

"I'm looking to see if someone stayed here in June of this year," he said.

Dawn leaned against the counter, taking in the garland strung along the second-floor balcony and the Christmas tree standing by the fireplace. "This would make for a nice Christmas movie. A lonely, cute soldier boy meets a wonderfully attractive and bright elementary school teacher, who is most definitely not looking for love. They meet, have an adorable misunderstanding, before he falls hopelessly in love with her."

"I'm sorry," the clerk said, "management has a pretty strict policy. Unless someone is in danger, we need a subpoena before we release guest information. I hope you understand, it's for the safety and privacy of our guests."

Dawn went on undeterred by the clerk shutting down her husband's request. "But she's had a terrible breakup with a jerk who cheats on her, and she's not open to love. But then, blah, blah, blah, they kiss in the falling snow, happy ending, love all around." She dazzled him with her smile. "What do you think?"

There was no use in arguing with the clerk who was doing her job, and Matt wasn't about to lie and mess up any potential evidence. He got out his phone, did a quick search, and pulled up a picture from the Flightline website. He showed it to the clerk.

"I know," Dawn continued, "it feels like all the other Christmas love movies, but I like it."

The clerk shook her head but said, "Maybe. I see a lot of people."

Dawn popped herself up on the counter, facing Matt, her legs kicking slowly back and forth. "If nothing else, we could role-play the movie and end it in a not very safe for work kind of way."

Matt's head snapped up to his wife.

"Got ya there, soldier." She went back to enjoying the decorations. "Go ahead, finish what you were doing, now that I've got you all worked up."

Matt blinked away his not safe for work thoughts and found the Facebook page he'd been looking for. "What about her?" he asked, showing the profile picture to the clerk. He had far less hope than with the picture of Everson.

"Oh, I know her," the clerk said, surprised, pulling the phone closer.

Dawn lifted her feet up under her and spun to face the clerk. "Wow. I'm impressed, babe. You're either very good or very lucky at this detective thing."

"Yeah," the clerk went on. "I talked to her a couple of times. I couldn't say if it was June, but she was asking about working in a hotel. What it's like, how much I got paid, and stuff like that. She was cool, and we talked for a while. She told me her whole story about being an addict and having two little girls and everything." She handed the phone back. "I remember because I thought how strong she was kicking drugs and thinking about how she could take care of her girls. I admired her." She stood up straighter and crossed her arms in a defensive posture. "She's not in trouble, is she?" Nikki had known this woman for minutes six months ago and still had managed to earn a sense of loyalty. The clerk was not about to give her up if she could help it.

"No," Matt said. "I'm sorry, but she passed away from a drug overdose last week. I'm looking into her death."

"Oh, shit," the clerk said, then apologized before she said it again.

"Ask if she stayed here, baby," Dawn said from her perch.

"Did Nikki stay here?"

The clerk, now looking a little sick, shook her head. "I don't know. Not that I know. She didn't register."

"Was she with anyone when you spoke to her?" Matt asked.

"No." The clerk stepped closer, her defensiveness gone. "Did that guy you showed me have anything to do with Nikki dying?"

"No," Matt said.

"Maybe," Dawn corrected him.

The clerk was at the computer terminal. "Do you want me to see if Nikki or that guy checked in?" Months ago and for minutes, and

178

the clerk was ready to risk her job for Nikki. Matt was tempted, but if this turned into something, he didn't need the evidence tossed or the girl to lose her job.

"Expect a subpoena," he said as Dawn slid off the counter.

"Kind of ruins the whole Christmas naughty time fantasy, doesn't it?"

Chapter 33

Everson was still standing at the window looking out onto the floor when Caddie knocked on the door frame. He turned slowly and gave a weak smile.

"Sheriff."

Drained is the word that came to Caddie's mind. She could only guess at what he was going through. Guilt over cheating on his wife? Regrets for not doing more to help her? Grief? Unfortunately for him, she had two overdose deaths to solve and a ticking time bomb between the Russians and Road Demons, and the always-present possibility that Nikki and Tracy would not be the last to die. "I was following up with some of your employees. We're still trying to get a better picture of your wife's last weeks. Is there anything else you've thought of that might help? Any particular issues she was dealing with? Any people she may have been talking to?"

"No, I'm sorry. You can see what it's like out there." He motioned with his head to the window behind him. "We have a large contract to fulfill, and we're shipping by the end of the week. It's horrible, but even with Tracy's death, we can't slow down and mourn her. Business doesn't work that way." He stopped to think about his next words. "I know that's part of the problem, believe me. If I had been more present, maybe she would still be alive. But it was our dream to turn Flightline into a real player in the field, and we need orders like this to get there. I never took my eye off that. That's my fault."

Caddie wasn't interested in holding Everson's hand while he worked through his emotions. She wondered if sending Matt to Decorah while she focused on Flightline had been a mistake. After losing Dawn, Matt probably had a better chance of connecting with Everson. It was at that thought, at her friend's loss and his wife, that she felt the buzz at the edge of her mind, again. Not a pain exactly. She pushed it away, focusing on Everson. "You can't blame yourself, Mr. Everson. Drug addiction is difficult to treat, and relapses are not uncommon. For what it's worth, I'm hearing from people here that Tracy seemed to be doing well when she left treatment."

"She was."

"But they also think something was bothering her the last few months. Something that kept her from coming into the office as often."

"I told you that. The pressure of work, I guess, or the drugs, or whatever."

Whatever? Caddie thought. "There's nothing specific you can think of that could have been bothering her?"

"No. Work, drugs, I don't know. And I don't know how that gets you closer to finding who sold her the drugs that killed her? Everyone in town is talking about this motorcycle gang, and there's the Russians. I told you, Tracy knew Nikki Moscow from rehab. I have no idea if they were in contact here. Tracy never mentioned it, but is it so hard to believe that Tracy used that connection to get drugs?"

"We're looking at everything, Mr. Everson. And I am sorry to keep asking you questions like this, but your wife's actions and state of mind could point to how she acquired the drugs that killed her. We don't even know if she knew she was taking fentanyl or thought it was another drug or unauthorized prescription pills like sleeping aids."

"What about the Russians and this motorcycle gang?" Everson asked, his voice rising a degree. "Are you looking at them, too?"

"We're looking at every possibility." She kept her voice modulated, which wasn't easy at the moment.

Everson turned back to the window. "I'm sorry. It's all just very difficult."

"I understand. Like I said, I'm sorry to press you on these things, but I can assure you, Nikki Moscow and your wife are my department's highest priorities."

"Good," he said to the glass.

"My investigator tried catching up with you unsuccessfully about your wife's phone yesterday. You said you found it."

"Yeah, sorry." He pointed to his jacket hanging on the rack by the door. "I was going to bring it by your department if nobody got it today."

Caddie retrieved the phone, saw a sticky with the passcode on the back, and slipped it into her jacket. "Thank you, this could help." She couldn't think of anything else, and Everson didn't seem in the talking mood anymore. She assured him again they were doing all they could, and she would keep him informed. She was about to excuse herself when Everson turned back from the window.

"I hope you make some arrests quickly," he said. "I'm not sure I could move on knowing someone out there all but killed my wife. And I would hate to see someone else die."

Caddie uttered another platitude before leaving. He was thinking of closure already. Maybe it was a good thing Matt went north for the day. Talk of closure less than two days after finding his wife dead would not have sat well with him. Heck, it wasn't sitting well with her.

Chapter 34

"What did you find?" Caddie stood with her back to the standing gas heater at the far corner of the nearly deserted patio of the Black Sheep Social Club. The Cedar Rapids federal courthouse faced them, sending the glow of eight stories of glass and golden metal across the parking lot. Matt handed her a beer from the bar inside before outlining what he'd found today, starting with Kashvi's description of Nikki and Tracy's relationship and finishing with his semi-successful attempt to see if Nikki and Everson met up at the Winneshiek Hotel. Dawn stood by his side, sleek and beautiful in a long red wool jacket with matching leather gloves.

Caddie agreed they needed to subpoena the hotel's records for June before asking the more pertinent question. "You think Kyle could be the source of drugs for both women?"

"We're looking for an ongoing connection between the two," Matt said. "It's possible they remained tighter than people think and one passed drugs to the other, or that Kyle was the link."

"Passing drugs from his girlfriend to his wife?" Caddie asked skeptically.

"Or vice versa," Dawn said. "Let's not automatically blame Nikki."

"Could be the other way around," Matt said.

"And Nikki ODs, and it doesn't stop Tracy from using from the same batch?"

"Drink, dear," Dawn said. She turned her back to Caddie and spoke softly, hoping not to set off a reaction from the sheriff. "And I know I shouldn't tell you to drink, but I need time. Caddie's question assumes Tracy knows her husband is having an affair with Nikki. Girlfriends sharing is fine, but that's a bit much. Second, addicts know you can die from using drugs, it doesn't stop them from using. Even Kyle admits he partied," Dawn used air quotes, "with his wife. He passes drugs one way or another between Tracy and Nikki before Nikki's death. It doesn't necessarily stop Tracy from using, particularly if she doesn't know it's the same drugs that killed Nikki."

Matt finished his long sip and repeated the thought, minus the air quotes.

"That's a heck of a theory," Caddie said. She filled Matt and their unseen partner in on her day, starting with retrieving Tracy's phone. "Claire jumped on it right away, but nothing so far. The problem is, she can't see anything that's been deleted. We'll have to wait for DCI to take a crack at it." Then she went into Kyle's Vegas adventures.

"Told ya," Dawn said. "He's a creep."

"He's a creep," Matt agreed.

"Gentry also mentioned taking export—," anything more was cut off as Caddie pulled a vibrating phone from her back pocket. "Rafer's here," she said, thumbing in a text.

"Rafer, not JT?" Dawn questioned her husband. "I want to know all the gossip, dear."

Rafer, a tall, broad-shouldered black man, stepped from the bar and flipped up the collar on his jacket before digging into his pockets for gloves. "Hey. Merry Christmas."

Dawn was the only one who answered him.

"It's cold out here." He stood as close as he could to the open flames.

"Would you rather have this conversation inside?" Caddie asked. Only a couple in the far corner of the fenced-off area joined them outside, and they weren't paying attention to anyone but each other.

"No, this is good," Rafer said. "Guess we just skip right over the holiday party niceties."

Dawn was the only one in the circle smiling. "Oh, there's history here. See what you miss when you spend half your time out of the country, dear? All the good gossip, and you don't even know." While Caddie was letting her frustration with the Rafer show, Dawn knew her husband's neutral expression was a mask. He wanted to ask where the FBI was on the investigation into Jimmy Dubcek, but he knew how important their current work was. That he could balance the two was progress.

"You have a party to get to and my mother expected me half an hour ago," Caddie said with no attempt to make things easier for

Rafer. "Why am I getting the stiff arm from the feds on basic cooperation on an outlaw motorcycle gang operating in my county?"

"Kind of rough, dear." Dawn snuggled close to Matt. "Glad she didn't take your breakup this badly."

"I'm trying to answer you, Caddie," Rafer shot back. She held out her hands like she'd been waiting all day, which she had.

Dawn popped an air kiss in Matt's ear, the grin all through her voice. "Smart to stay out of the crossfire, soldier."

"First," JT said, ignoring Matt and focusing his answer on Caddie, "none of our agencies have any intelligence indicating the Road Demons are involved in the opioid trade. None. Traditionally, they've been involved in meth and marijuana. Second, specifically dealing with Nikki Moscow and Tracy Everson, DEA, FBI, none of us have any information connecting the Road Demons, or anyone else for that matter, with their deaths. Finally, we're committed to fully supporting your investigation and will pass any information we gather that directly implicates the Demons or the Russians or anyone else."

Caddie was ready to spit back an answer when Matt's hand on her arm held her back. She took a deep breath instead.

"Good job, babe," Dawn said. "Now, stop touching her."

Matt was noticeably more friendly, which should have made Rafer suspicious. "DEA, FBI, Marshals, ATF have nothing on the Demons moving opioids in Fillmore County or anywhere in Iowa?"

"Matt," Rafer grinned at the friendly face, "if we have anything that helps, you'll be the first to know."

"Right," he said, still sounding friendly. "Traditionally, they've been into grass and meth and you know nothing tying them to two opioid ODs in Fillmore?"

"Right," Rafer was finally catching on to Matt being too friendly.

"It kind of sounds like you're waving us off the Road Demons."

"No," Rafer protested.

"Oh," Dawn said, "he's going to dig himself deeper."

Caddie picked up the ball from Matt. "You come here with a whole lot of nothing, nothing which you could have told me over the phone."

"And," Matt went on without missing a beat, "instead of DEA or ATF answering these questions, they send you."

"Guys," Rafer pleaded.

"You have a source," Matt said firmly. "You want to spoon-feed us because you're protecting a source."

"That's not enough," Caddie said, giving Rafer no time to respond. "We're getting the personal touch, so we stop pressing."

"We would tell-," Rafer tried before getting cut off.

"A really sensitive source," Matt said. "The kind of source you don't want to tell the local yokels about. Like maybe a UC?"

Caddie and Matt looked at one another, both raising their eyebrows. Dawn slipped between them. "I'm impressed, and it's almost cute the way you two work together, but I want you to knock it off. Me and you are cute, not you two."

"If you have a source, particularly if it's an undercover officer," Caddie said far less pointedly than she had been, "we need to know. I'm an inch away from arresting every Road Demon I see in the county to keep the place from blowing up. I don't want to expose a good source, and I certainly don't want to blow a UC op, but I have two dead victims; I don't want any more."

Rafer rubbed his eyes with the heel of his hands. "This can't go anywhere but between us."

"I'm not telling anyone," Dawn said as Matt and Caddie nodded agreement.

"ATF has a source with a support club," Rafer said, not denying or confirming the source was an undercover officer. "Not inner circle with Demon leadership, but they've provided good intel on guns. This is all built off tracing the weapons we believe Deputy Williams lifted off some busts."

Caddie's calm was gone. "The same deputy who attacked Claire, killed a fellow deputy, and shot and kidnapped me? You don't think we were owed that information?"

"A source ATF got because of Williams?" Matt said. "No wonder they sent you to take the bullet on that one."

"It was always the plan to bring you in at some point and share credit."

Caddie waved it away as a warmer breeze flickered the gas light.

"It wasn't my choice not to tell you," JT said, breaking ranks with his fellow feds. "I thought you were owed. But from everything we know, the Demons have generally stayed out of Fillmore County.

They're active in a line from Waterloo to Dubuque, have a presence in Cedar Rapids, and dealings in the Quad Cities and as far west as Mason City. But nothing in Fillmore."

"Your friend Frank keeps them out, dear," Dawn said.

"Because of the Russians?" Matt asked.

"The source doesn't know. What he was told was that there was an in with a Jones County deputy, then he heard it was Fillmore County, which matches Williams. On Fillmore, the only thing he knows is that at some point, the support club was told not to crap in Fillmore."

"They're doing more than that now," Caddie said. "What changed?"

"We don't know. Frank Moscow was doing time, and some of the cousins were busted in the steroid investigation. Maybe the Demons see the Russians as less of a threat."

"Frank won't take that lying down," Matt said.

"Babe," Dawn said, "try not to sound so sympathetic to your criminal friend."

"The Demons certainly wouldn't care about any warnings not to supply Nikki," Caddie mused.

"As far as we know, the Demons are not moving opioids in Iowa," Rafer said.

Dawn spoke softly to Matt as Caddie pressed the FBI agent for details. "Remember, JT is a friend. You want him in the room with the other feds arguing for you, not so mad he wants nothing to do with us. Get him to promise to pass anything along and give the guy a break. Besides, if this goes on much longer, Caddie may bop him in the nose."

Matt waited until Caddie took a breath before interrupting and getting Rafer off the hook. "I get the position you're in," he said. "We'll keep pushing any Road Demon intel your way, it could help keep your UC safe." Rafer didn't object that it wasn't an undercover officer, all but confirming it for Matt. "You guys need to do the same. A full rundown on MC members, focused on the leadership, could be helpful. And we've got local sources you don't. We may find connections your source isn't aware of."

"We can do that," Rafer said. He turned back to Caddie. "It may not seem like it right now, but we're on the same side, Caddie. I hear

187

even a whisper that the Demons could be responsible for the drugs that killed those women, I will tell you regardless of what ATF wants."

Caddie finished her beer and looked up into the cloud-filled skies. The low grey cover was holding in the day's warmth, but any Midwesterner knew it was temporary. "Okay," she finally said. "Anything we can get."

"As long as we're being all cooperative," Matt said. "The Jimmy Dubcek investigation? Is there one? Does the FBI plan on doing anything?"

"That's the reason I asked you to be here, too," Rafer said.

The news didn't sound like it was going to be good or bad, which, for Matt, meant it was bad.

"They've approved us opening a full field investigation on corruption in the Fillmore County Sheriff's Office connected to the building of your law enforcement center."

"It sounds an awful lot like that's going to come with a lot of qualifiers," Matt said.

"It does," Rafer said. "I'm sorry, Matt. I'm supposed to sell you the idea that this is good news. But you're not falling for that. All that talk about a federal task force and extra resources, that's all gone."

"The rest of it, JT," Caddie said. Dawn appreciated that the sheriff was looking out for Matt, too, trying to take some of the burden off him.

"For now, the scope of the investigation is limited to just that, the construction of the LE center. The school, the county government, the bank run by Jimmy's cousin they're outside the scope of the investigation. We come up with more, maybe we can expand."

Matt's head was down, his breathing controlled. Caddie spoke for him.

"What happened?"

"Politics."

"Fuck." Matt looked at Dawn for help. He needed someone to tell him the FBI didn't just quietly shit can the investigation into her death. Because if the FBI wasn't going to do it, he would.

She was more concerned about him than the investigation into her own death. "If Jimmy ends up in prison that's justice, Matt. Have

188

faith, you work with them, and you find out the truth. Within the law, you can still do it. For now, let's help Tracy and Nikki get their justice." Dawn wasn't entirely sure she believed it herself, but anything to keep Matt from making the mistake that would damn him.

"Let me know how I can help," he said very deliberately to Rafer, then held out his hand. He knew whatever happened in DC with the Dubcek investigation, JT was on his side. They shook, and Rafer retreated quickly, promising Caddie they would talk again.

Caddie let out a soft whistle. "I was worried there for a second. I'm surprised you let him off that easily."

"A voice told me to keep Nikki and Tracy the priority," he said.

"A sweet voice," Dawn added.

"Same goes for me, Matt. Whatever I can do," Caddie said.

"I know, thanks."

She dug into her pocket and came out with her keys, only to have Matt pull them from her hand.

"That was my first beer," he said. "How many for you?"

"Enough for me to let you keep those," Caddie admitted. "Drop me at my mother's?"

"That's nice," Dawn said. "You two look out for each other."

"Sure," Matt said.

"Come in and visit her for a few minutes?"

"Not a chance," Dawn said.

Chapter 35
December 28th

The Mannheim Medical Center Emergency Room was a scene straight out of a television drama. The lobby was packed, voices were raised, and a nurse in pink scrubs held her hands over her head, trying to quiet and push back the crowd. "This is a restricted area. You need to back up and give us room to see patients." Allison shouldered her way past two twenty-something-year-old girls who interrupted their crying long enough to stare daggers at her.

"Back up, back up," Allison raised her voice with each word as she moved deeper into the crowd toward the beleaguered nurse. "Back up or I'll clear the ER."

Heads turned in her direction as a few laughed at the threat. A room full of angry Russian cousins and hangers-on wasn't exactly intimidated by a lone female deputy at nearly two in the morning. It wasn't like she was going to pull her weapon and start shooting people.

"You should be out arresting Road Demons." Phil Moscow, standing closest to the nurse, turned his attention to Allison. As unpredictable as he was, he was the only thing keeping this from turning into a mini riot. "We got legitimate complaints, and you're in here harassing good folks."

Finally to the front of the crowd and facing one of the clan's patriarchs, Allison turned toward the room and put one hand up, imitating the nurse's futile gesture. She made sure to keep her other hand on the butt of her service weapon. She wasn't about to pull it out in the hospital, but she wasn't going to let someone else try to pull it either. "I know the staff here, I'm sure they're doing everything they can, but everyone crowding in is not helping. If you don't settle down and make room for other patients to get in, I'm going to get the entire Sheriff's Office down here and we'll clear the place."

"Good luck with that, sweetheart," came from deep in the crowd. Allison didn't love the sweetheart, but the laughter managed to break the tension.

"Please," she said more quietly. "Let me see if I can get you an update, and then we can figure out what happened."

"Road Demons happened," Phil said. Allison had noticed he didn't laugh at the sweetheart crack, and she was sure it wasn't because he was offended. "We know that. We got one of our own bleeding out back there, and you're in here—"

Allison grabbed him by the arm and started hauling him past the checkout desk. As soon as the situation had calmed down a degree, Phil was trying to ratchet it back up. The lobby behind them erupted in noise again, but no one followed. She pushed him into the first empty examining room. "Stay here." She forced herself to relax after realizing her hand had tensed on top of her weapon. Phil Moscow could have that effect on a person. "Give me two minutes to find out what's happening with Jesse, and I'll be back. Is there any family with him right now?"

"His ma."

"I'll be back." She shut the door behind her. She was two feet down the hall when the elevator at the far end opened and Doctor Serrano stepped out.

"Don't you ever sleep?" Allison asked.

"I was going to say the same to you, Deputy. I'm covering ER for a shift with so many on vacation."

"Where's Jesse Moscow?"

Serrano guided her into an open room. It would have been an exceptionally quiet night in the ER if Jesse hadn't been stabbed. "He's in surgery now. It's not going to be a murder, Deputy. The young man who brought him in did well in staunching the blood loss, which is the greatest threat in an injury like this."

"Who brought him in?" All Alison knew was what dispatch had passed on: Jesse Moscow had been stabbed and was at the ER. By the time she responded from the other side of town, the ER had managed to fill up with Russians.

"I don't know," the doctor said. "We were busy trying to save his life."

"Okay." Allison could figure that part out later. "Did he say anything that could be useful?"

"I don't think it would be betraying any confidence to say that he cursed the Road Demons motorcycle club very extensively before we sedated him."

"Anyone by name?" She asked. It would be too easy if he'd accused Squirts of stabbing him before he went under.

"No," Serrano said. "And after surgery, he'll be kept sedated for the pain. It will be hours before he can be questioned."

Allison wasn't looking forward to going back to Phil and the rest of the gang, but it seemed that was all the doctor had for her, and she needed to keep this moving. She also needed to call the sheriff regardless of the hour, but she figured delaying a few minutes to gather more information was worth it. "Thanks, Doctor Serrano. Merry Christmas."

"Merry Christmas, Deputy, and a happy New Year."

"Yeah, happy New Year."

Phil Moscow sat in a chair with an unlit cigarette hanging from his mouth. He didn't bother standing when Allison walked in. "It was the Road Demons," he said without asking about Jesse.

"He's going to be all right," Allison answered.

"He's a Moscow," Phil answered back. "I never doubted it."

"You said this was the Road Demons. Tell me what you know."

"I know it was them."

"Who else was there? Who brought Jesse in?"

Phil shrugged.

This was wasting time, and Allison had the odd thought of wishing she was talking to Frank Moscow and Matt was here. Security video would probably help identify who brought Jesse in, probably the same cousin from the Hawk's Nest the other night. Still, she pressed Phil for more information, knowing he would give none, before pushing him back to the lobby with instructions to let everyone know Jesse was in surgery and going to be okay. It took thirty seconds before he was out of the double automatic sliding doors with half the room in tow.

"Shit," Allison muttered. She slipped back into the empty examining room to make calls, sure Phil wasn't just stepping out for a smoke. She couldn't help thinking that Jesse's beating victim, Squirts, had a local connection and a solid motive for getting even.

192

She only hoped he was smart enough that he was nowhere to be found. At least for now.

Dispatch was sending Deputy Daniels her way. They would have to extend his shift, but Allison needed someone to watch over the Russians still in the waiting area. She debated calling the LT or the sheriff first, but decided this went straight to the top. The boss would want to know anyway, and at least the lieutenant could get a decent night's sleep. The voice that answered was appropriately groggy.

"Yeah."

"Boss, sorry to wake you, but it couldn't wait." Allison kept the description short, which was easy because they didn't know much. "I'm hoping the ER's CCTV can get me whoever brought Jesse in," she finished and gave the sheriff time to collect her thoughts.

"Um, darn it. I'm at my mother's, I can't get back to Mannheim tonight. Call Chris, see who else we can get on shift. Any Road Demons involved in the attack are probably lying low or out of the county by now, but let's get a presence on the road. We need to push this out to Blackhawk and Dubuque Counties. You know Jesse, find out when he can talk and question him. He probably won't talk, though."

"Do you want me to let Matt know in case he hears from Frank?"

"Shoot," she hesitated and let out a long breath. "Yeah, give him a call. But I do not want him heading out to see Frank until it's daylight. The Russians are going to be jumpy enough."

Allison thanked the boss, told her to get some sleep, and hung up.

"Yeah." Matt sounded more awake. Allison went through her spiel for the third time, adding in what the sheriff and lieutenant had said. This was exactly the type of situation where she expected Matt to start cursing. He'd never completely lost his Army-bred ability to drop an F-bomb. Instead, he repeated his, "Yeah." The next noise Allison heard may have been the most surprising thing she'd come across on a night full of surprises. It was soft, and she couldn't make out what she was saying, but she was sure she heard a woman's voice. She'd always thought Jager was hiding something, and she never one hundred percent trusted him despite Sam's affection for her uncle. But the one thing she thought she knew was that losing his wife had in some way permanently damaged the man. Not that he couldn't meet a woman and have a relationship, but he refused to. If he was dating someone, he was hiding it well. Unless it was under their noses the whole time. And he sure didn't sound surprised by the news of the attack on Jesse Moscow, which made her wonder exactly who he was in bed with.

"Unless you need me to do something," he said, sounding clear-headed. "I'm going to wait until morning and figure out next steps with Caddie."

She heard it again, soft and unintelligible. Matt Jager was not alone.

"No. I've got this for now," Allison said before letting him go. She couldn't help but wonder if the boss had just run a ruse on her by telling her to call Matt. She could understand the sheriff and Jager keeping a relationship private, but if they were together, she would resent being lied to.

Chapter 36

Matt woke to the sight of his wife in the wicker chair next to her side of the bed. She was dressed for the day, feet up on the mattress, eyes closed raised up to the sun streaming through a frost-rimmed window. A yellow light bathed her face and lightened her brunette hair. Her chest rose and fell in an easy rhythm. His breath caught as his heart sank. He'd loved her for so many years, and then she was taken away from him. He'd never recover from that, but he had gotten better. Crushing despair lifted only to be replaced with a seething anger. Dawn had saved him from that. But to what end? So he could lose himself in work. To let the investigation into Jimmy Dubcek and Dawn's murder sit at the mercy of bureaucrats in Washington who would sacrifice it in a heartbeat to the whims of politics. Together, they would discover the truth behind the deaths of Nikki and Tracy, then Dawn would fade away again. He knew that. But whatever came next, he would not lose focus on finding who was responsible for her murder. There was a time when he would have sought vengeance, but that's not what Dawn wanted. It would have to be justice.

Her lips twitched toward a lopsided smile. "What are you looking at, soldier?" Her eyes were still closed.

"A beautiful woman."

She opened her eyes and pulled her feet from the bed. "I knew that. I just wanted to hear you say it."

"How did you know I was awake? Hidden ghost powers?"

"I don't need ghost powers for that." The rising sun caught green in her eyes.

"What are you thinking about, baby?" he asked.

"You, me, Christmas, two women who should still be alive."

"That's a lot." Maybe they could stay here forever. He could watch the sun dance across her face, and she would talk to him. It would be enough for him to live in this moment. But that was a fantasy. "Any ideas? We can chase down leads on the Road Demons."

"No, dear." She pulled back hair that had fallen across her face, obeying laws of gravity she was immune to. "I want to focus on Nikki and Tracy. They're the victims. Nikki's connection to her girls is why I'm here."

"We think," he said.

"We think," she agreed. "Let Caddie chase motorcycle gangs. You and I, dear, should keep working this from the point of view of the victims. You said we started this looking for the common connection between them. There's two, their friendship and Kyle Everson."

Matt finally, reluctantly, crawled from bed. His bladder and the need to start the day pulled him from this dream. "An ongoing affair between Nikki and Kyle would explain Tracy withdrawing the last few months, and her concern about STDs. And it could mean he passed the drugs to one or both of them." He made his way to the bathroom, Dawn on his heels.

"Would that be a crime?" she asked.

"Federal felony to provide illegal drugs that lead to an overdose that causes death or requires medical intervention." He thought about Dawn's fussing when he'd make a mess of the bathroom and sat down to pee.

"That would be a good reason to act off and worry about the cops figuring it out," she said. "Is there enough to confront Everson about Nikki? I mean, there's not, is there?"

"We can demonstrate that he knows her from his visits to Decorah."

Dawn leaned against the doorframe, her arms crossed in front of her. "I'm not sure, but I think when we told him about Nikki's death, he said Tracy knew her. Not we or I, Tracy. That's another lie."

"Yep," Matt said. "Doesn't mean he did anything, but it's a lie. I could get the subpoena for the hotel signed today and served. If he's in their records, that helps. Then confront him about not mentioning that he knew her and claiming ignorance about her death."

Dawn thought while Matt washed his hands and started brushing his teeth. "Do that subpoena thing and then let's go back to looking at Nikki and see if there's a quicker way to definitively tie her to Kyle."

He glanced over to her, his face still over the sink. "I missed you," he said around his toothbrush. He got a smile as part of his answer.

"I know, dear."

Matt sipped tea and scrolled down the screen on command as Dawn sat in his office chair reading everything Claire had found on Nikki Moscow: extensive criminal history files; social media posts mostly with her daughters, a few with fellow students at Kirkwood College; long listings of relatives with criminal convictions; property records that showed she owned a good chunk of the land Matt had assumed her father held. She had taken over once he had the subpoena written and emailed to Caddie for approval. The setup in his private downtown office allowed her to have two screens up and her husband the ability to talk to her without raising worries that he was out of his mind.

"Can you get to the Patriot Inn's security footage from here, baby?" Dawn asked.

He brought it up and walked Dawn through the different views available on the surveillance system: front lot, two views of the lobby, a dining area that once offered a breakfast buffet but now looked deserted, and scattered shots of interior halls.

"Nothing in the back?" she asked, though she already knew the answer.

"It's out, along with sections of the hallways, including the one leading out back."

"Convenient."

"One way to look at it. I don't think they want to know what's going on in those rooms."

"What do you mean?" She looked up at him. Unable to resist, he bent over and kissed her on the lips, setting off a small static discharge. "Baby," she said.

"It's easier to deny any knowledge of drug distribution, prostitution, or common criminal stupidity if it's not on tape."

"Super convenient. I guess start with the lobby, best view of the desk, about an hour before we last see Nikki."

Matt leaned over and manipulated the program. "Let's call it midnight, then." Nikki Moscow appeared in washed-out colors on the monitor. The camera sat in the center of the lobby ceiling, giving a view of Nikki from above, her face still in view. A book sat open on the desk in front of her, most of it blocked from view by the high counter.

"Looks like a textbook," Dawn said.

"They found her backpack with psychology and business intro textbooks under the counter. There was more school stuff in it, but nothing that stuck out as interesting."

"I'd like to see the list." Dawn studied the young mother on the screen. It was hard for her to reconcile the image of the fit-looking student deep into a textbook past midnight while she worked with the addicted woman lying alone, dead behind the hotel. Like watching a movie you knew ended tragically, but you still pulled for the hero to survive.

Matt sped up the video, causing Nikki to turn pages and shift at speed without moving from the desk. "Nothing is going to happen until," he slowed to normal speed, "about now."

Nikki's head came up from the book, giving a clearer view of her face. The washed, gaunt look from her last mug shot for OWI was long gone and replaced by smooth skin, sharp features, and a full mouth. "She's pretty," Dawn said softly.

"Yeah."

Nikki reached forward, pulling a phone from under the counter. The video caught the screen at an angle, but it was completely unreadable. "Pause," Dawn said. "Can Claire do anything with that? Can you see what Nikki's reading?"

"No. She tried, but between the distance, light, and cheap camera, it's no use."

Nikki thumbed in a quick answer. "There was no text on her phone," Dawn said. "So she must be on that Yadda app. Maybe with the boyfriend Megan thinks she had."

"Yeah, which means whoever was contacting her and whatever they said was gone seconds after the messages were read."

Nikki set the phone back and returned to her books. Matt sped up the video again. "It's entirely possible that was her drug connection," he said. "Watch what happens twenty minutes later." He slowed to normal speed as Nikki closed her book, put a Be Right Back sign up on the counter, and turned away walking from her station. He stopped once she was gone. "That's the last we see of her."

"Go back," Dawn said. "I want to see all of that last bit at regular speed." Matt went back and hit play. Dawn bent closer, watching as Nikki smoothed her hair and touched her chest, letting her hand rest for a moment before she closed her textbook. "Back again," Dawn said in something close to a command voice. She watched it three more times before putting a hand up to stop Matt and standing. "She wasn't meeting a drug dealer, Matthew. She was primping herself to meet a boyfriend."

"Because she smoothed her hair?"

Dawn mimicked the movements, only slightly exaggerated. She smoothed her long hair, a hand running down her grey streak, finishing at the bottom of her shirt. Then she touched the center of her chest with one hand. "And she's touching a necklace. It's under her shirt, but she's touching a necklace."

"She wasn't wearing a necklace," Matt said.

Dawn gave a sly smile. "Whether she had it on that night or not, silly soldier. She had a necklace that meant something to her."

"She's touching a necklace from her boyfriend."

She stood on tiptoes, kissing him and setting off a second set of sparks in the last hour. "A necklace from a secret boyfriend who is about to give her a deadly dose of fentanyl in an area where the surveillance cameras don't work."

Chapter 37

Caddie felt pulled in two different directions. She very much wanted to keep the deaths of Nikki and Tracy as her overwhelming priority. As her favorite fictional detective liked to say, everybody matters or nobody matters. It would be easy for some to dismiss their deaths as the price paid for taking drugs, the more sympathetic lamenting the damage caused by addiction. But as far as Caddie was concerned, their deaths were murder. Someone gave them lethal doses of a deadly poison, intentionally or not. In doing so, they targeted people made vulnerable by addiction. It was like preying on the elderly for financial fraud. But after last night's stabbing, the threat of all-out war in her county loomed larger. Whoever was responsible for the OD deaths, the conflict between the Road Demons and the Russians promised a great deal more violence. And it wasn't like she was leading a large department with the resources to handle a range war. She needed to stop it now, before it got out of control.

She'd killed off half a forest printing everything Rafer had sent this morning. He'd come through on the jackets on the Demon's leadership and members, and even the Dirty Devils support club, one of whose members was feeding ATF intelligence. A few of the names were already familiar to her, starting with club president Jackson Strange, aka Strangler. She'd run into him twice already and knew in her gut they weren't done with one another. She sipped her coffee and picked up his packet again. Thirty-eight, born in Waterloo, made it through a year in the Army before getting booted with a dishonorable, then spent nearly two decades racking up an impressive record of arrests and convictions. Domestic assault, good old plain assault with a deadly weapon, a hammer in that case, multiple drug possessions, mostly dope but also coke and meth with the intent to distribute. Three stints in state prison lasting from thirteen months to four years. Nothing federal.

The rest of the leadership looked much the same: drugs, violence, convictions, and back out on the street. Another name stuck out, William Sexton, aka Squirts, listed as the club enforcer. That was a little surprising as he wasn't a particularly big guy, but if Allison's suspicions were right, he was responsible for stabbing Jesse Moscow as revenge for getting worked over outside the Hawk's Nest. Willing to do what needed to get done was probably a better qualification for enforcer than how big you were. The age and place of birth were interesting, too. Identical to Strangler's. Seemed like a good chance they'd grown up together, which meant they were tight. The counties listed for Demons' arrests blanketed the eastern third of the state without spilling over into Illinois. Fillmore was right in the middle of that blanket, and not a single arrest for anything. She accepted the idea that the Demons hadn't been arrested in Fillmore County, but it wasn't because they weren't active here. "Damn Jimmy Dubcek," she muttered to herself.

The lieutenant, geared up and ready to head out on patrol, stuck his head in Caddie's office. "You wanted to see me, ma'am?"

"Road Demons," she said, which brought him fully in. "Let's make them uncomfortable in Fillmore County. Don't let our guys make anything up, but any violations, rolling stop, muffler too loud, expired tags, anything. Pull them over, run them, cite them. And if anyone runs across William Sexton, who goes by Squirts, Allison wants to talk to him about the Jesse Moscow stabbing."

"Squirts?"

"Yeah, Squirts."

The LT shook his head. "They'll know we're watching them at any rate." He had a small grin, which was the LT's equivalent of overwhelming joy. "I looked at the schedule. I can get an additional deputy on the road the next two nights if you want to pay overtime. We're already scheduled heavy for New Year's Eve, so that gets us through the next three."

"Do it. I'll figure out the budget later," she said. "I'll even try to get out there myself."

"And the Moscow and Everson deaths?"

"That too," she said.

"You can't do it all, Sheriff," he said, softening to almost a personal tone.

She stood, ready to head out herself. She'd done what she could about the Demons and Russians for now. Back to the other priority. "They pay me to do it all."

"Not enough."

"No," she agreed. "Not even close."

The owner and sole instructor of the yoga studio knew Tracy and Nikki. Tracy remained a regular up to her death. She hadn't seen Nikki in months, with work, school, and her girls, yoga got squeezed out. "It's too bad. I thought the exercise and mindfulness—"

Mindfulness, Caddie thought to herself. *I'll stick with the exercise bike.*

"—were good for her. I sensed that she had a lot of healing to do. But I understood. Tracy was five times a week, every week, until about the last month, she trailed off a little to two or three times."

Through the woman's touchy-feely talk, Caddie latched onto something. "When did Tracy start with you?"

"We opened the end of June, right after the derecho. Tracy and Nikki were some of my first clients. I was very thankful. It's hard to start a business in a small town, and I can use every customer I can get. You should think about it yourself, Sheriff. Not just for you, but for your department. The combination of exercise and peacefulness could be very beneficial. I would offer a law enforcement discount."

Peacefulness. Caddie looked around the studio with its bamboo walls and long trailing plants. She wanted to make fun of it a little, but for all her 'nesses', the studio owner wasn't wrong about it being hard to start a business in a small town or that it might be good for some of her staff. Her head was feeling fine now, but she wondered if a little yoga might do more good than a doctor. "Send me something. No promises, but I'll let people know."

"Thank you, so much."

Back to the investigation. "Did Nikki and Tracy attend together?"

"Same morning class. I don't think they drove together, but they chatted and always worked next to one another. They were friends."

Then Caddie circled back to the remark that caught her attention. "Do you know why Tracy's attendance fell off?"

She had to think, which gave Caddie time to wonder how many shades of blonde the yoga instructor had streaked into her hair. She

202

also had a fleeting thought that she should introduce her to Matt. She was close to their age, fit, a business owner, and for some reason, she thought just the type to fawn all over a lawyer deputy who had money and stayed in shape. It wasn't nice, but she thought that's exactly what the yoga lady would like. She quickly threw the idea away; it felt like a betrayal, but for some reason not of Matt.

She shook her head. "I don't know. She still came to class, but she never gave herself completely to it."

Caddie had a few more questions, but wrapped up quickly. People kept singing the same song. Tracy was good, until she wasn't, and no one knew why. One explanation was drugs. The other was her husband having an affair with her best friend. Either way, it led to her death.

Chapter 38

The Patriot Inn made a half-hearted attempt at Christmas with a paper Santa and Rudolph taped to the check-in counter. The window facing out onto a wet blacktop lot held a Merry Christmas banner in Red, White, and Blue. A warming fog obscured the view of the highway, but the slush of tires across wet blacktop cut through to the small lobby.

"Not exactly the Winneshiek Inn, is it, dear?" Dawn was on the other side of the counter, peeking into cubbies and corners before the manager finally responded to the bell.

"Good morning, good morning, welcome to the Patriot Inn, America's favorite destination." The obligatory greeting wouldn't have bothered Matt so much if the man hadn't been so enthusiastic about it. Dressed for the part in blue pants, white shirt, and red tie, the manager sported what Matt estimated to be the last full comb-over in the county. "Will you be staying with us today?"

Dawn shook her head inches from the manager's. "Um, no, we will not. And you really need to vacuum better back here." Then she popped down, looking through open shelves.

Matt wasn't exactly sure what she had gone into full detective mode looking for, she was holding her thoughts close as she worked through them. He guessed he would have to respect the process. Luckily, he had his own questions for the manager. He flashed his badge. "No, not looking for a room. I'm Deputy Matt Jager with the Fillmore County Sheriff's Office. I'd like to ask you a few questions about Nikki Moscow and take a look around if that's not a problem." He didn't actually care if it was a problem, but it didn't hurt to stay on the good side of potential voters for Caddie.

"That was tragic." Some of the bravado from his welcome was gone, and the manager, Gary by his nametag, slumped a bit. "She was a good person and a really good worker. I'm still in shock."

Dawn popped up, a big smile for her husband. "Not seeing anything, babe. I want to look around the hotel after you and Gary are done chatting."

Matt tried not to smile at Dawn as she stood next to Gary, leaning over the counter and resting her chin on her hand. Maybe she should have slept more last night instead of watching him. "What can I do you for, soldier?" She winked. Then again, maybe she was just trying to find a moment of fun and flirt in the middle of what promised to be a short visit.

"Um," Matt said, thinking of what she could do for him. "Gary, did you see any signs that Nikki was using again? I know you answered these questions for the sheriff, but I was hoping something more may have come to mind."

"No." He shook his head, eyes down. "She never missed a day's work, was never even late. She always had everything tiptop when I came in in the morning."

Matt re-asked the questions Caddie hit already in the hopes that an answer would change, and he could pry something else out of Gary. Dawn, evidently bored and unable to command her husband's undivided attention, began wandering behind the counter. Her eyes casually passed over stacks of free drink coupons for the Hawk's Nest, a sticky note reminder in a woman's handwriting to order more ice melt, and a well-thumbed Land's End catalog. Then, she stopped and slowly held up her hand like a third grader who thought they might know the answer.

"Thanks, Gary. I appreciate the help," Matt said. "I'm just going to look around and then be out of your hair." He managed not to look at the comb-over when he said the last. Pulling his phone out, he wandered closer to the window and Dawn pretending to check his email. Gary didn't make things easier, standing there looking straight ahead for customers who weren't coming in.

"Dear," Dawn said, looking down at a monitor tucked into the corner of the desk, "they've got their surveillance feed going here. I can see the front and side lots, the halls on the second floor, and half the hall on the first." She looked up at him. "There are two blank black boxes. How much do you want to see what Gary doesn't want to see?"

He glanced back at Gary, who looked willing to stand and wait for work for as long as it took. "A whole bunch," he said very, very softly.

Matt snapped pictures with his phone. The little black balls in the ceiling of the first-floor hall, the short hall that led out the back to where Nikki was found dead, then the signs pointing to rooms by number. He let Dawn direct him, though by now he knew what she wanted anyway.

"Gary." Matt stood in the entry to the area behind the desk. His appearance shook the manager out of his waiting state. "You have a map of the inn's interior for guests?"

"Sure." He pulled a printout with the Patriot Inn logo, lots of red, white, and blue, and a diagram of both floors.

"Thanks." Matt took it and walked straight past the man to the security video monitor, Dawn right behind him.

"You're about to make old Gary very nervous, babe."

"Good," he said out loud.

Dawn pointed at the map and read off room numbers for him. In seconds, Matt had the area of the hotel that was effectively blacked out circled and turned to face Gary, who couldn't have given a cheery morning greeting now if he was paid better.

"Gary." This time, Matt was the cheery one. "Let's look at some rooms."

They stood under the black bulb that gave the video system a view of nothing, Gary protesting that this was all the fault of the corporate office for not wanting to spend money to fix the security system properly.

"Really," Dawn drew out the word.

"Really," Matt said, having more fun than should have been allowed in a death investigation. They were making real progress and he was with his wife, the love of his life and beyond. And it was Christmas. Even in this imperfect existence, there should have been so many more things he should be doing, but he wouldn't trade this moment for anything. "See, the sheriff is really good at her job, but she's been busy, and what with the holidays, she just hasn't had time to call Patriot Inn headquarters and confirm your story about the cameras. Why don't we save her the time? You give me corporate's number and we can clear it up right now."

"The shark is back, and Gary needs a bigger boat." Dawn was having as much fun as he was. If he could, he'd pull her close, kiss her like it was a black and white movie, call her dollface, and let the scene fade to black as they kept the rest off-screen.

"I don't know, with Christmas and everything." The collar of Gary's white shirt grew darker with sweat.

"Okay, Gare, let me tell you what I think," Matt said. "You don't want these cameras working. Maybe someone is dealing drugs out of these rooms, or an escort service sets up shop sometimes. Or, Gary has got something going on that corporate doesn't know about. Hooking up with a fling, maybe."

"Gary wouldn't do that," Dawn joined in.

"I don't know anything about drugs or hookers," Gary protested.

"Not sure I believe him, dear," Dawn said.

"I don't believe him either," Matt said to a confused manager. "And if I can prove someone was running dope through here and Gary knew and Nikki died because of that dope, Gary is going to go to federal prison for a long time."

Whether it was the accusation or Matt's insistence on speaking of him in the third person, the manager broke. "I don't know anything about drugs. This is a cheap hotel on a highway and people get up to all kinds of stuff here. That's not why the cameras are out."

"They're out because?" Matt asked.

Gary pulled a key card from his pocket and motioned for Matt to follow. "It's not what you think."

Matt insisted on entering the room first and making a quick search while he kept an eye on Gary in the doorway. Convinced the manager wasn't about to pull a hidden weapon and shoot it out, he relaxed as Dawn began searching the room. He lifted the covers for her to see under the bed.

"Yuck, but thank you." She made quick work of it.

"Okay, Gary," Matt said. "Talk."

"We had some minor flooding in this room a few years back, and we took it out of circulation to replace the carpet and fix the bathroom."

Dawn stood, brushing non-existent dirt off her jeans. "It's dusty and a little disgusting down there, but the carpet looks fairly new."

"And you never put it back up for customers," Matt guessed.

Gary shook his head. "No. Corporate seemed to have forgotten, and I was working a lot of night shifts, and we have apps on our phones that connect to the front desk buzzer, so I'll hear if someone wants to check in. I would come back here and catch a couple of hours of sleep."

"Or more," Dawn said.

"You told Nikki when she started working nights?" Matt asked.

"Yeah, not at first, but she was good and I knew she was busy with school and kids." Gary was back to looking sympathetically sad. "I was just trying to help her. A couple of hours' sleep can make all the difference."

"Was she meeting someone here?"

"I don't know."

Dawn wagged a finger in Gary's direction. "No, Gary. Truth now."

"Gary," Matt said.

The manager's face pleaded before he opened his mouth. "I don't know, not for sure."

"But," Dawn said. Matt repeated it.

The manager let out a long breath. "But, I think so. She didn't say, and I didn't ask, but even though she fixed the bed up after, it kind of looked like more than one person had been here. Plus, I knew Nikki drank diet pop, but sometimes there were regular Pepsi cans in the trash."

"Regular Pepsi is a clue, babe," Dawn said. "Mark that down."

Matt nodded; he'd mark it down. "Now that we're being completely honest, Gary. Is there anything you told me or the sheriff you want to change or add to? Is there any illegal activity, like drug trafficking, going on here?"

"Not that I know. As long as someone doesn't tear the place up or bother other guests, I'm not looking too close at what they're doing."

"You ever get the Road Demons motorcycle club coming through here?" Matt asked.

Dawn moved close to him. "Trying to bring it full circle, detective?"

"Sometimes," Gary said. "Ones and twos, no big groups, but sure, I've seen some over the years."

"Could you identify them?"

"No," Gary said with as much force as his morning greeting. Matt was sure that if Strangler himself walked into the room and confessed that Gary was his brother, the manager would deny ever having seen him before. But Dawn was right, while the circle wasn't closed, it was growing closer.

The back of the Patriot Inn was no less depressing without a driving drizzle. Dawn walked the space, keeping an eye on the ground, mainly to get a feel for where Nikki died. Matt supposed she was trying to keep a connection to the woman and her life. Eventually, she stopped and stood close to Matt, leaning her head against his shoulder. Unable to feel her weight, he kept an eye on their shadows to know that she was there with him. "So, what do you think?"

"It's sad," she said. "It seems like Nikki and Tracy were handling their sobriety very differently. Tracy was wealthy, with only the responsibilities she wanted to take on. Compared to Nikki, it looks like she had an easier path."

"It's never easy."

"No, and it only looks that way for Tracy. I don't think her husband loved her." She looked up at Matt, her eyes meeting his before they kissed, and the smallest of sparks replaced the feel of their lips. "Not like you love me. And not like Nikki's girls loved her. Heck, I'll even give Frank credit, for everything that is wrong with that family, and that's a lot, they love one another. Nikki had a purpose and a plan and fought every day to not only stay sober but to improve her girls' lives. I can't help thinking she stayed clean."

"You just want to believe that," Matt said. "Because you are kind and caring, and it's your way of protecting the girls' memories of their mom."

"Maybe." She stood straighter, shaking off the melancholy, and forced a smile. "So, do you want to know what I think?"

"Okay, Sherlock, what you got?"

"I'd rather be Nora. She wore great hats."

"All right, Nora it is. What's been brewing all day in that incredibly cute head of yours?"

She pointed back inside. "Nikki is at the desk studying while working an overnight job. And it's between semesters, which means she was reading ahead. That's a hard-working mom. Then she gets a message on an encrypted app."

"Suspicious."

"Not so much. She smooths out her hair and shirt, she reaches to feel a necklace—"

"There's no necklace in her clothes inventory," Matt cut in. "And you can't see one on the video."

"Right." She raised a finger, then a second. "There are two possibilities. She forgot to wear it, or she had it on under her shirt."

"Why would she—"

She went back to one finger, this time to tell Matt to stop interrupting her. "You wear a necklace under your shirt because you don't want people to see it. Maybe it's a religious medallion, or just maybe it's from a boyfriend and you don't want people to see and question it."

He interrupted her despite the finger. "You're saying the message was from a boyfriend, not a drug dealer?"

She let the interruption go, but the finger-pointing grew stronger. She would accept no more. "You don't make sure you're looking your best for your dope dealer. You do for the boyfriend Megan is certain her mother had. But Gary's secret room is the real clue, dear." She opened her hand, inviting him to speak now.

"Because that's where they hook up."

She let out a sigh. "Cruder than I would have put it, but yes. She and her boyfriend used the room. Claire already found that there are nights where Nikki is gone from the desk for an hour. Some of those may have been her getting a nap, some were her and whoever she was seeing. But, the poor girl was a smoker, so when they were finished, she came out here and had a cigarette."

"And died of an OD."

"The boyfriend was still here, Matt."

"He can't just run off after sex. They talk while she smokes. Then normally, she heads back to the desk and he leaves, but that night, he saw her die."

"He gave her the drugs, baby."

Matt let it sink in. This pointed them at one man, but that could be a mistake. "We have nothing solid proving Nikki and Everson were still together. We don't even know for certain that they had ever been together. And anyone who provided her drugs that killed her has motive to run. We could get a search warrant for the room and collect the sheets for DNA."

"Ick, but we could."

He was about to talk this all out with his lovely, bright wife when his phone pinged. He looked at the message and slipped it back away. "Got a mission from Caddie." He looked into his wife's eyes, burning the love he saw into his memory for the days when he would need it. "This feels like we are about to start moving very fast."

"It does, dear." And fast meant the end, and that meant Dawn would leave. But they couldn't let that stop them.

Chapter 39

Matt and Dawn waited in the common area as the staff member manning the front desk went to check if the Eversons were taking visitors. The tree and lights remained from the Christmas party, but Santa and reindeer had been replaced by paper streamers and plastic bells. The snowmen and stars survived the changeover, now under a banner reading HAPPY NEW YEAR.

"Bet nobody makes it until midnight for a kiss," Matt said, knowing the second it was out of his mouth, he was going to pay for it.

"Matthew," Dawn managed to speak and purse her lips at the same time, "be nice. We should have been so lucky." That hurt, and he could see Dawn also regretted it the moment it came out of her mouth. "Oh, baby. I'm sorry. That was mean of me. I promise you a New Year's kiss."

"Promise?" he asked, thinking of the ever-present fear that she could leave at any moment.

"Yes," Dawn said. She meant it.

The front desk person had been replaced by Denise, Barb's RN. Matt got a better look at her this time and was struck by the similarity to Tracy. Trim, athletic, blonde not entirely natural hair, but with more makeup than she really needed. She could have been Kyle's wife, only ten years younger. "Mr. Everson wasn't sure Barb was up to it, but when I told him that it was you, he said to tell you to come on to the room. He must like you, because that's about as excited about a visit as I've seen him get. It has been a long week with the holidays and all the excitement, so I'm not sure how alert Barb will be."

"Not to mention the death of their daughter-in-law," Dawn spoke directly to Denise, expecting Matt to translate. "I want to know about Barb's memory issues. Cognitive decline hits everyone differently." Not that he ever forgot, but his sly, sexy, angel wife held a Master's in Education. He'd always known she was smarter than he was.

"I know Barb has memory issues. Is it short-term, long-term? How does it work for her?" he asked.

"Exactly what I was getting at," Dawn approved.

Denise gave a nervous smile. "Generally, Barb's long-term memory is pretty good. We see this a lot. She can tell you about watching the moon landing on TV or how she worried when John was in Vietnam. But her short-term memory is very poor, and sometimes she's confused. She will tell you about John being in Vietnam like he's still there. Then, when he walks into the room, her heart just lights up. It's both very sweet and sad at the same time."

"Does she realize Tracy has passed away and how?" Dawn asked, and Matt passed it on.

Denise cleared her throat. "We had the counselor talk to her. She was very upset, but a half hour later, you wouldn't be able to tell. I expect in a few days she'll ask when Tracy is going to visit. Then we'll have to decide whether to tell her the truth and watch her get upset again, or push the answer off, knowing her mind will move on quickly enough."

Another question pressed at him. He told himself not to ask, but didn't listen. "What about her husband? Does she ever forget who he is or not recognize him?" It had nothing to do with the case; it was not a question that needed asking, except for Matt. The idea that he could ever forget his Dawn came as a sickening surprise.

"Never," Denise said. "I don't think there's a second that Barb doesn't know who he is or forgets that he's here for her."

"Never," Dawn whispered to him. "You will never forget me. I will be in your heart and head until the moment we are together again. I promise." The promise steeled Matt for what remained ahead. They would put this case to rest before his Dawn left him again. But the next part might not be pleasant.

John Everson met them at the door, welcoming Matt in with a handshake. The room behind them looked comfortably like a small apartment. A kitchenette held a small fridge, sink unit, and microwave. The rest of the furniture, minus the hospital bed at the far end, obviously came from the Everson house, the curtains were thick red, and out of date. Dawn liked the effect. It was a home.

"John, first, I want to offer my condolences on Tracy's death. I'm sorry, I was there in the house at the end. I know the EMTs did everything they could," Matt said.

"Thank you, come in. Barb's down the hall with physical therapy. You might as well take a seat. You're investigating Tracy's overdose?"

Matt quickly explained the law and a very incomplete outline of what they'd been looking at, including the death of Nikki Moscow. Everson took it calmly.

Matt sat on the small couch against the wall, while John took the worn leather recliner facing the television. He clicked the set off and turned to Matt.

"I'm glad you're on this. She and this other woman deserve someone looking out for them. I don't know what I can tell you, but go ahead with your questions."

"I'm hoping you might be able to fill in gaps during Tracy's final days and some general background information."

Everson nodded, waiting for the questions.

"Did Tracy visit often?"

"She did," John nodded. "She came to visit regularly, even though half the time Barb wasn't sure who she was. But she came and they chatted. She was a doll, brushing Barb's hair and talking about nothing for an hour."

Dawn wanted to let Matt work without interruption, but decided that was for when she wasn't here. "Not how Kyle talked about Tracy and his parents. Ask him about Christmas Day." Dawn did not like liars, and whatever else the younger Everson was, he was a liar more than once over. That put him on her suspect list on its own. Exactly what she suspected him of, she'd decide later.

"She didn't come for Christmas, though?" Matt asked.

"No, Tracy came Christmas Eve during the day. The girls chatted and had cookies. Barb recognized her right off, which was nice for both of them."

"Then Kyle visited on Christmas Day?" Matt asked. This was the moment that would cement any suspicions the senior Everson might have about Matt's visit. They were looking into his son's whereabouts at the time of his wife's death. Dawn wouldn't be surprised if Everson shut her hubby down.

214

"He did," he said, looking at the blank television screen. "He came by for twenty minutes or so in the evening."

"Did they often visit at different times?"

The line crossed, Everson could look at Matt directly again. "Tracy would visit during the afternoon, which was good because that's when Barb is at her best. Kyle visited less than Tracy. Usually, a quick stop in at night once a week or so."

"What time did Kyle leave on Christmas?"

"I don't know." Everson shook his head. "Early."

"Any idea where he might have gone from here?"

"No." Everson was back to watching the blank television screen. He'd crossed the line, but he didn't like being there.

"Oh, dear, baby," Dawn said. Her suspicions of the younger Everson solidified in her mind. He was the man having the secret affair with Nikki that Megan was sure of. He was there when she died. Then, days later, his wife takes a fatal overdose, and he lies about where he was. She whispered the words to not upset Matt's questioning, but they needed to be said. "It's murder, Matt. Two murders. Unless you have something really important, maybe that's it for now, dear. We all have a lot to absorb."

Matt's eyes flicked to hers. He paused before recovering. He thanked Everson and passed his card with the usual call if you think of anything.

"Tracy was a good kid," Everson said.

"These deaths are going to tear more than one family apart," Dawn said. Matt waited until they were walking out the door to answer.

"Murder has a way of doing that."

Chapter 40

It wasn't an argument. Matt liked to lie to himself and say that he and Dawn had never argued, not once. But that wasn't real life, and he knew he owed his wife more credit than that. Dawn could get angry and fuss at him and punish him with the cold shoulder, knowing that killed him. She could even, on the rarest of occasions, be wrong. But she wasn't this time and she stuck by what she'd said.

"It's murder, Matt. Kyle Everson killed his wife, one hundred percent. No doubt in my mind. He drugged her, waited until she was dead or nearly dead on the couch, and left the house for more than two hours, knowing there would be no helping her when he got back and called 911."

"And Nikki?" Matt parked on Main down from Jill's, so no one would look out the window and see him having an animated conversation with himself. "We don't know for sure that she was having an affair with him—"

"She was."

"She might have been. But what motive does he have for either of them? And where does he get fentanyl? Is he in with the Road Demons now?"

She crossed her arms and tightened her face. It wasn't a cold shoulder, but it let him know she was unhappy, though still in love, with him. "I don't know. But it's murder, I know it. And we need to go see your boss. Maybe she'll listen to reason."

"If she could hear you." Matt said, opening his door.

"Meanie," Dawn said, and meant it, even if just for a moment.

Caddie was already in the booth farthest from the door. Matt ordered a pot of tea, Caddie had her coffee, and Dawn told Bev not to worry, she wasn't having anything today. Bev, naturally, didn't react, but Dawn could have sworn Caddie's eyes flicked in her direction as her fingers went lightly to her temple. Time for another test.

"Hey!" Dawn yelled. Matt jumped in his seat as the sheriff stared placidly ahead. "Hey! Sheriff Lady, over here." Dawn waved her hand violently in front of Caddie's face.

"What's up with you?" Caddie asked Matt through Dawn's waving hand.

"Nothing. Thought I heard something."

Dawn snapped her fingers twice in front of Caddie's face, causing Matt to blink, but getting nothing from the sheriff. "I swear, baby. Caddie hears and sees me, but she doesn't think she does." She turned and scrunched her nose at Matt. "I think you broke the girl's brain. That's two things you're in trouble for."

Bev saved Matt with tea and warnings about it being hot. She stayed at the table and topped Caddie off.

"You two compare notes," Dawn said in a sing-song happy voice. "I'll let you talk while I gaze lovingly at my handsome, sweet, meanie of a husband." She got a quick look from Matt as Caddie reached into her pocket for her notepad. "What, you are sweet and handsome, a little mean, and oh so stubborn? But I love you."

He couldn't mouth it back with Caddie watching him from three feet away, so he pointed under the table at Dawn. "Thank you, dear," she said.

Caddie started off with her interview of the yoga studio owner and her observations about Tracy and Nikki's friendship, and that Tracy's attendance had trailed off near the end. She'd also stopped by Downtown Coffee, whose owner had the same story. "What bugs me," Caddie said, "is that this is at least the second time Everson hasn't been straight with us. He insisted Tracy and Nikki had no relationship after rehab, that's clearly not true."

"Maybe he didn't know," Matt said.

"Don't defend him, dear," Dawn tsked.

"Possible," Caddie admitted. "But he knew they were good friends at the clinic, then they're meeting multiple times a week for yoga for the first two months after release, and she doesn't mention that at all? Why downplay their relationship?"

"Because it points to a relationship between him and Nikki," Dawn said. "Plus, he killed them. Now, tell her about Kyle's Christmas lies."

Matt did exactly that, telling Caddie about their conversation with John Everson. "First, Dad denies any rift between Kyle's mother and Tracy. He said Tracy was nice—"

"A doll," Dawn said.

"A doll," Matt quoted, "who visited her mother-in-law a couple of times a week. Kyle had said that he visited his parents alone on Christmas because of mom's memory issues. That was not true. There's also how long he was there. He was gone from the house nearly three hours, Dad says he visited for twenty or thirty minutes."

"Boom." Dawn shot off a finger pistol. "Kyle Everson is a lying liar who killed his wife."

Matt cut Caddie off with a warning hand. "Not done. When you texted me about visiting the parents, I was at the Patriot Inn where I got an interesting admission from Gary the manager." He detailed the off-the-books room that was used for employees to rack out, and Gary's suspicions that Nikki had been using the room to see someone. "I think he's right. Whether it was because she was so busy, or to keep it separate from her girls, or to hide it all together, Nikki was using the room at the Inn for their assignations."

"Assignations," Dawn said cheerily, "nice word for a soldier. Don't forget to mention the necklace, that's a clue, dear."

"On top of that, there's a thing on the tape, too. Dawn had this habit of touching the little crucifix she wore, like this," he said, touching his chest. "Nikki does that after she got the message on her phone. I think her boyfriend gave her a necklace that she either forgot to wear or was under her shirt."

"That's a stretch," Caddie said, "but the room is interesting. If it was Everson, he had to be using the back door not to show up on the cameras."

"Sure," Matt said. "He parks his truck out back so no one sees it in front of the hotel at two in the morning."

"You came up with that quick, dear," Dawn said. "Too quick."

"I'll have Claire go back as far as possible on the hotel security footage and see if we can find a pattern," Caddie said. "Then there's Everson's home security camera. It would be too simple to see him leave the night Nikki dies."

"He's so darn busy, he sleeps at work a couple of times a week," Dawn said. "So darn busy having an affair, he meant." Matt passed it on.

Caddie started thinking through the case out loud. "Tracy and Nikki bond in rehab. Kyle doesn't visit a lot at first until he meets Nikki. Suddenly, he's the attentive husband."

"Creep," Dawn added.

"Tracy is discharged, and the clinic director sees Everson's truck outside a Decorah hotel. The hotel clerk confirms meeting Nikki. Nikki is released and reconnects with Tracy, but either there's a falling out between them or their lives just go in different directions, and eventually, Tracy's mental state seems to regress. She also gets tested for STDs because she believes Kyle is having an affair, whether she suspects Nikki or not. Kyle makes himself absent when Tracy dies and lies to us about it. Kyle is the link between them, but here's the thing—"

"Who was he seeing on Christmas?" Dawn asked. "Nikki was already dead."

"Who was he seeing on Christmas?" Caddie said. "Nikki was already dead."

"How many affairs do you think Everson was having?" Matt protested.

Dawn picked up their argument while Caddie sipped her coffee and thought. "He could have just stayed at Mom and Dad's, but didn't. I'm just mad I didn't see that, it practically bit us in the nose."

Caddie gave the slightest blink. "What if Nikki's OD was an accident? Everson is there, sees it, and thinks it's a good way to kill his wife?"

"Rotten turd," Dawn said, happy to have come up with another name for Everson.

Caddie shook her head. "Whatever exactly happened, we need a motive or a lot more evidence before we officially call this murder."

"He's a jerk," Dawn offered as motive.

"He's an asshole," Matt said.

"Not how I put it, dear."

"He is a jerk," Caddie said. "But I want more than that when we question him again."

It was during this back and forth that Matt slowly began to realize that denying Dawn's existence to Caddie was a mistake. He felt guilty for how he treated both of them. Dawn never deserved to be denied, and Caddie had more than earned the truth from him. He just had no idea how to fix it.

"You want motive," Matt said. "Let's look at the company. Everson says they're busy and growing. Does he want to take it public or sell it to a big defense contractor? Cutting Tracy out of that money could be a motive. Was he planning on divorcing her? What would that cost him?"

"That sounds like your area of expertise. Start with that tomorrow," Caddie said. "Plus, subpoenas for the bedding at Patriot's Inn, and see if the FBI can issue a preservation letter to the company holding Everson's security camera video before he deletes it somehow. The other thing we want to know before we go at him again, assuming we're right about all of this, is who else was he seeing. I think that starts with you talking to Kyle's father again."

"You already have me working up Flightline," Matt said.

"I know. I'd say you take the business and I take the father, but it sounds like you two have built a rapport."

"They're buddies," Dawn said, "which is an upgrade over Frank Moscow."

"Besides," Caddie sighed and pushed her empty coffee cup away, "involved or not, and I'm still not ruling them out, I've got the Road Demons to deal with, and until we put this investigation to bed, that's only going to get worse."

"It might get worse, whatever you do," Matt said.

Caddie slid to the edge of the bench, ready to head home, take some aspirin, and rest for tomorrow. "Merry frickin Christmas. You can pay." She called out a nicer farewell to Bev and was out the door.

"I like her," Dawn said.

"Me, too."

Dawn stood, holding out her hand for her husband to follow. "Just not too much, okay, soldier. You still belong to me."

Matt and Dawn walked the neighborhood. The cloud cover hadn't left and the air remained unseasonably moderate. A soft wind gently

220

shook trees strung with lights. They held hands that didn't touch, they kissed lips that only gave the smallest spark.

"I don't know how," Dawn said. "But we need to fix your friend."

"What about me?" he smiled.

"Beyond fixing, but still mine." She kissed him again and they walked on.

Chapter 41
December 29th

"This is boring." Dawn lay on the leather couch in Matt's office, arm over her eyes.

"No kitty cat show today?" Matt didn't take his eyes off the computer monitor, his fingers tapping away as the printer spat out more pages. The morning had been spent in the exciting work of drafting subpoenas and a search warrant for Patriot's Inn he sent along to Caddie, and a request for the ISP holding Everson's surveillance video to retain the data Matt passed to Rafer. He also worked up a batch of subpoenas for Kyle Everson's bank, credit cards, and DNA that he filed away for the future. Then it was on to research.

"Kitty cat shows are for cowboys. You're not very cowboy today."

"This is investigating, dear."

"No." She uncovered her eyes and dramatically turned on her side to face him. "Investigating is clues and chasing bad guys in dark alleys. It's in all the best shows."

Matt stopped typing and scrolled down a page on the screen. "This is interesting."

"Bet it's not."

"Flightline Avionics had three Suspicious Activity Reports filed on it during its first ten years of existence."

"Not interesting," Dawn said. "Not yet, anyway. Is that a bad number?"

"Not in the business they're in," Matt said. "These read like banks just being careful."

"Because we know how careful banks like to be." She sat up, but didn't look ready to leave the couch.

"The dollar amounts are reasonable, but they were overseas sales for a company that didn't have a record of that at the time. The banks were unable to confirm the original source of funds, so they filed reports, but I think the money was moving through legitimate brokers. But then, no reports for years even as the business grew."

"The banks stopped being suspicious."

"Yeah, the sales likely matched previous established history, no red flags raised."

"And then?"

Matt glanced up to see his wife sitting cross-legged on his coffee table, a bright smile on her face, a purple Santa hat perched on her head.

"And then, Santa Baby, two reports early last year for sales to a company listed in Cyprus, with the money moving through a bank in Panama. First one was for thirteen grand, another for forty-three thousand a month later." He smiled at her as if he'd found something worthwhile.

"And we find this suspicious because?" She winked at him in a silent, highly effective flirt.

"Because, you naughty little Santa, Everson said his business expanded into Eastern Europe. Clients Tracy helped him get. Remember Eastern European businessmen looking for a night on the town? If this is the start of that, why no banks or companies in Prague or Warsaw, or a dozen other major cities? Why a company in a small country with little in the way of an aviation industry and a bank in a country known for weak banking regulations?"

She shrugged and blew him a kiss. "I don't know, you tell me, detective."

He crooked his finger, motioning her forward. "Come here, you." She popped up, bounced to the side of his desk, and bent over for a kiss. The spark popped loud enough to open both their eyes wide. "Yowzah," he said. "Look here." He shrunk the PDF showing the banking reports and expanded a webpage from Flightline. The top read Business Partners. Scrolling down, Matt showed Dawn pictures of smiling customers, nearly all men in suits, with Kyle and Tracy. Intermixed were logos of avionics companies and regional airlines in the U.S. and overseas. "U.S. and Mexico, Peru, Italy, Sweden, and three German companies. You know what you don't see?"

"Anyone from Eastern Europe," Dawn answered. "So he was lying."

"Maybe not," Matt said. "Maybe it's just Eastern European countries you don't want people to know you're doing business with."

"And you gave me a hard time for deciding Nikki and Tracy were murdered." She put her hand on his shoulder, he pretended he could feel the weight. "You have what I believe you would call conjecture. You're going to have to prove all of this."

"I'd rather go home and play reindeer games with you."

She laughed a wonderful, full, happy laugh. The kind that made him want to cry and hug her at the same time. The kind that he would lock away in his memory and bring out months and years from now when he would need it to get through the night.

"Worst sex euphemism, ever," she said.

———

Caddie set a chai tea latte from Downtown Coffee on Claire's desk, followed by a strawberry muffin.

"Boss, you shouldn't have." She spun and grabbed both treats, pulling them in greedily. "But I'm so glad you did." She set the muffin aside to attack the latte. "Not to complain or brag, but I've been in since five this morning digging into the Road Demons."

"Sorry about that. Did you talk to Bob? If you really want to end it, he needs to hear it from you."

"Not, yet." Claire waved it away. "His family has tickets for Elf the Musical in Cedar Rapids tonight, but I told him that I probably couldn't make it with two deaths and a gang war ready to blow up. I know, I need to make a clean break of it. It just sucks that I didn't realize it until we were in the middle of the holidays. It really seems like the wrong time to break up."

"I am an expert at breaking up," Caddie laughed. "Trust me, there's never a good time. You just have to do it. It's the right thing for both of you."

Claire let out a long breath. "Not having a boyfriend is easier."

"Men can be fun at times," Caddie said. "Tell him you have to work tonight, that at least gets you out of seeing the play. But meet him for coffee tomorrow and just do it. I can make that an order if I need to."

"Thanks, I guess."

"Okay, enough love life advice from me. I want to hear what you've got on the Demons. They're not in the clear on the ODs, not by a long shot, and I'm afraid they represent a long-term problem, but what I really need is for you to dig into Flightline Avionics."

"What are we thinking?"

Caddie filled her in on what she and Matt had discovered over the last day, none of which had made it into a report yet, something they would have to fix. "I don't want to prejudge anything, but it's entirely possible that Kyle Everson was having an affair with Nikki Moscow. It fits with Tracy's concern over STDs, her pulling back from the business, and her general mental state. It fits with Megan believing her mother was secretly seeing someone. We don't know for sure, but it also looks like Tracy and Nikki weren't as close as they once were, whether that was from a falling out or their lives just drifting apart, who knows."

"But fits the pattern," Claire said.

"Right. If Everson is the person Nikki was seeing while she was at work, he was there when she OD'ed, and it looks like he has unaccounted for time on Christmas night and may have visited mom and dad to set up an alibi. The question is whether he's the cause of one or both of those deaths."

"Money?" Claire went for one of the two most common motives.

"That's what we need to figure out. I know Matt's digging into the company, but I need him out in the field, not at a computer. That's your job. Is Flightline getting ready to go public or be put up for sale? Any hints of divorce in the air? We could use anything pointing to a financial motive for Everson killing his wife."

"That wouldn't explain Nikki, though."

"No. And it doesn't tell us where Kyle got the fentanyl, but it could give us the leverage to figure that out."

Claire pushed the strawberry muffin further away and began scribbling notes on a yellow legal pad. "I need to know if Matt's found anything; he hasn't come in here yet today."

"Try his private office. You know how he gets."

Claire's face went from excited analyst to concerned friend. "You think he's doing okay? I know the holidays can be tough when you've lost someone. It's been more than ten years since I lost my parents, and I still miss them at Christmas."

In the middle of all of this, plus dealing with her own life, Claire couldn't help but care about Matt. Caddie knew that in some small way, she and Matt had become something like parents for Claire. Not replacements but people she could rely on.

"He told me he thought about spending Christmas in Singapore, even though he finished his job last week," Caddie said. "The idea of coming back to their house without his wife there was more than he wanted to deal with. The investigation is a distraction at least." But there was something else about Matt that Caddie couldn't exactly put her finger on, something lurking there, a combination of contentment and grief, which made little sense.

"Keep an eye on him," Claire said.

Caddie laid her hand on Claire's shoulder. "When you do find the right guy, he's going to be very lucky. Now, what about the Road Demons?"

"Well, one thing. None of their members has ever been arrested in Fillmore County. Ever. Not a speeding ticket, noise complaint, nothing. On the other hand, in every county touching Fillmore; Dubuque, Blackhawk, Linn, Jones, they've been arrested or cited for every kind of violation going back twenty years."

"Follows with what Rafer told us."

"But you have to dig deeper." Claire spun in her chair and retrieved a stack of reports. She was a screen girl, but knew the boss wouldn't read more than a couple of paragraphs if it wasn't on paper. "DEA intel on Demon activity from a decade ago describes one of the MC's main meth trafficking routes as secondary state and county highways between Cedar Rapids and Dubuque, which should put them running straight through Fillmore. Even older, DEA busted a smurf buying precursors for one-pot meth being brewed in Fillmore. What the charges don't show is that the meth cook was willing to testify he sold his product to the Demons. Until he couldn't testify because he was found dead in a ditch in rural Blackhawk County."

"Heart of Demon territory," Caddie said.

"Right." Claire tapped the stack hard with a finger. "You're really going to love the last one. Homeland Security was working a human trafficking case involving Chinese national women. The traffickers were moving the women from town to town, setting up temporary webpages for escort services and running them out of cheap hotels for a week or two before moving on. They liked small towns and low-cost hotels, and they used the Road Demons and other MCs as security to run interference with locals, provide drugs to the girls, whatever they needed."

"I see where this is going, and I don't like it," Caddie said. If HSI had been working on human trafficking in her county and didn't tell her, she was going to have a very uncomfortable conversation with their RAC and the U.S. Attorney. Might as well make all the feds mad at her.

Claire picked up on the sheriff's meaning. "No, this was under the old sheriff, but it gets worse. Deep in one of their reports is a list of hotels they used in Eastern Iowa."

"Including our Patriot Inn," Caddie said.

"Not only that. The Mannheim Patriot Inn was the last location in Iowa before the organizers, with the help of the Demons, moved operations to the oil fields in North Dakota."

"Jimmy freaking Dubcek warned the Demons," Caddie said.

"Timing is right anyway."

"Which one of us gets to tell Matt?" Caddie asked. If Jimmy looked to be connected to the deaths of Nikki and Tracy, Matt would lose his mind. "Then, of course, there's the ATF information on Demons buying weapons from Deputy Williams."

"Right, finally got to read that entire report. The source didn't know Williams by name, only that he'd heard talk that a cop had been a source for weapons the Demons sold on to other MCs. He was described as a long-time friend of the club."

"So Jimmy Dubcek's cousin supplies guns to a gang that runs drugs through, but not in, Fillmore County, provides security for prostitution at a Mannheim hotel, and just maybe gets warned off by the sheriff." Just when she thought this case was narrowing down, and they had a suspect in sight. "They operate in the county, Jimmy provides cover for a cut, as long as they don't go too overt."

"And now that Jimmy's no longer in charge," Claire said.

"They go overt," Caddie answered. "They take the Russians on directly. Sell dope that maybe kills Nikki and Tracy." Her coffee cup was empty, her head was spinning, and she wondered why the heck she wanted to fight to keep this job. That lasted about five seconds. "Okay, good work, as always. Dig into Flightline." She would focus on the target directly in front of them, Kyle Everson, wherever he got the drugs from. She wouldn't let the investigation get distracted. The

Demons weren't going anywhere, unfortunately. For now, it was a matter of finding out if they were responsible for the fentanyl that killed Tracy and Nikki. "All the financials, business transactions, anything you can find."

Claire had a grin when she asked. She wasn't trying to get out of work, she was excited about it. "Isn't that more Matt's territory?"

"Don't worry, I've got something else he'll enjoy more."

Chapter 42

Caddie filled Matt in on her plan as they walked up to the entrance to Flightline. He'd already emailed Claire everything he found this morning, and Caddie had hopefully dealt with the Road Demons for now by getting the LT to put out her pull-over and cite orders. Their decks were as clear as they would get. Dawn contributed by not screaming in Caddie's face and waving her hands wildly, though she really wanted to. She whispered to Matt that she would figure out a way to get through to the sheriff later.

"So, we're going to just act like we belong?" Matt asked as he held the door open for both of them.

"Act like we belong," Caddie agreed, passing him. Dawn walked through more slowly.

"I don't love that you two have shorthand," she said.

Matt winked at Dawn, only to get a friendly eyeroll in return. The front office ladies parked at the top of the stairs were another matter. The older waved, the younger stood dumbfounded, her eyes wide in shock as Matt returned the wave and followed Caddie onto the repair floor, ignoring the signs to check in at the office and that no unauthorized personnel were allowed. Matt squelched his law school education rambling to him about the Fourth Amendment.

From there, they split up, Caddie heading toward the far end and the walled-off working areas for sensitive electronic equipment, Matt and Dawn veering left into the ever-shifting labyrinth of crates, engines perched on repair stations, and movable metal tool cabinets.

"I would have rather gone with Caddie and talked to Gentry," Dawn said, two steps behind her husband, keeping her arms up and crossed below her chest as if the greasy equipment could stain her white jacket. "I have questions for every man involved in this investigation."

Matt tilted his head to read the lengthy shipping label in a clear plastic sleeve on a large crate. "That include me?"

"Be careful, soldier, you're on the top of my list for questions." She sounded happy to give him a hard time. "Like, first of all, what are you looking for?"

At the next crate, he pulled out the shipping documents and began skimming through the dozen or so pages. "Not entirely sure," he said, his head down and mouth obscured from view. "As best I can make out, this crate contains hydraulic gear. What it's actually for, I have no idea." He looked up, giving Dawn a smile. "My wife was better at school than I was."

"Well, she was a brilliant educator. Now, what is that rather expensive Marquette Law School education she paid for telling you?"

He stood straight, making no attempt to hide that he was reading through the documents. "That you could argue this is a warrantless search, or that it's not. But what I do know is that this lists a destination in Cyprus." He pulled out a notepad and jotted down names and addresses.

"You know your phone takes pictures, old timer?"

"Rather not have evidence on my phone, dear."

"Oh, my. Have we gone rogue, again?"

"A little bit. It's debatable anyway." Matt slipped the sheet back and walked to a dozen closed crates stacked and ready to go. He pulled another set of shipping docs. "Navigation electronics. Same company, same address in Cyprus. Generic sounding company, but the names don't sound Greek or Turkish to me." He looked up. "Unless Thomas Abner and Joseph Mandle are Greek or Turkish."

"Fake names?" She slid up next to him, looking over his shoulder, and answered her own question. "Fake or someone with those actual names from somewhere else set up a company in Cyprus?"

"Who knows?" Matt slid the sheets back into their pocket, waved at another approaching worker, and wandered like he belonged there. "Could be both."

"Would they use Cyprus for tax reasons?" Dawn asked. She waved at the unseeing mechanic, who finally decided he should tell someone and scurried off.

"Maybe, but there are better options," Matt answered. "But it's a lot easier to get away with redirecting your purchases of sensitive equipment in Cyprus than it is in the Isle of Man or the Caymans. Even better, it's a lot closer to Iran, Russia, or Belarus."

Dawn was surprised. Her hubby had been hinting at something like this, but for some reason hadn't said it out loud yet. Then again, she had Everson half convicted of murdering his wife in her mind well before uttering the words. She hadn't said it partly because of Matt's talk of people dealing with grief differently, and it nagged at her that it was unfair to judge. She knew measuring people against the pain and anguish of her sweet soldier was setting them against an impossible standard. She knew it when she was here, but he's certainly shown it since she's been gone. That boy loves her with every ounce of his being. Kyle Everson loving his wife more than a few degrees less didn't make him a killer. At least, that's what she had told herself.

"You have anything else to back up your theory there, Nick?" she asked, knowing he would love the comparison to Dashiell Hammett's Thin Man detective. He didn't disappoint.

"Maybe, Nora." He smiled and hurried them along as a man in clean coveralls, the sure sign of a supervisor, made as much of a beeline to them as the walls of crates and equipment would allow. "But you wanted to question Gentry, and you've been a good girl, and it is Christmas."

"Oh, joy."

———

Caddie banged insistently on the door to the restricted area until Gentry himself answered. "We need to talk," she told him without preamble. He nodded in resignation. Back in the same conference room, he let out a long breath. Caddie let him wallow in dread as she slowly pulled out a notepad, searched for a pen, then checked her phone for emails. The last wasn't just a delaying trick; she'd told Claire to shoot her anything she found of interest relating to Flightline the moment she found it. There was always the hope her analyst would load her up at the last moment with a magic bullet. Nothing like that, but Lieutenant Dubcek had sent a message that they needed to talk about the weather as soon as possible. She shook her head, which further unnerved the man across from her. Fillmore County, sometimes it seemed as if someone wasn't getting killed, the place was getting smacked by another storm. Glancing up, she decided Gentry had marinated long enough. She also decided she was picking up Matt's bad habits. Better to just go straight to getting the truth.

231

"Were you and Tracy Everson having an affair?" Okay, maybe not straight. The question set Gentry back. She had to press him on it, though she was nearly certain of the answer.

"No," he stammered. "I told you before."

"At a time when Tracy and her husband seem disconnected. When she drifted away from her sobriety partner, when no one I talk to in this town had more than a passing connection to her, you seem to have grown closer."

"That's not true," Gentry said.

It wasn't entirely true, Caddie knew. Tracy had remained loyal to her husband's parents, but the point still remained. Gentry was attentive to Tracy, where others she should have been able to count on weren't. "You drove out to the house to get her to sign for shipping."

"I told you that it was work."

"Shipping she didn't have to sign for when she was in Decorah," Caddie pressed. "Seems like someone else could have signed off just as well. Why did you feel the need to take the time to drive out there to get her signature on documents her husband could have signed?" Just admit that you were in love with her or had a crush or whatever, Caddie thought, so I can get to the fact that her husband was cheating on her and what you knew. But the exchange didn't go that way.

"I went out there to get Tracy's signature because I was told to," he said.

"By who?" She asked, though there could only be one answer.

"Tracy." The questioning wasn't going in the direction Caddie expected, but the result was the same, the barrier Gentry had maintained between them finally broke down, and he began to actually talk. "She didn't want to come in but wanted to keep working. She asked me to bring the paperwork out to her, so I did. Look, I admit, I liked Tracy. But we weren't having an affair, and I wasn't trying to. There aren't many jobs you can find in a town this size that pay like this one. I wasn't going to risk that by screwing the boss's wife. He slept around, that didn't mean he'd like it if his wife did."

"Let's talk about that," Caddie said. "You told me about Vegas, but you didn't say anything about Mannheim. Okay, you weren't having an affair with Tracy, but was she confiding in you at all? Talking to you about her husband?"

He shook his head, less in denial than in regret. "No. We weren't friends like that. It was superficial. What did you do this weekend, the weather, junk like that. You start talking to a woman about how her husband will chase anything in a skirt, that's a shortcut to getting fired. I saw her pulling back. Maybe if I'd asked or given her an opening, she might have talked. But she didn't."

"Any idea who Kyle may have been having an affair with?"

"Why?"

Caddie leaned on the table, bringing her closer to Gentry. She emphasized her words. "Mr. Gentry, I'm investigating the deaths of two women over the last week. As part of that, I'm looking at every possibility. That's why I pressed you about your relationship with Tracy Everson. It's why I'm asking about her husband. I'm not going to go into detail why, but I will tell you I need you to keep what we talk about between the two of us. Can you do that?"

He nodded. "I understand. Kyle wasn't as out there cheating on Tracy in Mannheim as he was in Vegas, but there were hints. Tracy would be looking for him, and he'd disappear for the afternoon. Kyle making a point of telling people he slept in the office the night before, like he was creating an alibi for not being home. Things like that, but I honestly don't know any details, and I haven't heard any rumors. I'd tell you if I did."

In the end, Gentry sort of confirmed what Caddie suspected, but without having anything close to concrete. She was about to wrap up when two quick taps on the door were followed by Matt walking into the room. He had that look. She might have made a little progress, but he was grinning like a cat with a fish in its sights. Then whatever was wrong with Caddie flared again, her vision blurred momentarily, and a slight headache spiked. This was actually beginning to worry her.

Matt sat down, glanced up to his right, pausing before he spoke. Caddie wanted to prod him along, but something paused her. When he came back, he glanced at her with a half grin and went straight at Gentry. "Who's responsible for the end-user certificates for the equipment you sell outside the U.S.?"

Gentry took a moment with the abrupt change in questioner and questions. "The buyer is responsible for filling out the EUCs. That's standard."

"Not what I'm talking about," Matt shot back. "The U.S.-based seller is responsible for issuing and verifying the end user certificate that demonstrates that the buyer is authorized to purchase sensitive equipment, which I'm going to guess covers an awful lot of what you sell, certainly navigation electronics, and probably hydraulic components. I'd have to do some research, but I know, depending on whether it's classified as military equipment or not, Flightline, the seller, has to file that paperwork with State or Commerce. Who in this office does that?"

"Front office." He looked to Caddie for help. She would disappoint him.

"Any of those shipping documents you drove out to Tracy to sign happen to be end-user certificates?" Caddie asked, not entirely sure what an end-user certificate was beyond knowing Matt had been working on them for HGS in Singapore.

The implications slowly fell on Gentry. "They were whole packets, shipping instructions, billing, and if it was overseas, end-user certificates."

Caddie had put it into her report, but she just realized she hadn't told Matt about Tracy wanting Gentry to leave the export documents with her for a few days at the house to look over before picking them up. She quickly filled him in.

"Why not have Kyle bring the papers in?" Matt asked. Gentry didn't have an answer. Matt paused, smiled at something, then looked back to Caddie, ignoring the man squirming on the other side of the table. "You warn him not to tell anyone what we're talking about?"

"Yes, but it wouldn't hurt to do it again." Bad weather, weird headaches, idiot motorcycle gangs, and local hoodlums all aside, it was moments like this with her investigative partner that reminded Caddie why she loved this job. Almost as good as putting a bastard like Kyle Everson behind bars.

———

Matt stopped outside the door to his Jeep and flipped up the collar on his wool jacket. The warm spell of the last twenty-four hours was rapidly disappearing in a bitter chill wind. Dawn matched him with a long, puffy white jacket extending below her knees. Caddie shrank deeper into her Sheriff's Office jacket.

"You want to tell me now?" she asked.

"You don't want to know," he said.

Caddie turned her back to the wind. "Aren't you an officer of the court?"

"Don't you have a motorcycle gang to worry about?" He smiled saying it. "Let me confirm a few things. If it doesn't pan out, no harm. Give me the next twelve hours. You keep following the means, who was the original source of the drugs. Let me work on the motive."

"And meet in the middle," Caddie agreed.

Dawn and Matt watched the sheriff pull away before hopping into their Jeep. Matt didn't want Caddie to see him leaving his door open for his unseen wife. Dawn turned to him after settling in. "You're going to have to talk to her." She was concerned. Her hubby had been too engrossed in questioning Gentry to notice, but she had. The squinting, the gentle touches to the side of her head. Six months ago, Caddie, wounded, beaten, and sprawled out on the floor of a dusty barn, saw through the veil that kept Dawn from being seen in this world. Whether it was because the sheriff had cheated death or that Dawn's love for her husband had connected her to this woman, she didn't know. But the one thing that seemed apparent to Dawn was that her husband's denying what Caddie had clearly seen broke something in Caddie's mind. She was not about to wait a minute longer than necessary to fix that.

Chapter 43

The roaring fireplace bounced reds and oranges across the Nativity set Dawn had Matt set up on the hearth where it belonged. "Better late than never," she said when he objected to the timing. The Christmas tree was lit, and the Vince Guaraldi Trio's Peanuts Christmas Special soundtrack was playing on the smart speakers. Matt opened his laptop on the coffee table and set his phone down.

"Ready?" he asked.

"Yep," Dawn bounced in her seat, happily surrounded by Christmas, ready to get back to work. "I always liked Teddy, him and his cute tiny wife and cute tiny kids."

"I think one of those tiny kids is playing college volleyball now."

"No." Dawn waved the idea away. "They were just little things last time we saw them."

The phone was answered with a heavy Carolina hill country accent. "Y'all calling to confess for your client?"

"Merry Christmas to you, too, Teddy," Matt said, a broad grin on his face from talking to an old friend. "I thought the Commerce Department was all about greasing the wheels of commerce. Where's your Christmas spirit?"

"Nah, y'all been bad this year, Matt. Nothing but coal for you. I'm still smarting over that Western Dynamic deal. You know, your boy was dirty as can be, and he walks away with a civil fine. Bet it took him a whole ten minutes selling stock to pay for it. But it is Christmas, so I'll be kinder than you deserve and ask what I can do for you?"

"It's what I can do for you, maybe," Matt said. "It's for my other job, though. I'm working two overdose deaths for the sheriff's office here in Iowa."

"Sorry to hear that. Least you're working on the side of angels for once. But can it wait 'till next week? I'm leaving the office in an hour, and the wife and I have plans to see the New Year in surrounded by mountains, not D.C. traffic."

"I'll be quick. I don't have anything solid, but I'm looking at a company, Flightline Avionics out of Mannheim, Iowa. They rehab aviation equipment, electronics and mechanical, for resale, including overseas."

"What's that got to do with overdose deaths?" Teddy already sounded invested, the two retired warrant officers were back where they started together twenty years ago.

"Looking for motive," Matt answered.

"Don't need a motive for an OD, brother." The soft punch of a computer keyboard being worked sped up, followed by a few unintelligible mutterings from Teddy Beacham, Deputy Assistant for Export Enforcement for the U.S. Department of Commerce, and one-time Army CID warrant officer classmate of Matt Jager.

"Yeah, I'm starting to think the ODs weren't accidental. Then I happened to see some shipping documents with a Cyprus destination and buyers with Anglo-sounding names who do their banking through Panama. There's a question, at least in my mind, about end-user certificates and if everything Flightline is doing is aboveboard. It might be that the wife who supposedly OD'ed was concerned, too. Can you see if they've filed for shipments ready to go in the next week or so? Not sure what your capabilities are."

"Looking. Depending on what the equipment is, they could be filing with State. Say, man, you doing okay? I know it's been a couple of years, but we all loved Dawn—"

She put her hand over her heart.

"—and I know the holidays can be tough."

"Thanks, brother." Matt air-kissed Dawn. "Started off a little shaky, but I'm doing okay now."

"Getting lost in the work. I hear ya." There was a pause on the other end. "Shoot," he drew out the word. "There's a flag on Flightline Avionics."

Matt and Dawn exchanged surprised looks. She made hand motions for Teddy to say more.

"Can you see what the flag is for?" Matt prompted.

"I'm looking. There's no orders to stop shipments or anything. Just a request for all information with a phone number and email address with HSI."

"If you had to guess?"

"I'd say someone opened an investigation, but there's not enough yet to do more than gather intel. You think the shipment you're looking at is going out soon?"

"They've got everyone working and packing crates the week between Christmas and New Year's, and my source says the first part of the shipment is scheduled for pick up Friday morning, New Year's Eve."

"Shoot," Teddy drew the word out even longer. "I need to call State and DHS, and touch base with the FBI to get to the bottom of this. And my wife used to like you. She is not going to be happy."

"That's what I'm here for," Matt answered Dawn's frown with a broader smile.

"Any chance you can delay them?" Teddy asked.

"Like I said, we're investigating two OD deaths. I just happened to see some shipping labels when I was at the plant."

"Uh-huh," Teddy answered.

"What I was hoping you'd do is give me a motive for the husband to kill his wife."

Dawn gave Everson a thumbs down.

"I don't see the tie," Teddy said. "Not yet anyway. But we'll be talking."

"I'll be here," Matt said before hanging up and expecting a final quiet night at home before the full weight of federal law enforcement resources turned their sights on a small Iowa company that might just be selling restricted equipment into one of a half-dozen world hotspots.

Dawn sat next to her husband on the couch, resting her head weightlessly on his shoulder, facing the fire. He was expecting her to say something sweet or silly. To bring them back to Christmas.

"It still doesn't explain Nikki's death, dear," she said.

"We're getting there," Matt answered, turning his head to kiss the top of her head. He made the kiss smack loud enough that he knew she would hear. "Ouch," he said as the spark zapped his head back.

———————

Caddie waited until Sue, the dispatcher on duty, made it into the deputies' bullpen before she started the meeting. Patrol schedules and holiday leave kept the in-office group small: her and Lieutenant

Dubcek, Claire, and Sue, plus Deputy Terry Schott, who was just coming on. The rest were attending by phone from the road or home, or wherever they were relaxing for the holidays. "Okay, folks, I'll keep this short, but I wanted everyone to get this straight from me. The weather system Chris has been warning us about for days hits tonight. We're looking at single-digit temps with wind chill below zero, high winds, and anywhere from five to eight inches of snow, with the possibility of more."

"Fun." Matt's voice came through the phone.

"You bet," Caddie said. "Matt and I are still focusing on the overdose investigations. Everyone else can expect to be dealing with the storm's impact. As always, Chris is leading the patrol efforts. Chris," she said, handing it off to her number two.

"Right. For those off-shift, make sure we can get hold of you if we need you to come in early. Allison?"

"Here."

"You're the senior deputy on tonight as the front moves in. A tow ban is in effect, so make sure anyone in an accident gets off the road and somewhere safe and warm as quickly as possible. Also, double-check any spots where homeless folks might shelter for the night. County social services still had some beds last I checked, and Saint Wen's is opening the basement with cots and hot food for a warming shelter."

"Do you need me to come in early?" she asked.

"No, you're going to have a long enough night," he said before moving on to his list of safety concerns for the public and his deputies. "I'll be the first backup tonight, so call me. Any questions?"

No one said anything, and Caddie moved to wrap the meeting up. They all had better things to do than drag this out. "I'll echo Chris. Please, be careful. I know you can deal with these conditions, we do it every winter. But people can die out in junk like this, let's make sure that doesn't happen. And if I don't see you before, Happy New Year."

———

Dawn snuggled up to her Matt, both pretending they could feel the warmth and weight of the other. They could definitely feel the

239

love. The speakers had shifted to soft Christmas jazz, the fire had grown lower, and the night had settled into a hazy dream of Christmas past. They were together, in love, inseparable. Their past, their present.

"I don't want New Year's yet," she said.

"No," he agreed. "It's still Christmas for me and you."

"There's nothing more we can do tonight, baby. I insist we stay by the fire and do nothing but be in love."

"We're very busy being in love."

"It's all we can handle tonight," she agreed.

Chapter 44
December 30th

A phone chirp pulled Matt from the confusion of a deep sleep before he realized he was lying on his back on the couch, the flames from the fire turned to glowing embers. For a fraction of a moment, he felt a weight on him. Looking down, he saw Dawn lying on top of him, her head resting on his chest. Then back in the world of the living, the weight and feel were gone, his wife an insubstantial ghost shadow across his heart. He reached for the phone, it chirped again, and Dawn sat up, blinking her own sleep away. "Unfair," she said.

"Yeah." He expected Caddie or a late-night call from Teddy telling him the lead to Flightline was hot and they had to jump on it. The voice on the speaker sat Matt up straight.

"Those sons a bitches took our little girl," Frank Moscow growled, every bit of recklessness and anger and danger the man could present filling his voice. "They hurt her, I'll kill every last one of 'em."

Dawn sat close, her hands clasped in front of her.

"Frank, what are you talking about? Took who?"

"Bella. Girl run off again to sleep in her own bed. We came down to fetch her home, and the door's busted open and Bella's gone."

Dawn was up first. Matt watched his wife's face as he listened to the desperate grandfather on the phone. Frank alternated between pleading for the Sheriff's Office's help and swearing he'd kill every Road Demon he could find. Matt grabbed his long wool jacket off the coat rack and pointed Dawn toward the back door.

"Ask for his wife," Dawn whispered.

Matt didn't have time to question or argue. "Is your wife there?"

"Yes, why—,"

"Put her on," Matt commanded, still looking at Dawn for instruction.

"Tell her to keep him there even if she has to shoot him," Dawn said.

Matt passed it on.

"Better hurry," the woman said, "before I send him out there myself."

Matt and Dawn were out the back door in a rush, only to be met by a wind gust that picked up the three inches of snow that had already fallen, adding it to the hard-driving flakes coming down. A home broken into, a child missing, a blizzard blowing through the county, and Matt felt nothing but optimism. Dawn was at his side. They could find Bella. They would have to.

Frank Moscow paced the trailer's living room like a jungle cat in a circus cage. "I swear to God, Jager, I will burn them to the fucking ground." Mary Moscow stood next to the kitchen sink, cigarette in hand, blowing smoke out a cracked-open window. She looked as mad as her husband, but under much better control. In a way, that made her scarier than Frank. Matt found himself in the unusual position of being the one trying to calm others down. Of course, it helped that Dawn was whispering in his ear.

"They're afraid, dear. Remember that. They lost their daughter, and now little Bella is gone. You know their pain, but you also know you need to think before you react." She smiled. "I taught you that."

"Frank," Matt said, trying to cut through the man's rantings, "the sheriff is organizing a proper search as we speak. She's even calling in other departments. I know you got folks out, but chasing down Road Demons isn't going to help find Bella."

Moscow spun on him, a new target for his frustration. "Bullshit, they came here, busted the door, and took our girl. I find a Road Demon, I find Bella."

Frank was right about one thing; the aluminum frame on the front door had been forced back around the handle. Someone had broken in and hadn't hidden it well.

"Baby," Dawn hung at his shoulder, "we didn't see any tracks in the snow coming in. I know the wind is blowing, but you'd think we'd see some signs of a car."

Matt turned to Mary as she stubbed her cigarette out in the sink. "Did you see any vehicle tracks when you came down to get Bella?"

"We weren't looking for tracks," she said, opening her purse for another smoke. "But I didn't see any. Winds blowing hard, you could park on the main road and be at the house in a couple of minutes if

242

you didn't want anyone at the house to see you." She lit up. "No tracks don't mean Road Demons weren't here." She took a long, deep pull, letting out the smoke as she talked. "And if it wasn't Road Demons, who took Bella?"

Dawn leaned closer and spoke lower. "Do not answer that, Matt."

"I don't know," he said. Mary squinted back through the cloud of burnt tobacco.

"She's not as trusting as your buddy Frank," Dawn said. "Baby, let's investigate instead of trying to convince two very angry grandparents that Caddie has this under control." She motioned him to follow her deeper into the trailer.

"Have you noticed anything out of place?" Matt asked as they passed into Bella's room. Mary kept vigil at the kitchen sink as Frank extended his pacing to include the hallway.

"Nothing gone far as we can tell," Frank answered. "We looked around, waiting for you to get here. Shit, I should have been out there searching. I should be out there now."

The scene looked the same as the last time they'd been there. A little girl's room full of pinks and purples, superhero girls, and princesses.

"Look, dear." Dawn made her way to the far side of the bed and a small end table wedged against the wall, holding a large picture of Nikki, Megan, and Bella hugging up against one another. "I think that little sweetie took this off the wall."

Matt nodded. There was nothing he could add. The poor kid was hurting, the kind of hurt that nearly kept him away from home for Christmas had driven Bella to surround herself with memories of her mother. He was about to ask Frank if he had any way of contacting the Demons, any mutual business partners who could act as intermediaries, when Dawn called him to the window overlooking the bed. "Matt, come here and look at this."

The world outside was fulfilling the night's forecast and more. The snow came down thick, pushed hard to the side by a steady howl of wind. A good night to be on the couch by the fire. Dawn pointed to a gap in the tree line not ten feet behind the trailer. "Look, right in there where that little path is, the trees are blocking the wind. Do you see what I see?"

"Shit." Matt pulled out his phone and thumbed redial to get Caddie. They wouldn't know until they got closer, but some of those tracks already disappearing looked too big for a small girl. Maybe the only thing worse than the Demons grabbing Bella was someone taking her into the woods in weather like this.

Snow swirled around Matt's face, then blew hard again. His long wool jacket and gloves would keep his body and hands warm enough, but his ears and feet were already feeling the bitter cold. He handed Frank one of the flashlights from the back of the Jeep. "The sheriff is setting searchers down along the roads surrounding the property. If Bella or anyone else comes out, they should see them."

Frank was only wearing a flannel jacket and ski cap, but he had his anger to keep him warm. "Not in this shit," he said. He adjusted his belt again, tightening it over Bella's jacket that Dawn reminded them to take.

The true test of the danger to Bella was that neither Caddie nor Dawn argued when Matt said he was going after her. "Take Frank with you," Caddie ordered.

"I'm coming too, babe," Dawn added. Mary would wait at the trailer while Megan and an aunt kept watch at Frank's house. The rest of the clan was driving snow-covered roads, hunting down members of a motorcycle club that hopefully had enough sense to stay home and out of the county tonight.

Matt grabbed an extra clip for his Beretta, slipping it into his jacket pocket.

"Gimme that twelve-gauge." Frank was eyeing Matt's Mossberg shotgun.

"I know this isn't going to work." Dawn moved between Matt and the Jeep. The wind that ripped at Matt and Frank gently tossed hair across her face. "But, I forbid you to give this man a weapon. I'm not a deputy, but I'm pretty darn sure that's illegal."

"Only use it if Bella's in danger," Matt ordered Frank as a way of explaining his decision to Dawn. "That's the only thing that matters."

"I don't like it," she said, standing aside.

Matt grabbed the shotgun and extended it to Frank. "Only if Bella is in danger."

244

"I heard ya." Moscow grabbed the gun, confirmed it was loaded, and pumped a round into the chamber.

"Not comforting, either of you," Dawn said, walking them around the back of the trailer.

Frank led the way through the woods. The footprints were increasingly difficult to find in the shifting snows, and it was quickly apparent that his experience hunting and familiarity with this stretch of woods made him the better tracker. It also gave Matt a chance to let the man get farther in front so he could talk to Dawn. He kept his voice low, knowing his wife, the woman he was eternally tied to, would be able to hear him in an AC/DC concert in a hurricane. "Could you lead us better?"

"I don't think so. I can see pretty good, but Frank is finding tracks I wouldn't know are tracks." They'd long ago left any semblance of a trail, the path winding one way, then turning quickly down another.

"Frank's better at this than I am, too," Matt said. "But I think Bella is running away from someone. If an abductor were making her walk, I think it wouldn't have all these crazy turns."

A dense clump of undergrowth with a thin layer of snow covering stopped Frank and sent him in small circles. "Stand back," he warned Matt. "No doubt, she's being hunted, and she lost him." He pointed at an area of barely discernible dips in the snow. "Son of a bitch is searching for her." He made his way to the far side of the clump. "She took off again." He motioned Matt forward with the shotgun.

"I hope he doesn't kill anyone, Matt," Dawn said. "That's not going to help anyone."

Frank picked up his pace.

"No, it won't," Matt agreed. "I need to stop Frank and talk. Any ideas before I do?"

Dawn stopped; she wanted her soldier to listen and understand. "I want you to turn around and go back to the house." She put a hand up. "I know you won't. I don't blame you. I'm just very worried for you and that little girl, and even that idiot Frank. If we had any sense, we'd give Caddie time to launch a full-scale search."

Wind flung snow across Dawn's face, the flashlight reflecting off its white. Her concern showed itself in a soft, caring smile. She knew her man. He would not stop. She loved that about him as much as it worried her. She wanted that little girl to be found and safe. She'd come back for that little girl, which didn't fit with her theory of being here to save Matt, but it's what they had for now.

"Jager," Frank called, crouching down. Moscow led them down a steep draw with heavily wooded slopes on both sides, a spring runoff creek creating a narrow, clear lane. He pointed at clearly defined tracks. He seethed. "She's running in her slippers. Son of bitch would have caught her, but she's quick and can dash between branches. She knows these woods, too. There was a spot back there, I think she was hiding for a bit. His footprints went back and forth. He must have found her, and she took off again."

"Kid is a Moscow all right," Matt said. Frank took it as the compliment it was meant to be.

Dawn stood on her tiptoes, searching the woods in front of them. "We're catching up," she said, then her breath caught. "Oh, Matt, I saw her." She turned to him, urgency in her voice. "Run, I saw her."

Matt took off, his legs pumping through snow and fallen branches, bursting through undergrowth. His lungs burned as Dawn urged him forward. He may not be the hunter Frank was, but Matt had always been a runner, and it paid off now. Frank cursed and stumbled after.

"Where?" Matt called to Dawn, who was moving swiftly, not changing her path and running straight through trees and bushes. If he'd had time, it would have bothered him.

She stopped and pointed to the right along the edge of an open field. That's when Matt saw her. Bella Moscow in long-sleeved pink PJs, her blonde hair frozen, a pallid face visible across the field as a sheet of white to match the storm. A dark shadow deeper in the woods grew, crashing towards her. They weren't thirty yards away. Matt stepped forward, weapon up.

"Bella is all that matters." Dawn was to his right, moving along the wood line toward the child. He knew she was right. This was a chance to catch whoever was chasing her, almost certainly the same person responsible for her mother's and probably Tracy's deaths. But Bella was all that mattered. The quickest way to end the danger was to chase the assailant off.

"Bella," Matt yelled at the top of his lungs. Afraid the sound wouldn't survive the onslaught of the storm, he stopped, yelled it again, and pointed his sidearm in the air. Two quick shots into the sky, and the crack of bullets cut through everything. "Bella," Matt yelled, "it's Deputy Jager. You know me."

Frank Moscow caught up, breathing hard, and raised the shotgun.

"Frank, no!" Dawn yelled, rushing back as if she could tackle the man. But the weapon's barrel continued its course up until it was pointed at the sky, and he let off a booming shot. He'd understood Matt's play and went with it. Bella was all that mattered.

"Bella!" her grandfather screamed, running along the edge of the field until she burst into the clear and flew into his arms. Dawn and Matt were two steps behind. The grizzled old con hung on to the child with everything he had.

Matt expected nothing but delight from his wife's face, but got shock and dismay. She pleaded with her husband. "Get her inside!" Matt nearly lifted Frank to his feet, Bella hanging tightly onto his neck as he tried wrapping her coat around her. "We need to get her back."

"The house is too far," Frank yelled. "We head back up the draw and hit the main road, and call your sheriff. She'll have people somewhere up there."

"Go," Matt shoved him back toward the draw, ready to follow. A glance over his shoulder changed everything. The firm shape of a shadow appeared on the opposite side of the clearing, then moved quickly away. "Oh, no you don't." Matt pushed Frank in one direction and ran the other.

———

Caught off guard, it took Dawn a moment to react. She chased after her Matt, that sweet soldier, dedicated cop, husband hurting over the loss of his wife. She hadn't considered that the moment he was released from the responsibility for saving Bella, he would focus all his energy and what little common sense the man showed at times on catching a killer. She'd thought he was beyond the need for vengeance; she hadn't considered that he would put justice before his own life. "Matt," she screamed, "get your crazy butt back here. You can't chase him in a blizzard."

The snow and wind didn't impede her the way they did Matt, and in a few strides, they were even. "Faster than you," she couldn't help saying, hoping a smile or laugh would bring him back to earth. Then a flash of blue against the darks and whites of a snow-filled forest hill caught her attention. Whoever Matt was chasing was struggling up the hill. Her boy just might catch him. In the middle of the open field, Matt's pace picked up, driving his legs in a sprint, snow flying behind him with each step. He'd seen Bella's pursuer. Dawn was a fraction of a second from actually cheering him on when the first sharp crack sounded. This time, there was no delay in her reaction. "Matt, stop!"

A louder, longer crack came as Matt's foot hit the hidden ice and his head turned to her. "Shi—" and he was gone in an instant.

———

The shocking cold grabbed Matt's feet and pulled him down as the sounds of cracking and the open field came together in his mind. The near-freezing days of last week gave way to two days of bitter cold, then another unseasonably warm day before the blizzard hit. It was as if Iowa set a trap to teach him a lesson. Plunging into darkness, freezing water enveloped him, sending shuddering waves of pain through his body. Seconds after his last breath, his lungs screamed for oxygen, his body told him to flee from the cold, and his mind yelled at him to swim.

Matt kicked and stroked up, but he sank still deeper from the surface. The wool jacket that had been instantly soaked now turned into a stone pulling him to the bottom. He twisted and struggled against weakening muscles to pull it off. He kicked, and a shoe floated away. Twisting again, the weight of the jacket eased and then slipped off. In a moment of deliberate calm, he kicked his legs and stroked, sending himself through the water.

———

Dawn ran and dived into water that was already trying to regain its form of thin ice. This was a reason she'd returned. It was the same reason she'd come back before. She was here to save Matt.

The cold had no effect on Dawn, but even with her sight, the pitch black of the water was disorienting. The hole in the ice above her was barely shades lighter than the darkness below. She was forced to search before finally seeing her Matt, who had drifted from under the opening above them. You never could tell how things worked between them, so she gave it a try, but yelling his name did no good. Even she couldn't hear it. She was closer now, watching as he struggled and shed his waterlogged jacket. *Smart boy,* she thought, reminding herself to tell him how sexy she thought his mind was. He grew up swimming in the Mississippi River; he could handle a pond. Then he kicked and stroked, sending himself lower, in the wrong direction. The fall and fight to get the jacket off had disoriented him.

Without considering what it could mean for her time here, Dawn knew one sure way to bring her husband to the surface. She concentrated on their love. The love that meant everything to them. The love that had defied death more than once. The love that would last forever. And she burned bright, sending beams of white light cutting through stygian darkness. An underwater Christmas star to light his way.

Matt spun in the water, and she could have sworn there was a smile on his face as he turned and swam to her. Swam to the surface.

Chapter 45

Ice caked instantly to Matt's hair and face as he broke the surface. His breath came in desperate gasps. Above him, Dawn crouched at the edge of the broken ice, glowing in a faint white that illuminated her hair in an effect that could only be described as a halo. "Hello, soldier," she said.

"My angel." Two strokes and he was to her, but his relief faded with the exhaustion in his legs and an impossible cold emanating from deep in his core. Ignoring the pain and biting wind, he reached as far out on the ice shelf as he could and kicked to bring himself up. The ice crumbled, and he plunged below the frigid waters again. Freezing cold pushed at his temples, sending waves of pain through his head. He forced himself to kick. Popping back up and grasping toward the ice's edge, he saw Dawn's beatific smile disappear.

"Come on, baby. Let's get you out of there." She forced an encouraging expression, but it didn't touch her voice. She was worried, and now he was too.

Matt put the pain away, forgot about the wind and driving snow, and the exhaustion from the fight to get to the surface, and concentrated. Reaching as far as he could, he kicked his legs, trying to force himself up and out, only to be met with more crashing ice and another dunk below the surface. Holding his mind together and kicking his legs was harder this time, his ability to concentrate quickly flowing away. He was drained and panic seeped into his attempt to steel himself. "One more," he could barely get the words out. The third attempt met with failure.

Pulling at the water, he surfaced and saw fear in Dawn's face. He'd been in the water too long; the freezing temperatures were shutting his system down and sapping what little strength he had left. "Sorry. I love…," was all he could get out. He wasn't sure if he actually told her he'd see her soon or if it was only in his mind. Despite her existence and promises of their next life together, he found that he was afraid of what was to come. Whatever awaited him, he wanted her face to be the last thing he saw in this world.

Dawn looked down at the ice around her and moved further away along the jagged opening. "Over here, Matt. It's a little thicker."

He didn't know that it would make a difference, but followed her, wanting more than anything to be close to Dawn if this was the end.

"Good job," she said, her smile filled with love. Then her face hardened and her eyes burned. His sweet, beautiful bride leaned over, set her hands on her knees, and snarled at him.

"Don't you dare quit, soldier!" she yelled without an ounce of sympathy. "You get your sorry ass out of that water this second! Do you hear me? Get up and out!"

He started to laugh, but reached out with one arm and pulled himself up. His shoulders clear of the water, he rested. She didn't.

"What are you doing? Do you think this is the Air Force? You are a warrant officer in the United States Fricking Army, get out of there now!" She leaned closer to his ear, her voice raging with anger at this soldier who wasn't doing his job of saving himself. Matt kicked off his remaining shoe and gently scissored his legs twice, bringing blood back to the muscles. "Come on, soldier, you can do this."

With the last bit of encouragement, Matt kicked and reached, the ice under his arm sagging, he kicked and reached further with the other arm.

"Kick, kick!" she yelled, clapping in rhythm.

He kicked and threw his back arm forward, pulling his stomach up and onto the ice. It cracked and started giving.

"This way!" Dawn yelled, stepping to her left, guiding him to roll to thicker ice. Matt rolled and kicked and pulled as the love of his life screamed like a Master Sergeant gone mad in his ear. "Go, go, go. Get your butt up here." He squirmed and low crawled until he could feel bitter winds on his feet. He kept crawling until he could crawl no more and turned over. A beautiful, beaming face met his, unfrozen tears running down Dawn's face. She bent over him and planted a huge kiss on his lips, the static charge cutting through the damp. "You're a good soldier, dear."

"You're a terrible drill sergeant, baby," he croaked back.

She kissed him again, and in his mind, if not his lips, he felt it. "I am a great drill sergeant. Now get your butt up before you freeze to death. Your work isn't finished."

Matt's jaw chattered as his body shivered uncontrollably. He had no shoes or jacket, and what remained of his clothes were frozen hard to his body. His phone and Beretta lay somewhere in the muck at the bottom of the pond. His vision constricted as snow froze his eyes shut. Stumbling forward, he concentrated on the dim but distinct light of Dawn in front of him. He wanted to say something to her, say he loved her, but he could barely put thoughts together, much less speak them. The drill sergeant gone, Dawn reverted to her natural, encouraging teacher role.

"Come on, Matt, just a bit farther. We can do it. You and me together like it's supposed to be. We'll get you a nice hot tea. You'd like that, wouldn't you? We'll put lots of honey in it and get you warm cookies and snuggle by the fire." She waved for him to follow. He stumbled and fell. She didn't yell.

"I love you and it's not your time, baby," she told him softly, the words cutting through the howl of the wind. "We will be together, I promise, but our time here is brief and a blessing. Your blessings are not done. Now, come on. Back on your feet."

She wanted him to fight. He wasn't sure why. They could be together now. But he'd pretty much always done what she told him. Guess keep listening to her. He pushed his hand down into the snow, the feeling in his fingers gone, and got himself to his feet to stumble forward.

Time and distance lost their meaning as his mind went numb until Dawn's raised voice cut through the fog. "A rock, Matt. You need a rock. I can't do this for you. You're almost done. I need you to concentrate." A rock? he thought, before he saw a padlocked door and a small structure in front of them and began to laugh.

"More fishing," he mumbled through frozen lips, digging through the snow. He found he was holding a rock in fingers that refused to feel. He swiped at the lock and dimly saw blood spreading across the back of his hand. Dawn encouraged him to try again, and on the second swing, the hasp holding the lock pulled out from the door. Another swing and it spun off into the snow.

Dawn's fading light had been replaced by the glowing red face of a portable propane heater. Matt's shivering hadn't stopped, but feeling was returning to the very tips of his fingers. They hurt. The ice fishing shack was fully prepped for the coming season with a full can of fuel for the heater and a stack of old blankets to keep laps warm. Dawn's gentle encouragement and professions of love had kept him going as he fumbled through starting the heater and stripping off his clothes. Finally, wrapped in blankets and curled up on the bench, he could think beyond the next few seconds. "Love you," he said through chattering teeth.

Dawn sat on the floor next to him so their faces were inches apart. "I love you, Matt."

"Christmas on a lake."

She laughed. "You could have picked better accommodations, dear."

"You said there would be tea and cookies."

"Later, tea and cookies, I promise."

Matt's eyes closed for a moment before what he'd just seen registered. He let a finger peek out from under the blanket as he pointed at the wall alongside the door and gave a little chuckle. "We owe Sam for the night."

"I love that girl," Dawn said, joining him in a soft laugh. A red and pink sign listed the rules for the ice fishing shack, number ten being "Have fun." At the bottom of the list, there was a cartoon image of their niece pointing at them in her Uncle Sam pose and the words Sam's Outdoor Adventures.

Matt came to with heat on his face and coolness to his back. He ached all over, and he was lying on something hard. He didn't remember where he was until he opened his eyes and saw his precious Dawn curled up asleep on the floor below the short bench he was perched on. A bright, clear morning light filled the shack from the single small window behind him. The noise that woke him came again, this time it was on the other side of the door.

"Wake up, Dawn," he said softly. "I think we have company."

Dawn sat up, stretching her arms overhead as a figure bundled in cold-weather gear and an orange ski mask opened the door, letting light flood into every corner of the room. Sam ripped off her mask, unbuckled her snow shoes, and, finally unencumbered, rushed to hug her mildly protesting uncle.

"I'm fine," Matt assured her, "Just let me get dressed."

Allison followed into the shack, closing the door behind her and radioing into dispatch that they'd found Matt. "Ice fishing shack on the south shore of Otter Pond. About a mile west of the intersection of County M and Pine Road," she said, though dispatch could get the location from the GPS on her radio. The voice on the other end changed with Claire taking over. "What's the health status of the subject?"

"Tell Claire we need tea and cookies," Dawn said. "For my hubby."

"I could use some tea and cookies," Matt said.

Allison gave a happy grunt. "He's himself."

Chapter 46

The fire was in full force, and the radiators in the old home cranked open enough that Matt started sweating sitting still in the living room. The fact that people kept throwing blankets on him didn't help. But it's hard to complain about being taken care of, especially when your wife is whispering in your ear not to complain. Caddie was walking them through last night's events in greater detail. How she'd found Frank Moscow as she drove up a county road, shining a spotlight into the woods. The storm had cut visibility to feet, and then, "He just popped out of the blizzard, that little girl wrapped in his arms." Caddie was nearly hugging her knees, sitting in Dawn's favorite chair. "I've been on the job a long time now, I think that's the first time I cried doing this. We got her in the truck and wrapped up when Frank tells me you took off after a suspect like a madman. He said you were fucking nuts."

"Not the language I'd use," Dawn said from beside him, "but I agree with the sentiment."

"From Frank, that's a compliment," Matt said as Claire rolled in from the kitchen with a large tray in her lap. Sam was two steps behind with another tray stacked with mugs. Dawn clapped.

"Cookies and tea for the hero," she said.

"You're the hero," he mouthed to her.

In seconds, he was loaded up with warm cookies and hot tea, and Sam threw the blanket back over his lap. In the four hours he'd spent in ER having Doctor Serrano nearly break her composure fussing over him, he'd had both, but this was far more satisfying.

"Let me catch you up," Claire said after she confirmed Matt had started drinking his tea. She wasn't the first in line to take care of him, but that wasn't going to stop her. "Once we knew you were safe, I went back on Everson's home security video. The system saves the last thirty days. At least twice a week, it looks like Kyle doesn't come home at night, including the night Nikki died."

"That's good," Matt said. "He's kind of covered himself with saying he works all night."

"We'll subpoena whatever surveillance they have at Flightline," Caddie said. "Let's find out if he thought of everything."

"He'll stop cooperating, and that will take time," Matt said. He glanced not very secretly at Dawn. "We need to do it, but I don't know how much time we have." Dawn blew him a kiss. He needed it.

"I have something else you'll like," Claire said, pulling her laptop out of the bag hanging on the back of her wheelchair. When up and running and in front of Matt, the screen held a frozen image of Nikki Moscow behind the front desk of the Patriot Inn. A small silver cross with a center covered in a triple diamond design was visible against a black sweater. "It took some looking, but I found her with the necklace twice in the last month. I think this is what she went to touch before she died that night. She does the same thing later in this video. She reaches up and touches it for a few moments. I don't think she was saying any prayers either."

"Someone special gave that to her," Dawn said. "And it was missing the night she died."

"We need to go back to Nikki's trailer," Matt said. "If it was Everson last night, that's what he was looking for."

"We already know it's Everson," Sam said from behind them. They all looked at her, and she shrugged. "What? I'm up to speed. He did it."

"Okay," Caddie said. "Everson gave her the necklace. Why would he break into Nikki's trailer in the middle of a blizzard to retrieve it?"

"The only answer is that it would lead us to him." Matt took a long drink of tea, grabbed two cookies, and threw off the blanket, standing. "I'm going to see Frank."

"Oh, joy," Dawn said, standing with him.

Caddie grabbed a cookie herself. She stood much more slowly. "I'm driving. I'm not letting you out of my sight."

"Oh, double joy," Dawn said.

———

Matt hesitated at the kitchen door as they waved to Claire and Sam, pulling out of the alley in Claire's van. Caddie wondered if exhaustion was catching up with him and he was having second thoughts about seeing Frank. She wanted to keep moving, but she understood how he must feel. From the moment she got his call last night that Bella was missing, she had been running non-stop: organizing a search for Bella, driving back roads in a blizzard, then rushing Bella and Frank to the hospital as she recalled search teams only to launch them again at first light, this time looking for her missing deputy. Between being sheriff and a worried friend, she was running on fumes herself.

"You can get some rest," she said. "I'll search Nikki's trailer."

"No." Matt shook his head, then looked away from Caddie but kept talking. "I know, I said we would." He paused. "Either that or she's going to lock me up."

"Matt?" *He's finally lost it*, she thought. An image rushed back to her. She and Matt had just met and were trying to solve two brutal murders. He was standing outside his Ford SUV, thinking no one was watching him, and opened the passenger door. He was talking to someone, someone who wasn't there. Then there were the small stolen moments when he seemed to be listening to a voice no one could hear or looking into a face that couldn't be seen. He finally admitted to Caddie that he still talked to his wife. She took it as figurative, spiritual, a mental exercise to retain a connection to the woman he loved. He talked to Dawn because he always had and still needed to. He said sometimes she talked back. And then he had smiled. But that couldn't be real, it was memories and emotional connections and a deep desire to know her again. It wasn't an actual conversation with his dead wife. Before Caddie could put any of this into words, her head throbbed in a pulse painful enough to force her eyes shut and shoot her hand to her temple.

Matt's hand on her elbow guided her to the kitchen island. "I'm sorry, Caddie. One way or another, this is going to be over in a minute. I trust you," he then added.

Caddie knew he wasn't talking to her. He was talking to Dawn. Talking to someone who only existed in his head, and at the thought, her temple throbbed again.

"But look at her, who's breaking her brain now?"

"Take a deep breath," he told Caddie. Her head hurt enough that it was making her nauseous, forcing her to take deep breaths to quell the uprising. Opening her eyes, she found Matt on the other side of the island, setting his phone in front of him. "It's okay." He pressed the screen, and, a split second later, the phone in her pocket rang. "Trust me, Caddie," he was looking at her, a pleading smile on his face, "you want to answer that."

She reached into her pocket, eyes fixed on Matt. She swiped to answer, automatically, saying, "Hello."

"Hi, Caddie."

She dropped the phone and just as quickly snatched it up again. She knew that voice. At her deepest, nearest death after being shot, she had heard that voice. It told her to fight. The woman's voice said that it was tempting to move on, but her time here wasn't finished. Then she said Matt needed their help.

"I know, it's a lot." The voice sounded so familiar, though she'd never heard it outside of her own head. "And, I'm sorry my husband messed up your brain by lying about me. He should have told his best friend the truth. Believe me, I let him know that wasn't nice."

Caddie's eyes moved quickly from Matt to the emptiness beside him. The space that until a moment ago wasn't registering, like it had been blanked out in her mind. Her head pounded, and her stomach threatened a full revolt.

"I have to thank you, Catherine Allemande. I've only been here for short spells since my accident." Her tone changed. "Well, not an accident, but let's leave that for later. You have been there for my Matt when he needed a friend. I'm a little jealous, but mostly I'm thankful, Caddie. If I can't be here, I can't think of anyone I'd rather have looking after him than you."

Caddie couldn't say anything. She couldn't answer the voice, but she was starting to see a face in her mind. She was in the barn after Deputy Williams nearly killed her a second time. A storm was raging outside, and Matt had rushed in, soaking wet, and knelt over her. He said it was over, Williams was dead. Then a woman appeared over his shoulder. A woman she recognized from the pictures everywhere in his house. It was Dawn, his wife, dead more than two years. As the memory faded in the days after, he pushed it further from her mind. It was drugs and pain, and her mind banished it from her memory because it couldn't exist.

"Now, I need you to concentrate on me," Dawn said, because Caddie knew in her heart it was Dawn.

258

Matt shook his head. "I don't think it's working, baby. She looks like she's going to have a stroke." His voice echoed through the phone.

"She can do it. Caddie, look at me. I'm right here. I'm Dawn Jager and I belong here. I'm real, in a way. There's a lot we have to talk about, but we need to help Megan and Bella by bringing in the man who murdered their mother. We need to help Nikki and Tracy by bringing them justice. I don't think I have a lot of time left here, and I want to meet you properly."

Caddie couldn't help herself. Between the gentle coaxing and a nagging sense in her mind that something, someone, was missing, she tried. She focused on the emptiness and Dawn's voice on the phone. She was reminding Caddie of the voice in the marshland who yelled no to distract a killer. Of the words of encouragement bringing Caddie back from the edge of this world. The face that shouldn't have been there.

Caddie's mind cleared. The pounding at her temples ceased. The emptiness wavered and was gone. Dawn Jager raised a hand and waved at her.

"Hi, Caddie." She gave Caddie a soft smile. "It's nice to finally meet you."

Caddie stood rooted in place, stunned, until she spun, rushed to the sink, and threw up.

Chapter 47

"You made me think I had a brain tumor or something." Caddie had alternated between ranting at Matt and what could only be described as gushing at Dawn the entire drive from Mannheim. Matt was in it deep for convincing her that she was out of her mind, the word gaslighting was thrown at him more than once. As for Dawn, she and Caddie had an immediate connection. The impossibility of Dawn's existence was immediately set aside. She was here, she was very real, and that presence neatly fit into a knowledge that had floated just out of Caddie's reach for months now. Matt's process of understanding was similar during Dawn's first visit. Once you accepted she was real, because she very much was, the rest was easy.

Caddie turned off the main road onto the snow-covered drive leading up to the Moscow house, changing back again to her friendly conversation with Dawn. "You literally lit the way for him? That's just so…"

"Angelic?" Dawn smiled.

Caddie slowed as they approached Nikki's trailer. "Yes, angelic. Don't let him call you a ghost again. You're an angel."

Dawn, who sat in the middle of the backseat, turned to her husband. "Do you hear that, dear? I'm an angel."

"How long is this going to go on?" he complained, but didn't sound too unhappy.

"As long as it needs to," Caddie said, pulling to a stop. Frank's extended cab truck was parked behind their Jeep, still in front of Nikki's trailer. Its hood and roof was stacked with more than a foot of snow, a reminder of the storm that dumped fourteen inches in a little less than twelve hours.

Dawn beamed both of them. "Okay, enough beating up of my sweetie, for now. We have a creep to put in jail. We're close, I know it, we just need a break."

"Later, then," Caddie said, but she had caught Dawn's grin, her joy at being here infectious. "Let's go make a break."

Frank stepped out of the trailer and met Matt at the bottom step. Dawn and Caddie gave them room. "Got a search warrant, counselor?"

"Frank. I hear Bella's doing good."

"Aw," Dawn couldn't help smiling, "you two are almost sweet."

Caddie opened her mouth, made a face, and closed it again.

"Hard not talking to me, isn't it?" Dawn said.

"The Mossberg?" Matt asked softly so Caddie wouldn't have to hear. She had enough secrets to keep.

"Ditched it before we got picked up. My nephew grabbed it. It's cleaned and oiled in the back of your Jeep."

Moscow stuck out his hand, when Matt shook it, Frank pulled him in close and spoke low. "Anything, anytime."

Dawn hung her head. "Forbidden, not that it's going to do any good."

"I'll take you up on that," Matt said.

"Forbidden," Dawn said even softer. She turned to Caddie. "These two are conspiring. You need to watch that." Caddie responded with an exaggerated eye roll. Like she didn't know that already.

"First thing I need," Matt said louder as they released their grips, "is for you to back off from the Demons. Give us time."

Frank let out a low growl and headed up the steps. "How long?"

Matt searched the face of his wife. She was smiling and warm and sly, and yet he could feel her time here was running low. She'd saved him and expended too much energy. He couldn't know for how long, but her time here was short. "Not long, Frank."

Frank perched on the edge of the recliner after Matt convinced him that someone from the Sheriff's Office needed to find any evidence to preserve the chain of custody. Caddie had taken Mary Moscow's spot next to the kitchen sink, minus the cigarette, though her arms were crossed and she had something of the same skeptical expression on her face. Dawn stood with her back to the broad front window. Clear afternoon sunlight reflecting off the freshly fallen snow outside created a halo around her entire body as if nature insisted on agreeing with Caddie. Dawn was an angel, not a ghost.

"Do you think it would help if I or the sheriff talked to Bella?" Matt asked. It wasn't his idea, but Dawn was the educator, and she thought she could gently question her through Matt and Caddie. It wasn't a bad idea.

"No." Frank was emphatic. "Girl has been through enough. 'Sides, she says she didn't see his face. She was asleep in her room. She'd even locked the front door. She heard someone break in and then noise in the kitchen. She hid under her covers, but when she heard him move down the hall toward her mother's room, she took off."

"Good girl," Dawn said. Caddie repeated it for Frank.

"Except he was at the end of the hall and saw her. She hightailed it out of here and thought she could make it up to the house through the woods. You know the rest from there. She found a hidey-hole for a bit, but the kid didn't have anything on but PJs, and it got too cold. She tried sneaking away, but he saw her again, and from there it was running and hiding."

"Poor babe," Dawn said.

"He must have assumed she saw who he was," Caddie added from the kitchen.

"Yep," Frank agreed. "I figure the wife and I didn't miss him by much, but that girl was out there in that storm for a good forty-five minutes." Frank shook his head. "That kid got an angel on her shoulder."

"She's got an angel, all right," Caddie said.

"Not me," Dawn said. "But very happy she does. Angels everywhere getting their wings."

"You sure she's okay?" Matt asked.

"Doctor Serrano says she's as right as rain. Her grandmother and sister are spoiling her as we speak."

Matt and Caddie had a few more questions for Frank before Dawn asked her first. "Ask your second-best friend there if Nikki regularly wore jewelry."

"Did Nikki wear jewelry?" Matt asked.

"Shit, I don't know. She's a woman, so sure. Tell you this, though, if she had good stuff, it was new. I caught her trying to pawn the TV when she was using. Wanted to whip her butt, taking her little one's TV like that. I know whatever she had that was real gold or silver was already gone. So if she had rings or something, it was junk."

Dawn shook her head. "That wasn't junk around Nikki's neck, trust me. What about men after she got out of rehab?" Caddie groaned at the question, Matt passed it on.

Frank's voice was softer than Matt had ever heard it. Something in the question had touched him. "Nikki was my girl. She loved her ma, but she was a daddy's girl. Daddy's girls don't tell their paps about men. I already asked Mary, and she doesn't know anything either. If I did, we wouldn't be sitting here having this conversation." That Matt believed.

"Baby," Dawn said, directing herself to Matt, then turned to Caddie, "sorry, you too. Guess I'm still getting used to this myself. Anyway, whoever chased after little Bella never got to Nikki's bedroom. I suggest we start there."

"We should start with Nikki's bedroom," Caddie agreed.

"See," Dawn said, "you're getting the hang of it, and you don't even look like you're talking to yourself."

Matt told Frank to sit still and motioned for Caddie and Dawn to follow him. In a minute, they were searching Nikki's room while Caddie and Dawn talked about him.

Caddie, on her knees looking under the bed, straightened up. "So, every time he has some brilliant insight, like Nikki was touching a necklace—"

"Or why 1899 meant Mannheim High School," Dawn finished, throwing it back as far as their first case together. She smiled. "That was me."

Matt finished his side of the bed and slid the closet door open.

"Maybe you're not half the detective I thought you were," Caddie grinned, getting into the feel of giving Matt a hard time.

"Now, Caddie—," Dawn stopped. "Oops, babe. I was about to defend your detecting abilities, but…," she stood at the head of the bed, pointing to the nearest bedpost and a dangling silver crucifix with a tri-diamond center.

Chapter 48

With the county still digging out from last night's snow, Allison parked by the new development south of town, ready to respond to calls for help and keep the speeding down until the roads improved thanks to clear skies and a strong late-day sun. Unfortunately, the reflection off unbroken white wasn't doing her already tired eyes any favors. On shift when Bella Moscow went missing, she had spent the following hours either driving through a blizzard or tromping through woods on snowshoes trying to keep up with Sam, who was a pro in incredible shape. They didn't stop until a convoy of Moscow cousins on snowmobiles retrieved them at the ice fishing shack and pulled a protesting Matt in a sled to the waiting sheriff. The entire episode was an adrenaline rush, but she eventually crashed out at Sam's place, got two hours of sleep, and then was back on duty so other deputies could get some downtime. She was feeling the cost of having corporal stripes.

Rubbing her eyes and blinking away the sun almost made her miss the truck coming from behind her. The first thing that caught her tired eyes was that it was a '70s Chevy, but it had a bright blue paint job that looked pretty new. The next thing she noticed was the passenger's patchy beard and long, ratty hair. She recognized the look, it was Squirts, the victim of Jesse's beating outside the Hawk's Nest, and a good suspect for Jesse's stabbing. Jesse was out of danger, so it wasn't going murder, but the assault was her case, which she appreciated, and she'd love to talk to Squirts about it. Besides, the sheriff hadn't retracted her order to harass the Demons out of the county, and Squirts was definitely a Demon. One way or another, it was worth pulling him over. She pulled out a half block behind the truck, waiting for an excuse. They didn't make her wait long, rolling through a stop sign fifty feet ahead. She called it in and flipped on her lights.

"Hey, sweetheart." She recognized the driver, too. Jackson Strange, Strangler, president of the Iowa chapter of the Road Demons. She read everything the FBI passed on him, and he was a piece of work. Allison liked her odds in a fight against Squirts, but Strangler was a big dude with nothing soft about him. Least of all his tone when he called her sweetheart.

"Driver's license, insurance, and registration, sir." The height of the truck made it difficult for Allison to see inside the vehicle and impossible to see their hands. It was broad daylight on a well-traveled road. Not the kind of place you'd expect trouble. Squirts was grinning at her like an idiot but said nothing. Strangler kept his cocky smile as he handed over the documents without a word or flinch. "I'll be right back," she said, before turning to her Sheriff's Office SUV. She hadn't seen anything in the truck that could support a search request. It would have to be a simple ticket unless something came back from dispatch.

Keeping one eye on Strangler and Squirts and another on the hardened laptop to her right, she processed Strange's information. No outstanding warrants, DL and registration up to date. She had a brief thought about giving him a field sobriety test, but without probable cause, that seemed a step too far. More of a Matt move than hers. She actually needed this job. She wrote out the ticket for failure to stop and approached the truck. She had to admit that it was a nice paint job, a kind of deep blue that wouldn't have been available when the truck was built. She wondered if it had been in an accident at some point or if Strangler just enjoyed a nice-looking truck. She handed him his documents and held out her electronic citation device.

"If you'll use the stylus to sign the pad, sir. I'm citing you for failure to stop. You want to be careful. The roads around here are pretty bad today." Strangler made dramatic motions signing the pad, his eyes on Allison the entire time. His leer told her he knew exactly what was going on. Squirts had decided to look out across the snow rather than at her. Maybe he was a little worried, she thought, packing that fact away in her mind. She hoped the message got through that they were being watched. If nothing else, getting eyed by a deputy would deter him from trying anything today.

She printed off his ticket and handed it to Strangler. She didn't have anything brilliant to ask Squirts, but she wasn't about to let the opportunity slip by without getting something in. "Hey, William, where were you two nights ago when Jesse Moscow was stabbed?"

Straight at it, and maybe she'd get a reaction. She got one. Squirts slowly raised his hand and gave her the middle finger. All while still looking out across the snow.

"Merry Christmas, beautiful," Strangler laughed. "We got a clubhouse up by Waterloo if you're in the mood for a New Year's kiss." Strangler puckered his lips before cranking the window up and pulling slowly away. At the end of the block, he made a show of stopping for a long time before turning right towards Cedar Rapids. Allison watched until the truck disappeared before climbing back into her SUV. She was surprised that he only offered a New Year's kiss and knew whatever happened with the overdose investigations, they weren't done dealing with the Road Demons. Not by a long shot.

Chapter 49

Denise hovered outside the door to John and Barb's room as the Sheriff's party saw their way in, Caddie leading the way. Dawn was in the rear, hushing the nurse as she went by. "I'm not really sure Barb is up to visitors," Denise protested, with no one paying her much attention before she turned and walked away as the door slowly slid shut.

"Surprised to see you here," John said. "I saw on Channel Nine how your office was searching for a missing deputy." He turned and took in Matt with his heavy jacket and Brewers knit cap. "That wasn't you, was it?"

"I'll tell you the story sometime," Matt promised.

"Well, not the whole story," Dawn said. "I'm going to go over with Caddie and visit Barb." Matt shot her a look. "I know, I know, but listen, I think I can help with Barb, and you and John are practically old Army buddies." She took in Matt's frown as his disagreement. "Trust me, babe."

Barb sat in her wheelchair near the center of the room, away from the television. "Hello." She gave a small wave without lifting her hand from her lap.

Dawn looked both ways between Matt and Caddie. She could swear the woman was talking to her. "Hi." Dawn waved. Barb smiled back. Caddie hadn't mastered hiding her reactions to Dawn and looked more than a little dumbfounded. Then whatever connection Dawn and Barb shared faded along with the light in the older woman's eyes. Caddie took it from there.

"Hello, Mrs. Everson. We met the other day at the Christmas party. I'm Sheriff Allemande. You can call me Caddie if you like." Barb shook her head and gave a laugh. She didn't believe the woman was a sheriff, but she wasn't about to argue.

John handed Matt a beer and sat in the recliner. Matt was about to refuse the bottle when he saw that it was non-alcoholic. "We can't have the real stuff in here. But this will do in a pinch." The television was playing a low-level college bowl game in front of a half-empty stadium. "The Hawkeye game was disappointing," Everson said, starting the conversation on safe ground.

"Not for me," Matt said. "I'm a Badger." The football talk out of the way, he moved on to the more delicate part of the conversation. "We're making progress in looking into your daughter-in-law's death."

"How's that?" John wasn't suffering from any mental decline. He knew this wasn't a courtesy visit to keep him up to date.

"I can't talk about details of the investigation." The next few questions would tip his hand anyway. "I need to tie down the timeline on the night of Tracy's death. You said your son was here for twenty minutes or so. Is that true?"

Everson took a pull from his beer as if it were the real thing. "It's true," he finally said. "I know where this is going, or at least what I think you're looking for. No, I don't know where John went when he left here. The fact is, he's not around much, and when he is, he doesn't stay long. But I can't believe he has anything to do directly with Tracy's death."

"What do you mean, directly?" Matt could feel Everson wanted to tell him something, he just needed to stay out of the way.

Everson nodded to Barb and Caddie, who were deep in conversation. Dawn stood over Barb's shoulder, a small smile on her face. She caught Matt's eyes and gave him an even smaller kiss.

"We gave him a good example, Barb and I," John said. "A strong, loving, respectful marriage. It never took. I'm not saying he didn't love Tracy, but it was no secret Kyle was unfaithful. He used visiting us as an excuse before and got caught by his mother doing it. Back when Barb was as sharp as can be. She gave him an earful. She loved Tracy. That was a good girl. I always thought part of her drug issues had to do with that marriage. Fair or not. I know he hasn't changed, and I do believe that had something to do with Tracy's relapse."

It may have been more direct than that, Matt thought, but let Everson keep talking.

"Where was he when he left here? I imagine he shacked up with some woman before he went home and found his wife dead. That's on him. Part of me is glad his mother doesn't understand everything that's going on. This would break her heart."

"Any idea who he might have been with?"

268

Everson lost himself in the bowl game and non-alcoholic beer in his hand. When he spoke, it was reluctantly. "I might."

———————

Dawn knew Caddie wasn't used to her constant input the way Matt was, and tried very hard to be quiet. She wasn't entirely successful. With Barb's condition, Matt insisted that nothing she said would ever get close to being admissible in court, but Dawn and Caddie thought talking to her could still be helpful. "As long as you don't ask her what she had for breakfast," Matt said, which got him an earful from both. He knew he deserved it. He blamed being tired and nearly freezing to death, which cut him a small amount of slack.

Caddie pulled up a stool from the little kitchenette. It put her higher than Barb in her wheelchair, but she didn't have much choice. Bending lower, she placed herself more on Barb's level. The woman gave her a broad, welcoming smile.

"You must be a friend of Tracy's," Barb stated, settling the question of who Caddie was in her mind.

Dawn crouched down so she was between the women. "Sorry, Caddie, it's sad, but you might as well go straight at."

Caddie nodded, thinking of all the times she saw Matt nodding to himself, and stopped. "You like Tracy a lot," she said.

"That's about as gentle a way to start as I can think of," Dawn said.

"Tracy's a good girl," Barb said. "She visits and does my hair, and we have tea. And she's very good with my garden. I grow the biggest, juiciest tomatoes and wonderful cucumbers. I'll get John to give you a jar of our bread and butter pickles. Best in the county." She turned to her husband. "John, make sure you give Tracy's friend a jar of bread and butter pickles."

Everson turned from the game and his talk with Matt. He looked happy to help his wife. "Yes, dear. I'm sure she'll love them."

"That's just sad," Dawn said. "But nice."

"Thank you," Caddie said. "That's very kind."

"Just try," Dawn said. "Who knows if it will help?"

"Did you see Tracy for Christmas?" she asked Barb.

Barb's animated answer included talk of preparing a Christmas ham with her special mustard sauce and service at Saint Mark's Lutheran Church over by the elementary school.

"Saint Mark's moved from there in the 80s," Dawn whispered. "Barb lives in a Mannheim that ceased to exist long ago. Matt was right, asking her about her life now was not going to get us anywhere."

Barb crossed her hands in her lap in a gentle pose that also highlighted an intricate gold ring on her right index finger. A clear green emerald was paired with two small diamonds. Like Caddie asking questions about today, Dawn didn't know if it would do any good, but what the heck. She pointed at Barb's hand.

"Caddie, ask about the ring. Then ask about the necklace."

The sheriff gave her the smallest head nod. It was a good idea. "That's a beautiful ring." She pointed at the emerald.

"Oh, that!" Barb looked surprised to see the ring on her finger, but quickly recovered, bringing Caddie into her confidence. "It's not the thing to show off, you know, but I do love jewelry. John's work takes him out of the country sometimes," she said, completely sure her husband still worked. "He works for a company in Cedar Rapids that makes those big air conditioners, and they send him out and he helps install them and teach the local folks how to maintain them. Well, they sent him to Colombia, of all places. He was there for three months, and Colombia has such lovely emeralds, and he bought me this ring." She looked over to see that her husband wasn't paying attention. "I needed to resize it, though. Bless him, he's a sweet man, but has no idea about ring sizes. And there were a pendant and earrings to match. That was a Christmas gift in 1978. We had a lovely holiday with my sister visiting from Germany. Her husband was stationed there in the Air Force."

Dawn wanted to let Barb live in a lovely 1978 Christmas, but this could go on for a while. "Redirect, Caddie. You need to show it to her now, or we'll hear all about her sister's visit."

Caddie slipped the clear baggie out of her pocket, letting the crucifix rest in her palm, the tri-diamond design face up. "Do you recognize this piece?"

Barb reached out slowly, slipping the baggie and necklace out of Caddie's hand. She turned it over gently. Somewhere in the

270

confusion of years, she understood that the woman with the badge in front of her was keeping the item, and her question had weight. John Everson, ever watchful of his wife, stood and joined their circle, Matt a step behind.

"Hi, babe," Dawn whispered, not wanting any spark of her existence to break Barb's spell. He gave her a small, sad smile in return.

"That was blessed by Pope John Paul II himself," she said as it slipped from her fingers into Caddie's palm. "Nineteen-eighty-seven, and John was sent to Italy, but not Rome. Where was that, dear?" she asked, looking up to him, admitting that she needed his help.

"Milan, dear heart," he said.

"Dear heart," Dawn repeated softly. She liked the expression. She liked it for this couple.

"Yes," Barb said. There was none of the innocence and nearly childlike wonder she had exhibited at the Christmas party. "Milan. I flew to Italy for a week and we went to the Vatican, though neither of us are Catholic. The pope was there in Saint Peter's Square giving his blessings. John had bought me this as a present and gave it to me when I arrived." Her fingers ran across the crucifix before they came back to her lap. She was done talking, a tired sadness coming over her. Dawn was sure that a clarity had come over Barb. She knew that so much of her life had slipped through her memory, and she would lose more. Barb held her hand out for her husband. John clasped it in both of his. Dawn turned away, the lost future of her and Matt, the promises and struggles that would have come with it, too much to contemplate. John picked up the answer they needed from there.

"When we moved in here, Barb kept some of her jewelry. She really likes the rings and won't lose them so easily. The rest we gave to Kyle. Tracy was in rehab then, we expected she would get them when she was out and better." John Everson held his wife gently in his gaze before turning to Matt.

"Now, if you'll excuse us, Barb needs to rest."

Caddie was pushing the door open to leave the facility when Matt caught up, gripped her arm, and pulled her back.

"Hey," Dawn said. "Hands off, buddy."

Caddie's look was more puzzled than irritated. Matt led them to the corner with the Christmas tree as the front desk attendant pretended not to watch the sheriff and the guy bundled up in a heavy jacket. "What?"

Matt turned his back to the desk. "I have a possibility of where Kyle was while his wife was dying."

"From his father?" Caddie asked.

"Oh, no." Dawn was looking back toward the room they had just come from. "That poor woman."

Matt wasn't exactly sure where Dawn's reaction was coming from; it certainly wasn't for the woman having an affair with Everson. "His dad came back to their room and caught their son kissing a staff member a few months ago. All three pretended no one had seen anything."

"Denise," Caddie and Dawn said at the same time. Matt nodded his head, but questioned both with his eyes.

"She was very interested in hearing our conversations," Dawn said.

Caddie followed her. "She didn't like us coming back today. She was looking a little sick under that layer of makeup."

"And," Dawn picked up, "that nice little heart-shaped pendant Denise wears. She clutched it like she was hiding it from us. I don't think Kyle would be so bold as to give his mom's jewelry to his mother's nurse, but necklaces for girlfriends is his move."

Matt's jaw slowly fell, his eyes darting back and forth.

"Close your mouth, dear," Dawn said as nicely as it could be said.

His mouth snapped shut just as Caddie muttered, "Shit," and looked back down the hall. Whatever had bothered Dawn had just hit the sheriff.

"I know, right?" Dawn said, following her gaze.

"Someone needs to explain this to me," Matt said.

"It gives us everything but motive," Caddie said.

"Do creeps need reasons to be creeps?" Dawn asked.

"Please," Matt said, "remember my brain was frozen. I'm not keeping up."

"Denise is the source of the fentanyl," Dawn said.

"Oh, shit. That poor woman," Matt said, finally understanding that the outpouring of empathy was for Barb Everson, not her registered nurse. Those months of pain and changing dosages were not about Barb's condition; it was about her nurse stealing her pain meds. "It's a diversion case."

"What's that?" Dawn asked.

"Diverting legally prescribed narcotics away from their intended use is a federal felony," Caddie said. "But we're not turning this one over to the feds to investigate. This is ours."

Matt approached the front desk. He took his Brewer's cap off, thinking he'd appear more friendly and in less of a rush if he didn't look ready to leave. And just maybe, he thought, he'd look better showing his short, gray-tinged hair. But after catching his reflection in the front door glass with his hair sticking up in random spikes, dark circles under his eyes, and his pale complexion, the hat went back on. He had questions, and it was his job to see if the front desk could track Denise down quietly.

He was not thrilled with the rest of their plan and objected when Dawn said she and Caddie were a team, but she promised if she felt like she'd wandered too far from him, she would "run my little butt right back." He'd have to trust her little butt on that. They were going to see if they could find Denise themselves.

He showed his badge again, his not-so-subtle way of reminding the staffer he wasn't just a family member asking about grandma. "I noticed you didn't have us sign in, but do you have a visitor's log or another way of tracking who comes in here?"

"Not for listed family members," she said. "This is a semi-independent living center. None of our residents are legally required to stay, but their safety is important to us. We have cleared family members on file with pictures, but once you work here long enough, you know regular visitors on sight. Anyone else, other than you and the sheriff, of course, would have to sign in, and we have the option of denying them entrance if we feel there's any potential issues."

"I remember you from the Christmas party," Matt said. It was partly a flyer. He thought he might remember her, but Dawn had a way of grabbing all of his attention. "Were you working the desk when the party finished?"

She said she was, before growing wary of Matt's questioning. He wanted to be more subtle, but, with the end in sight, asked straight out. "Did you see Kyle Everson that night?"

"He was here."

"For how long?"

"Not long, I think." She was looking down at the desk, though there was nothing going on there.

"Did you see him with anyone else while he was here?"

"Yes." She looked up from the desk. "I saw him with Denise Kohler."

"His mother's RN?"

"Yes."

"Keep going," Matt said, in no mood to drag this out.

She relented. "He left, and his car was parked on the far side of the lot. It's easy to see from here. He waited about five minutes, then Denise came out of the side exit of the building and got in with him."

"I want you to keep this between us," Matt said.

"Yes, sir."

Matt couldn't help thinking how the staffer suddenly started looking impossibly young, a kid barely out of school who just fingered a senior staff member for sleeping with a man whose wife died while they were probably in bed. He wished he had made it easier for her.

Dawn lied to her hubby, if only a little bit. She was nervous about leaving his side, not because she wasn't a big girl angel ghost, but she was finally admitting to herself that she was feeling tired. Not the fuzzy brain, a night of rest would cure tired, but weaker in her grip on this place. Her Matt's love, her anchor in life and after, was strong enough to keep her here for now, but even that soldier's love could only do so much. The time to leave was near, the explosion of energy she used to guide him to the surface of the pond drained her more than she would admit. And the pull of the other side, the overwhelming love that was calling her to complete her journey, was growing stronger in her heart. She would leave and she couldn't know if she and Matt would be together again in this place. That they were together already at the end of their journey didn't help Matt now, and that pained her.

274

But they had a mission here. She'd saved her boy, mission one complete. His lie to Caddie and the damage it had done were fixed. Mission two, check. It would set her heart easier knowing there was someone here he could care for and lean on, who knew what he carried in his heart. And if Dawn was finished making friends on this side of life, she was glad Caddie was the last one.

And now, they were closing in on solving the murders of Nikki Moscow and Tracy Everson. That mission wasn't complete, but they were getting there, and Dawn wanted to see it to the end. She was more than a little angry over the deaths of these women. They'd struggled through addiction to set their lives right; they had a chance for happiness, people loved them, and they had futures. Kyle Everson took that away. For Dawn, who'd spent her life caring for little ones as an educator, the pain he'd caused Megan and Bella made it very personal. Those girls would carry the scars her Matt carried. That made her mad. Dawn would do whatever she could to see Everson behind bars before she had to go.

"Ready?" Caddie whispered.

"Let's get this over with," Dawn answered.

Caddie rapped gently on the door. She waited and was about to do it again when the soft sound of rustling of feet could be heard.

"Sheriff." Mr. Everson stepped into the hall, closing the door behind them. His shoes had been replaced by slippers. "Barb's sleeping now. She doesn't understand everything that's going on, but I'm pretty sure she knows something's wrong. And honestly, I think we've helped you more than you could ask of us."

"I understand the position this puts you in, Mr. Everson," Caddie said. "And believe me, I don't want to cause you or your wife any more trouble, but I have two young women dead. I'm going to figure this out sooner or later."

"Then you don't need more from us," Everson said.

Dawn spoke softly, afraid of waking Barb. "He feels guilty. He knows he helped point us at his son. Maybe a little forgiveness and gentle encouragement, not shark mode. Wait, do you have a shark mode? Yeah, I can see you in shark mode, like going after FBI supervisors shark mode. Let's save shark for later. I know someone who will need it."

Caddie wasn't going shark, though she had it in her, but it was still a tough road. "I need your help if I'm going to prevent another death. He's going to start panicking, you know that. There's one person who links him to those deaths, whether she knew what he was planning from the beginning or not, I don't know. She could be in danger. I think you may have figured out where we're going on this. Now, I can take what we have and go to the judge and get a search warrant, come into this facility and seize your wife's medical records."

"I want you to leave Barb out of this," it was half plea, half demand. "In her state, she can't help you, and if she understands any of this that's going on, you'll only hurt her. She hasn't got long." He cracked, and tears welled in his eyes. "We haven't got long, Sheriff."

"Oh, my," Dawn said. "I'm so sorry, Mr. Everson. But I promise you this, a place waits for you and Barb to be together. I know that. Look deep into your heart and you'll know it too. Your love will survive. But my friend here has to stop more pain. She has to give some sense of justice to two little girls. Please, help us."

Caddie had waited to speak, whether it was to let her invisible partner talk and somehow connect to John Everson at a fundamental level or to let him think, it was working on him. She gently pushed him. "I think we can finish your involvement right here and now. Denise is not going to last five minutes under questioning; then your involvement is finished."

"Except for watching my son be arrested for murder," he said.

"For seeing Tracy get justice," Caddie said, then got to the point of their return. "Mr. Everson, what pain medication is your wife on?"

He hesitated, his face hardened. They would confirm what they already suspected.

Caddie went on. "Denise was diverting it. That's why Barb was in pain for several months. She probably didn't steal it all the time, and sometimes another nurse would provide it, but she was stealing your wife's meds. She needs to pay for that."

Everson nodded. "Fentanyl," he said softly.

"Thank you," Caddie said. "And don't worry, Denise's time here is finished."

Everson said nothing, simply turned and walked back into their room and let the door shut behind him. He would have to live with knowing he'd failed to protect his wife, and that his son was responsible for her pain and the death of two innocent women.

"It's a tough business you're in, Caddie Allemande," Dawn said.

"This sucks," Caddie mumbled.

"It does suck."

A movement at the end of the hall caught Caddie's eye. "Get your husband to cover the front." She turned, walking forcefully before breaking into a run. Dawn, lost in her thoughts about John and Barb Everson, took a second before she spun on her heels and ran.

Matt was at the end of the line of questions that a front desk attendant could possibly answer, except for the whereabouts of the woman they needed to talk to. "Could you tell me where…,"

Dawn came sprinting around the corner, waving him wildly toward the door. "Run, Matt. Go, go."

Matt's head spun watching his wife in full sprint before looking back at the attendant, shrugging, and running after Dawn. She was waiting for him outside on the parking lot barely cleared of last night's snow. "It's a chase. Caddie took off after Denise." As she said this, the nurse appeared around the far end of the building, her head down, walking as quickly as she could without running.

"I don't think it's going to be much of a chase," Matt said. Whether she understood what he said or not, Denise heard him. She looked up, stopped walking, and let her head drop back down. Caddie appeared around the corner behind her. Dawn began walking forward.

"Try not to let the fact that she's attractive blind you to the fact that she's evil," she said.

Matt was about to protest, but thought his wife, once again, knew his mind better than he did.

Chapter 50

Caddie put a Fillmore County Sheriff's baseball cap on Denise and threw the same blanket she had wrapped Bella in over her shoulders before bringing the nurse in the back door of the Law Enforcement Center. It wasn't the world's best disguise, but it might keep a random passer-by from recognizing her. She left her in a conference room with Matt and Dawn, which was still hard to wrap her head around, before she headed to her office to secure her weapon. Chris was waiting for her when she came out.

"There's only one person in the women's lockup. Laney Hillman is in on a drunk and disorderly and petty theft."

"Again?" Caddie asked.

"Yep. She was three sheets to the wind in Casey's, causing a scene, and ate two slices of pizza without paying. Then she vomited on the floor."

"Good, Lord, that woman. Laney is going to kill herself one day, just pass out in a snowbank and freeze to death." Caddie considered letting her stew in jail for her own good, but she had higher priorities today. "Kick her loose. I want you to drive her home and read her the riot act. I'll pay her Casey's tab."

"I got Casey's," he said. "I still owe you for that nice bottle of whiskey for Christmas."

"When this is over, I expect an invite to enjoy a glass with you."

"Yes, ma'am," he said before taking off to clear the jail for the prisoner they needed to keep under wraps for the next twenty-four hours.

———

Caddie came back into the conference room with Matt's Marquette travel mug steaming with hot tea. It was sugar instead of honey, but he wasn't about to complain, just like he wasn't going to admit to Dawn or Caddie that deep down inside, he was still cold.

"Thank you, Caddie," Dawn said. "He won't admit it, but I think he's still cold." She slid onto the table, crossing her feet beneath her and spinning to look at Denise cowering on the other side. She caught Caddie's look. "Guess you didn't realize. I've been sitting on your furniture the whole time. You should try it. But not now, it will undercut your authority."

Caddie set a sheet of paper and a pen in front of Denise. "Please read that and let me know if you have any questions. Those are the same rights I read to you earlier."

Picking up the pen, Denise read, her hand shaking. She looked up at the sheriff and quickly shifted to Matt. He had to admit, the big, tear-filled eyes and soft blonde hair did tricks on his system. But it wasn't hard to remember the evil she had done.

"I heard you're a lawyer. Do I need one?" Denise asked.

"Let's be clear, I'm an investigator for the Sheriff's Office. I have a law degree, but I'm not here to provide you with legal advice. But I'll give you a tip. You decide to talk to us, tell us nothing but the truth. Lies are only going to hurt you. Do not doubt that at the end of the day, we will prove you diverted a Class III narcotic from at least one of your patients, if not more, and that drug was used to kill two people."

Denise's hand dropped to the table, the pen rolling away across the paper.

"What's more," Matt went on, "those are federal crimes. You will do years, long years. There's one option to lessen that time and maybe lessen the crushing guilt you will feel looking at the ceiling of your cell at night. Talk to us now and fully cooperate. Then, when the time comes, plead guilty. That can cut a third off your sentence, and you still get a life. A life you took away from Nikki and Tracy. A life you do not fucking deserve."

"Ouch," Dawn said. "I forget how scary shark mode is."

Caddie stood, retrieved the pen, and put it back in Denise's hand. "That's all the legal advice you're going to get from us. You want an attorney; ask for it. We'll stop this interview right now, and by morning, when we arrest your partner in these murders, we won't need your cooperation. Maybe Everson will be the one to earn a few years off by ratting you out."

Denise's eyes flashed between the two in vain search of a safe harbor.

"I'd sign," Dawn said. "These two have me scared, and I'm an innocent ghost lady."

Caddie decided to open the questioning herself, not sure if Matt would go too hard or too easy on Denise. Not that she didn't deserve a hard interview, but this was about servicing the case, not their need to punish her. At least not yet. "Let's start at the beginning. When did you meet Kyle Everson?"

Denise gave one last pleading look to Matt, but seeing no sympathy, turned to Caddie. "When his parents moved into Valley View, earlier this year, February, I think."

"When did you become romantically involved?" Caddie felt odd about using the word romantically; it wouldn't have been her first choice. She wanted to say screwing.

Denise started with her and Kyle talking and becoming friends. He listened to her after a hard day dealing with patients. He helped pay for a car repair when money was tight. All while Tracy was trying to get her life straight in rehab, and he was meeting Nikki for the first time.

"Poor, baby," Dawn muttered. Caddie couldn't have cared less either. This was all about Denise trying to feel less guilty. She and Everson didn't grow closer and fall in love, he played her. He had a target, and he hit it. Denise finally put them in bed together in June, about the same time Everson was checking into a Decorah hotel with Nikki Moscow.

"Busy freaking creep," Dawn said. Matt seemed content to let Caddie do the questioning and Dawn the commenting, so the Sheriff went on.

"When did you first divert narcotics from patients' use?" She left the rest of the question wide open. When did Everson ask you to steal fentanyl? Did he tell you what it was for? Did you care about the pain you were putting Barb through?

"August." A one-word answer. Denise had drug out the story of her and Kyle. How she put elderly patients in pain was going to be pulling teeth. Matt cleared his throat and took a sip of his tea.

"I think my hubby wants to play now," Dawn said. "You might want to warn her."

Caddie decided to let her friend pull the teeth and waved him in.

"I gave you legal advice, don't ignore it," he said. "What did Kyle tell you the fentanyl was for?"

Denise looked down, tears running off the tip of her nose. No one offered her a tissue. "To kill Tracy," she whispered.

The room was deathly quiet; even Dawn didn't want to break it. Matt spoke softly. "Go on."

"He said she was going to kill the business. I don't know what it's all about, but he said they had customers the government can't know about. Drug cartels or something, I guess. I didn't ask. Anyway, she changed her mind about selling to them and started arguing with Kyle when she went back to work. He said if she told the government, we would lose everything and he would go to prison."

"We?" Matt asked.

Denise nodded. "We were going to be married. He would have just divorced her, but then she would for sure report him."

"Whose idea was the fentanyl?"

"His, but I told him about lethal levels and how I could short his mother." She looked up now. "She never went completely without, I swear."

Matt waved for her to go on, he wasn't interested in her attempt to make herself feel better.

"He had enough for a while now. I wasn't even sure he was going to do it, then Nikki died."

"Why?" It was Dawn and she was mad. Caddie repeated it in the exact same voice.

"I knew he had been seeing her on and off. She was still friends with Tracy despite sleeping with her husband and being so busy. He says she felt guilty about it and threatened to break it off, but she also really liked him. He could be like that. He told me he was with Nikki because we needed two ODs so the cops wouldn't look too close at his wife and would think it was just a strong batch of drugs out there."

Dawn cursed, which got both Matt and Caddie's attention. "Sorry, go on," she said.

"How did he kill Nikki?" Matt asked.

"He soaked her cigarette in fentanyl. Just a little at a time so it wouldn't mess it up. Then, when she went to smoke after, you know, he switched it out on her. I told him I didn't want to know about how it happened, so that's all I know."

"And wine with Tracy?" Matt asked.

Denise nodded. Matt took a drink of tea, looked at his two investigative partners, his wife, and his friend, and pulled his legal pad closer. "We're going to be here for a while. Can we get Ms. Kohler a drink and some tissues? I want to start at the beginning, in detail."

———————

The deputies' bullpen was oddly quiet despite the room being half full. The hour had grown late, and everyone seemed lost in their own thoughts. The death of Nikki and Tracy, the attempted abduction or, more likely, killing of Bella Moscow, the tinder fire that was still burning between the Russians and the Road Demons, all set off by one man. They had everything tied down but the motive, and even that was beginning to come together. Tracy was threatening to report her husband for illegal sales. But it wasn't going to be drug cartels. It would be connected to Cyprus and mysterious Eastern European buyers. Matt was surprised that even Dawn had grown silent; he missed her running commentary on his life. The room stirred as Allison rejoined them.

"She's tucked in for the night all by herself in the women's lockup," she said before plopping down in a chair. "I asked them to keep an eye on her, but I don't think she's suicidal."

"Letting her patients suffer like that and then helping kill two women." Claire had stuck around despite not having anything to research for now. Everyone was gathering for the final moment. "That's evil."

"U.S. Attorney's Office in Cedar Rapids had a case a few years back with an anesthesiologist who switched out meds from fentanyl to something weaker. Some of his patients didn't go all the way under," Matt said.

"During surgery?" Claire asked.

"Yep. They felt everything."

Dawn, who'd been sitting on the desk that Matt was leaning back against, rested her head on his shoulder. "I'm tired, baby," she said. "Sorry."

Caddie squinted at Matt and motioned with her head for him to go. He wanted to cry. His Dawn was leaving again. She had saved him, and they were about to arrest Kyle Everson for crimes that would send him away for the rest of his life. Nikki's girls were safe. It was time for his wife to go. He wanted out of this room with all its people so they could spend their last moments together. He wanted to grieve all over again, by himself, hoarding his pain.

"What do you want to do, Sheriff?" Lieutenant Dubcek asked. "You didn't keep Kohler's arrest a secret for no reason."

"I want to know everything." Caddie sat slumped in a chair, her legs out in front of her. "Exactly what was Tracy threatening to report her husband for? I don't think drug cartels are buying used airplane engines. It has to be with the export docs that Gentry left with her."

"Doesn't matter." Matt shook his head. He would stand and leave the room, but Dawn hadn't moved her head, and he could almost pretend in his mind that he could feel her against him. "He gave Tracy and Nikki the drugs that killed them. We don't even have to prove it was intentional."

"Look, I know you're right," Caddie said. "We could get an arrest warrant signed tonight and arrest him before sunrise. We could build on what we have from there. It's a really strong case. But a motive makes it ironclad. I want ironclad. I want to know what he's doing that was worth killing Nikki and Tracy over."

Caddie pulled herself up but didn't stand. "He has no idea we have Denise. His father isn't telling him, I don't think, and if I were him, I would avoid Denise for a while. We have a day, maybe, before he knows," Caddie said, then her energy picked up with an idea. "Have you heard back from your Commerce guy?"

Matt dug into his jacket pockets.

Dawn spoke without moving her head. "Your phone is at the bottom of a frozen pond, dear."

"No phone," he said. "His contact info is on my laptop at home. It's past midnight in DC now. Perfect time to call him."

"Okay." Caddie stood. "I'm going with you," she cut herself off before she said 'two.' "You're on tonight, Chris?"

"Yes, ma'am."

"Do your best to check on Everson's property and Flightline without tipping your hand. You see any activity at all, arrest the bastard."

He picked a black wool cap off the desk and adjusted his belt, ready to go out on patrol. "Yes, ma'am. Night all," he said before leaving.

"Claire."

"Yes, boss?" she asked expectedly.

"Go home, go to bed, and deal with that issue we talked about tomorrow. Those are orders."

"Yes, ma'am," she said, mimicking the LT.

Caddie pointed at Allison. The deputy answered without being asked. "I'm off now, I'll be back first thing to support the investigation or arrest."

"Good, go."

The room cleared in seconds, leaving Matt, Dawn, and Caddie in a tight circle.

"You okay, Dawn?" Caddie asked. Matt's heart appreciated the care in her voice.

"Peachy," she said.

"Is there anything I can do to help?"

"Sure," Dawn said, standing. "Arrest Kyle Everson." She wanted more, but that would have to do for now.

Chapter 51
December 31st

The kitchen was a brightly lit, pushing the windows to near black. The smell of coffee and tea mixed with microwave bacon and frying eggs. Caddie had two breakfast sandwiches ready to go, joining them with a warning to never expect her to cook for Matt again. Dawn sat cross-legged on the kitchen island, radiating a reinvigorated happiness. As tired as she was an hour ago, being home where she could talk openly with Caddie and tell Matt how much she loved him gave her new energy. She still needed to rest, but it could wait a bit longer. The two cops listened to the teacher as they fueled up.

"I want him busted for trying to get Bella, too," Dawn said. "We know it was Everson at the trailer looking for the necklace, then chasing that poor girl through a blizzard. Plus, causing my crazy husband to drop into a frozen pond."

"We can't prove it," Caddie answered. "At least not yet. As far as I know, no one saw him or his vehicle anywhere near the Moscow property. And there was not much out there for traffic, the weather was just too bad."

"He ran there," Matt said, the idea just coming to him. "I was on one of those trails earlier this week. It's the old railroad right-of-way trail that runs from Dubuque to Cedar Rapids. I bet it passes within a couple of hundred yards of Everson's house at the bottom of their drive, then right along the east side of Otter Pond. I should have thought of it before. It would have been safer than driving and being seen."

"Pretty bad weather for a run," Caddie said.

"I've seen this one go in weather almost as bad," Dawn said.

"Weather wasn't going to bother him, too much," Matt said. "He's got the right running gear, and with the trail, he wouldn't have had to worry about getting lost. Run to Nikki's, that's a couple of miles, find the necklace, get home. Any tracks would disappear in the storm. If he hadn't chased Bella, he would have been there and back in an hour with zero chance of anyone seeing him."

The rhythm of the conversation, the back and forth, along with the coffee and sandwiches, was waking Caddie up, too. "Okay, then we get his home video of him coming and going, that'll help."

"Nope," Dawn said. She was up now, following Matt and Caddie into the living room. "His cameras only cover the front of the house. He goes out the back door, and he's free and clear, no little video of him creeping out in the middle of the night like a creep."

Caddie stopped as Matt took up position on the couch. "Fine, we'll keep working the attempted kidnapping angle. But with Denise, we have more than enough probable cause to arrest Everson on state murder charges—"

Matt grunted with some level of uncertainty. "You're the one who wanted to nail down the motive."

"Hush, dear," Dawn said.

"Yeah, Matt, the women are figuring this out," Caddie said. She and Dawn couldn't help themselves. They barely knew each other, but they had been through life and death situations together more than once. Whatever happened next, they would forever remain friends. "I'm not saying it's perfect, but it's enough to keep him detained while we get the U.S. Attorney's Office to indict on federal charges. Either way, he doesn't get away or hurt anyone else."

"As my hubby has noted, you did say you wanted a motive, other than Everson being a complete jerk," Dawn said. "You weren't wrong."

"I know." Caddie sat in Dawn's favorite chair. "It's late, we're tired. Let's get the motive."

Matt flipped open his laptop and took a bite of his breakfast sandwich, trying not to get crumbs everywhere. "Okay." He took a big swig of tea to wash it down. "Let's make Teddy's wife even madder." He read Teddy's number off his laptop contact and punched it into Caddie's phone. Dawn made a hush noise all for herself.

The phone went to voicemail, but the prompt was cut off before it could finish. "Hello." It was Teddy.

"Hey, brother, how are you doing?" Matt said.

"Matt?"

"Sorry, did I wake you?" Matt grinned. Ted's response was quick and profane.

286

"Hey," Matt said. "I thought you were a Christian man, that's not good language."

Caddie's chuckle allowed Dawn to let loose.

"I spent half my day trying to call you, the other half on the phone to HSI. You know the hornet's nest you kicked over?"

"I hope it's a big one. Sorry, spent last night on the lake and lost my phone." Teddy softly cursed him again. "Trust me, it wasn't fun. I'll explain later. Meanwhile, I've got Sheriff Caddie Allemande here with me."

"Hi, Ted. Sorry about the hour," she said.

"And me," Dawn whispered. "Hi, Ted."

"Before you tell me about the hornet's nest," Matt said, "you should know, we found the source of the fentanyl that killed our two victims, and she ties it directly to Kyle Everson, the owner of Flightline. She also says this is about Tracy threatening to report something about Flightline's sales to the government."

"Give me a minute." They could hear Ted apologize to his wife and the sounds of moving through his house. "I'm back. I don't have everything in front of me. I'm at home and it's, what, nearly three in the morning? Good Lord, Matt. Anyway, HSI in Saint Paul received a call last month from an unidentified number, apparently the user was on some app disguising her location and number—"

"Yaddah," Dawn said.

"She had questions about sensitive aviation equipment potentially going to Russia, including embargoed landing gear components and high-quality navigation electronics. She doesn't give up more, but the agent looked up the equipment she mentioned, and it's commercial-grade stuff that's easily modified for heavy-lift military transports, fighter jets, and even guided missiles."

"It was Tracy," Dawn said.

"That's right, Sheriff," Ted responded.

"Sorry," Dawn whispered to Caddie.

Teddy continued. "She called back ten days ago and began sending images of end-user certificates and equipment listings and shipping docs without final dates. She made allegations that at the behest of her husband, she met with third-party dealers out of Hungary last year. It was clear from their questions that their clients were fronting for Russian buyers. HSI had plans to set up a formal interview with the source in January."

"There's your motive," Caddie said. "Maybe Everson got wind of Tracy keeping the export docs at the house."

"Which she was taking pictures of using her anonymous app and sending to the feds," Dawn said.

"It makes me wonder if Tracy talked to Dr. Prijat about her husband's business. If getting out from under illegal sales was part of Tracy getting straight," Matt said.

"It makes sense," Caddie agreed. "But this was more than her getting cold feet or threatening to tell the government. She was actually gathering the proof to do it. He was going to lose everything and go to jail for evading military sanctions. He knew her phone passcode, but with Yadda destroying the images when she sends them, Everson can't be sure whether she's talking to the feds yet or not."

"It was the final push that led to her murder," Dawn said.

"He's not taking chances," Matt said. "He kills her to end the threat."

Dawn picked it up, "And Nikki dies just so he can make it look like there was killer dope out there."

Matt finished the thought, "He clears the field, his business keeps booming by dealing embargoed equipment, and he's home free."

"Unless he decides to kill Denise, too," Caddie said. "We might have saved her life."

Teddy's voice was fully awake now. "If I got this right, you have Everson's fentanyl source. When do you plan on arresting him?"

Caddie looked to her partners, who happened to be her best friend, the other an angel with an irresistible charm. "Today?"

"Yeah, today," Matt said.

"Today," Dawn's answer was softer, sadder.

"Shoot," Teddy said. "Any idea what's actually in the shipment going out today? We would love to catch him in the act of actually moving embargoed goods."

"I don't know," Matt answered. He hit mute. "Pictures of the shipping docs on my phone are in the lake."

"Aren't your phone and laptop synced, baby?" Dawn asked.

He tapped the phone quickly. "Teddy, call you right back, man. We may have an idea that will make everyone happy and get this bastard locked up today."

Teddy signed off, and Matt, Dawn, and Caddie crowded around the laptop as Matt pulled the pictures up. Hydraulics and navigation equipment all going to the front company in Cyprus. Exactly the equipment Tracy was warning HSI about. Despite the certainty that the end of the case and the waning of his wife's energy meant only one thing, Matt couldn't help a sense of excitement from entering his voice. "Let's wake up a lot of people and wish them a Merry Christmas."

"God bless us, everyone," Caddie said.

"You two suck," Dawn laughed.

Chapter 52

Lieutenant Dubcek had mixed emotions pulling his Sheriff's Office truck up in front of the Moscow house. There was a time when the office wouldn't send a deputy out here without backup, and his mission wasn't what he wanted to be doing this morning, not with everything else that was going on. But the sheriff wasn't wrong in sending him. Frank Moscow was still a wild card that needed to be accounted for. He gave it a minute before turning off the engine. The home was awake under a heavy blanket of snow, a curl of smoke coming from the chimney. Darn near a picture postcard. The LT stepped out of the truck as Frank opened his front door.

"Morning, Frank."

"You here to babysit me?"

"Something like that," Dubcek admitted. "You know what's going on?"

Moscow nodded. "I know Jager and the sheriff arrested a nurse from the old folks home, and there's a lot of feds in town this morning. Not hard to figure a trail out from there. Since you're here, I figure they're arresting Everson."

Dubcek shook his head. "Someday, you're going to have to tell me how you know these things."

"Someday."

"Matt Jager wanted me to explain the rest to you, at least as much as I'm allowed. He said we owe you that much."

"Appreciate that." Frank stepped back, still holding the door open. "You might as well come in. Coffee's fresh, and Mary and the girls are making monkey bread."

"Thanks." Chris reached into the truck, coming out with two brightly wrapped and ribboned boxes before closing the door. "I'd take credit for these, but it was my wife's idea." He held them up. "Just a little something for the girls."

"Taking gifts from cops." Frank motioned Dubcek in. "You're going to ruin my reputation."

Dubcek made his way up the stairs, greeted by the smell of coffee and baking bread. "You'll fix that," he said.

———

Claire's eyes didn't stray from her laptop despite movement all around her. DEA's analyst was helping her FBI counterpart hook into the Sheriff's office Wi-Fi. An FDA OCI agent was dropping off his laptop bag before heading back out to join up with the rest of the team. HSI would be represented by an analyst by the afternoon. He'd left early, but Saint Paul was a five-hour drive under the best of conditions. Claire didn't normally mind being in the office while Caddie and everyone else were out on the streets investigating and patrolling. It was her role and where she could be most effective, but today she wished the boss would have bent the rules, even a little. It may have been thrown together in eight hours, but this was the most exciting operation she'd been a part of, and with a small, mostly rural county, there was no telling when something this good would come around again. She also envied Caddie and Matt. She'd only seen them for a few minutes, but they were acting like two kids with a secret. Part of her wished they would get together; she thought they'd be perfect. The other half of her thought it would be sad for them to lose what they had. She shut out thoughts of Bob and the breakup she hadn't the heart to tell him about yet. At the moment, she got to happily lose herself in the job.

A soft ping announced a new email a fraction of a second after it appeared on her screen. The subject line read Search Warrant with a return address of the U.S. Attorney's Office. She hit print and wheeled off toward the printer down the hall. If everything went to plan, it wouldn't be the last search warrant they got today.

———

"Two semis headed your way," Caddie's voice came over Allison's radio. "Trailers are red with MTX International Shipping on the side." Allison waited before replying as the tension inside her cruiser built. Will Pencheck, a Cedar Rapids detective working with the FBI's Joint Terrorism Task Force, cranked around in his seat, looking back over the narrow, snow cramped country road. There was one other possible route, but this was the straightest shot to the highway, and there was no reason for the shipping company, which had no idea they were hauling materials designed to evade sanctions, to take any other route. If they didn't show in a minute or two, Allison would lead her two-vehicle detachment in pursuit.

"There they are," Pencheck said, turning around, grinning away.

"We see them," Allison radioed back. When the front semi was a hundred yards away, she pulled out of the farm field road she'd been waiting on, turned on her flashing blue lights, and slowed down. Pencheck turned to look out the back again.

"He's wondering what you're up to, all right," he said.

"He'll figure it out in a second."

As the second semi cleared the road Allison had been on, Deputy Dan Taggert and an HSI agent pulled out in a SO cruiser, blue lights flashing. Allison kept her convoy at a steady thirty-five. As they approached the gravel lot surrounding a grain elevator, empty on this winter holiday, Allison stuck her arm out the window and motioned for the semi to follow her. Once they were all safely off the road, Allison and Pencheck approached the first driver whose window was already down.

"Commercial vehicle safety compliance inspection," she said.

The driver's puzzled expression said enough.

"I'd get comfortable," Allison said. "It might take a while."

"If this is going to delay me, I'm going to have to call it in to my dispatch," he warned.

"I'd appreciate it if you hold off on that for a few minutes. It won't be long," Allison said. "I'll be able to explain everything then."

"Okay." He motioned to the truck behind him. "Mind if I go tell my partner?"

"Not at all," Allison said as she and Pencheck turned toward the warmth of her cruiser.

"Hope this works out," Pencheck said.

"Knowing the boss," Allison said. "You can count on it."

———————

There was no more need for subterfuge as Caddie gathered eight Fillmore County deputies and federal agents in the parking lot of Flightline Avionics. She was fairly certain staging behind the high school gymnasium had kept their hastily formed task force from drawing too much attention, but it was a small town. That was over now, everything from here on was straightforward, or at least as straightforward as it could get. She waited as JT pulled in with the FDA agent. They were bringing the last piece of the puzzle, physical copies of the search warrant. Dawn was chatting with Matt, who was grinning a bit like a goof.

"So cute," Dawn said. "Back all dressed up and with nice bright blue running shoes." She smiled over to Caddie. "I tried to get him to bundle up, but I think he secretly wants to look cool."

Matt was, in fact, back in his uniform with a long wool jacket, dress shirt, jeans, and running shoes from a brand Caddie didn't even recognize.

"You do love expensive running shoes," the sheriff said.

"He does." Dawn nestled closer to her husband, standing alongside Everson's black truck with the Flightline personalized plates that helped unravel his lies. Caddie could easily imagine that when these two met, Matt didn't stand a chance of resisting her charms. She'd feel sorry for him if Dawn weren't the best thing that had ever happened to him.

"In his defense, when he was an MP sergeant and I was still in school, he bought the cheapest running shoes he could find at the PX and didn't toss them until they were practically falling off his feet," Dawn spoke to her like they were old friends. It had been that way all morning. They had known each other for less than a day, and Caddie would already miss her when she left. "At least they have the parking lot plowed and he doesn't have to get his pretty shoes dirty."

Rafer started handing out copies of the warrant. Caddie reluctantly turned from the couple. "Everyone, we have a search warrant for the premises," she said loudly without yelling. "We're searching for evidence in connection with the murders of Nikki Moscow and Tracy Everson. Read it over before you join the search. Remember, we're authorized to look for evidence connecting Kyle Everson to the deaths of Nikki and Tracy: communication devices, notes, letters, any actual evidence of the drugs themselves. If you find something, call a DEA or FDA agent over; they'll take pictures and collect it so we can keep a tight hold on the chain of custody."

Dawn spoke to Caddie as everyone took a minute to give the warrant a final look. "You don't know how long I've wanted to tell you how good you are at being sheriff. I'm really glad we ended up on the same team." She turned to Matt. "Your turn, babe."

Matt raised his voice for everyone to hear. "If you see any potential evidence of additional crimes not covered in the warrant, stop what you're doing, get me or the sheriff, and we'll evaluate it. We are not getting evidence tossed because it's not in the warrant. Okay?" Everyone agreed, they'd all heard the same spiel an hour ago. The other deputies and agents didn't know exactly what was happening, as far as they'd been told, it was a search in an OD case that had turned to murder. But they were all looking forward to finding out what was really going on.

Caddie closed in on Dawn and Matt as the others filed into the building. "Sure you don't want to go in and get Everson?" she asked them.

"Thanks," Matt answered, "but it's cleaner this way. I called Teddy looking for intel on Flightline, which is true. He tells me about the source who's now been murdered, another federal crime. And I have expertise in export cases. I can testify to all of that, plus the night of Tracy's death. It's not as fun as throwing cuffs on, but it's better this way."

"Our boy is maturing," Dawn said. "But thanks for the offer, Caddie. Besides, he would waste time flirting with the ladies upstairs."

"He is a flirt, isn't he?" Caddie joined in.

"I regret you two meeting," Matt said as he held the door open for Dawn and Caddie, the last to enter Flightline. He didn't mean a word of it.

Matt walked onto the repair and maintenance floor and held up a copy of the warrant for the Flightline employees to see. There was nothing magical about waving a piece of paper at everyone, but it had the effect of impressing upon them the seriousness of the situation, as if the deputies in uniform and feds with badges weren't enough. "Fillmore County Sheriff's Office. We have a warrant to search the premises for evidence in connection with the murders of Nikki Moscow and Tracy Everson." The warrant said overdose deaths, but Matt liked the word murder better.

The announcement sent a visible shock through everyone on the floor, stunning them into silence.

"I heard a gasp," Dawn said. "I'm not sure I've ever heard an actual gasp before." The Flightline employees took an involuntary step back from the equipment and crates. A forklift driver near the open bay doors turned his machine off.

Matt turned to find Deputy Schott near the back of the group. "Terry, could you escort the Flightline folks to the conference room at the far end. Get names and contact information and let them know we'll probably release them soon."

"But, they're not detained," he said, walking past Matt.

"No. If they want to walk, they can walk. But I don't think they will."

Jason Gentry stepped forward, suggesting they lock up the semi-trailers and close the doors. Matt was good with that, and it was clear Gentry understood there wasn't going to be any more shipping out of the building today, if ever.

Matt and Dawn wandered through the maze of engines, machine equipment, and wood crates until they found one sealed up and ready to go. It was tall enough that the shipping documents and scanning code were at nearly eye level. "This is it, babe," Dawn said. "As soon as you do this, it's out of your hands."

"That's okay," he said so low that no one else heard. "It's the right thing for everyone." He raised his voice and waved to JT, who had been waiting at the back of the room. He pointed at the shipping label as the FBI agent joined them. "I recognize this company and address from a DHS intel alert I've been made aware of concerning Flightline Avionics. There are allegations that this third-party company is passing restricted technology to the Russian Federation." Allegations that came from a woman who was dead, who could never testify, whose statements may or may not be inadmissible hearsay at this point.

"Mr. Gentry," Matt called to him as the bay door dropped, cutting off the cold air coming in from outside. "You want to come here for a second?" He pointed at the crate. "What's in here?"

Gentry didn't need to look. "Landing gear hydraulics, they're specially made for very heavy aircraft."

"Like military transports?" Matt asked.

"Yes."

"Agent Rafer," Matt said. "That DHS bulletin specifically mentioned equipment for military transports. I think this is potentially evidence of an effort to evade U.S. export restrictions."

Rafer waved his hands over his head. "Everybody, stop what you're doing. We need a new search warrant."

"I guess that's us done," Dawn said. "It's up to the feds now. Let's go see Caddie. She's probably already thrown the cuffs on Everson for diverting drugs from his mom and killing two women. Which is still so darn hard to believe."

"Nice to have an unexciting end," he said under his breath.

"It's not over yet," Dawn joked.

Caddie was halfway up the stairs when the front office ladies appeared, pressing up against each other, something very close to terror etched on their faces. Between their babbling, Caddie couldn't make out actual words, but she understood their general meaning. She waved her deputy and a DEA agent to go on ahead. "Tracy's desk is the large workstation on the near end. Start there."

"No one is being arrested," she counseled the ladies, which of course was a lie, but they weren't being arrested, which made it close enough to the truth. "I have a search warrant for evidence in connection with the overdose deaths of Nikki Moscow and Tracy Everson."

They wailed the names, and the older one went into a slow-motion collapse to the floor. Luckily, it was carpeted, her office mate helped her down, and it was a very slow-motion collapse. Dealing with these two wasn't on her Christmas list, but she couldn't exactly leave them out here if one of them really was having some kind of cardiac event. After a few minutes of reassurance and Caddie making a trip to the breakroom on the first floor for two Sprites from the machine, the women settled down but didn't look to be moving on from their spot on the upper landing. It was out of the way and no one needed an ambulance, so Caddie figured this was a good a place to stash them as any. When she walked into the office, the search had progressed from Tracy's work station to the storage cabinets lining the far wall.

"Her desk is clean," the DEA agent said. "I figured you'd want us to wait for you before we went into Everson's office."

"Thanks," Caddie said. The drama from the landing behind her, she was fully back in cop mode and feeling comfortable. She was a little surprised Everson hadn't come out yet, but she suspected he was watching Matt and his team on the factory floor below knowing his world was ending. She should have detained him before he saw that, but the front office ladies had thrown off her timing. That was on her, not a mistake she would make again. She knocked firmly on the door, stood to the side, unsnapped his holster, and placed her hand on the butt of her sidearm. "Mr. Everson, this is Sheriff Allemande. I have a search warrant and I'm coming in."

She turned the doorknob, but it didn't give. It was locked. She rapped harder. "Mr. Everson, I need you to open the door." The worst-case scenario flashed across her mind: Everson with a rifle, opening the window overlooking the factory floor, and firing on the officers below. All because she'd put together this operation too fast and they hadn't thought through every possibility. She had waited at the door long enough. It didn't look like that tough anyway. Taking a half step back, Caddie raised a foot and kicked alongside the doorknob as hard as she could. The door cracked and, with a second kick, gave and flew in. Her weapon out, Caddie stepped quickly through the opening, moving to the side as she scanned the room. It was empty.

The front office ladies went back into hysterics, claiming that Everson was in his office and they didn't know anything. Them not knowing anything, Caddie believed. As she hit the first step heading down, Matt and Dawn were coming off the floor, their part of this little drama supposedly over. Caddie shouted down to them. "Everson's not in his office."

"But his truck's outside," Matt said, stopping.

Dawn took another step and spoke more slowly. "His truck is outside on the plowed parking lot."

"The airstrip." Caddie came hurtling down the stairs. "The airstrip is plowed. Dammit, the airstrip is plowed." Matt was past her the moment she was through the door.

"Good thing he's got running shoes," Dawn called to Caddie as Matt ran across the lot, headed toward the small hangar positioned halfway down the concrete strip two hundred yards away.

Running faster, Matt remembered to keep his center of gravity above his legs. The experience of hours running in the cold on snow and icy trails was coming in handy.

"Try to be careful this time, Matt." Dawn was keeping pace with him as he turned from the short drive connecting the lot to the airstrip and picked up speed. He wanted to argue, but between his time in Singapore and Dawn's return, he hadn't been putting in the miles. He needed all his breath to keep going.

"So much for a quiet ending, huh, dear?"

He could smile at that. Dawn wasn't worried, so everything would be fine. Just needed to get Everson before he hopped in his plane and headed to God knows where. They'd catch him eventually, but, dammit, he wanted the man in cuffs and headed to jail in Fillmore County. He wanted Caddie to get the credit and those girls to know their office had done everything they could to bring their mom's killer to justice. Twenty yards from the open hangar door, Matt slowed and pulled his Beretta from the holster clipped to his belt. He always knew it was a good idea to own more than one sidearm. The roar of a propeller engine jumped from the building.

Matt glanced back but didn't see the sheriff anywhere. He had no idea what had happened to Caddie, but he was ending this now. He range walked forward, weapon out front, ready to get out of the way if a Cessna started coming at him.

"You got this, dear," Dawn said, still in encouragement mode.

Fully in line with the door, Matt could see the four-seater pointed out of the open bay, the propeller spinning into a solid disc. If he had to, he could put a couple of rounds through the windshield before getting out of the way.

"Baby," Dawn nearly squealed with delight. "He's too slow. Look."

She was right. Everson was hurrying from a back room with a large, heavy-looking canvas bag over one shoulder.

"Oh, poop," Dawn said. Everson let the bag drop as he brought the rifle in his other hand up. Matt wasn't sure what kind it was, but

298

the camo body and solid barrel told him it punched holes in animals larger than him.

"Drop it," Matt shouted, his weapon up and pointing at Everson.

"No." Everson wasn't a raging madman. He was calm, matter-of-fact. That was not reassuring. "I'm getting on this plane and running. Maybe they catch me, maybe they don't. I let you take me in, there's no chance. Put down the gun, Matt, and you get to live."

Dawn was unnaturally calm. "Let's cut to the chase, dear. I'll skip the speech about you trusting me, and you slowly put your pistol down."

He glanced at her.

"Trust me," she said gently.

Matt eased out of his firing stance. She did say slowly. He raised both hands. "Okay," he said. "No reason for either of us to get hurt."

"Put it down," Everson said.

Matt crouched slowly, set the weapon down, then stood.

"Good," Everson said. "Kick it to the side, gently."

Matt slid the weapon away with the side of his foot. "No one needs to get hurt."

"No, no one gets hurt," Everson said. He leaned to the side and grabbed the strap on his bag while keeping a finger on the trigger of the rifle still pointed in Matt's direction. Dawn stuffed her hands in the pockets of her wool coat and nearly bounced in place. Her happy waiting position.

"No one gets hurt." Caddie Allemande stepped out of the back room, her pistol up and pointed directly at Everson's head. She was close enough that there would be no missing. "Slowly put the weapon down."

"Yay." Dawn clapped. "Gotcha, freaking creep. Hope you rot in prison for all the people you've hurt." She turned to Matt. "I saw her heading toward the back door. We got your back, baby."

All of the air went out of Everson, and Caddie ordered him again to put the weapon down and put his hands on his head. Matt retrieved his sidearm as Dawn continued to cheer. Everson was on his stomach by the time they approached.

"I wish I could let you put the cuffs on," Caddie said to Dawn.

"Thank you, that would be nice, but you go ahead. If it's not me or my hubby, it's good that our best friend does it."

"You're under arrest for the murders of Nikki Moscow and Tracy Everson, freaking creep. Hope you rot in prison for all the people you've hurt," Caddie said so Everson would hear exactly what Dawn thought of him.

Chapter 53

Downtown Mannheim was filled with people as the early winter evening settled in. Isabella's and Jill's were full. The weather was brisk without the pain of deep freeze, the skies clear with a quarter moon showing overhead. The yoga studio was having a champagne, strawberries, and stretch night, which didn't sound entirely legal to Matt, but he didn't care. The Hawk's Nest was getting warmed up for a long night. The parking in front of Matt's office was taken, so he turned to take the alley and the back entrance. He would rather be home, his selfishness reasserting itself. He wanted Dawn all to himself, but he learned the more he shared her love, the more he got back. She was an alchemist creating an unending supply. They knew their time was measured in hours, but she had people's lives she needed to touch. Starting with her niece.

Light flooded out into the alley. The garage door to Sam's Outdoor Adventures was wide open, the storefront window ablaze. The alleyway was lined with cars. "I think our niece is having a party," Dawn said. She was giving him her pursed-lipped smile, as much satisfaction as joy.

"Should I play the dad and yell at everybody and threaten to tell their parents?" he asked, pulling over.

"No, dear. But, I wish you had had the chance," she said about their imagined future with little ones and a life wonderful but unlived.

He turned to her, wanting Dawn to know he meant this from the bottom of his soul. "You would have been the greatest mom."

"Thank you, Matt. I know."

Sam hugged Matt hard around the neck without letting go of her beer. It wasn't her first. "You managed to arrest someone without getting shot at."

"Well, it wasn't for not trying," Matt joked to a frown from Dawn.

Allison, still in full uniform, approached, extending a hand. "That was good work," she said with a shake.

"Thought you'd still be babysitting semis," Matt said.

"DHS had the driver take them back to Flightline. They're locked up and the feds' problem now." She held up a can of Pepsi. "I've got two hours off before I'm on patrol."

"It stinks," Sam said. "The rest of us are heading upstairs for a Star Wars original trilogy watch party and pizza. You can join us."

Matt looked around at the eclectic-looking mix of twenty-somethings. "No, you have fun."

Dawn turned away to hide it, but Matt saw her wipe a tear. "Give her another hug."

Matt hugged Sam again, then slipped a blue folder into her hands. "Give this a look tomorrow. It's the plans your aunt had for rehabbing the rest of the building. Apartments, upgrading the electric, permitting process, everything. She even thought about a shared deck space on the roof. Come get those power tools and see if you can save a few bucks on the job."

Sam hugged it to her chest like a treasure. "Thank you. I don't know what to say."

"Say you'll do it right. Call it Dawn Loft Apartments or something. I'll get the accountant to figure out how the company pays."

Sam hugged him again, the folder of her aunt's plans between them. "You mean, you'll pay."

"I expect you to get us into the black." Matt reached into his pocket and came out with a thin stack of folded twenties. "Here's a hundred. I owe you rental for a night in the ice fishing shack and a broken lock."

"I shouldn't take this," Sam said, taking the money. "But we need to turn a profit." Matt thanked her for the offer of movie and pizza again before moving on for his Dawn.

They walked back down Main talking about nothing, just the way that they wanted it. Claire's van was in front of Jill's with Frank Moscow's truck behind it. Passing by the plate-glass window, they could see the group sitting at one of the round tables in back. They were all digging into oversized sundaes, including Frank.

"I don't know how that man stays so skinny," Dawn said. "I swear, the way he eats."

"Healthy living," Matt said, and got a laugh.

Matt got a New Year's kiss on the cheek from Bev, and Dawn told her to back off, and they walked back to Claire's table. Megan gave a small, unsure wave. Bella reached for a hug from Matt. "Thank you," she said softly.

"So many hugs, so little time," Dawn said.

Matt crouched down and got a hug and kiss on the cheek from Claire. "We did good," she said.

"We did," Matt agreed. "Caddie told me about your dilemma. With everything that was going on…"

"An hour ago," she said. "Breaking up with someone on New Year's Eve stinks."

"Not as much as not breaking up if you're going to."

"That's okay," Claire said, looking at the girls at the table. "I had a better invitation, and with this one, I'll get a decent night's sleep."

Matt set the presents in his hands on the table. "These are for you two. Wait until you get home, but I hope you like them." Bella pulled them both close with one hand while the other kept digging into her ice cream.

"I don't know if you remember her," Matt said.

"Oh, goodness," Dawn said. "Maybe this was a bad idea." Matt kept going.

"But my wife was Dawn Jager. She used to be your vice principal. I know she thought you were both wonderful girls, and I know she would be proud of you."

"I remember her," Bella said.

"You need to get the bastards that killed her," Megan added.

"They are Frank's grandkids," Dawn said.

Frank lit his cigarette, waving to the girls on the other side of the window. They'd be heading home when they finished their ice cream. "Anything you need, anytime you need it," he said to Matt.

Dawn shrugged, her hands deep in her pockets, her face turned up to the stars that grew brighter by the moment as night took hold. "I give up with you two. You're going to do whatever you want anyway."

Matt didn't respond to either. He knew Frank meant it, and he had a feeling he'd take him up on it at some point. He also knew Dawn was right, he shouldn't. "How are you and the Road Demons? Do I need to warn the sheriff about anything?"

Frank shook his head. "No. That's over. We're all good now."

"One of yours got stabbed." Matt didn't believe for a second Frank was the kind of man to leave an unbalanced sheet.

"They'll make it right."

Matt regretted prying. "I don't want to know."

"No, you don't," Frank said.

Matt waved to the girls through the window and told Claire he'd talk to her tomorrow. If they didn't have work to do, he'd find another excuse.

Matt and Dawn walked away. She held onto his arm, and he reached deep into memory to feel her weight pulling on him. "I don't know, dear," she said. "Seems like we collected little ones without even noticing."

"Wait here, dear." Dawn shushed Matt's protest with a kiss, the electric spark weak but there. Caddie stood in the open front door of her home. She gave a small wave, then shook her head at the sight of Dawn passing through the Jeep's passenger door. Matt would have argued with making the stop if he'd known he wouldn't be included in this conversation, but Dawn had things she needed to say to Caddie that were just between them.

They greeted each other awkwardly.

"Caddie Allemande," Dawn went on, "I wanted to say goodbye and to thank you."

Caddie tried waving both away.

"No," Dawn said. "I have to go, but I couldn't leave without letting you know how much I appreciate what you mean to my Matt." She looked back at him. "He can be vain and stubborn and rushes in when he should wait." She turned back to Caddie. "But he is sweet and smart and cares and more than anything, I love him. You've saved my husband in more ways than one. Thank you, Caddie. My boy needs someone like you in his life."

304

Caddie looked down, then gave up fighting back the tears. When their eyes met again, they were both crying. "I think your husband is the best friend I've ever had, and you've both saved me."

"It's what friends do for each other."

Caddie nodded. "Will you be back?"

Dawn looked back at her Matt again. "I don't know. I don't know if I can do it again." She turned to Caddie. "If I can't..."

Caddie nodded. "I know. I will. I'm glad we got to meet, Dawn."

"Me, too, Caddie. It's been a heck of an adventure."

Chapter 54

They stood in the front sitting room, the rounded corner of the house giving them a view of the city around them. Lights from their Christmas tree reflected off the windows, giving a shifting pattern of close-in stars for their final night together. Dawn was dark against the glass, dressed in a long, flowing robe of dark green that appeared nearly black, her hair giving the effect of a hood. Every moment had been filled with their love, whether it was silent or in soft talk. He could not tell her he loved her enough. She thanked him for their lives together. By a small grace and miracle, neither cried.

The air outside began to pop and crack as neighbors let off fireworks into the sky. A rocket climbed through the tree cover and burst into reds and greens seemingly over their heads. "I can't believe, I'm glad fireworks are legal in Iowa now," Dawn said.

The grandfather clock that had once belonged to Dawn's nana had struck eleven times an hour ago. Matt dreaded the striking of twelve. It shouldn't matter, this wasn't *A Christmas Carol* with its timely ghosts. He didn't need to learn lessons about the meaning of Christmas. He understood its promise that he would be with his Dawn again in another place. But that didn't stop the pain of her leaving him now.

"Tell me you'll come back," he said. It was asking too much, asking what she could not guarantee, but he asked it anyway because he desperately needed to believe that she would return to him. The reflection in the window betrayed that she was crying. He reached out a hand and she held it, though neither felt it.

"I can't promise, baby. I love you and I wish I could. But it's just so hard. I just don't know."

"One more time," he begged. It was unfair and selfish to ask. And as untrue as any promise would be, he wanted that promise. "I need you to come back to me one more time. I know, I could make it if I could see you one more time. If I could hear that you love me. If I could look into your eyes once more and know I've made you happy. I could finish my time here."

Her chest heaved, she cried, and she lied to him. "I promise, I will come to you one more time."

They turned to one another. The crash of fireworks grew as the moment drew near. In his mind, it was the Fourth and the sky was filled with falling cinders of light. Tears ran down his face. "I love you so much. All of this pain, all of my longing for you. It's all been worth it because you love me."

"I will always love you." Her voice was soft, almost distant. "Never forget, I have always loved you. I will always love you."

He kissed her. She pressed her hands against his chest. He felt it all, every sensation of her being here was with him. Whether that was real or a memory didn't matter. He could feel her lips, and she leaned into him, and they were together for that moment. When his eyes opened, she was gone, and the fireworks in the sky were poor imitations, and the house was cold and quiet.

Chapter 55

Matt held up the twelve-pack of Leinenkugel's as Caddie opened the door. "Sorry about the hour," he said. "But I could use a drink, and if I get drunk alone, that means I'm an alcoholic."

"I'm sorry, Matt," she said. Caddie was dressed in jeans and a Cubs sweatshirt, not looking like she was ready for bed. "I was afraid you would need to stop by."

He turned away so he wouldn't cry again. He'd cried enough for one night.

"Come on," she said. "It's cold out. Besides, we have time now, I want to hear the whole story."

He stepped into the house and slipped his shoes off so he wouldn't track snow and dirt in. "It started when you wanted to arrest our niece."

Caddie shut the door behind him. "No, Matt, the whole story. Start at the beginning."

Despite the tears clouding his vision, he looked at Caddie. "You're a good friend."

"I know," she said, shutting the door behind them.

"I was stationed in Korea and coming home on leave for my sister's wedding…"

Chapter 56

Kyle Everson let out a deep breath. Yankton, South Dakota, was no one's idea of paradise, particularly inside a federal pen. But it was a warm summer day, and his attorney had managed to get him a minimum-security designation in return for cooperation on the Russian exports. That took some doing, but Kyle had names and connections that were invaluable to some three-letter agencies. In the end, they were happy to make a deal. And he was finally out of Iowa. Finally, beyond the reach of that maniac Frank Moscow. He had heard whispered threats even in the federal lockup in Iowa, but that was all behind him now. It was almost like a new lease on life. Only his second day here and he already knew his routine for good weather days. Starting with a long walk.

With time to think, he'd almost come to regret killing Nikki. It had been easy enough; the woman smoked like her life depended on it, and he knew she'd puff away half a cigarette before she realized it had been doped up, and by then it would be too late. It was a little trickier than fixing up Tracy's wine, but she was an addict and wasn't supposed to be drinking anyway. Easy enough to switch the glass and bottle out. But he was sure he needed Nikki dead. She was supposed to get the cops looking at local drug dealers, she was related to enough of them. And she would have been suspicious of Tracy's death. Nikki knew better than anyone that his wife had kicked the opioid habit as good as it could be kicked. He hadn't let on about the Russian deal to Nikki, but he did talk about the money that was coming in. It wouldn't have been too hard to put it all together. Besides, two deaths made it look like there was bad dope in the community. That was the idea, anyway. He was back to being convinced that Nikki's death was unfortunate but necessary.

Lost in thought and the feel of the sun on his face, Everson didn't register the presence of the other prisoner until a sharp pain exploded in his side. Looking down, he was surprised to see an arm pistoning in and out of him. A hand holding a crude knife was drenched in his blood. He looked up at his killer's face as shock set in. Kyle Everson fell to his knees as a rough voice bent over and whispered in his ear.

"Frank Moscow says he'll see you in hell." The last image before Kyle lost consciousness and his life was the tattoo on the man's forearm of a demon riding a motorcycle.

Tammy and A Christmas Carol
The True Story

We had been married nearly a decade when the Army moved us to Japan. It wasn't long after that when Tammy became pregnant with our first child. She was tired and uncomfortable and subsisting on unfrosted vanilla cake and milk. It was our anniversary, December 1st, and she just wanted to go to bed and sleep. She curled up facing me.

"Turn the other way," I said.

"Why?"

"Just turn the other way."

Her eyes opened wide enough to give a suspicious look. "This isn't going to get weird, is it?"

"A little," I said. "Trust me."

She did, but not without a second look back. With her finally facing the other way, I reached into my nightstand, pulled something out, and cleared my throat. "Marley was dead to begin with. There is no doubt..."

She spun back, eyes wide. "You're reading to me!"

"Yes, bear. But I'll feel weird if you're watching me. You have to face the other way."

She kissed me, fluffed her pillow, and plopped down happily facing away. "Start over, I don't want to miss any of my story."

I read to her every night until we had finished Scrooge's journey. Then every year after, starting on our anniversary, I read to her. Cozy Christmas mysteries set in snowy English towns, Christmas poems filled with faith and love, and more than once, back to *A Christmas Carol*.

When we had been together for thirty-six years, my baby lay in a hospice bed fading away from me. We kissed and said I love you in the morning, then the pain meds sent her down. A little after nine at night, I could see she was coming to the surface, not awake but nearly so. I told her how much I loved her. I repeated my promise that I would love her forever and we would be together forever. Eventually, I grabbed my iPad and found her favorite book of Christmas poems and read to her again about faith, love, and family.

When her awareness turned to grimacing pain, I called the nurse, and they gave her pain meds.

I fell asleep in the chair next to her. We were holding hands. It was ten minutes to midnight when I woke. "Tammy, are you gone?" I asked. She was. She had waited for me to go to sleep because she always took care of me. She loved me. She loves me still. Reading *A Christmas Carol* to her all those years ago gives me hope I was worthy of that love.

Acknowledgements

A heartfelt thanks to everyone who read A Spirit of Murder and A Spirit of Vengeance. Whether you purchased it, checked it out from the library, or got it passed on by someone else, I hope you felt a touch of the love that Tammy and I share, and my grief at her loss. And hopefully, you enjoyed the series as a good old-fashioned romantic mystery with a touch of the supernatural along the way. That you would take the time and emotional energy to read these stories means more to me than this writer can express.

A special thanks to Tommy Lewis, as always, for his insightful feedback and suggestions. They never fail to make for a better story. And to Mary Springman for the unenviable task of editing and proofing me, then having to listen to me talk even more about the story. Thanks to Kelsey and Matt for watching out for their dad. And most of all, thank you, Tammy. I will love you forever, but you already know that.